Secrets Kept

World of Nälu

The Short Stories

Desert Rose
Dragon Thief
Indestructible
A Princess No More

The Hidden Dagger Trilogy

Secrets Kept

Secrets Kept

THE HIDDEN DAGGER TRILOGY

BOOK ONE

J. L. MBEWE

BrokenSeed
Books

Secrets Kept
The Hidden Dagger Trilogy
Book One
Second Edition

Published by BrokenSeed Books
A division of Pala Press
Lindale, Texas

ISBN-13: 978-0692432976
ISBN-10: 0692432973

DEDICATION

To James
Who gave my dream wings
Zikomo mwamuna wanga
Nikukonda muyayaya

Acknowledgements

I will be forever grateful to the following:

James for your constant support and belief in me.

Mom for making me take keyboarding back in the day, instead of the art class I wanted.

Dad for introducing me to the world of fantasy.

Jennifer for my second childhood and the many afternoons spent reading the story out loud.

Preston, what can I say, thank you for your input and humor, even if you did move to the other side of the world, and back again.

My first critique group: Mike, Kassy, Kymberly, Chris, Kristen. For all the input, critiques and laughs. Miss you guys.

To my early readers: Ben, Rachael, Jo, and Hannah: Thank you all for reading and your input.

To Becky Minor for a manuscript swap and for the helpful critiques.

To Lynn, Bethany, and Kessie, who gave me more insight to what I was doing wrong. Ha!

And I have to repeat my thanks to Pauline and everyone at AltWit Press for taking a chance on my writing. Thank you for all your hard work and input on bringing SK to light.

To the readers who have picked up the short stories and are eagerly waiting to find out what happens next. You encourage me. Thank you!

I can't thank Anne Elisabeth Stengl enough for her support. I am overwhelmed with gratitude, blessed beyond belief. Thank you!

To #mywana tweeps, you guys rock. I've learned so much from y'all this past year, my head is still spinning!

And to God. Thank you. This long journey all started with the question: "What are you doing with what I gave you?" The answer: Writing. This is it. Ten years in the making. Hope you all enjoy it!

Secrets Kept, second edition.

A big thank you to Ralene Burke who helped tighten the second edition and to Robert Mullin for his help in formatting. And to the SCAWALAG who helped me stay sane through this entire process. I so appreciate y'all. Thank you!

Now go have an adventure!

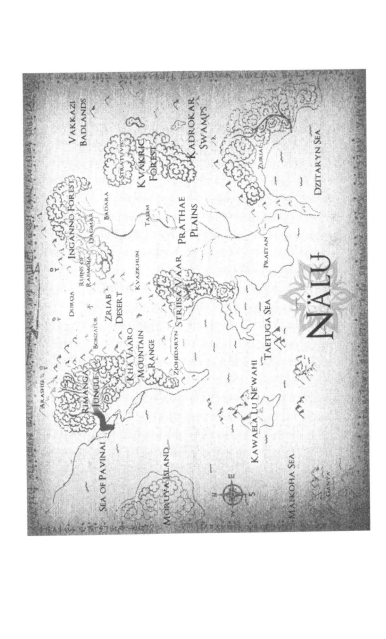

1

TODAY, SHE WOULD ask him. If she didn't, her mother would have her way, and then Ayianna would be stuck among the humans for the rest of her life. She latched the gate and picked up her lantern and the milk pail. Ivory froth filled the pail halfway, down an inch since yesterday. At this rate, they wouldn't have enough milk for the winter.

The morning lingered between the half-light of dawn and the shroud of night. The darkness obscured much of the forest and the dirt path behind her house. A cold breeze hissed through the odd, bushy silhouettes and spindly evergreens, whispering fear into her heart and provoking images of creatures hiding among the shifting shadows. She shivered and quickened her pace. Would she ever get used to living here?

Her lantern swung in her hand as she made her way back to the front yard. Its yellow glare skimmed the clumps of vines twisting up the back wall. Her house was almost as big as the village governor's, which would have put her family at an advantage if her father hadn't been an elf.

She sighed.

What kind of future could she hope to have here?

None.

She clenched her jaw and gripped the pail's handle tighter. Enough wondering. She needed to hurry and speak with Father before the porridge was ready—before Mother's presence could interfere.

At the end of the goat pen, where the path curved left to the front of the house, a sharp cry pierced the lingering darkness. Ayianna jumped back, upsetting the milk in her pail. She bit back a curse.

"Liam?"

No, the cry didn't sound like a wolf. Ayianna scanned the underbrush, the autumn trees above. Behind her, the goat bleated, but went back to nibbling on the grass. She shrugged, her eyes still scanning the bushes as she turned to go.

Leaves rustled, and the bush's slender limbs shuddered. Shadows veiled the intruder, the light of the lantern unable to penetrate the layers of dry leaves and stems. Ayianna peered closer. A dark mass burst out of the bush toward her face. She flung her arms up. The milk pail slammed into her head, and its warm contents splashed down her face, neck, and clothes. The lantern rocked on its hinge, the flame flashing and flickering. The intruder screeched, and a rush of wings brushed against her skin.

Ayianna lowered her arms.

A large bird ruffled its dark feathers and made to settle its wings, but one hung at an odd angle. Its round, ebony eyes ogled her.

Could it be?

"Fero? Is brother home already?" She glanced around, but her eyes failed her in the half-light. Her wet clothes clung to her skin, and the breeze grew colder. She shivered and glared at the bird. "Brother or not, look what you made me do? Now, I've got no milk, and I'm all wet."

Fero jerked his wayward wing back and hissed.

"Are you hurt?" Ayianna lifted the lantern, and its glow washed over the falcon, revealing dark stains on his ribbed underbelly. She reached out to touch him, but he snapped his curved beak at her. The branch shifted, and the bird thrashed about, trying to regain his perch, but then he broke free and soared haphazardly into the red-tinged sky.

Atop the bush, a strip of cloth fluttered where Fero had sat. She tore it free. The fabric was damp, soiled, and stunk of decay. It stained her fingertips red. Blood?

"Ayianna!"

Her mother's voice wrenched her from her thoughts. Ayianna tossed the cloth aside and darted up the path to the fire pit where her mother bent over a pot and stirred. The steam and smoke swirled into Mother's pinched face. Her head covering hung loose over her shoulders, revealing her messy braid and stray hairs.

Ayianna's stomach knotted. Should she say something? What would she say? Her brother's crazy bird had stopped for a visit and left a soiled piece of cloth? It was probably nothing. She shivered again in the morning breeze.

Her mother straightened, wiped her hands on her apron, and wrapped the scarf around her head. Her blue eyes narrowed. "What happened to you?"

"I tripped and spilled the milk."

She clucked her tongue. "Well, the porridge is ready." She held up three steaming bowls. "Take these inside, I'll be in soon. Once you're done, you'll need to start on the garden right away. We don't want to risk an early frost and lose everything we've worked for."

Ayianna nodded. She set the lantern aside and placed the milk pail in the attached shed. Sacks of threshed wheat sat at the back, waiting for the colder months where she would have to grind them into flour. Barrels filled with brine and cabbage lined one wall. Bundles of herbs hung from the thatched roof;

their spicy scents stung her nose and mingled with the souring cabbage. The smell turned her stomach.

She ducked back outside and accepted the bowls from her mother. Balancing them in her arms, she kicked the door open and slipped inside. She'd have to clean up later or lose the opportunity to speak with her father. The thin door clicked shut behind her.

"Morning," her father said. He sat on the edge of a bench and pulled his boots on. Thick streams of silver swam through his shaggy hair. Another sign that village life didn't agree with him.

"Morning, Father." Ayianna set the bowls on the small table in the center of the room and eyed him. Was he in a good mood, or should she try later? She took a deep breath. "Did you sleep well?"

He rubbed his face and stifled a yawn. "As well as I might, I suppose. Porridge again?"

She nodded.

Her father made a face and then smiled. He gestured toward the ceiling of the three-room house. "We have a roof over our heads and food in our bellies. What more could we ask for?"

Ayianna fidgeted with a chair. Here was her opportunity, if only the words would come. She opened her mouth to speak, but clamped it shut again. She grabbed one of the bowls of porridge and plopped down. Her soul writhed against the silence and would spew out recklessly if she didn't follow through. She took a deep breath.

"Father?"

He looked at her and smiled, but his eyes gave it away. He was bracing himself, knowing already what she was about to say.

She straightened her shoulders and plunged ahead. "I was wondering, you know, when Teron returns, if you—I mean, what do you think if Teron wishes—"

"The porridge tastes better when it's hot, you know."

Drat. Her mother stood in the doorway with a wooden spoon in her hand. She pulled off her scarf and hung it on a peg by the door. "You two better hurry. Lord Ramiro will have a fit if Father's late."

"We have plenty of time," her father said. He stretched and joined Ayianna at the table. "We were just waiting for you so that we may give thanks together."

She pursed her lips. "I don't have time for this. I must finish Lady Mara's order before the end of the week." Despite her protest, she sat down at the table. Her once tawny hair looked more like the splotchy coat of a roan horse, more white than brown.

Ayianna's father bowed his head, and she did likewise.

"*Lrasam zuyo, Osaryn, tahe dzitaryn, taary, asar roworyn.*" The elvish words poured from his lips as he prayed to the elven god, Osaryn, thanking him for the provisions. He lifted his gray eyes. "*Rodzijo unue.*"

Ayianna repeated the refrain aware of the tension radiating from her mother. She brought the wooden bowl to her lips.

"Why do you cling to Osaryn when he has done nothing for you but exile you from your homeland?" Mother asked.

Ayianna closed her eyes and swallowed the bland porridge. Would the fighting never end? She took a couple of slow gulps before putting the bowl down.

Her mother stood and crossed the room to her personal shrine of the Nuja, the four gods and goddesses of the plains people. Her people. She picked up the gilded statue of the goddess Natata and kissed it. She recited a chant in an undertone, almost musical way. Ayianna couldn't hear the words, but knew their meaning nevertheless: a giving of thanks, a request for favor, and a promise of sacrifice. Always the same day in and day out, but her mother's zeal for the Nuja had almost become maniacal since they had left Zurial.

Her mother replaced the statue with a slight bow of her head, and then returned to the table, drained her porridge, and dropped the bowl into the basin by the window. Without another word, she strode to the back of the room where her work bench sat nestled between tall drawers full of every bead, stone, and charm you could think of. Although the more costly gems have long since been sold—not that the plains people could have afforded them anyway. Above her bench, wooden dowels ran along the wall, and from them hung spools of silver, gold, flax, hemp, and cotton. Her mother removed one of the drawers and sat down at her desk.

Ayianna cleared her throat. "Don't you think your designs would fetch a higher price back in Zurial?"

"No." Her mother didn't look up, but continued to twist the strands of silver together.

"Well, at least the elves would appreciate your skills more."

"They didn't then, and they wouldn't now."

Ayianna frowned. "I thought you liked Zurial."

"Why are you bringing this up again?" Her mother bent closer to the table and slipped several red beads on to the strands, but not once did she raise her eyes.

"Well, it's just that . . . I was wondering," Ayianna rubbed at the knot in the table, "what you two thought about returning to Zurial when Teron comes back from Dagmar?"

There. She had finally said it. She took a deep breath and exhaled.

Mother looked up and turned her glare on Father. "You haven't told her yet?"

Her father's eyebrows furrowed, creasing lines across his smooth, tanned face. He set his empty bowl aside. "Don't you think Teron should be here for such an announcement?"

"Time is running out." She twisted the silver around the beads. "It could be the end of the week before Teron is here."

"This isn't the elven way."

"In case you haven't noticed, we are no longer among the elves. We are among my people now. Perhaps you would like to tell her why."

"What are you talking about?" Ayianna glanced to her mother and then to her father. "What haven't you told me?"

He took her hand. "Don't worry, Ayianna. Your mother speaks about things she doesn't understand." His eyes softened as he studied her. "But one thing is for certain, you have grown into a lovely lady."

Warmth crept into her cheeks, but she held his gaze as he continued. "Your mother and I have decided, since we are living among her people, that it was time for you to marry."

Her stomach sank. "But—but what about Zurial? At least I could return."

"And what would you do there?" Her mother raised her eyebrows.

"I'd be a stargazer."

Her mother chuckled. "Silly girl with silly dreams. Only pure-blooded elves can achieve that. You must accept your station in life, your responsibilities to your family and society."

"Gilana, that is enough." Her father stood.

"Either way, we can never return to Zurial." Her mother turned her glare on Ayianna. "And don't ever mention it again. We were never there. We came from Praetan, remember?"

Ayianna clenched her teeth. "Why?"

"Ask your father." She turned back to her work.

Ayianna sat in silence, waiting for an answer that wasn't going to come.

"It's for the best." Her father gripped her shoulders.

She glanced up at him. "At least tell me why?"

"There are some things better left unknown." Her father sighed. "For your own safety."

Ayianna stood and shrugged off his hands. She gathered the bowls, dumped them into the basin, and began pumping water. Marriage? How could her parents decide when it was time for her to get married? She was half-elf. How could the same age restraints of the humans apply to her?

Maybe her mother was right. Maybe she was more human than elf. She had been silly to think she could have been a stargazer. Her anger slowly dissipated, and once again she became aware of the tension vibrating between her parents. What was happening to her family?

She let go of the pump's handle, and the gush of water turned to a trickle, then disappeared altogether. She dried her hands on a towel and turned around. "So did you two have someone in mind?"

Her mother set aside the necklace she was working on and smiled. "Of course, dear, he is a charming young man with an eye for the courts of Badara."

She stiffened. Had she expected a different answer? She wrapped her arms around her waist and tried to remember all the eligible bachelors her mother had pointed out for the past five years. Was it Alberd with the missing front teeth, who was old enough to be her grandfather? Or the shaggy-haired Bodik with the square face and a nose like a vulture's beak. She was almost too afraid to ask. She swallowed. "Have I met him?"

"Yes." Her mother stood. Her eyes sparkled, and her face broke into a wide grin. "He is the nephew of Lord Ramiro. A draper of the finest silks and weaves, and he has friends among the nobility. This is truly a fine opportunity for you."

"Desmond?" Her mind reeled. The handsome blond? The one she had glimpsed a time or two on her trips with her father to Lord Ramiro's castle? The one the village girls had fawned over, but knew he'd never stoop so low as to look for a wife among the Karim villages? "But wouldn't I be considered beneath him?"

Her father shook his head. "Never think you are above or below anyone."

"The Nuja allow some people to rise above their circumstances." Her mother draped an arm around her shoulder. "And you, out of all the young women, have caught his eye."

"You mean, he's already asked? But he . . . " Ayianna stumbled through her words. "But I haven't really met him. I hardly know him."

"We do things differently here in the plains." She released Ayianna from her grasp and went back to her desk. "It's a good thing, too. You can't rely on feelings to secure a stable future. I should know." She stooped over her workspace and pushed the beads and pendants around in their wooden trays.

"Well," her father said. "Lord Ramiro will be expecting me early if I am to get a head start on the inventory. Ayianna, you will accompany me, I'm sure he would like to see you. I suppose to go over the preparations and betrothal arrangements."

"Now?" Her mother straightened.

"Why not? Since we've told her, he'll like to make it official as quickly as possible."

"She's not going there as she is—looking like a hireling." Her mother scurried about the rooms, gathering ribbons and a brush. "Wash your face, girl, and change your clothes. Wear your green dress."

Her father opened the door. "Be quick about it. I won't be long in saddling the horse." He winked at Ayianna and walked outside. The thin door snapped shut behind him.

Ayianna scrubbed the dried milk from her face. She rushed into the adjoining room and pulled out her green dress trimmed in black and silver—the nicest dress she owned. Was she going to see him today? She quickly changed, her mind running through all the things she might say to this man. Did he approve of her? Of course he did, why else would he have requested their betrothal? Would she refuse him? Could she?

Her mother yanked her into the main room again and set her in the chair. Ayianna studied the swirling wood grain in the table while her mother pulled a brush through her long hair. Mother chatted about betrothals and weddings of the plains people, and of social etiquette, but Ayianna's thoughts clouded out her mother's voice.

Betrothed . . .

The handsome nephew of a lord, Desmond had chosen her.

Excitement fluttered through her, but it did not surmount the growing unease in her stomach.

2

AYIANNA WRAPPED HER arms around her father's waist and rocked with the sway of their old mare, Brona. A few shafts of the early morning glow filtered through the limbs, barely lighting the well-worn path to Lord Ramiro's. She leaned her head against her father's back and closed her eyes, reveling in her father's earthy scent.

Marriage . . . her future secured in the hands of a stranger. Her dream of becoming a stargazer of the Esusamor elves, gone. No longer would she be under her father's protection. No more would she lay her head on his back and ride to Ramiro's. Tears sprang to her eyes.

"There are some things we need to discuss," her father said after riding for a while.

Straightening, Ayianna swallowed the knot in her throat and waited for him to continue.

"I do not believe Desmond is aware of your . . . heritage."

"What?" Ayianna straightened. "You could pass as a human."

"Are you suggesting I lie to him?"

Her father hesitated. "No . . . only don't bring it up. If he asks you, then answer how you want. The men of the plains regard their wives differently."

"What do you mean? Doesn't Lord Ramiro know you are an elf?" The lengthening silence confirmed her suspicions. "How could you?"

"I have my reasons."

"Father . . . " But Ayianna couldn't continue. Instead, she roiled in her thoughts and tried to accept what her father was saying. "Do these reasons of yours have anything to do with what Mother was talking about? About being exiled from Zurial?"

Her father tensed. "I wasn't exiled."

"Then why did we leave?"

"We made a choice to leave." He shook his head. "It's in the past, let's forget about it and think about your future."

"A future built on lies!" Ayianna ground her teeth. "This goes against everything you ever taught me."

His shoulders sagged. "Sometimes we are forced to choose against truth for a greater purpose. This is your burden to bear. You must forget about what might have been and live with what is."

Ayianna rubbed the edge of the faded saddle in front of her. How could he do this to her? No, it wasn't him. It was her mother. Why did her mother's bitterness have to wreak havoc on everyone else? Some elven maidens never married. Not that she didn't want to, but to enter into such an intimate relationship with a stranger was appalling.

"Desmond has sought your hand in marriage, with Lord Ramiro's approval, mind you. So we shall proceed and accept his proposal."

"Don't I get a choice?"

"I don't—" Her father shook his head. "Not this time."

She pulled back and slumped behind the saddle, refusing to lean into him. She ached for the simpler times back in Zurial when all that mattered was attending to her studies, hunting for dove eggs with her brother, and basking in the comfort of her father's presence and the peace that once was their home.

The trees receded as the land gave way to harvested fields. The night sky faded as the eastern horizon burned red. Wisps of fog clung to the ground where the warmth of morning met the cold earth. Other villagers appeared out of the thickets, hauling baskets and shovels over their shoulders and heading for the potato fields. Dirt stained their tunics and mismatched patches dotted drab leggings. Hirelings.

Ayianna peered around her father's shoulder. Lord Ramiro's fortress broke from the tree line and towered above the flat fields surrounding it. With new eyes, she admired the stout walls and ramparts overlooking the orange and yellow canopy of trees. A tingle of delight danced down her spine.

Nearing the fortress, her excitement gave way to nervousness. She had only seen Lord Ramiro from a distance. A tall man with chiseled features, he kept the operations of his lands under tight control. She took a deep breath and exhaled through her nose. The air reeked of fermenting cabbage, manure, and freshly overturned dirt.

Bustling activity inundated the area. Horses snorted as servants took hay and water into the stables. Hirelings stooped over the fields, filling their baskets with potatoes. Goats bleated to be milked, and a rooster heralded dawn's arrival. The whole place droned of animal sounds and servants' chatter.

Inside the stables, her father reined Brona to a stop. Ayianna slipped off the horse, landing on the hard packed dirt. She straightened her dress and adjusted the green scarf around her neck. Her father dismounted. His old cap slouched on his head and covered his pointy ears. How did Lord Ramiro not notice?

Her father led Brona into a stall and unsaddled her. He handed Ayianna one of the knapsacks.

"There is more for us to talk about." Her father scanned the stable and the bailey. "Now is not the time or place for it. But I'd suppose there will never be a time and place for the secrets I harbor."

"What are you talking about?" Ayianna stared at her father. His gray eyes were wistful, though he gazed at her, he looked beyond her. She touched his elbow.

His face softened as he wrapped his arm around her shoulders and squeezed. "Come, Lord Ramiro is waiting."

Ayianna stood in front of Lord Ramiro like a horse on parade. Maidservants came and went. Some took measurements; others pulled and tugged at her clothes, perhaps doing their best to make her presentable for their lord.

Polished marble floor met dark mahogany walls. Tapestries displayed men on horseback hunting bears and deer, and a large black cat that looked suspiciously like a Haruzo of the desert. On the opposite wall, a tapestry portrayed a different kind of hunt. Three women clad in pale silks raced through flowering gardens, chasing a white horse with a gold horn protruding from its forehead.

The bustling of the maidservants ceased, leaving Ayianna and her father alone with Lord Ramiro. He returned his quill to the ink pot and lifted a parchment—probably the betrothal. Burgundy silk draped his arms beneath a black velvet jerkin. He had blond hair like Desmond, but he lacked the charm his nephew possessed. Her gaze crossed his and she quickly looked away.

Had she seen a speck of approval in his blue eyes? She didn't dare chance another look. Instead, she studied the cracks in the polished marble floor, her mother's warning still ringing in her ears: *Keep your head covered. Don't look men in the eyes, nor speak unless spoken to, unless you want to be mistaken for a wench at some filthy brothel.*

"A fine choice." Lord Ramiro's booming voice rang throughout the hall. "I must say, my nephew has great taste. No doubt it is her exquisite beauty that far outweighs the other ladies-in-waiting of a much more noble breeding."

Ayianna cringed inwardly and glanced at her father. He stood rigid and quiet next to a huge window. The light pouring in washed across his tan face. His brown tunic dulled in comparison to the lord's velvet and silk attire.

"Arlyn," Lord Ramiro said after the last of the maidservants had left. He strolled across the marbled floors. His boots clicked louder in the growing silence. His gem studded belt and pendent caught the sunlight, flashing prisms of color against the polished stones.

He shook Father's hand and grasped his elbow. "You are a good man and have been one of my best stewards. I am certain Desmond's father would have welcomed this venture. You and your family shall move onto the grounds. Your wife may continue her jewelry making as Desmond sees fit. As for your daughter, she will begin her preparations for the revealing at the harvest jubilee. Do you have any objections?"

"No, sir," her father replied.

"Then you will take the next few days to move your family here. When Desmond returns from Badara, we will host a private feast and finalize the betrothal arrangement. You may go, but I'll expect you back here for the evening meal." Lord Ramiro nodded and strode from the room. A final flash of color and light, and then his footsteps echoed down the hall.

Servants scurried past the door, peering in at Desmond's new bride-to-be. Ayianna held her breath as whispers filled the corridor until they faded into silence. Did they approve? If they didn't, how could she live among them?

Ayianna lifted her head and looked at her father. A sad smile softened his jawline, but a storm of emotions swirled in his gray eyes.

Once outside, Ayianna left her father in the stables and continued out of the gates. He wouldn't need her to saddle the horse, and she needed some time alone. Perhaps she'd find Liam. At least the wolf would listen to her.

She surveyed the potato fields. Hirelings worked the soil and filled their woven baskets with dirty, round potatoes. Some hauled their brimming load toward Lord Ramiro's cellars, others prepared for the midday rest. The sun now hovered above, still plenty warm for fall.

Ayianna's thoughts turned to Desmond. She barely knew this man who had asked for her hand in marriage. He was a merchant's son, following his father's footsteps while she, on the other hand, was a daughter following a path chosen by her father.

Ayianna traced the lettering on her father's leather knapsack. Her mind strayed back to Zurial and its glittering sea, green mountains, and bright stars. She closed her eyes against the tears. Desmond was the death of her dreams.

Why did her father leave Zurial? An honored scribe, he took great care in preserving the ancient books of the elves. He had no enemies. He had loved his homeland, but he had chosen to settle in a nameless village that had no future. Why? Had he committed a crime in Zurial? Had he been exiled like Mother said?

Ayianna headed toward the woods and scanned the area. *Where is she? She should be here by now.*

A commotion near the front gates brought Ayianna's attention back to the castle. A woman with a baby slung across her back pleaded with Ramiro's chief servant. She moved closer.

"Please! Let me work for your master."

"Absolutely not! Lord Ramiro won't hear of a Durquian working his fields."

"Perhaps he'd allow me to glean after his workers have finished."

"There had better not be anything left to glean when they've finished. There are consequences for such negligence."

The baby began to cry, and the woman adjusted the colorful fabric strapping the child to her back. "But my family is starving."

"Do you not have fields of your own to work? Livestock to attend to?"

"Please, Baldor, my brother, the fields of Durqa are arid and barren. The earth consumes the seeds we plant."

Baldor clenched his jaw as his face flushed red. "Do not address me so. You have no brother or father among us. How you escaped from the confines of Durqa alive is your own business. You know the laws. Be gone from us for there will be no bloodshed today." He wheeled about and charged through the castle's gates.

The woman slowly turned and made her way along the stout curtain wall surrounding Lord Ramiro's holdings. The baby's cry echoed off the brick barricade and pierced Ayianna's heart.

She shuddered. Her father's knapsack suddenly felt heavy. She darted after the woman. She rounded the wall just in time to catch a glimpse of her disappearing into the woods.

"Madam! Madam of Durqa," Ayianna called after her.

The woman spun, and her desperate eyes narrowed. Her hand grasped a slender dagger hanging from a braided rope at her waist. Dark smudges covered her pale face and arms. Dressed in a red-brown tunic and leggings, the Durquian stood a head taller than Ayianna.

"Take this, it isn't much." Ayianna offered her knapsack to the stranger.

The woman looked at the bag as tears welled up in her eyes. "May the Chai bless you. What is your name?"

Ayianna hadn't heard of the Chai before. Hopefully, it was a nice deity and not easily angered like the Nuja. She didn't want strange people lifting her name up before strange gods, but she didn't want to be rude either. She stuck her hand into the pocket of her dress and grasped the worn talisman her mother had given her. The polished white stone was cold and smooth in her hand. "I am Ayianna, daughter of Gilana and Arlyn."

"I am Marjeta. I will not forget your generosity, Ayianna." The woman bowed her head and pulled a leather cord free from her neck. "My gift in return. I hope it blesses you as it has me." She handed Ayianna a small wood flute and strode off into the trees.

Ayianna fingered the small flute. Delicate carvings wove their way around its barrel. She tied it around her neck and brought it to her lips. As she prepared to blow, something crashed through the bushes and knocked into her. Her heart leapt into her throat, but her fear quickly dissolved.

"Liam!" Ayianna grabbed the silver wolf into a huge hug. "Where have you been? I had so much on my mind this morning and then—oh, I have so much to tell you."

Liam sat on her haunches, her long snout cracked open in a silly smile. She panted happily, swishing her tail back and forth.

Ayianna buried her face in the lush fur. "Father's betrothed me to Desmond, and we're moving to the castle. Life is changing too fast, too soon." Ayianna pulled away and scratched behind Liam's ears. "So, where have you been? You're feet are all muddy. You better not have been playing in the—"

"Ayianna!" Her father's voice echoed off the castle's wall.

She straightened. "Come on, Liam."

Ayianna darted toward the front gate, passing several older hirelings who had stopped working, their gaze following her.

An old woman bent with age and years of hard work leaned on her shovel. Her cold eyes peered out from the folds of her wrinkly skin. "You'll bring curses on us, ya miserable lil' whelp!"

Ayianna shrank back from the woman's harsh glare. "What do you mean?"

"We've not'ing to do wit'em Durquians," an older man said. He stomped on the shovel's edge, sending it deeper into the dirt. "You'd do best to avoid 'em."

"The whole lot of them wicked and bloodthirsty," another villager drawled as he spat on the ground. He lifted his brown, weathered face and glowered at Ayianna. He rested on his shovel. "Thieves and murderers."

"She was hungry," Ayianna said. "How can you deny someone—"

"Bad blood, little one, bad blood. They'd be dawdling in things that one ought not to dawdle in. The horrors that haunt 'em. They'll haunt you too, if you be too friendly with 'em. Ever hear of the mutats, dithza-mielis, hütas?" He sneered. "Creatures who'll kill you in your dreams, or drive you to do it yourself, I've heard. I'd stay clear away from 'em if I were you." He heaved a large basket of potatoes and hauled it toward the cellars.

Ayianna clutched her talisman again. Mutats? Dithza-mielis? Hütas? Maybe he was just trying to scare her. She turned away and sought her father, ignoring the icy stares.

3

"LET'S STOP FOR the midday rest," Ayianna's father said as he reined in the old mare.

"Oh . . . "Ayianna dismounted and turned to face him. "I—um—I gave the food away." She twisted the scarf's ends in her fingers.

His brows furrowed.

Before he could say anything, she quickly added. "She was hungry, and she had a baby. I don't think they had eaten in a while."

Her father's puzzled face gave way to a grin. "You have a good heart, Ayianna. It won't hurt us to go hungry for a little longer. Still, let's walk a bit." He led Brona down the path in silence, and then chuckled. "Well, I am glad I gave you the knapsack containing the food and not your betrothal gift."

"What?" She dropped the scarf's ends and stared at him.

He brought Brona broadside and dug in the knapsack hanging from her saddle horn. A smiled tugged at the corners of his mouth as he pulled out a delicate package. "From your mother and me."

Ayianna took the slender gift and unwrapped it. Within the folds of a lace handkerchief sat a hairpin unlike any she'd seen before. A dark blue sapphire glittered amidst bronze petals. A weaving of copper and silver threads spun around the flower's base and attached it to three strands twisting around a center prong. Mother's signature design.

"It's beautiful. Thank you!" She embraced him.

"Here." Father took the pin from her. "Let me show you how the great elven ladies of Zurial wear their hair." He took off her scarf. "Well, I'm not going to undo your mother's handiwork, but let's see. They twist their hair like this, and then like that." Her father slid the pin into her hair and stepped back to admire his creation. "Then again, maybe not. We'll just slide it into the ribbons, and let your mother show you how to pin it with your scarf."

She laughed as tears stung her eyes. "Thank you, Father."

"Better put your scarf on before your mother catches you without it. She won't let you hear the end of it."

Ayianna rearranged the scarf around her head. "What's bothering Mother?"

"She is upset at me for uprooting the family."

"Why did you leave Zurial?"

Arlyn looked away and continued strolling along the path, Brona clopping behind him. Birds twittered somewhere among the autumn-colored trees.

Ayianna kept pace and her tongue. He hadn't changed the subject or demanded the conversation to end. Perhaps he'd tell her if she didn't interrupt or seem too eager. Beneath her feet, dried brown and red leaves crackled. Then again, maybe he wouldn't.

He twisted the reins between his fingers. "Some things are better left unknown. With knowledge comes responsibility and wouldn't life be better lived in ignorance?"

"Perhaps, but ignorance breeds fear and dooms one to a life of failure."

"Well spoken." Her father continued for a few steps and then asked, "Ayianna, do you believe in Osaryn?"

She hesitated. "Yes."

"Then why do you carry your mother's talisman in your pocket?"

She turned her attention to the path before her. Tufts of brown grass lined the indented road where wagon wheels had eaten into the dirt.

"The world is at war with itself," her father said.

"But we live in peace, relatively speaking."

"Some battles we can see, such as the struggle to survive among the animals and people groups here in Nälu. And then there are others beyond our realm of knowledge, such as the ones fought by the guardians."

"What does this have to do with you leaving Zurial?"

"Well, some of us are chosen to guard secrets rather than fight battles." Her father took a deep breath and blew it out slowly. "I am one who guards a secret. Like my father before me."

Ayianna tried to meet his gaze, but he stared straight ahead. He clenched and unclenched his jaw.

"Secrets are dangerous." He stopped and faced her. "The enemy got too close, and we had to leave."

"Does mother know?"

He nodded.

"Teron?"

He glanced away and nodded.

"Why didn't you tell me?"

"You know how your mother is, but it's for the best."

"How?"

"You'll marry Desmond and have nothing to worry about."

Ayianna scowled. "Except to hide under lies for the rest of my life. Did you ever think about what I want?"

"Sometimes circumstances don't allow us to choose our paths or the burdens we must bear."

She looked away and blinked back tears. Was there no other way? Was this her life's path? A path forced onto her because of who her father was. Her gaze met his, and the depth of sorrow churned his gray eyes almost black. He didn't want this anymore than she did. She took a deep breath and straightened her shoulders. She would bear this burden for her father. If only her heart could agree.

Her father slipped his arm around her shoulders. "You won't have to do this alone. We'll be with you." His eyes gained a faint sparkle. "And you'll get a fine view of those stars from Ramiro's towers."

Ayianna smiled. She could do this, for him. And maybe it wouldn't be so bad. The burden seemed lighter already. Besides, all the other girls had found Desmond desirable, why couldn't she?

Arm in arm, they strolled down the path without speaking. The sun shifted in the sky, and the trees blazed orange and red. Yes, she could live in the plains. Zurial couldn't compare to the plains' array of autumn colors.

"Does mother know about our move to Lord Ramiro's estate?"

"Not yet, she'll be pleasantly surprised, though. Once Teron . . . " He pulled away. His face hardened as he scanned the trees.

"What—"

He held up his hand and tilted an ear toward the forest.

Ayianna scanned the underbrush, certain it was Liam her father had heard, but the silver wolf was nowhere to be seen. Had she not followed them?

"I sense some men of ill-intent not far away," her father finally whispered and handed her his knapsack.

Ayianna's eyes widened. "Thieves?"

"I doubt it. We're too close to the villages and Lord Ramiro's lands."

Ayianna glanced over her shoulder, trying to sense the presence her father spoke of, but found nothing. A pure elf would have been able to sense them. Could she learn?

"What should we do?" she asked.

"Keep on walking." Her father stooped and picked up a tree limb as wide as his wrist. He stabbed the ground with it as if it were a walking stick. He rubbed the bark off, snapping branches as he slid his hand along it.

Ayianna hung the bag over her shoulder. "Why don't we—"

The underbrush around them exploded.

Brona reared. Ayianna's father allowed the mare her head, then eased her back.

Six men dressed in red and black clothes fanned out in front of them, brandishing short, fat swords. Black scarves hid their faces, except for their pale eyes.

Ayianna pressed into her father. They didn't stand a chance against so many armed men.

"You've been a hard one to find, elf." One of the men stepped forward, his voice muffled behind the scarf.

Arlyn pressed the reins into Ayianna's hands. "Take Brona and go." His glare never left the advancing men. He balanced his newly acquired walking stick in his hands.

Ayianna couldn't leave him outnumbered. Why didn't they just mount up and flee together?

"Kill the girl, but she wants him alive." The man ordered as he lunged and slashed his sword in front of him.

Arlyn swung the tree limb and clipped the man's hand, knocking the stout blade from his fingers. The other men charged. Arlyn whirled around Ayianna. He wheeled the tree limb above and slammed it down atop another man's head.

The man twitched and slumped to the ground.

Her father whipped the limb back around, catching another one in the gut.

Brona pranced away from the skirmish, yanking Ayianna with her. Ayianna tugged the horse's head back down and grasped the bridle. She glanced at one of the fallen men. Perhaps she could get one of the swords.

She reached for one, but Brona struggled against her, unwilling to move closer. The mare spun around, jerking Ayianna off balance.

A man approached. His black scarf had been pulled away from his face, revealing a dirty moustache and beard.

Ayianna glanced at her father, and her heart sank. Three men surrounded him, and he was doing his best to keep them at bay.

The man continued to advance.

Ayianna swung Brona around and tried to use her as a shield, but the horse shied away from the man and pushed Ayianna toward the fighting men. Her father still held his ground against them, but for how long?

Suddenly the man was next to her.

She jumped back, but tripped and hit the ground. His sword flashed above her, and Ayianna screamed.

She closed her eyes, expecting pain, but felt nothing. A huge weight fell on her, and she struggled to breathe. She snapped her eyes open.

Her father's pained expression hung over her, pleading with her. "Go to your brother," he gasped. "Tell him . . . the sun has set."

"No." Ayianna wiggled out from under him and grabbed his face. "No, Father, you're not dying. You can't . . . "

Defeat twisted his face. Fear and pain burned in his gray eyes, the fire slowly fading from his gaze. His hand brushed her cheek. "Tell him the morning star is forever locked in stone."

"No, Father, I can't leave you like this." She dug her hands under his shoulders and tried to lift him. His body sagged, and he slipped through her fingers. She slumped next to him, laying her forehead on his back. This was all her fault. The blade had been meant for her. If she had listened, she could have gone for help. Instead, her actions had killed her father. They had wanted him alive. Her eyes burned, and her vision blurred.

"Go!" He gasped and coughed.

Tears poured down her face as she squeezed his hand one last time. She couldn't think about it. She had to go, to leave him and do what he said. She willed herself to obey. Where had Brona gone?

She eyed the group of men. They argued and called each other profane names. She spun around. A couple of yards away, the mare struggled in the underbrush, the reins tangled in the limbs and thorns.

Ayianna darted to her side and yanked the reins free. She mounted quickly and chanced one more glance at her father's prostrate body, the hilt of the sword protruding from his back. Her chest constricted, and she gasped. How could she leave him like this?

"You fools, the girl is escaping!" one of the men yelled, and they rushed toward her.

Ayianna wheeled Brona about and pressed her heels into the mare's flanks, hoping the men didn't have horses hiding among the trees.

4

RAYS OF GOLDEN light leaked through the branches as Ayianna guided Brona over the rocky terrain. She had ridden hard through the night, skirting the edge of the Prathae Plains and resting the horse only when necessary. The old mare would have done her father proud.

Ayianna stretched in the saddle, her backside numb, and her legs threatening to cramp. She kneaded her thigh and tried to see beyond the clusters of evergreens and oaks. She blinked the drowsy haze from her eyes. *How much farther?*

She urged the horse on. Perhaps she'd make it in time to join her brother for the morning meal, but then she'd have to tell him what happened and deliver her father's message.

A fresh wave of tears spilled down her cheeks. She blinked them away and tried to focus on maneuvering between the trees. She gritted her teeth. They had better leave her father's body alone. One thing was certain, he would receive a proper burial as soon as she and her brother returned. She swiped at the tears with her scarf. Her face burned, her skin raw from the constant rubbing.

Brona tugged against the reins. Ayianna patted her sweaty neck and murmured words of praise. Ahead, a swift river severed their path, and the horse halted. She flicked her ears and threw her head.

"Come on, you can do it." Ayianna dug her heels into the mare's belly, and the horse plunged forward.

Once across, she patted Brona's neck. "Good girl, that wasn't so . . . " Ayianna trailed off. The forest was too quiet. Her words out of place, swallowed up by the silence.

An odd stench drifted on the breeze, growing stronger. Smoke hung heavy in the air and clung to the trees. She buried her nose in the crook of her arm. Then she caught sight of Dagmar's gates, broken and splintered. Her heart stopped. No.

She urged Brona onward and glanced about, searching for movement, for life. Mangled bodies of men and women covered the bailey. Hundreds of creatures the size of dogs, but with bodies like deformed men covered in wiry fur, lay among the dead. Bloody gashes ripped aside their dark fur and exposed the white of their bones.

Her stomach churned. She tried calling for her brother, but the cries died within her knotted throat. To the right small buildings ran along the curtain wall until it curved out of sight. The fortress loomed above them all, its windows blackened and void of life, like a mother grieving the loss of her children.

Who would destroy a place of learning? She adjusted the bag's strap around her shoulder, slid off the horse, and crumbled to the ground.

The horse flinched, her eyes big and round. Her nostrils flared, and she jerked her head up.

"Easy there, Brona." Ayianna forced the words out and reached out to touch the horse's neck, but the mare bolted, tearing the reins from her grasp. Ayianna stumbled after her, but the horse was gone.

Ayianna gripped the stone wall next to her. *I should leave. Go for help—but where?* She closed her eyes for a moment and then turned back toward the gates.

A man's vacant eyes stared at her, his neck oddly twisted, his throat torn. Another held what was left of his stomach, his intestines spilled across the ground. Bodies atop bodies hid the ground. A blanket of flies buzzed about the corpses, crawling in and out of their gaping mouths and bloody wounds.

Bile seared her throat. She took a step and collapsed. Dry heaves forced her to wretch until nothing remained.

She wiped her mouth and pushed up from the ground. The metallic stench of blood and acrid smoke threatened to make her wretch again. She gritted her teeth and picked her way around the bodies, through the bailey, and into the inner courtyard. A vacant, crystal basin sat above the dead like a silent sentry.

A shadow flitted across the edge of her vision. She whirled around, scanning the buildings and the courtyard. Had she seen something? Or was it just the haze of smoke wafting on the breeze? She inched toward the fortress, but her eyes darted back and forth.

A clank resounded beyond the inner courtyard, and she halted. Had somebody survived? Or was the enemy still there? She dashed up to the fortress's large wooden doors and shoved against the coarse wood.

The school was in disarray. Broken tables and chairs lay upside down, shoved against the walls. Remnants of banners smoldered in the center of the room.

From the rafters hung an ominous black flag. Two golden triangles gleamed from the dark fabric, a gold snake curled in the center of the banner, weaving through the angled points of the triangles. The banner of Stygian.

Dread crawled up Ayianna's spine. It couldn't be . . . Stygian remained in the Abyss, held back by the Perimeter. He couldn't have led this attack.

She passed through the corridor into Dagmar's famed library. Ayianna stared. The beautiful wooden bookshelves had been hacked to pieces and scattered throughout the room. The library's vault sat open and naked, its guarded secrets gone. Heaps of ashes littered the marble floor where the remains of books and scrolls lay charred and useless.

She turned and rushed back outside.

"Teron?" Her voice caught in her throat. She darted through the dormitories and the outer buildings. Every door she opened, every window she peered in revealed the same horror. Death in some twisted form had seized the lives of Dagmar's inhabitants. She tried to take deep breaths, but the stench of death burned her lungs.

Ayianna stumbled toward the last stone hut and tripped over a body, falling headlong into a furry carcass of one of the hideous creatures. She struggled to free herself from the tangle of arms only to roll into a crumpled body of a young woman. Blood stained her dress and hands. Ayianna spun around and came face to face with her brother's staring eyes—his head severed from his arrow-studded body.

How—her brother—his head. She screamed. She shoved her brother's corpse away, his body cold and limp. She staggered to her feet and tumbled through the doorway of the hut. Shrieking, she raked at her arms and body, but could not remove the feel of his icy skin against hers, nor the vision forever seared in her mind.

A mud-caked hand clamped around her mouth and smothered her cries.

Ayianna fought and kicked. Breaking free, she fell forward and hit the ground. She rolled out of the way and snatched a discarded sword from the grass. She leapt to her feet, but black spots crowded her vision. She swayed, blinking her eyes. Where was he?

A shadow slipped to her right, and she whirled to face her attacker. Disheveled black hair hung past his shoulders, but didn't hide the scar over his left eyebrow or the gold earring in his right ear. Pirate.

She clenched her teeth and swung the blade. He blocked her blow, knocking the sword from her hand. Ayianna jumped back and massaged her stinging palm. She refused to look away as he leveled his sword at her throat.

"Who are you, and what are you doing here?" he demanded. His gray eyes bore into hers, daring her to give him a reason to kill.

"What's it to you?" She wrapped her arms around her waist. Nausea churned her gut, her throat burning. Maybe she'd vomit on him instead of fighting it.

"Look, I do not wish to harm you." He stepped back, threw his sword to the ground, and wiped his hands on his brown pants.

Ayianna studied him. Blood and dirt stained his ivory tunic. His dark complexion was out of place in the plains, like her father. An elf, no doubt. "Why should I trust you?"

"I haven't killed you, have I?"

Ayianna weighed his words. She straightened, but never took her eyes off him—just in case.

"My name is Marjeta," she said, picking the first name that had come to her mind.

"Marjeta, huh?" His eyes narrowed. "And what are you doing here, *Marjeta*?"

"Looking for someone."

"Don't you think it's a little foolish to be wandering the plains alone, and without a head covering? One might think you were up to no good." He ducked back into the hut and returned shortly with a few items. He placed them inside a bag.

"What are you doing? Scavenging?" Ayianna asked. "Were you part of the sick evil that slaughtered these people?"

He whirled around and pressed the edge of the blade against her neck. "I'd be careful about throwing around unfounded accusations." He withdrew and shoved the dagger into his boot. "Go back to where you came from." He grabbed a yew bow, unstrung it, and slid it into a leather casing.

"Were you here when it happened?"

"What's it to you?"

She gritted her teeth. He turned away while he tied his hair back, revealing his upturned ears. No surprise there.

Ayianna glowered and crossed her arms. "I want to know who is responsible."

"Go home." He shoved more things into a bag. "It isn't your responsibility."

"And it's yours?"

"I . . ." He hesitated. "I was a guard. I'm supposed to be here, unlike you."

"A guard, huh? Well, great job you did . . . guarding!" Ayianna exploded, but no sooner had the words tumbled out than she wished they had died in her throat.

The elf's face hardened, his brows furrowed, but he didn't reply. He finished strapping a scabbard to his waist, then he snatched up his sword and sheathed it with an air of finality.

Ayianna whirled around. Tears burned her cheeks again. *What should I do? Where do I go?* She stormed across the courtyard, unseeing. Home. She should return home. She must tell her mother what happened. Her stomach lurched.

In a flurry of feathers and a piercing cry, a falcon swooped out of the sky.

Ayianna looked up, and the warmth of familiarity washed over her. Her brother's bird spiraled haphazardly toward her, and then landed on her shoulder, his long talons pinching her skin.

"Fero . . ." Her voice cracked.

"Liar!"

She startled and glanced back at the guard.

Recognition blazed in his eyes. "You are Teron's sister, Ayianna."

"What makes you say that?"

His eyes narrowed. "You're not the only one who knows Fero."

"You . . . you know my brother?"

"Knew. He's dead, remember?" The guard clenched his teeth and started for her. "What are you doing here?"

Ayianna fell back. Mounting pressure squeezed her head, her mind reeled. Her brother and father dead—Dagmar destroyed—the guard—Fero. Her disjointed thoughts spun in sorrow's vortex. Her limbs refused to move—words escaped her. The elf came toward her, saying something, but her ears roared. Ayianna sank to her knees as tears burned her face again.

"Kael? What is going on here?" A rich, deep voice broke through her daze.

Ayianna glanced up.

An elderly elf approached. Dirt and dried blood smeared his wrinkled, bronze face, nearly hiding the dark runes marring his cheekbones. The sorrow in his amber eyes tore at her heart. He turned his gaze to the guard.

Kael shook his head. "Headmaster, this is Teron's sister, Ayianna."

The Headmaster raised his thick, white eyebrows, creasing even more wrinkles into his balding head. He looked back at Ayianna and held out his hand. "Why are you here?"

She swallowed the knot in her throat and took his hand. "I was looking for my brother—my . . . my father sent me."

"A strange mission to send a young woman on alone, I would think." He tugged on his braided beard.

"I'm sorry, but who are you?" she asked, hoping he wouldn't push for more details.

The elderly elf bowed his head. "I am Saeed. High Guardian, and, before yesterday, Headmaster of the Kayulm'sa Nutraadzi."

She stared at him. "I've never met a Guardian before. Do you really do magic?"

Saeed shook his head. "Not magic, no. We do have gifts the great Vituko has bestowed on us."

"Vituko?"

"This is neither the time nor the place to discuss the divine," Kael said. "We must hurry if we're to reach Badara before the festival starts."

Saeed tugged on his long, white beard again. "We cannot leave Dagmar like this."

"What are you suggesting?"

"We must burn them."

Kael clenched his jaw and nodded. "What about the girl?"

"Don't worry about me." Ayianna straightened. "I'm going home."

"Out of the question," Saeed said. "I cannot, in good conscience, allow you to traipse across the plains by yourself."

"I have to. My mother will need to know what happened."

Saeed shook his head.

"You don't understand. She might even be in danger. I must go."

"In danger of what?" Saeed raised an eyebrow.

She glanced back and forth between Saeed and Kael, and gritted her teeth. "At least allow me an axe to help build the pyre."

Kael's eyebrows shot up. He opened his mouth to speak, but Saeed spoke first.

"So be it. Kael, find us some axes, and I will go get the oil."

Several hours later, Ayianna's muscles burned and her hands bled. She gripped the axe harder and chopped the dead tree into smaller pieces.

"We have enough."

Ayianna whirled around, her pulse pounding in her head. It was only Kael. She lowered her axe and pushed the air out through her nose.

He stooped to pick up a few logs and straightened. "I didn't mean to startle you."

Ayianna dropped the axe and gathered up the severed branches. The last thing she wanted was to talk to him. She strode through the gates, trying to ignore the throbbing of her head, back, and arms. She threw her load onto the makeshift pyre and started back for more.

Suddenly, the world shifted, and she stumbled forward. She reached for the wall and steadied herself. The cool stone soothed her burning hands, but her vision kept spinning. What was happening? She tried to blink the haze from her eyes. Her legs buckled, and she collapsed.

"Are you all right?" Kael's face hovered above her.

Ayianna blinked. "I . . . I'm fine." She sat up, but the world pitched again. She closed her eyes and leaned against the stone.

She felt his hands on hers. "Your hands are bleeding."

She jerked them away and glared at him. "I'm fine!"

"No, you're not. Here, drink." He held out a waterskin.

She eyed him, but finally took it and gulped down the water. The warm liquid rushed to her empty stomach.

"Not too fast." He pulled it back. "When was the last time you ate?"

She struggled to order her scattered thoughts. "Yesterday . . . morning."

"Here." Kael tugged a chunk of bread and some smoked meat from his knapsack and handed it to her.

"Thank you." She devoured the bread and meat.

He leaned against the wall and inclined his head toward Saeed. "He'll light the fire soon."

She glanced into the courtyard. The elderly elf poured oil over the pile of wood and bodies. She swallowed and tugged at the hem of her dress, her movements painful. Laying her hands in her lap, she stared at the broken blisters.

"He'll probably say a prayer, if you'd like to come."

She didn't want to be any closer to the mound of death than she already was. Still, her brother was in there somewhere. Tears stung her eyes again. She nodded slowly.

He stood and helped her to feet.

After Saeed prayed in a tongue unfamiliar to Ayianna, he lit the pyre. The flames lapped at the dry timber, escalating as they engulfed the oil-soaked wood. Her brother and father. Gone.

She closed her eyes against the tears, but they still came. She fell to her knees and cried. *Osaryn, if you are real as my father has taught me, help me!*

A hand gripped her shoulder firmly and pulled her to her feet. She looked up. Saeed's face was wet, his eyes red. "You must hide. Someone comes, and we know not if he is a friend or foe."

"How many do you think?" Kael gripped his sword's hilt. He clenched his jaw, causing a vein in his forehead to bulge.

"Maybe five or more."

Ayianna heard the pounding hooves growing louder over the roar of the flames. She scanned the area for a hiding place. How could an old elf and the guard survive against so many? She glanced at the splintered gates. One hung from a hinge and rested against several barrels. She quickly ducked behind them and waited. Her heart hammered in her ears, competing with the thunder of the coming horsemen.

"She couldn't have gone far." A deep voice growled.

The horses' pounding hooves slowed as they passed through the gate. "What happened here?"

"Who cares," another man said. "Find the girl."

It couldn't be. Ayianna held her breath. Who else would they be looking for but her?

"Hey, you there," a voice shouted. "Yes, you, old elf, have you seen a young girl pass through here?"

"I have seen many young girls here, and, as you can tell, many have lost their lives and burn now on the pyre. If you wish to investigate the dead, you may do so."

"Don't be smart with me old elf. She would have passed through this morning sometime."

"What business do you have with her?" Kael asked.

"So you don't deny you saw a girl."

Ayianna had heard enough. She had to get out of there. Behind her, the hanging gate created a space near the ground just large enough for her to squeeze through. She dropped to her knees and crawled toward it, but her dress restricted her movement. Cursing, she grasped its hem.

Swords clashed, and her heart plummeted. Kael and Saeed would die on the account of her.

She hated it . . . hated it all.

She clenched her teeth. At least Kael and Saeed stood a better chance than her father. Without a second glance, she crawled through the opening. Almost to the other side, something grabbed her dress. She spun around, expecting to see a grisly face looming over her. Instead, her dress had snagged on the splintered gate. She ripped it free, scrambled to her feet, and sprinted into the trees. The clanging swords faded as she rushed through the underbrush. Branches whipped her face, but their sting only drove her on.

Deeper in the woods, the clash of battle ceased. Had Kael and Saeed survived? Or would death claim them instead of her? Her mind dove back to the hut, reliving the horror of her brother's broken body. She pushed herself harder and harder, desperately wanting to outrun the images that burned behind her eyes.

Run. The word echoed in the hollows of her mind, her consciousness slipping away. *Run.* How long? How far? She didn't know, she just ran. Her lungs burned, fighting for air. Her mind grew fuzzy. She ran until her ears ached and tears stung her eyes, and still she ran on. Exhaustion weighed down her legs. Her knee buckled and she tumbled.

Ayianna struggled to her feet. Warm blood oozed down her face.

Horses' hooves crashed through the brush behind her.

She couldn't outrun them, but maybe she could hide. She darted through the trees, looking for sanctuary. She stumbled and hit a tree. Tears blurred her vision, her limbs trembled. She couldn't go on much longer. Pain ripped through her side, and she toppled to the ground as darkness enclosed her in its icy grip.

5

BUILT FROM WHITE, speckled granite, the castle of Gwydion stretched high, its towers piercing the sky. The setting sun glinted off its polished white and green-flecked walls. The Sorceress ran her gloved hand along the chipped battlement and breathed deeply of the autumn air. The world seemed at peace and in dreamy slumber.

Earthy, rich tones of burning muskroot, olibanum, and the sweet raklichi plant drifted from the courtyard as the priestesses burned the evening's incense in worship to the goddess Raezana. They weaved through the gardens and disappeared into the temple.

Imps scampered through the outer courtyard. Their attack on Dagmar only partially successful. Nevertheless, fresh blood whetted their appetites, and the fallen fairies hungered for more. They screeched and shoved one another as they fought over the very best spot—a spot which would allow their yellowed eyes to once again see the man who took pity on them.

Derk.

Semine lifted her eyeglass and scanned the horizon from her lofty perch. A few scraggly trees dotted the rough terrain.

To the north, she could almost see the glowing orbs of the Great Perimeter and somewhere beyond, the land of Nganjo. She glanced away. She dared not risk a glimpse of the orbs for fear of being blinded.

A gust of wind buffeted the tower, and Semine steadied herself against the rampart. Her white robes billowed, but a gold belt anchored them around her waist. A crown of fiery copper hair swirled and danced about her pale face like the tendrils of flames lapping at a sacrifice in the temple's stone altar. She pushed the curls away from her eyes, wishing she had tied them back.

The autumn's chill crawled down her neck and into her toes. She rubbed her gloved arms for warmth and paced the battlement. Where was he? She should've tried the uisol stone, but she was afraid of what she might see.

A horn blew.

Semine peered through the eyeglass and caught a glimpse of an advancing caravan. Grinning, she turned and descended from the tower's heights, adjusting her robes and hair as she went. For years she had planned for this very day. Raezana would be pleased with her.

She waited at the top of the steps leading down into the courtyard. Lush green shrubbery lined the paths that crisscrossed below her, evergreen against the waning colors of autumn. Fitting for a goddess of fertility and life.

Beyond the gardens, the white dome of the temple rose into the sky like a woman with child in her ninth month. Raezana had given birth to the humans, despite what the guardians taught, and Semine was determined to let the world know. The delicate carvings and mosaic murals adorning the dome glinted in the late afternoon light.

Semine blinked away their glare and turned her gaze back to the advancing caravan. For too long, Derk had avoided her and hid among the thieves and outcasts. Not anymore.

Raezana's time had come. She straightened her shoulders and lifted her chin.

A horn echoed off Gwydion's towers as the caravan poured through the gates and parted to one side or the other. A hush fell over the imps. Four black horses, their heads adorned with black and gold plumes, pulled a carriage made of dragon bones. Hooves and wheels clattered over the cobblestone street and halted before Semine.

The driver, a wiry elf, jumped from his seat and opened the coach's door. Lord Derk stepped out, flourishing a polished, black cane, and dressed like a king in a black doublet, a matching cloak lined with fur, and a ringlet of silver on his head. Still as handsome as the day Semine had first laid eyes on him, Derk displayed little sign of aging except for a few strands of silver streaking his thick black hair and goatee.

A handful of crows scattered at his approach. Their flapping wings and guttural cries broke the silence.

"Lord Derk!" Semine proclaimed. "Welcome to Gwydion, the temple of the lovely Raezana."

Her servants stepped from the shadows and knelt.

Derk nodded in return. He turned to Semine, his silky doublet reflecting the glare of the sun.

Semine searched his eyes. Had he forgiven her? She raised her gloved hand, and a servant stepped forward. "Take Derk's men to the barracks and attend to their needs."

The servant nodded and trotted down the steps.

"Shall we proceed inside?" Semine asked.

After leading Derk through a short tour of the great hall and keep, Semine took him to her private chambers. A large fire crackled in the hearth. It warmed the cold marble floors and diminished the chill in the room. Two elaborately carved oak chairs, covered in red-and-gold patterned velvet, sat in front of the fireplace. An archway led into an adjoining room where Semine's bed towered above a large bear rug, its head still attached. Dark wood posts spiraled to the ceiling. Heavy blood-red drapes enclosed the bed.

Semine settled in one of the chairs next to the blazing fire and loosened her robe. She motioned for Derk to join her, the chair ample enough for the two of them. Instead, he sat across from her.

"It is true, then? You have the pearl?" Derk rested his black polished cane across his knees.

Semine sulked. "Business already? We have barely been reacquainted."

"What is to know, Semine?" He glanced round the room. "You have been feasting like a queen, while I have been scavenging like a dog in Durqa."

"Scavenging?" She raised her eyebrows. "You manipulated your way into lordship. You reign as king over thieves and murderers. I must say, you have done rather well for yourself."

"You haven't suffered like the rest of us."

"You have no idea how much I've suffered." Semine clenched the chair's arm. "Did you think Raezana would let such transgressions go unpunished? No. I paid for my failures as well as yours and Nach's." And she would continue to pay for Nach's betrayal. She took a deep breath and squared her shoulders. "But I remained faithful. Where were you while I was maintaining the temple? I was the one who planted the seeds of doubt in the heart of Nälu, and like tares among wheat, the seeds grew. The plains people have embraced the false divinity of the Nuja, and now they will embrace the Goddess Raezana. And what did you do?"

Derk twisted the cane in his fingers and smiled. "You don't still blame me, do you?"

"If I had, would I've sent for you?" She relaxed her grip on the chair and leaned forward. "Let's not dwell on past mistakes when we have the opportunity for vengeance, and the victory is certainly ours!"

"You said that last time and look where it got us. Do you even know what happened to Nach?"

"He got what he deserved." Semine ground her teeth. "He was supposed to be Raezana's chosen one."

"Doesn't friendship mean anything to you anymore?" Derk shook his head. "While you were feigning innocence in your little temple, he crossed over into Nganjo and made a pact with the queen of the underworld. He wants nothing to do with you or your feeble goddess."

Anger darkened her thoughts. She stood. "Have you turned your back on Raezana, too?

He stared at her, his dark eyes smoldering.

"I have not seen you among the faithful pilgrims paying homage to her these past thirty years." Semine narrowed her eyes. "Have you forsaken her?"

"How do you expect me to traverse the countryside when there's been a bounty on my head?"

Semine lifted her chin. "It didn't stop you today."

"Then delay me no more that I may go to the temple right now and pay homage to the great goddess who seems incapable of escaping her confines."

"Raezana is a jealous goddess. Do not mock her." Semine rubbed her temples. Such blasphemy! How could he disrespect the goddess like that? Perhaps, she should have disposed of him than risk the fires of the Abyss. No. She would not think like that. He had been her friend until Raezana entered her life. So many years had passed since their time in Ganya, and the rift grew deeper and wider between them. Could she ever restore it? Had not Raezana promised to? She exhaled her mounting frustration. "I don't expect you to understand the complexity of her situation and what it will take to free her. But in your simplemindedness, do not anger her or you will be worse off than Nach."

"May Raezana have mercy," Derk glared at Semine, "for my anger is not directed at her, but her high priestess."

Semine cocked her head. "And what have I done to deserve your anger?"

"Look, I didn't come all this way to argue over the past."

"And have I brought any of this up?"

"It's just that, we were a team: you, me, Nach. Doesn't it bother you in the least what happened to him, to us?"

She glanced at the flickering flame and weighed her response. "Nach made his choice." She faced him and tried to read his eyes. "Of course, it bothers me, but don't you understand why I had to do what I did?"

Derk clenched his jaw and tapped his cane against his boots. Finally, he glanced up. "You did it for Raezana."

"Yes." Semine returned to her seat and crossed her legs. "So, are you or are you not interested in hearing what I have to say?"

He sighed, but nodded.

"Thirty some years ago, Raezana gave me a vision of a child born beneath the dark star. She marked him to undo the chains that bind her in the underworld."

Derk narrowed his eyes and leaned forward. "Who is he?"

"All in good time. Let us not get ahead of ourselves, shall we?" Semine smiled. She had, at least, captured his interest. She relaxed against the smooth upholstery. "If my sources are correct, we have found the whereabouts of the dagger keeper."

He rubbed his goatee. "So with the dagger and this supposed marked one, you plan to free Raezana?"

"Yes, and resurrect Stygian from the Abyss. Raezana will want her mortal lover at her side."

"How are you going to do that?"

"There are ways. Ways we have only dreamed about until now." Semine's thoughts drifted as she rubbed her gloved arms. "I have delved deep into the Tóas Dikon . . . seen things you would only imagine in your worst nightmare. Yes, there is always a way, but how much are you willing to pay? For every desire met, a sacrifice must be made . . . "

"Semine?"

She blinked and her focus returned to him. She had been lost in her thoughts again. "I have at my disposal new resources, fresh information, and, best of all, a spy."

Before he could respond, she beckoned with her hand, and a young man stepped into the room. A silky black robe flowed from his shoulders to the ground. His blond hair had been slicked back into a black band at his neck, and a scabbed laceration cut across his nose and left cheek. He bowed before Derk and straightened.

Semine stood and draped her arm across his broad shoulders. "I would like for you to meet my new apprentice, Imaran."

Derk huffed. "You mean your new bed fellow."

Semine rolled her eyes and withdrew her arm. "Jealous?"

"Hardly." Derk stood and studied the young man. "What happened to your face?"

Imaran eyed him. "Wounds are expected in battle."

"He has secured the Book of Records and the old Tuqua scrolls for us as well as the Sacred Pearl." Semine ran her hand along his shoulder.

"The Pearl?" Derk rolled the cane between his fingers. "Does Karasi still remain with us? Have you seen her?"

Semine shook her head. "Karasi hasn't emerged from the Pearl in three centuries. I would think she had died if it weren't for the strength of the Perimeter. As it is, the Perimeter stones remain strong, and the barrier will continue to prevent Stygian's return until Karasi dies." Semine settled back in her chair. "She's worthless to us, but Raezana believes otherwise. She wants to see Karasi suffer before she kills her."

"And how do you kill a spirit being like her?"

Semine shrugged. "Raezana knows."

Derk turned his gaze back to Imaran and cocked his head. "Were you studying to be a Guardian?"

Imaran's hand pressed against the Nevin's mark on his neck.

"An apprentice, huh? Already in your third term. Still, I have to wonder . . . " Derk lifted the cane toward Imaran. "What possessed you to leave after so long?"

"What possessed *you* to leave when you did?"

Derk stabbed the cane into the ground. "I did not wait six hundred years to be marked as one of them. Now answer—"

"Derk," Semine interrupted, "that hardly seems necessary."

"How do you know we can trust him? I'd rather not make the same mistake we made with Hadrian."

Semine traced the gold pattern on the chair's arm. "I underestimated the dwarf, but that was then. This is now. Imaran has already proven himself as far as I'm concerned. Besides, he has my old mentor's blessing."

Derk huffed and settled in his chair. "Don't tell me you're still sleeping with him."

Semine clenched her teeth. Like it had been her choice. Would Derk never forgive her? Why did she bother with him?

Because he is part of my plan, Raezana's voice whispered in her mind. *He will be the seed. A mortal vessel for my beloved, and through you, my eternal glory shall return once more.*

She couldn't lose focus, no matter how irritating he could be. She couldn't fail Raezana again.

"Semine?"

56

Her attention snapped back to Derk. "No, I'm not. And it isn't any business of yours, now is it?"

"Calm down." He raised his hand. "I came all the way from Durqa to assist you. Do you think I care who you are bedding?" He crossed his legs and laid his cane across his lap. "So what are your plans, Semine? We have no army, no weapons. The Guardians aren't going to just let us sacrifice a human and bring back the dead."

Semine dismissed Imaran with a nod and sat back down. "Badara and Praetan, the two great cities of the plains, are influential throughout Nälu, and they are ready for change." Semine smiled. "How would you like to be king, Derk? King of Badara?"

He raised his eyebrows. "King?"

"Yes, and perhaps one day king of all of Nälu."

"And what about you?"

"I am Raezana's high priestess. I desire nothing more than to serve her. Her word is my command. Find a king, she said, and I chose you. Of course, I can choose another, if you'd prefer."

"No . . . no, I am interested in hearing more of what you have to say."

Semine reclined in her chair. "Have you heard of the Twammurt Curse?"

6

AYIANNA'S EYELIDS FLEW open. Her heart hammered. Where was she? What happened? Her brother's severed head flashed in her mind. It all came rushing back—the guard, the old elf, the horses! Her chest constricted.

She bolted upright. Her head spun, and a wave of nausea twisted her stomach. A rough wool blanket fell from her shoulders. A small fire crackled and popped. Its shifting light revealed a man—no, an elf—reclining against a tree. It was Saeed, and across from him sat Kael.

They had survived! An intense urge to grab their necks and kiss them swept over her, but fled just as quickly as guilt slammed into her. They could have died because of her.

Kael lifted his gaze to meet hers. His gray eyes drew her in and chilled her. Currents of sorrow swirled behind his icy glare like rivers in winter. He turned away.

She pulled the blanket around her shoulders and inched closer to the orange flames. The heat warmed her face, but not the hollowness of her soul. Closer still, she inched, until her skin burned. If only they'd consume her and purge the memory of her brother, her father, and the sorrow threatening to drown her. She didn't want to remember Dagmar, or the words they had shared. She didn't want to think anymore. Instead, she wished to shrink away into the darkness and disappear. Numbness seeped across her body, like the north wind passing over the waterways, freezing and hardening.

"Ayianna?" Saeed tugged the braids of his soiled beard. His lined face could have belonged to any grandfather as he sat there, absorbed in his thoughts and in the glow of the fire. Still, he was probably much older than any grandfather she had ever known.

"How are you feeling?" he asked.

"I have felt better." She drew her knees to her chin and wrapped the blanket around them. "What happened back there?"

"They attacked, we fought," Kael said as he whittled away on a stick. "Why did you run?"

Ayianna looked back into the dying fire. "I had thought . . . well, with so many and only two of you . . . "

"You were afraid they would find you." Saeed's amber eyes were gentle, but weary. "Why were they after you?"

She hesitated. She detected no ill-will or anger from him. Still . . . her father had his reasons for keeping secrets, but what should she tell him? It wasn't like she knew the secrets her father harbored, and she didn't even know if they were connected. But Saeed was a guardian.

"They killed my father."

Kael glanced up from his whittling.

"They didn't want him dead, though." She twisted the blanket in her hands, not wanting to go on.

The silence lengthened. Both Saeed and Kael watched her, their eyes glimmering in the firelight.

She took a deep breath. "After they had attacked, they . . . um . . . my father told me to find my brother. They must have followed me."

"Why?" Saeed asked.

"They were supposed to kill me, not my father."

"It doesn't make sense." Kael threw the stick into the fire. "They don't sound like regular thieves to me."

Saeed ran his hand along his beard. "I agree. Ayianna, do you remember anything more? Did they say why they were looking for your father?"

She closed her eyes and tried to remember. "One of them said, 'kill the girl and keep him alive.' Someone wanted him. That was it. I don't remember much else, except that they had been looking for my father and that after they kil—" The words stuck in her throat, and she took a deep breath. "They started calling each other names and arguing."

"If they wanted him alive," Kael said as he studied Ayianna, "then mostly likely he knew something they wanted to know."

"But I don't know anything that someone would kill for."

"I'm sure your father didn't trust you with all of his secrets."

She glared at the guard, too stunned and hurt to reply.

"Time will reveal all things." Saeed's gaze passed from Kael to her.

Could he read her mind? She dug in her pocket for her mother's talisman, but guilt pierced her as she remembered her father's admonishment.

She opened her mouth to say something, but Kael held up his hand. He rose to his feet and drew his sword, his eyes scanning the forest. Patches of moonlight seeped through the trees and bathed the long, wispy grass in an icy-blue gleam. A rustling of branches and grass whispered beyond their campsite.

Ayianna held her breath. Were there more thieves and murderers? She glanced around. Saeed sat against a tree, his eyes closed. What was he doing? She started to stand, but the guard shook his head. She strained her eyes to form objects out of the shadows.

A silver wolf slinked into view.

"Liam!" Warmth flooded her grieving soul, and a wave of fresh tears coursed down her cheeks. Liam bounded through the campsite and bowled her over. Ayianna buried her face in the wolf's thick fur, hiding her tears.

"Ayianna," Saeed said.

She lifted her head and dried her face with the edge of her skirt. Her raw skin burned against the rough fabric.

Saeed stood next to her and touched her forehead. "We must go."

"Right now?"

"Yes." Kael rolled his blanket up and stashed it in his pack. "We must reach Badara at daybreak."

She dropped her hands in her lap. "I don't think I can go another step on foot."

"Then it's a good thing we have horses. Their owners won't be needing them anymore," Kael replied. His somber face didn't reflect the dry humor lacing his words. He dipped into the shadows and returned with three horses, a roan and two sorrels.

The last shades of night faded into an early morning haze as Ayianna, Saeed, and Kael reached Badara. Square towers and battlements rose up from behind the large walls of Badara. Soldiers stood along the top of the wall with their hands resting on the hilts of their swords, watching the coming and the going beneath them. Green banners fluttered atop the towers.

Perhaps Dagmar had only been a nightmare.

Ayianna urged her horse on, following Saeed and Kael through the swarm of activities. Merchants and farmers poured through the gates and organized their goods for market. Little donkeys pulled heavy carts laden with fresh produce and various grains. Farmers herded animals of all kinds into wooden pens outside the white walls of Badara. Bleating of sheep and goats, neighing of horses, and braying of donkeys filled the morning air.

Was it always so busy in Badara? So many different people from all over Nälu converged along the road, between vendors, and into the city. Elves and dwarves. Dark-skinned and light-skinned. All mingling with the humans, such a contrast from Lord Ramiro's manor and neighboring villages.

Hadn't Lord Ramiro said Desmond was in Badara? She scanned the crowds for him, but then shook her head. He wouldn't be outside with the smell of the cattle and fowl. He was a draper of expensive cloths and hides. Could she even find him among so many people? Perhaps it would be better if she didn't.

Ayianna followed Kael and Saeed through Badara's large gatehouse. Sharp spikes of the iron portcullises hung overhead, and small slits in the wall glared at her. She shivered and pressed her heels against the horse's sides.

They weaved their way through the growing crowd. Cramped stone buildings lined the narrow cobblestone street. Wooden signs dotted windows, advertising herbs, trinkets, or vacancies. The sweet smell of cinnamon and yeasty breads hinted at a bakery nearby, but barely masked the odor of hay and manure.

They approached the merchant's square, and Ayianna glanced around, trying to see everything at once. Not even Zurial could boast such a varied mix of nations and merchandise.

To her right, an elderly woman sold colorful, woven scarves, smocks, and kirtles. A dwarf across the street sold iron tools and weaponry. Farther in, an elf adjusted the jewelry rack after making a sale. Ahead, a skinny elf with mahogany-colored skin paraded several beautiful horses around a corral. Muscles rippled under their polished coats, boasting of strength and speed.

"Those are the nithzads, the fastest horses in Nälu. They ride like the wind." Kael reined in his mount next to hers.

"They are beautiful. Where are they from?"

"The Zriab Desert," Saeed said. A small smile creased more wrinkles into his bronze skin. "The Saryhemor elves raise them." He turned his horse away and continued up the cobbled street.

Kael leaned in his saddle toward Ayianna. "He is a desert elf and proud of it."

Ahead, Saeed wove his horse between clusters of shoppers who chatted away like chickens at feeding time. The hair on top of his head had thinned enough to expose a small patch of brown scalp gleaming in the morning sun. His remaining hair was bound in leather and brushed the rump of his horse. If elves weren't supposed to age, how old was he really?

She turned back to Kael. "Are you a desert elf too?"

"No, I'm an Esusamor elf from Zurial."

"Oh . . . " She should have known that. He wasn't as dark as Saeed, and he didn't have a beard.

They urged their horses on to catch up with the Guardian and passed a boy selling smoked fish. At first, he looked like an ordinary boy, except for the V-shape edging around his forehead, and his skin glimmered in the sun. Short, brown tousled hair grew from behind the ridge and bounced as he shifted curled seashells and dried fish atop various large, wooden barrels.

Behind him, a mountain of barrels loomed over them. A man stood on top, tying a rope, securing them to large wagon. He wore large, floppy boots and a silver vest. Green feathery fringe grew from his opalescent skin and stretched the length of his arms. He called down to the boy and threw him the end of the rope. Ayianna didn't understand the words, but his voice flowed over them like the sea lapping at the shoreline.

The boy craned his neck to look up at the man. The movement revealed three faint slits beneath his jawline—a Kaleki! She couldn't believe it. She had only glimpsed their silvery sails and slick sailing vessels from the cliffs of Zurial, but here, right in the middle of the plains, were two merfolk. What were they doing so far inland?

The boy flashed a smile at her.

Her face and ears burned. How long had she been staring? She straightened and pressed her heels into the side of her horse. She pulled alongside Kael and rode in silence. The heat in her cheeks subsided, and her thoughts returned to Dagmar and her father. Questions somersaulted in her mind until she could no longer keep quiet.

"What are we going to do?"

"We? Saeed will see that you are safely returned home." He goaded his horse forward in the ever crowding streets.

She glared at the back of his head. "But what about Dagmar and . . . and those men hunting me?"

"You'll have protection in your village."

"Right, like the protection that Dagmar had? My village doesn't even have walls."

"What happened at Dagmar is none of your concern."

"None of my concern?" Ayianna gripped the edge of the saddle. "My brother is dead, burning in a mass pyre. My father's been murdered, his body left for scavengers! Yet you say—"

He turned, his glare fierce. "Your brother's death was an unintended casualty, one of many who were killed. He was not the focus."

Ayianna bit her lip, fighting back tears. "I—I didn't mean to lessen another's death."

But her words were lost to him as he kicked his horse into a trot. She followed after him. He was right. She needed to go home, but what would she find? Her anger dissipated into guilt. It gnawed at her like a dog chewing a bone. *Oh, Osaryn, protect my mother!*

Kael halted in front of the stables and dismounted next to Saeed.

Ayianna didn't know what to do. Her stomach twisted in knots. She wanted to turn the horse around and ride home.

"Come now, Ayianna," Saeed glanced up at her, "rushing back to your home would be foolish."

She stared at him. "How did you know?"

"Your face reveals a great deal." Saeed patted her leg. "Now, off you go. Your mount is in need of rest as well."

Ayianna slid from her horse and fell to the ground.

"Don't ride much, do you?" Kael offered to help her stand.

She brushed his hand aside. "I'm fine." She stood and wobbled into the stables, pulling her horse after her. Kael and Saeed followed.

"Morning, elf-folk," a stable boy said. He rubbed his hands on his drab tunic. "That'll be ten dlaquis per horse. You three look mighty rough this morning. Did ya have a run in with thieves or something?"

"If thieves could do this much damage, then we would all be lost." Saeed counted the dlaquis to the boy. "What news can you tell me about Badara and her king?"

"Depends on how much that information is worth to ya." The boy grinned. He took off his cap and scratched his head.

His hair, the color of dirty straw, stood askew. He flattened it and replaced his cap. "Well?"

Kael frowned. "We aren't interested in purchasing information that you gathered for free."

"Your loss." The boy shrugged. He took the reins and led the horses toward the corral.

"To think we'd have to pay for the latest gossip." Ayianna shook her head.

Kael looked past her. "Darin will have more information than a mere stable boy."

"Perhaps," Saeed said. "But unlike Darin, wherever the boy goes no man thinks to guard his tongue in his presence. You would be surprised the information he could gather."

Kael turned his attention to Saeed. "What are you planning to do?"

"I will seek an audience with King Valdamar."

"What?" Ayianna raised her eyebrows. "Looking like that?"

Saeed gave her a sad half-smile. "It would not be so easy for him to dismiss the death of many if I approach looking as if death itself spit me back out."

"What would you have me do?" Kael asked.

"Find Nevin Darin and tell him what happened—tell him to alert the other guardians and prepare for an assembly." Saeed tugged a braid as he scanned the crowded streets. "He is overseeing the festival preparations. He should not be difficult to find."

Kael nodded. "What about the girl?"

She gritted her teeth. The sooner she was away from him, the better.

"She is in your charge until I have met with the king. Then we will accompany her to her village. I have a few questions I would like to ask her mother. Perhaps she will have some answers." Saeed turned to Ayianna. His eyes softened. "And I would not ask anyone to deliver such news as you have to bear alone, my dear."

Ayianna's throat knotted, so she nodded her thanks instead.

Saeed turned to leave. "If all goes well, I shall meet you two this evening in Darin's quarters." Then he stepped into the street and disappeared among the people crowding the market square.

Kael rounded on her. He opened his mouth to speak, but then closed it, clenching his jaw until the vein bulged. She stared at his scuffed up boots, wishing the ground would suddenly open up and swallow her. He spun around and marched away. She hurried after him.

She kept pace for a few strides, but then he stopped and faced her.

"Women walk behind men in the plains. Or weren't you aware of that?"

"I . . . " Ayianna stared at him and then quickly lowered her eyes. "I'm sorry. I didn't mean to offend you."

"You didn't offend me. You're offending the citizens of Badara. I suppose you haven't lived among the human's long enough for their society to convert your mind."

Was it that obvious? Wait, how did he know? She dared a glance at him and, not only did she see his grim face, but also the disapproving looks of those passing by. *How am I ever going to adapt to this way of life?*

She caught sight of the crimson blood staining the sleeve of his ivory tunic. "Kael! Your arm!"

He turned away. "A scratch. It must have reopened."

"It will fester if you don't clean it. Then you could get lavi aezar and lose your arm. We need to take care of that right away." Ayianna pulled him into the first building they came to—a blacksmith's shop.

Soot blanketed the walls, ceiling, and floor. Flecks of iron crunched underfoot. Coals smoldered in the forge, emitting heat. The smell of hot metal and sulfur saturated the air. In the corner, a burly man hammered away, sparks erupting with each stroke. The blacksmith was just as filthy as his shop. Sweat rolled down his blackened face, and grease and dirt smeared his leather apron. The blacksmith turned and shoved a glowing spike of iron into the coals.

"Can I help you?" the man asked as he wiped his hands on his apron. His voice louder than normal, but still friendly.

"Could you boil some water?" Ayianna asked.

"You'll have to speak up, I'm a little hard of hearing."

"Could you boil some water?" Ayianna asked a little louder.

"Eh?"

"Hot water!" Ayianna shouted pointing at Kael's bloodied sleeve.

The blacksmith nodded and ducked from the room.

"This isn't exactly a place for tending wounds." Kael tugged his shirt off and sat on a wooden bench. Several old scars lined his back and chest.

She gasped. "What happened to you?"

"Run in with pirates."

"So, you're not a pirate?"

"No."

She frowned. "Then why—"

"Look, I've got things to do." He stood, but she pushed him back down.

Warmth flooded her face. She quickly removed her hands and stepped back. "Darin isn't going anywhere." She pulled her gaze from his chest to his arm.

A crusty gash cut across his upper arm, the surrounding skin was red and swollen. Fresh blood oozed from the reopened wound.

"That is not a scratch. What happened?"

"Are you going to mend my arm or just stare at me?"

"I was only inspecting the wound." Ayianna poked the edge of the skin, a little warm to the touch, but not hot. Hopefully, she wouldn't have to sew it up.

The blacksmith returned with the water and a towel.

Ayianna dipped the edge of the towel into the hot water and swirled it about. She dribbled water into the gash and pressed the cloth against it to soften the dried blood.

Kael tightened his jaw, but didn't say anything.

She continued cleaning as gently as she could while the blacksmith rummaged through his cupboards. He came back and handed her a roll of gauze. She wrapped Kael's arm, and as she tied the ends, a booming voice rang through the air.

"Ayianna!"

She jumped back, knocking over the water. She scrambled to set the bucket right and keep the hem of her dress dry.

A man towered in the doorway, his blue eyes locked coldly on Kael. A shiny, burgundy doublet flashed beneath a short black cape. His wavy blond hair settled around his narrow face.

Desmond.

The two men stared at each other, neither saying a word until Desmond turned his attention to Ayianna.

"What are you doing here? Look at you, your face—your clothes," Desmond said, his eyes sweeping the height of Ayianna. "Where is your head-covering? People will think you're some kind of whore. Razi!"

A young boy dressed in a green tunic and leggings appeared in the doorway.

"Bring me a scarf from the wares," Desmond said, and the boy darted from the blacksmith shop.

"I'm sorry." Kael stood. "But who are you, and what business do you have here?"

Desmond rounded on Kael. "Excuse me, but she belongs to me. She is my betrothed."

"I don't recall Teron mentioning that."

Ayianna twisted the cold, wet rag in her hands. The elf obviously knew more about her brother than what he had told her.

Desmond smiled. "And why would he?"

"Have we met before?" Kael asked. "Have you been to Dagmar?"

Desmond eyed him before answering. "Possibly. I have passed through Dagmar a time or two."

"One hardly passes through. I am sure I would have remembered you."

"My religious pilgrimages are a private matter. Perhaps you should put your shirt on now and go."

"Desmond." His name felt strange on her tongue. "Kael saved my life."

His head snapped her direction. "Saved your life? What were you doing that you needed saving?"

"I was looking for my brother, but Dagmar had been attacked." Her voice choked, but she remained composed and braced herself for what he would say.

"What possessed you to traipse all over the countryside alone? You know better than that."

"But there were these people, and my father—"

"Enough," Desmond said, "Your mother is probably half-sick from worrying over you."

"Yes," Ayianna mumbled. She lowered her eyes as guilt burrowed holes in her resolve.

Razi reappeared with an orange and yellow banded scarf. Desmond took it and gave it to Ayianna.

Chagrinned, Ayianna slipped the scarf over her head and around her neck.

Desmond turned to Kael. "I must repay you for bringing . . . " He cocked his head and then added with emphasis, "my betrothed safely to Badara."

"That won't be necessary," Kael replied, still shirtless. He gave Ayianna a curt nod and stepped out of the blacksmith shop.

Ayianna watched him go, longing to ask him questions about her brother, but he vanished amid the growing crowds of people.

"What is this?" Desmond asked.

Ayianna turned to catch Desmond's glare settling on Liam. "Her name is Liam, and she belongs to me."

"Right. Well, I have work to do. You can clean up and rest at Cuthbert's Inn." Desmond turned to the blacksmith and added loudly. "I will return later to pick up my uncle's order."

Desmond ushered her out of the blacksmith shop and into the scores of people flooding the streets. The exchange of coins rattled in the scales, bartering voices swelled. Hundreds of people wandered the streets of Badara, trying the wares like cows grazing on a warm summer day.

Ayianna's skin crawled as if someone were watching her. She glanced back and sucked in a breath.

A tall man in a long, black cloak leaned against the blacksmith shop. He shifted his weight, but didn't move. His eyes seemed to follow her every move. But then, everyone seemed to be watching her.

7

AYIANNA KEPT PACE three feet behind Desmond and tried to remember the proper protocol of city life. Desmond hurried up the cobbled street. He waved off pleasantries as people parted and shouted greetings above the din of the crowd. Ayianna focused her eyes on the heels of his polished black boots.

Finally, he stopped in front of a tall, stone building on the edge of the market square. Layers of dirt and grime lined the crevices between the gray, oblong stones. A weathered sign swung from the awning. The words Cuthbert's Inn had been burned into the wood. Desmond shoved open the swinging latticed door, and a bell jingled, announcing their arrival.

A tangled mix of body odor and sweet ale collided with her nose. Thick candles burned on long wood tables that lined the dim room. To the right, a thin spindle railing followed the stairs and wrapped around the floors like a snake curling around a tree. At the back of the room a small counter stood in front of a wall littered with keys and hollows. To the left, archways led into private areas partially blocked by velvet curtains trimmed in silver.

"Aye, and who do we 'ave 'ere?" an old man asked as he hobbled up to the worn counter.

"Hello, Cuthbert. This lovely, young lady is my betrothed," Desmond said.

"Oo'wee!" Cuthbert's grisly face broke into a wide grin. "I didn't know you's a gettin' married."

Ayianna lowered her eyes and stared at the wooden floor boards, thankful the lighting was dim enough to hide her damaged, soiled clothes—Desmond probably more so.

"Yes, it's about time I settle down and take a wife," Desmond said with a half-laugh.

"Sure it is, with the prince on the throne soon an' looking for eligible men for 'is courts." Cuthbert rapped his knuckles on the counter and chuckled. "Speaking of the courts, there's a sealed letter for ya from the prince 'isself."

Cuthbert ducked under the counter and reappeared with a thick envelope, complete with the king's stamp and green ribbons of the court. Ayianna had seen a few letters bearing the crown's seal, mostly edicts concerning taxes and tithes.

"Kind of 'eavy. Sure don't receive many of these around 'ere."

Desmond only smiled and took the letter from the innkeeper. He tucked it into his belt and allowed his cape to swing forward, hiding the yellowed parchment.

"She sure's a pretty one."

Ayianna cheeks burned at the innkeeper's comment.

"Yes, old man." Desmond's hand rested on Ayianna's shoulder. "She will need a meal, a room with a bath, and her clothes laundered." Desmond plopped several dluas on the table. "And something for the dog."

Wolf! Ayianna bit down on her tongue and kept her eyes on Cuthbert's brown, worn boots.

"Eh! I will make an exception for you, but, Desmond, two shozals would be plenty to cover these expenses, I'd not 'ave enough coins to do ya proper," Cuthbert protested, shoving the coins back toward Desmond.

"Keep the rest, Cuthbert. You are a good man." Desmond leaned closer and whispered into Cuthbert's ear.

Ayianna tried to listen, but could only catch the words, "watch," "find," and "later." She shuffled her feet with irritation, and glared at Desmond—what could he be saying that he had to hide from her?

"Of course, of course," Cuthbert replied, nodding. "I see and 'ear most things coming and going. I 'ave more tales to tell then minstrels 'ave songs to sing."

"Don't forget to launder the clothes as well." Desmond's eyes roved over Ayianna's damaged clothes. "On second thought, throw them away. I will send up new ones."

"Aye, Desmond, that I will." Cuthbert backed into the door behind him and yelled, "Mairi! Soup and a bath! We've a paying customer!"

Desmond glanced at her. "Until evening then."

"But—"

Desmond pressed his fingers gently against her lips, and a tingle ran down her spine. She stared into his bright blue eyes, too stunned to move or look away. He bent down and kissed her forehead.

Ayianna stood, breathless, as he rushed out into the busy courtyard, his dark cloak swishing after him.

The old man took a key from the wall and limped around the counter.

"Ya 'ungry?" he asked.

Ayianna nodded. She kept her eyes lowered, remembering her mother's social drills. She reached into her pocket, grasped the talisman, and whispered a prayer of protection.

"Mairi!" Cuthbert bellowed.

An old woman popped her head around the corner of the door, her sweaty face red. Her eyes bulged behind shaggy eyebrows. "Yes, ya old coot?"

"Are ya deaf? We 'ave a paying customer! Soup, bath, launder—get busy in there. I want to 'ear some banging pots."

"I'll bang some pots all right, alongside your 'ead. Soup's a coming," she growled.

The innkeeper shook his head, an exasperated expression deepening his wrinkles.

Mairi ducked back into the kitchen, rattled some pots, and quickly returned with a steaming bowl of legume soup and a chunk of dark rye bread. Its pungent smell made Ayianna's stomach growl as she took a seat at a table.

After eating, Ayianna followed the old man upstairs to the rooms. Cuthbert unlocked the door, handed Ayianna the key, and disappeared down the stairs.

Inside the room, a darkened lamp sat on a set of drawers next to a pitcher and bowl. A small chest lay against the wall to the left. A plump mattress rested atop a wooden box beneath the opened window. Fresh linen lay folded at the edge of the bed, awaiting its next customer.

Ayianna cringed. Had she ever slept in another's bed? Light streamed through the window, casting long shadows in the room. Noises drifted in from the busy courtyard below. To the right, a thin door stood ajar, exposing an adjoining room where a large, wooden basin had been filled with hot water, and a pleasant aroma wafted from the bath area. Several candles mounted on tall, iron pillars flickered, giving light to the bathing room.

Such luxury! Ayianna stripped and crawled into the oval barrel. Her scratches burned in the hot water, but the heat soothed her achy body. She dropped her long braid over the side of the barrel and closed her eyes.

A knock at the door startled her. She jerked forward and sought a covering, but found nothing. No towel, no robe, nothing except her dirty dress. How could she be so foolish? Did she lock the outer door?

"Excuse me, Miss." A female voice drifted through the open doorway. "I've been sent to fetch your clothes. I have a fresh towel for you. May I come in?"

"Ah," Ayianna stammered. She moved closer to the edge of the barrel. "Yes."

A maid entered, dressed in a simple, gray smock. She nodded her head and placed a dingy towel and folded nightgown on the chair by the door. "I will take your old clothes, Miss. Is there anything else I can bring you?"

Ayianna shook her head as she squeezed closer to the side of the tub. "Could you lock the door, please?"

The maid smiled and nodded. She scooped up the dirty clothes and left.

Ayianna leaned back against the barrel. How could she have been so foolish to forget to lock the door?

Liam's nails clicked along the wooden floor and poked her wet nose over the barrel's edge.

"Oh, Liam, what are we to do? I can't imagine what we will tell Mother when we return. I can hear her now. 'Where have you been?' 'What were you thinking?' And then, when we tell her about Teron and Father, she'll certainly lose her mind. She'll really be expecting me to save the family by marrying Desmond. It's hopeless, isn't it? Or maybe hope doesn't look like hope. It sure doesn't feel like it."

Ayianna glanced at her faithful companion and smiled. Liam sat there listening, her tail sweeping the floor. Ayianna closed her eyes and allowed the hot water to ease the ache and stiffness from her body. The broken blisters on her hands throbbed beneath the hot water.

Sleep tugged at her mind and scattered her thoughts. She slowly sat up. The last thing she wanted was to fall asleep in the bath and drown. The thought of people finding her dead and naked horrified her. With new vigor, she scrubbed the dirt off and ignored the stabbing pain arising from the broken blisters on her hands.

After the bath, she dressed in the nightgown and closed the shutters. The room darkened—perfect for sleeping. She dragged her tired body onto the bed. A faint lavender scent lifted from the mattress. At least it smelled clean. She yawned, hugging the pillow to her head, and slipped away.

8

KAEL CRANED HIS neck to see over the throng of people preparing for the Feast of Daeju. They hung boughs of flowers and shrubbery from one cramped building to another. Large, white columns rose above the inner courtyard like sentries guarding the way to the king's castle. Tantalizing smells of fresh baked bread and roasting pig saturated the air. Kael's stomach twisted in hunger, but food would have to wait.

He plunged through the crowd. Somewhere in all the commotion, he would find Nevin Darin—a half-giant would be difficult to miss.

A dull, throbbing ache continued to assault his arm and nerves as Kael made his way toward the great hall. Ayianna had cleaned it well under the circumstances, but was it good enough? He'd have to visit the apothecary later. His pace slowed. Without the dire need to defend himself or another, a sleep-deprived, battle-weary haze seized his mind and consumed his energy. At least he wasn't having to keep an eye on the girl. She would have slowed him down, and he didn't have time for playing nursemaid. Despite Desmond's timely arrival, the lack of having her near bugged him. Was it the promise to her brother? Or was it her overwhelming grief . . . a grief that mirrored his own? He'd check on her later. Not that she wasn't in capable hands by the look of Desmond's attire and forthrightness. Still the situation nagged him. Why hadn't Teron mentioned the betrothal?

Her brother's ring! How could he have forgotten? He had to return it to her . . . another reason for him to check on her.

"Pardon us," a gruff voice said behind him.

Kael's attention snapped to the present. He stood in the middle of the road, blocking traffic. He shook his head and stepped out of the way of a group of humans carrying a long table. He had to focus.

Wreaths of pine and cedar adorned the long rows of tables for the king and his guests. A disjointed melody lifted above the clamor of the crowd as a group of minstrels practiced with their lutes and horns.

An eight-foot-tall man appeared out of nowhere. Kael pushed toward him.

The half-giant's voice thundered over the others as he instructed various servants on matters pertaining to tomorrow's festival. Dressed in leather pants and a sleeveless buckskin vest, Darin towered above the people. He was bald and wore a dark patch over his right eye, his other eye studied his surroundings and then rested on Kael.

Kael touched his fingertips together and bowed. "*Prözam*, Nevin Darin."

"*Prözam*, Kael," Darin replied as he grasped Kael's shoulder and tipped his head. "You look terrible. What brings you to Badara?"

"Urgent matters. May we speak in private?"

"Yes, of course. King Valdamar has provided the guardians with a small study when we are here in Badara. We may use it."

After delegating a few tasks, Darin led Kael to the north tower, where a flight of stone steps spiraled up to a cramped study furnished with a desk, a few shelves, and a loft for sleeping. Darin's towering frame took up most of the room and dwarfed the scant oak furniture.

"Home away from home." Darin smiled and patted the loft's straw mattress. "It is meager, but it serves its purpose. Centuries ago, when Badara had looked to the guardians for tutoring their young princes, you would have found a much bigger room and not located in some far tower. Alas, times are changing. Priorities change . . . " He sat down on a bench, his knees nearly reaching his shoulders. He motioned for Kael to sit. "What urgent matters have brought you here?"

Kael shook his head and tightened his grip on his sword belt. "Two nights ago, Dagmar was attacked. Imaran, one of the pupils finishing his second phase, stole the Sacred Pearl and fled with the aid of a dragon. The school has been ransacked, the secret vaults have been opened and their contents stolen. Saeed wants you to notify the other guardians, to form an assembly."

Darin's brow furrowed, cutting deep grooves into his forehead. He did not avert his gaze, but simply stared at Kael as if he could relive the battle through another's memory.

Kael shuddered. He swallowed the lump in his throat and waited.

Darin leaned forward, and an ebony pendent set in twisted silver dangled from his neck—the lenjía. All the guardians had one, except Saeed. He had two. "What about Unai, the other teachers, the pupils?"

"Many are dead. I don't know what became of Unai. Saeed thinks he might have tried to get some of the students to safety. To where, I don't know. We didn't see him or anybody else on our way south. Saeed is seeking audience with the king as we speak, and then he will meet us here this evening if all goes well."

"Good luck with that. The king has not been seeing anyone these past couple of days. His officials claim he has been busy mediating between the Nuja pilgrimages and the festival goers."

"Well, I'm certain the destruction of Dagmar will demand his attention."

Darin frowned. "I doubt it, unless it proves a threat to him personally. Any idea of who did this?"

"No, but the Muzal banner hangs in the school."

"The Muzal, you say?" Darin rubbed his bald head. A leather vambrace wrapped around his forearm and curved to a point toward his fingers. Runes of Pyamor, the Pauden language, scrawled across the large knuckles of his hand. "What kind of a fool would do such a thing?"

"Imaran."

"I doubt he did it by himself."

Kael shrugged. "I didn't recognize the men—if they were men—nor their colors: red and black."

"You said he escaped by dragon?"

Kael nodded. He walked over to the narrow window and looked out. Beyond the curtain wall, clumps of autumn trees and evergreens littered the edges of the plains. He could see nothing of the festival decorations or the people. Darin hadn't been jesting when he said this was the far tower. He turned to Darin. "Do you think the Kaleki are in on it?"

"No, they would never go against the old alliance. Even if the other nations break away, the Kaleki will not." Darin put his hands behind his head and leaned against the wall. He gazed up at the high ceiling for a while and then turned his attention back to Kael. "If the items in the vault are gone, then I would have to assume whoever is in charge has their sights on dark things."

Kael's eyes narrowed. "What was in those vaults?"

"Well, the Book of Records, which is really just history and genealogies. I doubt that will be much use to them. No, it is the Tuqua Scrolls I'm concerned about. They could be dangerous in the wrong hands. They are full of incantations and curses. The first Guardian Circle claimed they belonged to Lord Stygian himself. The words in those scrolls are the very breath of the Tóas Dikon, and they stand in complete opposition to the Yenzo Tanil."

"Why did Saeed have them at the school in the first place?"

Darin fingered the pendent hanging from his neck. "The headmaster before him used those scrolls to instruct pupils on matters pertaining to what some call the 'Corruptive Gifts.' He believed guardians needed to know what they were up against, in case the perimeter was to fail or someone unleashed the Tóas from the underworld. Made sense, coming from his day and age, but Saeed disagreed. He thought that only guardians accepted into the Circle should have access to that information, guardians who have proven themselves trustworthy and have received their gifting from Vituko. Therefore, when Saeed became headmaster, he locked the scrolls in the vault and only those within the Circle know about them."

"Then how did Imaran know about them?"

Darin shook his head. "Your guess is as good as mine, but someone must have told him."

Kael sat down in the chair and closed his eyes. His head was starting to spin. He had too much to process right now, and he didn't want to think about the implications of Darin's words. He opened his eyes.

After studying him for a moment, Darin rubbed his face and stood. "I will alert the others. It will probably be a month before we can convene." He clasped his pendent. "Do you know if Saeed contacted Nerissa yet?"

Kael shook his head. "He refuses to use the lenjía and asks you to do the same."

"Saeed suspects one of us, then." Darin walked over to the desk and pulled out an inkwell, quill, and a piece of parchment. He scrawled a note.

Kael was only half aware of Darin's presence next to him. The scratching of the quill kept his conscious anchored to the tower. He longed to release the tension and the grief, to sleep and wake up from this nightmare. The scratching stopped, and Kael blinked his eyes. Had he nodded off?

A large golden eagle dropped from the height of the ceiling and landed on Darin's vambrace. He stroked the feathers and murmured softly as he secured a small silver tube to one of its legs. Then the eagle stretched its wings and took flight, soaring out of the tower's narrow window.

Darin's hand clamped on Kael's shoulder. "Sleep, friend. I've got to make sure everything is ready for the festival."

Kael nodded.

Darin ducked out of the room, leaving Kael alone with his muddled thoughts. Exhaustion weighed upon him like a heavy fur blanket. He crawled into the loft and collapsed.

9

AYIANNA PEERED INTO the shadows of her room, but only found Liam curled up in the corner. What had awakened her? If the thundering of her heart wouldn't subside, she'd never hear if someone was in her room or not. Liam continued dozing, which was a good sign. There was nothing to worry about.

Was it evening already? How long had she slept? Ayianna slipped out of bed and stumbled to the water jar. She splashed her face with cool water. Her vision swirled, and she gripped the edge of the chest.

She rested her head next to the jar and sunk to the cold floor until the vertigo lessened.

Finally, she rose and lit the oil lamp. Its faint glow cheered the room and calmed her nerves. She leaned against the wall and curled her arms around her knees. Her thoughts drifted to Saeed. Had he seen the king already? Would the king even care about her father's death? And what of her mother? Safe. She had to be. The men had followed her instead, but unease crushed her hope. She would not have peace until she saw her mother again.

Liam yawned and stretched her front paws before her. She padded over to Ayianna, her toenails clicking on the wood. The only sound in the quiet shadows. The wolf nuzzled her shoulder and reclined next to her, closing her eyes again.

Ayianna sighed. Why did she fret? It was over, wasn't it? Now she'd return home with her betrothed, tell her mother the devastating news, and they'd carry on as planned. She swallowed the lump in her throat. Maybe she could—

Alarmed voices carried into the room from below. Ayianna stiffened. What was going on down there? Were there more men after her? Liam lifted her head, her ears twitching, but she didn't move any farther. No. The speakers could be alarmed for any reason. What if it was about Dagmar?

Her unease mounted. Ayianna crawled over to the door and eased it open. Its hinges whined in protest. She cringed.

"What!" a rough voice hollered.

"Let him talk," another voice drawled. "Let him talk. Can't you see he is a bit shaken?"

"There were so many of them, wretched, smelly creatures. They crawled right over the walls! We didn't stand a chance," a younger voice replied.

Ayianna's breath caught in her lungs.

"Right over the walls, you say, what manner of beast was it?" the rough voice interrupted again.

"I don't know. I'd never seen them before!"

"Nobody can be safe if they climb walls like trees!" the rough voice bellowed.

"But that wasn't all—they had a giant troll!"

"A what?"

"Who would do this?" another voice piped up.

"Can you not guess who?" a hoarse voice replied. "Evil lurking in the shadows, Dagmar destroyed, the pearl stolen?" Silence answered the man. "It's her who never sleeps, moaning in the depths of the Abyss, waiting for the Perimeter to weaken, waiting to return and reclaim what was taken from her.

"You're just trying to scare us."

"Am I? Mark my words: whoever stole the pearl is a pawn in the underworld's return to power."

The inn shuddered with the explosion of garbled voices as the men downstairs tried to talk over each other.

"You simpletons!" roared a voice. "Have you never heard of the Dagger of Raemoja?"

"Yes, the traveling bards sing of it quite often," a soft voice said. "It is said that any man who possesses the dagger would have power beyond the guardians."

"No," another voice protested. "The dagger brings only death and destruction to the bearer."

"Fools, you weary me with your tales."

"Who are you calling a fool?" a small voice asked. "Didn't you hear what the boy said? It's hopeless!"

"Hopeless? Have you forgotten the Guardian Circle? Isn't it their job to protect and guide Nälu?" a calm voice said.

"Did they even survive the attack?" the rough voice asked.

"I-I don't know," the young voice stammered, "I didn't see them."

"It would take a lot more than a giant troll and a handful of imps to destroy the guardians." The calm voice was familiar, but Ayianna couldn't place it. Was it Kael? But why would he be down there?

"What good would it do us if they did survive? They're just a bunch of old fools who have outlived their purpose," a hoarse voice said.

"Old fools, eh?" the calm voice said. The voices fell silent again. Chairs squeaked as the men shifted in them.

"What's your name, boy?" the calm voice asked. A chair scuffed the floor as if someone stood up. No, it wasn't Kael. Desmond? He didn't seem to be the type to be interested in matters pertaining to the guardians, but then, she hardly knew him.

"I am not a boy," the hoarse voice responded.

"By my standards you are. You sure know quite a bit about the dagger and the pearl."

"And you know quite a bit about the guardians. Perhaps you are one of them," the hoarse voice said. "If you'll excuse me, I have other matters of greater concern than the tavern's latest gossip. Good evening." His footsteps, one heavier than the other, exited the tavern.

Ayianna pulled back from the door, but froze as heavy footsteps climbed the stairs. Her heart pounded, but the footsteps disappeared into one of the rooms. Ayianna heaved a sigh of relief and closed the door.

She darted to the window, hoping the man had lingered in the street.

Several crows scattered as she opened the shutters. Shadows mingled together in the streets. Merchants closed down for the night. Farmers disappeared over the horizon, returning home with their profits and newly purchased supplies. Stars twinkled in the heavens. The white city glowed in the moonlight, but no lone stranger walked down the street.

Ayianna exhaled the pent up tension. How beautiful and peaceful it seemed! How ordinary it all appeared—Dagmar's nightmare seemed so distant. If it hadn't been for the conversation she had just overheard, she might have doubted the reality of the horror that haunted her.

Tears stung her eyes, and she blinked them away. She sank to the bed.

Liam ambled over and laid her head on Ayianna's lap.

Ayianna scratched the wolf's ears. Tears slid down her cheeks. "Father and Teron are . . . gone."

Liam jumped to the bed and curled up next to her.

Ayianna buried her face in the thick, white fur. She gritted her teeth. Anguish pierced the core of her being. The ache so sharp, so real, she thought her heart would fail. She needed a distraction.

She stood and paced the room, hugging her waist. But the more she paced, the more her thoughts fixated on the one thing she fought so hard to avoid. Would she suffocate in her own room?

Liam stretched out across the bed and rested her head on her paws, her pale eyes following Ayianna back and forth across the room. She flipped her tail as if to voice her disapproval of her master's pacing.

Ayianna halted. "What do you expect me to do? I can't leave this room and roam the city by myself." She slumped next to Liam. "We need to get home to Mother. She's probably worried herself sick." Her thoughts dove back to her father's death and the blade meant for her. "How can I bring such news to her?"

Liam nudged her nose under Ayianna's arm and Ayianna sighed, trailing her fingers through Liam's fur. She would do it. Her father's death would not be in vain. She'd make it right, make her father proud.

"Mother will know what to do and what Father's message meant." Ayianna straightened. "Perhaps I can find Saeed. Maybe he could make arrangements with Desmond, and we could go home tomorrow."

Liam's ears perked up. She twisted her neck toward the door, and a few moments later a knock came.

"Madam, your clothes." The door creaked open, and a thin maid entered, her dress twice too big for her and gathered to her waist by the strings of her apron. A brown scarf covered her hair and wrapped around her neck. She nodded and held up a large bundle. "Master Desmond has requested your company for dinner this evening. He asks that you wear the burgundy one." She curtsied and left.

Burgundy one? Ayianna closed the door and unwrapped the package. Two dresses slipped out. One was a plain green, the fabric and design typical of the plains people. She placed it on the bed next to its matching headscarf. The other dress was burgundy, its fabric soft unlike her own garments. Delicate embroidery lined the blood-red bodice and gave way to a layered skirt below.

She shook her head as the silky layers slid through her fingers. A dress fit for a lady. Her stomach fluttered and then fell flat. How could she pass as a lady of Badara?

No, she would learn. Her father's death wouldn't be in vain.

She yanked the nightgown off and slipped the new dress on. Its light fabric slid over her skin. She lifted her arms, and the flared sleeves shimmered. She swirled around the room, the dress billowing at her ankles.

"What do you think, Liam? Isn't it beautiful?"

Liam burrowed her muzzle under her paws and flipped her tail again. Ayianna smiled—perhaps she should unbraid her hair.

Someone pounded on the door, and Ayianna jumped back. She bumped into the wooden box, causing it to screech loudly across the floorboards. Her heart jumped into her throat.

"Ayianna?" a muffled voice asked through the closed door.

She took a deep breath and opened the door.

Desmond's smile turned to concern. "Are you all right? You look a little flushed."

"Yes—yes, I'm fine. Thank you." She calmed her racing heart and smoothed her new dress, suddenly feeling naked without her usual woolen apron.

"You look beautiful!" His eyes swept the length of her. "But you are forgetting something."

Oh. Of course. Her face burned even hotter. She returned to the bed, snatched the matching scarf, and wrapped it around her head and neck.

Desmond smiled and held out his arm for her.

She hesitated. "Aren't I supposed to walk behind you?"

"Not when we are courting."

She slid her hand under his arm. A spicy smell assaulted her nose. Had he just washed up, or was he trying to cover the stench of a busy day? She studied him out of the corner of her eye as they made their way down the stairs.

His short blond hair had been smoothed back. His slender face ended in a square jaw, which at the moment, he was clenching. Was he just as nervous as her? Or was he angry?

She stumbled, but he steadied her with his other hand. Heat crept into her face. How could she be so clumsy? Falling down the stairs and taking him with her was not how she wanted to start out the evening. For the rest of the way, she focused on the descent.

He led her through the inn's main dining area and under the wide arches to a private table in the back. A small candle flickered in the middle of a setting for two. A delicious aroma of roasted fowl wafted throughout the room, and Ayianna's stomach growled. Desmond pulled a chair out for her, and when she had sat down, he seated himself across from her.

"Did you sleep well?" he asked as he pulled out a large square cloth and tucked it into the neckline of his doublet.

"Yes, thank you," Ayianna said, copying his actions.

Desmond shook his head. "Ladies are supposed to lay the cloth over their laps."

"Oh." Her face grew hot, and she shifted in her seat. "I-I'm sorry." She removed the cloth and draped it over her dress.

He carved into the small bird and slid a portion onto Ayianna's plate. "Do you like duck? It's Cuthbert's specialty."

"I've never had it before."

"Well, eat up." His face broke into a bright grin, revealing two dimples in the center of his cheeks. He grabbed the bird's leg and bit off a chunk.

Ayianna took a bite and chewed it slowly, savoring the tender, salty morsel. She couldn't remember the last time she even had meat. "I like it very much."

"I knew you would, but we must take great care in introducing such fine foods to you, otherwise you will get sick."

She tried not to frown and slowly nodded. Humans and their odd customs. She might not have had duck before, but she had lived among the elves. Of course, she probably shouldn't mention that, so she pierced a roasted potato chunk with her fork and stuck it in her mouth instead.

They ate together in awkward silence for a while. Ayianna tried to think of something to say or ask, but then she remembered her mother's social etiquette—ladies do not speak unless addressed and in proper fashion. What was proper fashion? At least she didn't have to break the silence.

Desmond didn't seem to be disturbed by the lack of conversation. He dined eagerly as if he hadn't eaten all day. He devoured most of the duck and emptied his wooden goblet of wine twice during the course of the meal. Once finished, he wiped his hands and face on the square cloth. He picked up his goblet and swirled its contents.

"Ayianna," he said, finally breaking the silence. "I had almost forgotten how lovely you are . . . " He drank deeply and set the goblet down. He pointed to her untouched wine. "Drink, it's good for your stomach."

Ayianna lifted the goblet and sniffed the dark liquid inside. A sharp fragrance of berries and mint stung her nose. She took a sip. The wine, sweet and bitter, burned as she swallowed. Warmth spread from her throat to her stomach and to the rest of her body.

Desmond leaned back and crossed his arms. "Integrity, trustworthiness, honesty, obedience . . . words that define a lady. The lady of a castle must carry out her duties and fulfill her roles as such, especially in the absence of the lord. Otherwise, why would the lord choose her to be his wife?

"I understand that you are ignorant of many things above your station in life. For you, there is grace, but correction remains inevitable. How else shall you learn?"

Her stomach sank. What had she done wrong?

"I'm disappointed in the choices you've made. From my understanding, you had plenty of chores to do with the harvest season coming to a close, but, instead, I find you traipsing over the countryside like a common whore. If this behavior continues, you will bring disgrace to your family and to me."

She gritted her teeth. "But my father—"

"And, I would like to add," Desmond continued, "you are betrothed to a man above your station, yet you are found in the company of a shirtless half-breed?"

"Half-breed?" She choked on the words.

Desmond shook his head. "Obviously, you don't know the significance of your actions. Perhaps, after a couple of days in the city, you'll see for yourself."

"But I can't stay here another day. I must go home."

"My business trip won't be finished until the end of the week. You will have to wait until then."

"But . . . my mother? I can't—"

"You should have thought about that before. Now you will have to wait till I've finished conducting my affairs."

Ayianna leapt to her feet. The chair fell backward and crashed into the stone floor behind her. "My father told me to go to Dagmar and find my brother. What was I supposed to do? Disobey him? You don't even care what I have been through. You sit here spouting trite, overbearing laws. I've seen horrors . . . death and cruelty! People dead, blood everywhere! Dagmar destroyed!"

"Ayianna!" Desmond faced clouded. He stood, his gaze darting down the hall. Voices rumbled in the main dining area as the evening guests ate their meal. He placed his hands on the table. "You must cease this outrage."

"No!" The tears came, spilling down her cheeks. "My father is dead. My brother is dead! Do you even care?" Ayianna shook and her trembling legs buckled.

Desmond's scowl slipped from his face, instead concern flickered in his eyes. He reached for her just as she collapsed. Sliding to the floor beside her, Desmond held her tight against his chest.

She struggled to push him away, but her strength failed. Grief ruptured her thin façade, and she cried in his arms.

"Ayianna," Desmond murmured and stroke her forehead.

She opened her eyes. She was back in her room, laying on the plump mattress. Desmond sat next to her, her hand in his. Had she fallen asleep? She struggled to sit up, her vision swimming, but Desmond shook his head, brushing her cheek with his finger.

Ayianna lay back down, looking up into his handsome face, now ashen with concern. She looked away, ashamed of her outburst.

"Ayianna," he said. He lifted her hand to his lips and kissed it. "I was hoping that our first meeting could have been different."

"Desmond," Ayianna began, but he pressed his fingers against her lips.

"You wear your father's betrothal gift." Desmond fingered the hairpin's delicate petals.

"Why me?" she asked.

He raised his eyebrows. "What do you mean?"

"Why did you choose me out of all the other girls?"

"Well, you were different. Most of the other girls threw themselves at me. I was like a hunk of meat to a pack of ravenous dogs to them. You, on the other hand, didn't see me at all. You ignored me."

"I did not."

"Who is telling the story here?" His face broke into a smile, revealing his dimples, his blue eyes twinkling. "You are a hard worker, dependable—so my uncle tells me. And I thought to myself, now here's a girl for me. Trustworthy, beautiful . . . must I go on?"

Ayianna smiled. She could look into those blue eyes forever.

Desmond leaned over and kissed Ayianna on the forehead. "Tomorrow is the Feast of Daeju. You can watch the parade from the balcony if you want. I have some business to finish, but I'll return in the evening."

"Feast of Daeju?"

"You should sleep."

"Please, tell me about the feast."

"It is a feast honoring the Sacred Pearl and commemorating the fall of Raemoja. If you believe all the stories and legends the bards sing about. Nowadays, people welcome any reason to come together and celebrate. Others, like me, look forward to it because people's moods are brighter and they tend to lighten their purses quicker. Quite a lucrative time for us merchants, I must say."

"Oh, in Zurial we have a similar celebration, but we call it *Zjóhedzi*."

"Zurial?"

Her throat closed up. What had her father told Lord Ramiro? Wasn't Praetan supposed to be her birthplace? She swallowed, hoping her face didn't give her away. "We spent some time there."

"Oh, of course." He smiled. "Well, it's late and time for you to rest."

Placing the betrothal pin beside Ayianna, Desmond stood. He closed the shutters and dimmed the lamp. "Sleep well."

Then he was gone, out the door and down the stairs, his footsteps disappearing into the night.

Ayianna lay there for a few moments, her heartbeat the only sound echoing in her ears. That was too close. How could she keep up with all the lies? She exhaled the mounting tension and turned her thoughts to Desmond.

He no longer seemed a stranger to her, but a friend who cared for her. Perhaps everything was going to be all right, if she could manage to remember her father's lies. Her father . . . her brother. How could she even think like that? Tears stung her eyes again, and she curled into a ball. Her thoughts and feelings threatened to consume her.

Nails clicked on the floor. Liam sprang into the bed and stretched out next to her. Ayianna buried her face in the wolf's musky fur.

No. She wouldn't think right now. Instead, she would cling to the memory of her father, her brother and their faith. If Osaryn truly existed beyond the land of Nälu, her father's death would not be in vain. She could endure the path set before her. One day at a time.

10

LOST IN THE brilliant display of colors below the balcony, Ayianna allowed her thoughts to drift. Her grief dulled. Beneath her, a procession of jugglers staggered past. Knives and flaming torches spun in the air around them. Two of them opened their mouths and spewed fire. A tumult of shrieks and laughter echoed off the buildings as the onlookers below exploded in applause.

The third floor patio was the best way to see the parade, Desmond had insisted. Why would anyone want to be down in the streets? Except for Ayianna that is. Her first time in Badara, the city of the king, and here she was locked way in an inn.

A giant creature swayed under her perch. He was so big she could almost reach over the railing and touch his wrinkly skin. Two long ivory tusks protruded from the sides of his mouth and another pair curled out above his temples like horns. A long, flexible trunk swung from the animal's face and hoisted a bright orange and blue banner.

"A letanili of the Pauden," a voice behind her said.

Ayianna jumped. She turned around and sucked in her breath. Kael stood beneath the archway leading to the balcony. Cleaned up and dressed in traditional elven attire, he looked every bit an elf and perhaps a vision of her father in his younger years. Grief wrenched her heart.

She averted her eyes. She couldn't help but think the white embroidery lining the slate blue tunic seemed out of place on Kael despite the fact he was an elf. Maybe it was the scar across his brow or the small gold earring. More likely, it was his behavior she hadn't expected from one who hailed from a race who valued courteous and graceful conduct.

"Forgive me for intruding," he said as he touched his fingertips together in the traditional elven greeting and bowed.

"You shouldn't creep up on people like that." She looked away and exhaled her frustration.

"And you should be more aware of your surroundings."

She pulled her scarf around her head tighter. "Are you still here?"

"Enjoying the parade?" He stepped out onto the balcony next to her.

She slid away from him. "I was until you showed up."

"Where is Liam?"

"In the room."

"And Desmond?"

"Busy." She focused on the acrobats bouncing down the street after the parade.

Civilians and foreigners alike poured out into the cobbled streets and followed the parade as it disappeared around a corner. The festival would finish with spectacular shows and a gigantic feast, and she wouldn't be able to see any of it. She tried to hide her disappointment.

"The rest of the festival is held in the inner courtyard." He twisted his hands around the polished wood railing. "You're welcome to join me, unless you're content with staring at the dirty streets below."

Ayianna's breath caught. Had he read her mind? She fished in her pocket for her talisman, but then chided herself. *Elves don't read minds.*

"You know," he faced her and leaned against the wood, "a talisman only works when you wear it around your neck."

Ayianna spun around. "How did you know?"

"Besides talismans, amulets, and other protective charms are for lazy people and scheming peddlers wanting to make a quick fortune. You can learn to guard your thoughts without their use."

Ayianna stared at him. She wasn't sure if she was more upset that he could somehow read her mind or the fact that he had just called her lazy.

"Why are you here?" she asked, finally finding her voice.

"I was just passing by and saw you, so I thought I'd say hello, seeing how we didn't meet on the best of terms or parted on them either." He pulled his eyes from the street and met hers. "And I would like to thank you for cleaning up my arm."

"It was nothing. I—uh . . . " How could she be so ungrateful? She met his gaze. "You saved my life, it was the least I could do. I guess we are even then."

"Not quite, unless you call a life and an arm fair trade." He cocked an eyebrow

She shook her head. "I guess not."

"Are you interested in seeing more of the festival?"

"I . . . " Ayianna glanced away. The ruckus of horns and voices had faded. A faint melody drifted down the deserted streets. "I shouldn't."

"Of course. I understand," he said. "When are you going home?"

"I have to wait for Desmond to finish up his business here." She leaned forward on the railing. "About a week."

"A week?" Kael touched her shoulder. "Your mother will be worried sick."

Her ache deepened at his touch. She blinked back the tears and straightened. "I have no choice."

He stood next to her, the silence growing longer. Finally, he cleared his throat. "Well, I . . . " He eyed her, his expression unreadable, but his gray eyes darkened. "I guess this is goodbye then." He turned to leave.

"Wait." Ayianna faced him. "Did Saeed meet with the king yet?"

"No, the king isn't seeing anyone right now. Saeed is furious."

"How can the king not be concerned what happened at Dagmar?"

He shrugged. "Dagmar is considered outside of his jurisdiction."

"But what about the men that murdered my father? We are under Ramiro's lordship, thus under the king's jurisdiction."

"The king isn't going to bother with a mere peasant's death."

Ayianna gaped at him. How could he be so . . . so irritating!

"I didn't mean . . . " He frowned and crossed his arms. "I meant that is how he views it."

"What about Saeed?"

He leaned against the archway. "He doesn't have much to go on. Have you remembered anything else about the incident?"

"I've been trying to forget it."

"I'm meeting Saeed in a while. I could take you to him."

Ayianna looked down the street. Did her brother's death make her message obsolete? If Saeed knew her father was a secret keeper, then perhaps her father's death would be honored and some sort of justice brought about.

She pursed her lips. How angry would Desmond be if she went? But if she was back before he was, then there would be no need for him to know. She had to do it for her father.

A handful of women swirled in the center of the courtyard to a lilting tune of horns and lutes as Ayianna followed Kael through the throng enjoying the show. She clutched the carved talisman, hoping to ease the nerves twisting her stomach. She scanned the sea of turned heads and swinging hips for Desmond. Would he even be among the celebrants?

Without a glimpse of her betrothed, Ayianna tightened her head covering and hurried after Kael. Was she doing the right thing? Maybe she should turn back before Desmond caught her. No, she had to talk to Saeed. Desmond would understand. He'd have to.

The aroma of smoked turkey legs and cinnamon buns hung heavy in the air, and her stomach growled, scolding her for missing the afternoon meal. She couldn't let that distract her. She'd eat, once she had talked to Saeed.

But what was she going to tell him? Her father had been a secret keeper, but of what? Maybe Saeed wouldn't believe her or wouldn't be able to help, and she would have risked the scorn of her future husband for nothing.

Kael and Ayianna skirted the edge of the courtyard where large fountains and green shrubbery made a circular pattern. Kael had explained that it was built to confuse the king's enemies and slow their progress toward the great hall. Ayianna thought she'd be sick if they didn't reach the inner courtyard soon. Apart from the dizzying path, the clipped hedges towered over her and cast the afternoon in shadows. No entrance or exit in sight, just rows and rows of leafy bushes. Had anyone lost their way in the maze? Did Kael know where he was going?

But before panic could grip her, the stone path ended. The inner courtyard sprawled beneath them, hemmed in by a second curtain wall and steep sides of the great castle of Badara. Below, the dancers gyrated, and the chaotic multitude broke into applause. Angular towers crowned with crenellations rose behind them to varying heights and surrounded the king's keep. Mounted above the towers, a green and gold banner flashed in the afternoon sun. Ayianna couldn't help but notice the difference between the sharp angles of Badara and the sweeping curves of Zurial. A twinge of longing for her childhood home swept through her, but she quickly brushed it aside.

Kael pressed on through the packed courtyard, toward the great hall. Ayianna did her best to keep up, but only managed to fall farther behind. The boisterous assembly writhed with laughter, spilling ale from their mugs. They didn't care if they bumped into her or sprayed her with the nauseating drink.

She looked for Kael, but he was gone. She called for him, but her voice was drowned amidst the clamor of instruments and voices. A shiver raced down her spine. How could she have lost him?

The music changed to a soft, luring melody and drew her attention back toward the center stage. The people stilled as the dancers began to sing, their voices fluid and hypnotic. Words twined with the lutes' gentle, rhythmic strums.

Ayianna didn't recognize the language, but she understood its power. The song tugged at her, calling to her grief-stricken heart. It breathed of peace and freedom. The crowd surged forward and swept her along like a leaf in a stream.

The dancers, with their colorful silk scarves and dresses, flickered between the bobbing of heads. The song, like a balm, soothed her sorrowful heart. Doubt and worry disappeared.

A hand grabbed her arm, and she flinched. She didn't want to be stopped. She needed to see the dancers. She jerked her arm free and plunged forward, pushing through the men and women. Where was the peace the song promised? Bodies jostled against her, pushing her back, muffling the strains of the melody.

Hands grasped her shoulders and spun her around. She yelped. Balling her hand into a fist, she swung, but her aim was poor. A flash of slate blue blocked her blow. It took a moment for her to recognize Kael's icy glare.

"What are you thinking?" His grip tightened on her shoulders. His gaze broke from hers and swept across the area. "You nearly gouged my eye out."

"What were you thinking, grabbing me like that?" She eyed his hardened expression. "Is there something wrong?"

His jaw tightened, his gray eyes darkened. "Stay close, I'm certain Desmond wouldn't approve if I lost you."

She planted her hands on her hips. "And he wouldn't approve of you being with me either, but that didn't stop you, did it?"

"Nor did it stop you."

She glared at him, but the song called to her, and she turned away in search of the dancers. Now she was even farther away, standing on the outskirts of the crowd next to one of the fountains. She flung her hands up. What a fool of an elf, he was!

"Tuthiyenat ení lul élelTanil rul nina lélel."

Ayianna caught a glimpse of a staff as the lead dancer held it high—a bright red glow swirled above it. The mesmerized throng wavered in a captivated trance. The light faded to orange, then yellow, and formed an orb above the dancer's staff. Warmth pulsated from the dancers like the rays of the sun on a summer day. She didn't want the song to end, but to continue in its swaying tranquility.

The dancer hoisted the wooden staff high into the air, but this time the orb burned white.

The staff descended as the music hushed, the words hanging in the air.

"O dilu za uzanaleta tanil
Eja o niotu za uzanaleta twanil
Ruza zatuiso kol tiuthil nina isür."

Strong arms seized her from behind and shoved her into the pool of water. Ayianna kicked and thrashed, but she couldn't break free. Finally, the grip gave way, and she resurfaced. Sputtering and coughing out water, she spun to face her attacker.

Kael. He stood next to her, drenched.

"You!" Ayianna balled her fists. "What are you doing?"

Kael wiped the water from his eyes and squeezed his hair dry. "I saved your life."

"By trying to drown me?" she asked, but her words were lost in cheers and clapping, the uproar near deafening.

"Keep your voice down." His brows tightened. He glanced away and scanned the area.

"As if they could hear me."

He glared at her. "That was a spell. I'm sure of it."

"Really?" She drew up her waterlogged dress and waded toward the edge. "And next you'll say, we're all under attack, and you'll try to drown me again."

Kael offered to help her out, but she shoved his hand away. She dragged herself out of the pool and did her best to wring out her dress. She faced him and opened her mouth to unleash an angry tirade, but stopped.

Everyone had grown silent.

"Are you all right?" He climbed out of the pool.

"I am soaking wet! What do you think?"

"A little water never hurt anyone." He shook his shirt out and tried to press the water from his pants legs.

Ayianna shook her head. "You were trying to drown me."

"I wasn't—listen. If that was a spell, and I think it was, you would've been cursed or something worse. The water blocked the spell. If I'm wrong, we're just wet. But if I'm right, then I protected you."

"You think?" Ayianna stood on tip-toe, trying to peer over and between shoulders. The people stared ahead, mesmerized and unmoving. Why had everyone gone silent? "How do you know so much about spells?"

"Keep your voice down," he whispered harshly and grasped her arm.

"Get away from me!" She shoved him aside and pushed through the bodies. This time they didn't push her back. What was going on? She came upon an opening between a plump older man and his shorter companion, a woman wrapped in a purple head covering and a lavender dress. Ahead, she caught the flicker of colorful scarves. The dancers!

"Lord Wistan!" someone announced. Male or female, she couldn't tell.

A man arrayed in Badara's green and gold joined the women. One of them removed a silver cup from between the prongs of the ornate staff and presented it to him.

"Citizens of Badara!" the man exclaimed, holding the silver cup high. "A cup of ale for all!" The crowd erupted again with cheers and applause. "Let the feast begin!"

"Ayianna, you're not yourself." Kael's voice sounded distant. "It's the spell."

What did he know? She clenched her teeth. Why did he irritate her so? She wove her away between the stiff humans. She had to meet the dancers. They had to sing again. Maybe she could make a special request, if she could ever reach them.

The crowds shifted, and the stage they had been dancing on came into view, but there were no dancers. Her heart sank.

Kael touched her shoulder.

"What?" She pulled her attention from the empty stage and glanced up at Kael. His gray eyes were as cold as ice.

"We need to go."

She frowned. "No, I'm done with you. If Saeed still wants to see me, he can come by the inn and make arrangements with Desmond. This is ridiculous." Ayianna shook her head and shoved past him.

What was she thinking? She had to get back and cleaned up before Desmond returned. She gritted her teeth and entered the winding bushes.

11

AYIANNA TRUDGED DOWN the vacant street, her dress sloshing against her legs. She entered the inn and stormed up the stairs. Wet, cold, and with no other clothes to change into— the burgundy dress didn't count—what a day it had turned out to be.

Liam wagged her tail in greeting.

Ayianna slouched on the floor and hugged her. She caught sight of the crumpled nightgown on the bed. She straightened, peeled off her wet dress, and draped it on the empty basin. It would take all night to dry. How was she going to explain this to Desmond? Excuses swirled in her head, but none of them seemed plausible.

Hooves thundered in the street outside.

She donned the nightgown and darted to the window. Men rode by on horseback, carrying the black and gold banner she had seen in Dagmar. She gasped, gripping the windowsill. What were they doing here? Where were Badara's guards? A legion of fur-covered creatures scampered behind them and disappeared into the lengthening shadows.

She jumped back from the window. Should she run? Where? Find Kael? Why Kael? She shook her head. Maybe she should talk to Cuthbert. She yanked open the door and something crashed in the inn below. She shoved the rising fear down and peered over the thin, serpentine railing.

Several armed men dragged Cuthbert from the kitchen and shoved him to his knees before a tall man in a long, black cloak. Had he been the man watching her from the blacksmith shop?

"Get those filthy imps out of my inn!" Cuthbert shouted as he struggled against his attackers.

The man in the cloak snorted and leveled his sword. "We're looking for a girl. She'd be new to the area."

"Aye, this 'ere's an inn. It's full of newcomers!" the old man said.

"She's a pretty thing—long dark hair, a peasant of sorts, has a wolf for a pet."

Ayianna's chest tightened. The pounding in her ears drowned the innkeeper's response. She forced herself to breath slowly. How did they find her?

Movement beneath the tables caught her eye. Furry creatures scampered about, their noses to the floor like dogs sniffing out a rat. Imps? One of the creatures froze and turned its yellow eyes her direction, its deformed face and body like a human. Dagmar!

"This way!" its scratchy voice called to the others as it charged up the stairs.

It speaks! Ayianna slammed the door and locked it. Why were they hunting her? What was she going to do? She dashed to the window—too high to jump. Liam snarled, and Ayianna spun around as claws ripped into the wood.

She swallowed a scream and dragged Liam into the adjoining room. The wolf fought her, growling and lunging. Ayianna kicked the door shut and shoved the empty basin against it. She sank to the floor in the darkness. She pulled

Liam closer and tried to think. No lights, no weapons, no exit—trapped. She sucked in her breath and listened.

The bed screeched across the floorboards and crashed against a wall. The imps had broken in, and it didn't take them long to discover where she and Liam hid. Claws tore along the walls and the door. Rays of dim light sifted through shredded wood. The smell of death overwhelmed the small, dark space.

Liam broke from her grasp and charged the door.

Ayianna backed away and her hand hit something—the iron candle pillar. She stood and grabbed it, knocking the thick, unlit candle to the floor. With both hands, she hoisted the heavy pillar in the air.

The first imp broke through, and Liam tore into it.

Another one charged her. Ayianna swung the iron pillar, and it collided with the imp's body, knocking it aside. Shrieks erupted in the other room as more imps poured through the broken door, clawing over each other to reach her.

She swiped at the oncoming charge. They slammed into the basin and toppled to the floor. More imps leapt upon her. Sharp claws raked across her shoulder. She fell back against the wall and scraped the imp off.

The battered door exploded as a man stepped inside and plowed through the imps.

Desmond! Relief flooded Ayianna. She swung at the imps with renewed strength.

Soon, the last imp crumpled to the ground. She leapt into the man's arms, tears streaming down her face.

"Not mad at me anymore?" he asked, pulling away.

Ayianna looked not into Desmond's blue eyes, but Kael's gray. "You!" She recoiled.

"Who'd you expect? Desmond's obviously got more important things to do."

"You are unbelievable!" She pushed her way past him and tripped over the imps strewn about the floor. She collapsed on the bed and clenched her hands together, but they wouldn't stop shaking.

He wiped the blood from his sword on the fur of an imp sword and sheathed it. Kicking a few of the dead imps out of his way, he strode out of the room.

Fine, just leave me here for the next batch of filthy, smelly creatures! She eyed one and immediately wished she hadn't. The almost human-like face glared at her from an odd angle. Blood oozed from its nose and mouth. She gagged and quickly looked away.

Kael reappeared in the doorway. "Come on."

"But . . . what about Desmond?"

"Don't be foolish. This city is crawling with imps, and I bet your dearly beloved wouldn't even stand a chance if he were here."

"I never said he was my dearly beloved."

"Aren't you betrothed to him?" Kael crossed the room and peered out through the windows.

She clung to Liam. "Not by choice."

He returned to the doorway and faced her. "If we don't leave now, we'll be trapped."

Ayianna glanced at the scattered imp carcasses, hoping Desmond would walk through the door any moment.

Liam pulled away, sniffed, and pawed at them. Then the wolf sauntered over to Kael and sat on her haunches.

Traitor. Any minute now, Desmond would rush in . . . Seconds slid by but he didn't appear.

"We can't wait for him," Kael said and patted Liam on the head.

The wolf looked at her master and tilted her head. Ayianna scowled at her.

"Where are we going?" she asked.

"We will meet Saeed at the stables."

"But . . . " Ayianna glanced at her wet clothes hanging on the windowsill. "I'm wearing a nightgown."

"You have no choice." He jerked a robe from the chest against the wall and threw it to her.

"You can't be serious."

His eyes narrowed. "Do I look like I'm jesting?"

The rest of her protest withered. She tugged the robe on and followed Kael from the room. Hopefully, Desmond would find them soon.

The inn was empty, except for the few dead bodies lying beneath remnants of tables and chairs. No sign of Cuthbert, though. Ayianna cringed as the stairs creaked beneath her feet.

Kael didn't seem to notice as he and Liam were already waiting for her at the entrance. He didn't wait long. As soon as Ayianna drew near, he pressed through the swinging door. She pulled the robe tighter and ducked outside after him. Darting from shadow to shadow, they made their way to the stables.

The Feast of Daeju was winding down. The people lingered, filling their bellies with food and ale, unaware of the calamity that had crept into the city. Hanging lanterns lined the cobbled street and burned dim as the sun dipped behind the trees, casting the cramped buildings in a crimson glow.

Ayianna watched the people laugh and eat. "Maybe we should warn someone?"

"Darin is taking care of that," Kael said. He slinked toward the stables. His silent, graceful movements reminded her he was an elf.

"Citizens of Badara!"

A man in a green and gold uniform stood on a platform for all to see. He held up a gold goblet. "A toast . . . "

The people roared in agreement as they raised their own worn mugs and held them high.

"You, who have waited, longed for this day!"

Ayianna took a step back toward the courtyard and peered around a slouching man's shoulders. The crowd drained their mugs in unison.

"Lord Wistan." Kael's hand gripped her elbow. "He should be concerned for the safety of Badara and its king."

Ayianna glanced around at the large stone towers looming above them, empty and dark. Where were the guards? Kael tugged, and she pulled her attention away from the captain and followed.

To the right, a low building stretched along the curtain wall next to a large corral. The earthy smells of hay and manure drifted on the breeze. They sprang from the shadows and hurried inside the stables. The thud of hooves echoed off the buildings, and wheels ground across the cobblestones outside.

Ayianna peered through the wooden boards as several dark-clad men on horseback galloped past. A procession of imps shuffled before a carriage constructed from what seemed to be massive black bones. Liam growled, and Ayianna placed her hand on the wolf's back.

At the edge of the courtyard, the bone carriage rumbled to a stop, and a man stepped out. A murmur rose through the crowd. The tall stranger joined Lord Wistan at the top of the dancer's stage. Black hair and a goatee trimmed his handsome face. He smiled and held his hand over the crowd as if greeting his subjects. His charm drew her in, yet repulsed her.

"My Lord Derk, it is ready," Lord Wistan said, offering the gold goblet to him.

"Thank you, friend." Lord Derk accepted the goblet. He flung his black cloak back and held his hand high. "People of Badara, may I present to you the Book of Thar'ryn."

Several noblemen approached, hoisting a leather-bound tome on a platform.

"*Nijal!*" Derk exclaimed. Bright orange flames erupted from his outstretched hand and consumed the book.

Ayianna gasped.

The crowd watched it burn. An unnatural silence gripped them as if no one dared to move or breathe.

"May the ancient laws of the Sacred Pearl disintegrate just as the book in which they are written burns. Today, we forge our own destiny in freedom, a new liberty for the Prathae Plains."

The crowd stared on as the man drank from the goblet. A soft chant rose from behind him. Was it the dancers?

"Dusíruja thiköza shoza kotat lul thüta nilétu
Okóqual oletu thöl lul göleth luza rulétu.
Thüta'th taelu ath ale
Lul quathith ení thile.
Mäta! Mäta!
Lul thütath quathithtud tuíso thile!"

"What's going on?" whispered Ayianna.

"They are hailing that man as the new king."

"But what about King Valdamar? Where is he?"

"Darin will find him. We'd better get these horses saddled." Kael withdrew to the shadows. "Badara closes its gates at sundown, we don't have much time. Saeed will be here soon."

Kael grabbed a couple of bridles and a saddle from the tack room. Ayianna located the stall where their horses had been bedded down. They pawed the straw and threw their heads, their eyes wide, their nostrils flared. Could they sense the tension in the air? Or was it something else?

"Easy there," she whispered and unlatched the gate. The horses burst through, knocking her against the wall.

"What are you doing?" Kael grabbed a rope off the wall. "You'll lose our mounts!"

Ayianna gritted her teeth. She scrambled to her feet and yanked another saddle off the large wooden barrel protruding from the tack room. She lugged it toward Kael, who had secured the sorrel. She plopped the saddle on the ground.

He finished saddling the one and went after the roan.

Liam paced the aisle. The stable opened into a corral to the right. Behind them, stalls lined the wall and contained several horses. They shifted, restless.

Something was wrong.

With teeth bared, Liam slunk past Kael as he placed the bridle on the roan. The wolf headed for the corral, growling. What was she sensing?

The horse jerked away from Kael, snorting and pawing the ground.

"Easy there," Kael said as he lunged to catch the horse's reins.

Imps dropped from the rafters. The stable exploded in chaos. Horses bucked and kicked, racing around the corral. Ayianna stumbled backward. Why were the imps after her?

One of the horses reared, breaking away from Kael. The other one bolted.

Kael dodged the terrified horses, leapt over the imps, and unsheathed his sword. He swung, the blade hissing through the air until it crunched into bone.

Ayianna tripped over a saddle and fell. Bile burned her throat. Was this how she would die?

The roan reared up, striking the air with its hooves where she'd been standing. An imp tore at the horse's neck.

Ayianna spun out of the way just as the horse's hooves came crashing down. She sprang from the ground, but tripped on the hem of her robe. How clumsy could she be! She jerked her robe free and ran toward the gate.

An imp landed on her shoulders, knocking her to the ground again. Its claws ripped into her face. The wound burned and warm blood trickled down her cheek.

She shoved the imp away and scrambled to her feet.

The imp tumbled into the straw. It spun around and snarled. Spotting a pitchfork against the wall, Ayianna grabbed it and waved it in front of her. *Kill it!* She couldn't. Its yellowed eyes held an intelligence that neither bird nor beast had, albeit a twisted one. And it could talk. She plunged the fork at him, but her attempt was weak, and he batted the tines away.

"Ye can't kill me." The imp pranced and made crude gestures with its clawed hands. "Ye can't—"

Kael's blade sliced through the imp's neck, and its head toppled to the ground. He swung around and caught the last imp through the gut. He wiped his blade on its furry carcass. "Weak—you stall like that again, and you're dead."

Tears stung her eyes and her hands and legs trembled. She wanted to throw accusations back at him, but her jaw refused to unclench.

Hooves pounded into the stable.

Ayianna stumbled over the straw mound, away from the new assailant. She glanced over her shoulder.

Kael stood, brandishing his sword. A hooded figure stooped in his saddle and reined in his mount.

"Kael, now!"

Saeed. Relief flooded her.

Kael sheathed his sword. He cornered the skittish roan and leapt atop.

Ayianna scanned the stables. Where had the sorrel gone? Her heart plummeted. They wouldn't leave her behind, would they?

Kael wheeled his horse around and barreled toward her. He leaned over, his hand outstretched.

"No, wait—"

He jerked her up into the saddle behind him, and urged the horse to gallop.

Several more imps dropped from the ceiling. Kael yanked the horse left.

Ayianna lost her grip and toppled off. She slammed against a stall and slid to the floor. Her right side burned.

"Get up!" Kael yelled at her.

She scrabbled to her feet.

He grabbed her and hauled her back on the mount a second time. He kicked the horse's flanks. They raced through the stables into the corral. They were trapped, but Kael urged the horse faster.

"What are you doing?"

"Hold on."

They sped toward the wooden fence.

She grasped him around the waist and leaned into his back. The horse lurched. It leapt, but pitched forward as its hind hooves caught the railing. Despite her fear, their mount landed firmly on the other side.

They raced through the narrow streets. The roan's hooves clattered against the cobblestones and echoed off the buildings.

The shrill sound of metal grinding against metal jolted Ayianna. She peered around Kael's shoulder.

Ahead, Saeed galloped through the gatehouse. The portcullis fell.

Kael snapped the reins, and the horse lunged forward. Ayianna buried her face into Kael's back, squeezing him tighter. The giant iron grid slammed shut behind them.

12

FOR TWO DAYS, they rode west, camping once beneath the stars. By midmorning of the third day, gray clouds had consumed the sky. The air breathed of moisture, dampening their clothes, chilling them. Kael clenched his jaw against the cold. Ahead, Saeed reined in his horse.

A spindly, wood fence encircled Ayianna's village. Huts made from cut sod squatted along the outskirts, bordering the communal vegetable and herb gardens. To the far left, a handful of pigs grunted and nosed around a compost pile. Did humans let their pigs run free? He shook his head and bought his horse alongside Saeed.

Deeper inside the community, buildings constructed from wood lined the dirt-packed road. The governor's two-story house rose above them, sitting next to the Nuja temple and village's bell tower.

A plume of smoke rose into the damp air from a dug fire pit off to the left of him. Where were all the people? The small village should have been buzzing with activity. Instead, an eerie calm covered it like a green film on a stagnant swamp. A child cried in the distance. Moments later a shrill voice screamed curses for the child to stop.

A strange, unseen prison locked the inhabitants in a dreary world—the weather didn't help. Clouds draped over the plains and clung to the trees. Autumn's chill seeped through him. At least he had Ayianna's warmth to fight off the cold. Saeed didn't.

Kael couldn't help but wonder how he would have viewed this place if Teron and his sister had still been alive. What kind of welcome would Arlyn have given them upon discovering Teron's engagement? Would he have returned to Zurial? Kael shoved his meanderings away. It didn't matter now. They were dead—all of them.

Saeed turned in his saddle. "Ayianna, where is your home?"

Ayianna stirred behind Kael and lifted her head from his back. A rush of cold, damp air replaced her warmth, sending a shiver down his spine. She pointed toward a well-sized house past the governor's, near the edge of the village.

He obliged and urged the horse on. They passed several smaller huts along the way. Their thatched roofs drooped over doorways and windows, their shutters closed and uninviting.

Kael stopped in front of the house.

Ayianna slipped off, but as soon as her feet touched the ground, her legs buckled. She reached for the saddle and missed, grabbing his leg instead. She quickly pushed away and waddled toward the hut.

He shook his head. *So much death for one so young. Poor girl.* He dismounted and joined Saeed.

"Do you think the mother will have any information?"

Saeed shrugged. "I doubt it, but it is worth a try. We should hurry though, I do not—"

A shriek erupted from the house. "No, no, no!"

Kael rushed to the doorway, his hand on the hilt of his sword.

Ayianna lay crumpled in the middle of the floor, sobbing.

He clenched his jaw as his vision adjusted to the darkness. Tables and chairs had been knocked over. Broken dishes littered the floor. Cupboards and chests lay bare, their contents strewn about the room. Where was her mother?

Saeed pushed Kael aside. He maneuvered between the shards of pottery and lumps of clothes until he was at her side. He knelt and put his arm around her.

Kael turned away and pushed open the shutters. Perhaps he should question the neighbors. He strode outside and knocked on the first house he came to.

Silence answered. He knocked again.

The door creaked open, and a red-headed boy peered up at him.

"My name is Kael." He rubbed his thumb over the knuckles of his left hand. "A friend of Arlyn and Gilana, your neighbors. Could you—"

The door slammed shut.

He drew in a deep breath. "Can you at least tell me what happened?"

No response.

He shook his head. What was wrong with these people?

He was about to move on when the door opened and an older man stepped out. Frayed patches adorned his pants and tunic. He rubbed his nose. "We don't need your kind around here . . . nothing but trouble you are."

Kael glimpsed movement behind the sourly villager. A woman's head, cloaked in a scarf, peered beside him. "Gilana wasn't, she—"

"She wasn't an elf." He continued glaring at Kael. "Married a good-for-nothing. He couldn't plow a field straight even if a wall marked his way. I should've known he was an elf. But she got what was coming to her for throwing in with your lot."

"Can you tell me what happened to her?"

118

"What does it look like?" The man looked over Kael's shoulder. "No mind between your pointy ears, eh?"

Kael tightened his fists, but took a step back. "I'm sorry to have bothered you." He turned to go.

"Did you hear the pretty song?" the woman asked. She kept her head down.

Her husband clenched his jaw, but didn't say anything.

Kael returned to the door. "What song?"

"It was faint, but a song upon the wind, most beautiful if I have ever heard one—so luring, so pensive. I wish it hadn't ended . . . " Her voice faded, and then she whispered softly to herself, "*Quathith ení taelu.*"

"No, ma'am . . . I didn't hear any songs." He bowed slightly, but the man rolled his eyes. He ushered his wife back inside and shut the door.

Kael walked back to Ayianna's house, taking the long way around. He drew in a deep breath. The dampness clung to his lungs. Dread burdened the air, but was it coming from him or something else? How did they hear the song the dancers had sung at Badara? It had to be a spell—no, a curse. And the angst and despair he tasted on the wind must have been birthed two nights ago from the souls of the dancers.

Entering the house, he found the tables and chairs had been set right. Piles of broken dishes and torn pillows lined the wall now, leaving a large path to the other rooms. Ayianna lifted her head at his approach, her eyes red and puffy. Saeed reclined in one of the chairs next to her.

"Well, the neighbors refused to help." Kael sat across from the two of them. "Somehow, they heard the song the dancers were singing. It had to be a spell of some sort, or worse, a curse. The woman said it was beautiful and luring. She quoted something in the ancient language. I doubt she knew what it meant, but maybe it was part of the song, '*Quathith ení taelu*'."

"Kiss of death . . . " Saeed's bushy eyebrows knitted together as he stroked his beard with a gnarled hand. A habit Kael had seen many times.

Ayianna cocked her head. "But that's impossible. Badara is so far from here, no one could've heard the music."

"Distance does not matter," Saeed said. "The spell weaver determines where and who the spell is for, and the more adept he or she is, the stronger the spell."

"Oh . . . "

Saeed cleared his throat. "Why are these people after you?"

She rubbed her temples, just missing the scabs on her cuts. "I . . . I don't know."

"I cannot help you otherwise."

"They wanted something from your father." Kael leaned across the table toward her. "Teron knew something, but he is dead and of no use to them, and now your mother is missing. Did she know something?"

Ayianna stared at him. A mixture of confusion and anger flashed across her face. She nodded slowly. "Everyone knew but me."

"Knew what exactly?" Saeed cast a sideways glance at Kael, but turned his attention to Ayianna.

Kael resisted the temptation to squirm in his chair. He had been under the scrutiny of those amber eyes before. Digging and exposing, the Headmaster saw things no one else could. He studied the girl before him, wondering what Saeed could see. The likeness to her brother was uncanny, though, she appeared more human than he did. Lighter skin, the same hazel eyes, rounder ears.

Her gaze darted between the two of them. Fresh tears spilled down her cheeks, and she wiped her nose with the edge of her scarf. "My father . . . " She choked. "He was a secret keeper. But I don't know what secret he was guarding. He only told me to find my brother and warn him."

Saeed tugged one of his braids as he studied the girl. Kael held his tongue. That much Teron had told him, but a secret keeper of what?

"Warn your brother about what? What did your father say?"

Ayianna bit her lip and looked up at the ceiling. "Something about the sun setting. He said, 'the sun has set . . .'" She sniffed. "But I can't remember the rest."

Saeed leaned forward. "Whoever is after the secret now has your mother. It would be helpful if you could remember your father's last words." He stood and turned to Kael. "Her wounds should be cleaned again, double-checked for infection, and dressed if need be."

He opened his mouth to protest, but Saeed walked outside.

He grabbed an empty jar and filled it with water from the hand pump. *She is Teron's sister. I at least owe it to him.* He grabbed a rag and sat down next to Ayianna. Working in silence, he cleansed the grime from her face. He rinsed the rag out and began dabbing the cuts around the edge of her cheek. Her skin was red and puckered where the imp's dirty claws scratched her, but displayed no signs of infection yet.

She grimaced with each stroke of the rag. He tried to be gentle, but gentle didn't remove filth. Her gaze shifted.

"Will I have a scar like yours?"

Kael set his jaw and allowed the silence to lengthen. She looked away.

"You're lucky the imp missed your eye. The cuts aren't too deep." He rinsed the rag again. "We won't bandage it. The air will do it some good and speed the healing."

"Thank you," she said and reached up to touch her face.

"Don't touch it!" Kael grabbed her hand. "Your hands are dirty."

She pulled away. "What do you know about my brother? And my father being a secret keeper?"

Kael stood. He flung the dirty water out the window, refilled the jar, and turned back around. "Take off the robe."

Her eyebrows arched, and her lips parted. She might have said something, but he was too flustered to hear her. He set the jar of water down and threw the rag inside. "I didn't mean— look, I need to check your shoulder."

Her face was bright red. She pulled one arm out of its sleeve, but clutched the rest of the robe tightly around her chest.

Kael took a deep breath. He peeled back the nightgown to reveal a nasty gash. He swabbed it, less gentle this time. She flinched. He blocked his mind from the torrent of anger and embarrassment boiling within her.

Saeed strode through the doorway. "I must find Darin before he sends out the messengers."

Kael jumped back. "Er—why?"

"If the people here have heard the song, then I am certain the people of Talem have heard it as well. The plains are no longer safe. The Guardian Circle must meet elsewhere."

"But where?" Kael rinsed the rag quickly while his mind buzzed, hardly hearing a word Saeed had said.

Saeed scratched his right eyebrow. "We will move the meeting to Raemoja."

"What?" Kael's mind snapped to attention. "Why? There's nothing there. Why not Zurial?"

"Zurial is too far. And I would prefer not to have to deal with people at the moment." Saeed peered out the window. "You and Ayianna will go on ahead."

Kael stared at the Headmaster. He shook his head. "You can't expect me—I'm not a wet nurse."

"I am not a baby. I don't need you or a wet nurse." Anger surged from her and slammed into him, but he didn't care. She turned to Saeed and yanked the robe back over her shoulder. "I can't just leave. What about my father's body?"

"Until we have further information, there is nothing we can do." Saeed's voice was gentle, but firm. "Right now, we need to keep you safe."

"She is betrothed," Kael said. "Why not let him take care of her? I'd rather not traverse weeks' worth of land with a girl."

"He is not here, nor do we know if he has succumbed to the spell or not." Saeed peered outside again. "Take the old Naajiso trail through the Inganno Forest. Remember the old bard's tale about Trygg and the battle of Raemoja?"

"Yes, but—"

"It will take you only a few days to cross through, no more. Stay on the trail and no harm will come upon you."

"Nevin Saeed, you can't be serious."

"Do I ever jest?"

Kael frowned. "Sometimes."

A small smile brushed the Headmaster's lips, and Kael thought he might have seen the old twinkle in Saeed's eyes again, but it disappeared so swiftly he doubted it.

"Do not linger here," Saeed said as he turned to go. "I think the villagers are up to something."

Kael followed him outside.

Saeed pulled his hood over his face and mounted his horse. He touched his fingertips together in an elven salute, then jerked the horse around and galloped out of the village, disappearing into a cloud of haze.

Kael's gaze settled upon the villagers. Men and women in dirty, tattered clothes huddled around the neighbor's house, conversing in low terms. Though he couldn't hear what they were saying, he could sense their intent. He shut the door and glanced at Ayianna.

"Get dressed and pack what you can for food."

Ayianna stood without acknowledging him and began pilfering through the piles of clothes and rubbish.

Kael peered through the window at the huddled group of villagers. How much time could he spare?

He turned his attention back to the girl. She dumped a half loaf of bread, a broken jar of dried fruit and a brick of cheese onto the table.

"Could you hurry?"

Ayianna placed her hands on her hips. "You could help."

He gritted his teeth. He glanced at the villagers and then back at her. "What do you want me to do?"

"Put the food in this." She grabbed a leather knapsack and threw it at him.

He caught it before the metal buckle hit him in the head.

She stuck her chin out, turned, and disappeared into the adjoining room.

I probably deserved that. He stuffed the food into the sack. *Why couldn't Saeed have taken her?* He kicked a pile of clothes across the floor.

"Do you have a waterskin?" he asked.

"Somewhere in all this mess." Her voice drifted from the room. "We usually hang it by the door."

Of course. He spotted the corked water bladder hanging from a peg. He pumped water into the waterskin and looked out the window again.

The fire pit at the center of the village was now filled with wood, and small flames danced along the logs. A few of the villagers held sticks in the fire. They pulled back and hoisted fiery torches.

Kael's stomach sank. *Fools.*

Movement drew his attention to the east—two horsemen rode into the village. One was dressed in the finery of a prince, the other he recognized. More complications . . . or maybe not.

Maybe he could leave Ayianna behind after all. Saeed would understand, wouldn't he?

Kael capped the waterskin and set it on the table.

Ayianna entered the room and shoved whatever was in her hands into the bag.

"Desmond is here."

"Really?" Her face paled.

Kael stepped outside as Desmond arrived, followed by the lavishly adorned horse of Prince Vian. Emerald green robes draped over the prince's shoulders and across the flanks of his dapple gray mount. He carried himself with an air of authority and peered down his nose at the village. His presence shamed the dirty villagers.

Ayianna's betrothed jumped from his horse and bounded toward Kael, his face red. "You!" he bellowed and balled his fists.

"Desmond!" Ayianna shouted.

He spun toward Ayianna, his hand still raised. For a moment, Kael thought he might hit her, but he froze in mid-stride. "What happened to your face?"

Kael rested his hand on the hilt of his sword. "Where have you been, Desmond? A lord who fails to protect his *possessions* is no lord at all."

"That is none of your business." Desmond glared at him.

"How did you leave Badara?" Kael asked. "The gates close after dark."

"My friend here," Desmond pointed to his companion, "is Prince Vian of Badara. We have the liberty to go where we please, when we please."

"Forgive me if I do not bow—a true prince would not flee in danger, but stand to defend his kingdom."

The rider's pale face flushed a deep red, almost matching his cropped hair.

"How dare you talk to the prince in such a manner, half-breed." Desmond unsheathed his sword.

"Desmond, don't waste your energy," the prince said. He readjusted his purple doublet and turned in the saddle toward Kael. "What news have you of my kingdom?"

"Were you in such a hurry to leave that you didn't hear the crowds hailing a new king?"

The prince raised his eyebrows. "Perhaps you've mistaken the boisterous celebrants for supplanters."

"Lord Wistan has betrayed your father. The Book of Thar'ryn burns in the great white city of the plains, but no one protests it."

"I don't know what you are talking about." The prince shifted in his saddle and glanced at the huddled villagers. "What are you staring at? Get back to whatever it is you peasants are supposed to be doing."

Kael arched a brow. "What are *you* doing here?"

"Is that how you address his royal highness?" Desmond interrupted.

Kael frowned. "Unless you—"

"Desmond, we are wasting our time." The prince jerked his horse around. "You've found your girl. Let's move out. We must make it to Talem before the assembly."

"If you are seeking the guardians, you won't find them there."

The prince cocked his head. "What would you know of them?"

"You're pathetic. When the High Guardian comes to see the king, he is denied, but when your little lives are threatened you come running to the guardians to make it all better."

"The king is missing." The prince's pale face twisted in anger. "And, yes, Badara is in upheaval. That much was obvious when the celebrants broke curfew and tried to attack

126

me. Then, to Desmond's dismay, we came upon Cuthbert's demolished inn and—"

"Enough, Vian." Desmond glared at him. "We don't need to explain ourselves to him."

Kael eyed the prince. He did seem a little disheveled: his robes were wrinkled and his horse's green plumes broken. "The guardians are meeting in Raemoja."

"The city of ruins? How in the fiery abyss are we to find them now? What good are the guardians when they are unreachable in the time of need?" The prince's green eyes narrowed. "Why would they go there instead of Talem?"

"When the High Guardian orders it, I don't ask why."

The prince pulled the reins to the right and turned his horse around. "Then we must travel to Raemoja instead."

"I am headed there." Why did he say that? Traveling with them was the last thing he wanted.

"No, no, no!" Desmond shoved his sword away. "No half-breed is going to be joining us."

"Stop calling him that," Ayianna said.

"Stay out of this!" He rounded on her. "And I will deal with you later."

"We have a common destination," Prince Vian said. "So logically, we should travel together."

Kael scanned the villagers. They had shied away, but continued mumbling among themselves, casting furtive glances at the prince. "It seems that way."

"What is your name?"

He turned his attention to the prince. "Kael, son of Lord Aiden of Zurial."

"And how does an elven lord from Zurial know the way to Raemoja?"

"I am not a lord." Kael rubbed his thumb over his knuckles. Should he tell him about the short cut? But why? He could be a free elf. Ayianna had her betrothed, he had the prince. Surely the three of them could figure out how to get to the ruins without him.

Vian pursed his lips. "When do you plan to leave?"

"Vian!"

"Only as far as Raemoja," Vian said. "Everyone knows it is safer in numbers."

"Right, but we have the numbers."

"He knows the way." Vian leaned forward in the saddle. "And from the looks of the inn, he's good with the sword. I won't take any chances."

Desmond's eyebrows shot up. "But you will take a chance with a complete stranger?"

"Enough." The prince held up his hand. "The way to Raemoja has been lost to us. It would take too long for us to search every mountain on this side of the Zriab Desert. If this elf can take us, so be it."

Kael crossed his arms. "The way is difficult. You'll have to trust me."

The prince nodded.

"Then we leave right away."

Desmond turned his glare on Ayianna. "You had better have a good explanation."

Ayianna's face flushed scarlet. "I was attacked in the inn . . . and . . . "

"And Kael just happened to be there." He clenched his jaw. "Get dressed. We'll talk about this later."

She fled into the house.

Kael mounted his horse. He should've said something to restore her honor. Since she was still in her nightgown and with another male, he could see where Desmond's thoughts went, but the draper wouldn't have believed him.

Several minutes later, Ayianna returned, dressed in her brother's old clothes and hat. Kael choked back a laugh at Desmond's livid face.

13

THREE DAYS LATER, the travelers reached the Thzadi River. Its lazy waters slurred past the mossy banks like a giant, black snake. The spindly limbs of oak and maple hung low, their autumn colors already fading.

Desmond dodged their overreaching branches and pulled his horse to a halt.

Ayianna slid off, careful not to touch him anymore than she had to. How much longer would she have to endure his silence? Whether on horseback or setting camp, he had only spoken when necessary. She didn't have to be an elf to sense his fury. Ayianna looked around. If she didn't have something to do, the guilt would suffocate her.

Kael pulled the saddle off his horse and deposited it at the base of large, gnarled oak tree. Desmond did the same, but Vian led his mount over to Kael and walked away.

"The horse isn't going to unsaddle himself," Kael said as he sat down at the edge of the clearing.

"Pardon me?" Vian blinked and raised his eyebrows.

"Your horse."

"I can't unsaddle my horse."

"You mean you won't or you don't know how?" Kael reclined against a tree. "Because we can remedy your ignorance promptly."

The prince's mouth dropped. Desmond unsheathed his sword and leveled it at Kael. "Tend to his horse."

Ayianna's eyes darted between Desmond and Kael. Surely, a mere merchant wouldn't stand a chance against Kael.

Kael's gaze didn't falter. "No."

Desmond lunged, but Kael sprung like a cobra. A dagger flashed and blocked Desmond's strike. Desmond slashed again. Kael spun, sword in one hand, dagger in the other.

"Stop this!" Ayianna shouted. She whirled to face Vian. "You're the prince, do something!"

Vian shook his head, his eyes wide, taking in the fight.

Metal clanged, snapping Ayianna's attention back to others. She veered out of the way as Desmond swept past.

He swung, but Kael stepped aside. Kael brought his sword down on Desmond's blade and pressed the dagger against his throat.

Ayianna held her breath as the two of them glared at each other.

Desmond's eyes glittered. His face burned a furious shade of purple.

Kael shoved him back. "The prince will unsaddle his own horse."

Desmond huffed and marched off. He stopped near a thick bush laden with red berries and turned around. "Ayianna, unsaddle his horse."

She stared at him. "What?"

"Consider it punishment for your lewd behavior."

"I have never—"

"When we get back, I will lead you personally to the stocks."

She gaped at him, opening and closing her mouth like a fish out of water.

"No," Kael said. "She hasn't done anything wrong."

Desmond raised an eyebrow and barked a mirthless laugh. "Your words are rubbish to me. She has shamed me—look at her blush as if she were still a maiden, but she's nothing but a whore!"

Hot tears stung Ayianna's eyes. "And there's nothing I could say that would change your mind."

He stared at her. Hurt replaced the fury in his eyes. He lifted his shoulders in a feeble attempt to shrug.

"If you can't trust me, then why did you choose me to be your wife?"

Desmond frowned. He turned around and stalked off into the forest.

Ayianna refused to look at the others. She moved over to the prince's mount and began to undo the girth, but Vian stopped her.

He cleared his throat. "I'll take care of this. It can't be too hard now, can it?" He flashed a small smile at her and untied a thick roll of blankets and several leather bags. He carried them over to a tree and dumped them at its base.

Ayianna stood there, uncertain what to do or where to go.

Vian came back and loosened the girth the rest of the way. He pulled the saddle off, but its weight yanked him down. The horse jumped aside as the saddle sprawled on the ground. He brushed his hands on his pants. "Well, that does it."

"Perhaps we should have a fire." Kael sheathed his sword and dagger.

"I'll find some wood." Ayianna took off into the darkening forest before anybody could say otherwise.

How could Desmond say that? A whore! Of all things he could have called her, he chose that. How dare he! She inhaled the earthy smells of dirt and trees and tried to shove the anger and humiliation surging over her. What kind of crazy standard did the plains people have for their women? But then, he had found her in her nightgown with another male. She cringed. He had every right to reproach her.

But if he had known her, he would have never accused her of such.

Ayianna plunged deeper into the wood, but kept the river to her left. Patches of the dry vegetation shone gold in the evening sun. The lengthening shadows splayed atop the dying grass and prickly bushes. Everywhere the plains bowed to winter's oncoming death, but not without the promise of spring's rebirth. Live and die. Nature was simple, unlike people.

She searched beneath the overarching trees for dead branches and stacked what she found in her arms. Liam padded next to her, darting in and out of the thick underbrush. She bent over to pick up a small log, and the little wood flute swung into her line of vision.

She set down her bundle and leaned against the tree. The tips of the grass tickled her nose. She brushed them aside and slid her fingers over the flute. Delicate carvings wove their way around its barrel. She brought it to her lips and blew. A sound, rich and tranquil, lifted from the instrument like the wind ruffling through leaves on a cool, autumn day.

A small creature dropped out of the trees and plopped at her feet.

Ayianna jumped. The bark of the tree bit into her back and jolted her injured shoulder. She grimaced, but held her tongue.

"Hello." The creature cocked his head. His voice was airy like the breeze through the treetops. He stood about three-feet with brown, rough skin like bark and had no clothes. Deep green leaves grew from his head and rustled with each little movement.

"Who . . . what are you?" asked Ayianna, staring at the strange creature.

"I am a dryad. My name is Ashby." The creature bowed, and a wooden flute similar to hers swung from his neck. "Now, if I may ask you a question, how came you upon such a flute? For I am sure you know not the significance of it."

"I'm afraid not. A woman gave it to me. Um . . . what's a dryad?"

"Can you not guess?" The dryad's lips cracked in a smile. "We are the protectors of trees."

"Are there many like you?"

He gestured with his arm to the surrounding woods. "We are as many as there are trees."

"Oh, I've never seen anything like you before," Ayianna glanced around at the shadowy forest. She should really get back to camp soon.

"Humans and dryads have been in conflict since ancient times. Humans expand their territories without thought, taking down young and old trees alike. Of course, not before we have a little fun with them first." The dryad chortled.

Ayianna didn't know what to say. "Oh?"

The dryad swayed with excitement. "Each dryad is connected to the tree they protect. You see that tree over there? Well, that is my tree. If someone cuts that tree down, they cut me down. I die."

"Oh . . . I'm sorry."

"Do not be, it is a part of life. I have been here for hundreds of years. By the time someone comes to take my tree, I will be ready to go."

"But think what history you've seen. You'd be better storytellers than our bards."

"Yes, history." The dryad grimaced. "We were once storytellers."

Ayianna waited as Ashby became quiet and still. His eyes dimmed, and his body grew transparent. She was afraid he'd disappear altogether without telling her about the flute. "Ashby?"

The dryad shook himself. "No matter, never good to mourn the passing of days, but to celebrate the ones you have. That is where history is made."

"So this flute I have, does it call the dryads when played?"

"Yes, and more." He rubbed his leafy head. "Do not let such a flute fall into the wrong hands. For if one of the races bears a dryad flute it is thus said the bearer is friend to all dryads. An ambassador one is, yes, and a keeper of secrets."

Ayianna rolled the flute in her fingers. *More secrets . . . and an ambassador for what?*

"Goodbye friend-Ayianna."

"Wait!" Ayianna looked up, but the dryad had already disappeared. Liam's wet nose nudged her neck, and she pushed it away.

"What are you doing out here?"

Ayianna leapt to her feet and tucked the flute under her tunic. "I was gathering firewood."

"Looks like it." The shadows couldn't conceal Desmond's scowl.

Ayianna scooped up her bundle of sticks and turned away. "Wait."

She glanced back at Desmond. His blue eyes sent shivers down her spine. She looked away and gritted her teeth.

"I owe you an apology," he said. "How can I not have faith in my own decisions? So, what did happen in Badara?"

"I was attacked by imps. I don't know why Kael was at the inn." She shifted the wood in her arms. "I had actually thought it was you coming to my rescue. I was there, alone, I didn't know what to do, and Kael was going to meet Saeed at the stables, so I went with him. I had hoped Saeed would be able to do something about my father's death, him being a guardian and all." She chanced a look at Desmond.

He leaned against a tree. "Our world is changing, isn't it?"

"I don't know so much about changing. The heart of what Nälu stands for has been attacked, the Sacred Pearl kidnapped, and the legacy of the guardians near destroyed. Innocent people have died. You call that simple change?"

"I didn't mean it was good change." He rubbed his face. "Sometimes tradition needs to be defied in order to survive."

Ayianna raised an eyebrow. Had she expected him not to have brains behind his intriguing charm?

"So, did you get to see the parade?" he asked.

She nodded and told him all about the jugglers, acrobats, and the giant letanili while they gathered dead branches.

She turned to Desmond. "What about you? Did you get to watch the parade?"

He shook his head and smiled. "I was busy making money."

"What exactly does a draper do?"

"Well, me personally, I specialize in the rare, expensive fabrics."

"Oh, like what?"

"Well," Desmond said as he took the bundle of sticks from her and tucked them under his arm. "There's the silk from the elves of Striisa Vaar and the mohair from the Klovan dwarves."

"Do you get to travel to these places?"

He nodded. "Although, nobody really goes into Striisa Vaar. I get my silks from a third party in N'dari. When we get back, I need to go to Zurial and see if I can't get my hands on the Kaleki's silver fabric. Don't know what it is, but I hear it is amazing—the water doesn't cling to it but slides off."

"Zurial." Ayianna looked up at the sky and saw the first couple of stars twinkling in the fading light. "I had hoped to return."

"And what would you do if you had returned to Zurial?" Desmond asked.

"I'd learn to read the stars."

"What about marriage?"

Ayianna glanced at Desmond. "Well . . . of course."

"But not me?" He scratched the back of his neck.

"Well . . . " Ayianna fumbled for a reply. "It's not that you're . . . it's just that you—I mean . . . "

"You do realize that an elf's lifespan is different than a human's. Take Kael, for instance, he could be a hundred years old, and where would that leave you? And then there's the racial tension your offspring would create. Are you even thinking about your children?"

She choked. She couldn't swallow past the lies of her father. "I . . . I hadn't given that much thought."

"I'm sorry, Ayianna, but there is no future for you in Zurial. You're among your own people now. You must accept your heritage." Desmond tucked strands of her dark hair behind her ear. "Your time among the elves wasn't wasted. You could say it has made you more than a simple peasant. How many peasants can read? None. We can't let that go to waste, can we?"

Ayianna stared into his blue eyes. Chills crawled down her spine and into her toes. His nearness chased away any coherent thought she might have had.

"We should probably get back to camp." He turned away.

She slumped against the tree. Could she really keep up this disguise?

Back in camp, a blazing fire warded off the cold evening. Ayianna reclined against a tree and ran her fingers through Liam's thick fur. She glanced at Kael. How old was he really? He stood at the edge of the clearing, staring at something across the river. She followed his gaze. The darkest of night devoured the other side, even the flickering light of the fire. What did he see? Did he sense something?

"Desmond, have you told Ayianna your great news?"

Vian's voice jerked her attention back to the camp. He unrolled a large bear rug and spread several thick blankets on top of it. She had never seen anyone carry so much on a trip, much less someone fleeing for his life.

"What great news?" Desmond shook out his blankets.

"Come on, now. I can't believe you hadn't told her yet," Vian said. "You know—your new position with the king?"

"Ah, that great news . . . " Desmond's face broke into a grin. "Well, I wouldn't want to brag, but since you've mentioned it—I will be made the Councilor of Merchant Affairs."

"What is that?" Ayianna asked.

"I will oversee all the merchant guilds and farmers who come to sell in Badara. Of course, this means we will move to Badara after the wedding. Vian has made arrangements for us to live within the castle."

"The castle?" repeated Ayianna. A smile tugged at the corner of her lips. It wasn't Zurial, but what little girl hadn't dreamed of living in a castle? She glanced at Desmond.

He was smiling as he crawled under his blanket. He looked up and winked.

Heat flooded her face, and she looked away.

Ayianna curled up next to Liam. Exhaustion weighed heavily on her, but the events of the last couple of days inundated her mind and kept her awake. So much death, so many secrets. And now her mother was missing and the king had been overthrown. She shuddered. What was going on? Was it all connected somehow?

Desmond's news floated on top of the swirling grief like oil on water, refusing to penetrate the dam she had built to keep the sorrow from swallowing her up. Once they reached

Raemoja, the guardians would have the answers, and then she would return, marry Desmond, move to Badara, and live like royalty. The spark of hope flickering in the midst of her grief felt foreign to her.

Ayianna stared up at the starry sky, and an old blanket of familiarity draped over her. She and her brother had spent countless nights under the same stars as he filled her head with amazing stories of fairies, dwarves, and unicorns. Obviously stories he had heard from Rashid, the old bard. But, oh, the tales that he would weave—dragons, sorcerers, and dark lords, the constant battle of good and evil.

Some nights after the tales were told, she swore she'd seen a harpy swooping in the skies or an imp peering through the trees, and her brother had to carry her home because she had been too afraid to walk.

Now she was living it.

14

KAEL LAY WIDE awake in the predawn hours, listening. What had woke him? Every nerve in his body tingled as he pushed his awareness through the darkness, searching for any sign of disturbance, but his brain was sluggish and fuzzy. Sitting up, he glanced around the campsite. The others were still fast asleep.

Maybe water would clear his mind. Kael started for the river, but found his direction disorientated as he peered into the dark trees. He turned around. He must have slept hard. He couldn't remember the last time he had his directions mixed up. How could he? Elves were notably good navigators. Blame it on the other half, he mused dryly.

He splashed his face with the icy river water. He glanced back at the trees as wisps of a gray mist oozed between the bent and wrinkled trunks. A premonition tickled his muddled mind, but he shrugged it off. He rose from the bank and awoke the others.

"Oh!" Prince Vian groaned. "It's still dark!"

"Up," Kael said, "we're crossing the river before dawn."

"What's the hurry?" Desmond stretched his arms above his head in a yawn.

Ayianna sat up without complaint and began folding her wool blanket. Liam strolled around the campsite and sniffed the air.

"We move through the Inganno Forest as quickly as possible," Kael said and tied his rolled up blanket to his pack.

"What?" Desmond leapt to his feet. "You never said anything about the forest."

"It would take a month to go around."

"I've heard stories about the forest." Ayianna hugged a wool blanket to her chest. "Stories filled with horror and evil creatures."

"Nobody who goes in comes out alive," Vian's wide eyes darted around. Then he bent down and tried to roll up his furs and blankets.

"Sure, they don't." Kael swung his pack over his shoulder. "And where do you think the stories come from?"

Vian glanced up. "Aren't you scared of the forest?"

"Not nearly enough." Desmond shook his head and stuffed his blanket into his pack. "Did you sleep well, Ayianna?"

She nodded and shrugged her pack over her shoulders.

Kael's gaze rested on the river as it gurgled past. What had transpired between her and Desmond? One moment, he was ready to throw her away, and the next they are talking like nothing happened. He shook his head. She was nothing like her brother.

"Kael!" Ayianna's voice pierced his muddled thoughts. "The horses . . . they're gone!"

"I let them go last night."

"You did what?" Vian whirled to face him. "How dare you release the royal horses?"

"The trail isn't wide enough for horses."

Vian's nostrils flared as he crossed his arms. "But how are we to return home?"

"I guess that would be your problem, wouldn't it?"

Vian's jaw dropped as he glared back. "But—what about thieves? And—and—"

"No one will risk expulsion upon the account of the king's branded horses wandering into their village when there would probably be a reward if they're returned."

Vian stared at him and then turned away in a huff. He dragged his blankets into a pile and threw his robes on top while the others continued to pack.

Unease turned Kael's stomach, but he couldn't figure out why. He looked up. The sky across the river lightened in dawn's approach, and clarity stung his head like a hammered thumb. They were on the wrong side of the river. The night before, the Thzadi River had separated them from the forest; but now, nothing stood in their way. How? What kind of dark enchantment were they facing?

He slowly exhaled the unease. The last thing he wanted was to inflict fear on his blundering travel companions. It would only make his job worse. "We've already crossed the river."

"I would have remembered that," Desmond said as he fumbled with his sword belt.

"Somehow, we've been moved to the other side." Kael strapped his quiver of arrows across his back and picked up his bow.

Ayianna's eyes widened. "Perhaps it is the curse of the forest."

"The curse of the forest?" Vian stared at the trees, and then the river. "But what about breakfast?"

"No time. Carry what you can, leave the rest behind." Kael kicked dirt over the smoldering embers in the small fire pit.

"Preposterous! I can't leave my robes and blankets!" The prince lugged an armful of blankets and clothes onto his shoulders, a sleeve of a robe trailing behind him. "Any chance of someone carrying this for me?"

Kael raised his eyebrows. "What do you think?"

"Couldn't hurt to ask." Vian forced a fragile smile.

Kael turned away and buckled the sword belt around his waist. He then pulled out a small orb from his knapsack and whispered, "*Yetakoith taheza.*" A light sprang to life within the orb like the morning sun pushing through a darkened horizon.

Desmond jumped back. "What sorcery of the Abyss do you bring down upon us?"

Kael shook his head and stepped away, scanning the ground for remnants of the Naajiso trail. What exactly was he looking for?

"Well?"

"If a small charm of the guardians bothers you, then perhaps you should go back."

Desmond's lip curled. "Caution isn't wasted when one can't distinguish friend from foe."

"Perhaps you should figure that out first. We don't have time for mistrust."

"Don't worry, Desmond. I appreciate your caution, even if it is a little misguided," Vian said with a smile. He staggered under the awkward bundle of blankets and robes that he had managed to cram into large lumpy mess.

Kael rolled his eyes and turned away. A few yards away, a sliver of polished black stone glinted beneath a layer of dead leaves. Above it, large twisted trees stood like sentries guarding the entrance to the Forest of Inganno. Gray mist hovered over the ground and clung to their crumpled bark.

It breathed of dark magic and death.

Kael looked over his shoulder.

Vian stood behind him and stared up at the trees. He sucked in his breath. "Let's hope we don't return horrified and stricken with disease."

"Or never return at all," Desmond said. He clasped the prince on the shoulder and glared at Kael. "People avoid this forest for a reason. I should know—this is my uncle's land."

"It belongs to no man." Kael eyed the formidable trees. An ancient force lingered at the edges of the forest like the foul stench of a beast. The unseen vapors tugged at him, threatening, demanding. But what could a forest demand of him? He tightened his hand on the hilt of his sword, and words from the sacred text flitted through his mind.

But to whom I belong, he abides in me. For he is the true one, and truth is stronger than he who abides in the world of lies.

Too bad he and Osaryn weren't on speaking terms. If he even belonged to the elven god anymore. An overwhelming sense of hopelessness drowned his grief. No, he could not think like that. Not when he stood on the threshold of his demise.

Kael took a deep breath. To enter the forest meant death, yet Kael was about to lead a spoiled prince, an arrogant merchant, and a girl through its dangers. And what was he?

"*A few days, nothing more . . .* " Saeed had said. "*Stay on the trail and no harm will come to you.*"

Kael held up the orb and entered the forest.

"This path is cumbersome!" Desmond's voice drifted through the thick silence for the hundredth time.

Kael clenched his jaw and focused on the narrow trail beneath his feet. The orb's orange glow lit the ground and the gnarled trees nearest to him, but the rest of the forest disappeared into a dark abyss. The curse even swallowed light.

Apprehension curled the edges of his thoughts and crawled down his spine. Perhaps Saeed had miscalculated the trail through the forest. Or they were walking slower. They had hiked for most of the day without a hint of progress. Maybe they had taken a wrong turn somewhere or had gotten on the wrong trail. Had the fairies laid more than one pathway with black stones?

Kael swept a curtain of cobwebs aside. Their sticky strands clung to his face and body. He swiped them from his face and rubbed his hands on his pants. What was Saeed thinking, making him drag Ayianna, Desmond, and Vian through this forest. Of course, it had only been the girl at the time. They were slowing him down. He clenched his fists and took a deep breath. The moldy air filled his nose, tickling his lungs. He suppressed a cough.

What if it was the forest? Perhaps the curse had consumed more land, expanding the ancient forest's boundaries, making it more difficult to navigate. And now they were doomed to wander forever lost. He shuddered.

The old trees crowded around him, their mangled branches stretching above him, ready to snatch him up for trespassing. He pushed the thought way and reminded himself—the forest couldn't harm them as long as they stayed on the trail.

He doubled checked the ground. Moss covered everything—no polished stones anywhere. His heart leapt into his throat. But as quickly as the fear strangled him, it released him. Beneath his boots, where they had scuffed the moldy carpet away, the black stones glittered from the orb's glow. He kicked the debris from the path and revealed more of the Naajiso trail.

He bent down and rubbed a finger over the stones' smooth surface. Specks of light glimmered deep within like stars on a moonless night. What kind of creation was this? This was no natural stone.

"What is it?"

Ayianna's voice broke Kael from his reverie. He stood. "Nothing."

"The stones are pretty, aren't they?" She gazed down at the cleared pathway.

He shrugged. "Come on, we must keep moving."

Ahead, thorny vines hung between the trees, blocking their way. Kael pulled out his hunting knife and hacked the vines apart. Why hadn't he thought to grab a hatchet?

"Who made the trail?" Ayianna asked as the others joined them. "Why is it here?"

"The Naajiso laid the trail down a long time ago. Before the Great Fairy Rebellion and before the Tóas had consumed the forest." Kael swept the vines aside. A couple of the long spindly thorns bit into his hands and arms. He tightened his jaw.

Vian stepped into the glow of the orb. "Well, I heard some of the bards say the Naajiso created it as a pathway to Raemoja, moved hundreds if not thousands of soldiers and weapons into strategic locations to overthrow the malevolent Lord Stygian."

"Bard's tales." Desmond sniffed and draped an arm over Ayianna's shoulder. "Shouldn't we be moving forward?"

"Agreed," Vian said. "I do think the strategy was brilliant. No one would logically plan an attack like that, but it worked. Simply brilliant, really."

Desmond shook his head. "It's a bard's tale."

"The guardians believe it and teach it." Vian wiped his forehead with the back of his sleeve. "Of course, the bards tend to be a little more poetic and romantic for my taste, but still there might be some truth behind those tales."

"If I were you," Desmond cocked his head, "I wouldn't rely on poetry or fables to lead my kingdom. I would stick to what's been proven—the mighty shall rule the weak, and those with more money are mightier."

"I don't think—"

"Less talk, more walk!" Kael pressed deeper into the forest, and the others filed in behind him.

Time ceased, and silence suffocated Kael's ears. His aggravation heightened. They should have made better progress, an incline in the path, colder air, less trees. Where were the mountains?

He peered around him, but the scenery hadn't changed at bit. Snake-like vines coiled and twisted across the trail. Wrinkly trees towered over a decaying carpet of moss, dead leaves, and branches. Thick cobwebs hung on the trees and draped to the ground. Beyond the orb of the light, he saw nothing but a black abyss.

He shuddered. *Should I risk seeking life forms?* Cautiously, he opened his senses and reached out into the darkness. He slammed into a whirling vortex. A hollow vacuum pulled at him, sucking his breath away. Kael quickly retreated and fortified his mind. He gasped. What was that?

"Are you all right?" Ayianna asked, coming up from behind him.

"Yes," he said a little too harshly.

A frown creased her forehead. She opened her mouth to say something, but he moved away.

He clenched his jaw. "We're going too slow."

He tried to rub the forest's musty smell from his nose, but he couldn't rub the guilt away. He reached into his pocket and rolled Teron's ring between his fingers. He'd have to tell Ayianna eventually, but not yet. The pain was still too real, too close. Tears stung his eyes, but he gritted his teeth and attacked the vines in front of him. Shoving through them, Kael relished the pain their thorns inflicted on his skin.

15

HOURS SLID BY, but Ayianna couldn't tell how long they'd been hiking. Her legs and her back burned. She tried to ignore the hunger gnawing on her insides and focused instead on the impossible trail before her. The old trees continued to snag her attention. Their gnarled, twisted trunks towered above her; their crooked limbs entwined with the next and closed in on her.

She took deep breaths and tried to keep the familiar panic away. Liam nudged her hand. She ran her fingers through the silver fur. Her mind settled, and the panic subsided for the moment.

The lethargic forest seemed to pacify Desmond and Vian. They had finally stopped asking Kael when they would rest. Still, Ayianna heard occasional snippets of murmurs and complaints.

An unnatural silence clutched the ancient forest and compressed the sounds of their progress. Kael hacked through the thorny vines crisscrossing the path and moved farther ahead. The broken vines swung in his wake. She raised her hands to deflect them, but they slipped through. Their thorns tore at her clothes and hands, again.

Tired and miserable, she blinked away the tears and pressed forward. She strained to see the path ahead of Kael—nothing but inky blackness. His silhouette glided over the black stones with eerie grace as he worked his way through another clump of vines.

Silvery cobwebs swayed loosely among the trees like tattered curtains of the dead. Where were the spiders? How big would they be to create such a large web? Their thin fibers stuck to her face as she pushed through. After a while, she gave up trying to clean the sticky web from her hair and clothing.

Ayianna's skin crawled. Something flickered to her right amid the thick trees. She peered into the forest. The darkness swallowed up the orb's glow like a black velvet cloak, leaving the shadows to her imagination. The trees crowded closer and closer together. Forward, backward, right or left. There was no way out.

Panic clasped its clammy hand around her neck and suffocated her.

She closed her eyes and took a breath. Liam brushed against her leg, and Ayianna bent over, running her fingers through the wolf's fur. She exhaled slowly. *We will find our way out.*

"All right there, Ayianna?" asked Vian as he came up behind her.

She glanced up. Kael had stopped, and everyone was staring at her.

"We need to rest," Desmond said. "Can't you see she is exhausted?"

Kael's jaw tightened as he eyed her. His gray eyes looked almost purple in the orange light. He didn't need another reason to detest her.

She straightened. "No, I'm fine, really. Each step is a step closer, right?" She tried to smile, but the muscles in her face trembled. Instead, she clamped her mouth shut.

"It shouldn't be much longer," Kael said. He turned away and continued on.

"You've got a strong one there, Desmond," Vian said.

Desmond smiled and clamped his hand on her shoulder, giving it a squeeze.

This time, Ayianna managed a smile as warmth blossomed in her chest and filled her with energy. She could have walked another hundred miles.

She hiked on with a little extra bounce in her step. She could do this. She'd show Kael and make Desmond proud. She'd—

Her foot caught on a protruding root. She stumbled forward, landing on all fours like a dog. Her enthusiasm shriveled up like a prune. She pushed herself up from the trail and brushed the dirt off her scraped hands. Glancing up, she caught sight of a light in the distance.

"Look!" Ayianna cried out. "A light!"

Desmond peered into the trees. "I don't see anything. Maybe your eyes are playing tricks on you."

"But it was right there." She pointed where she had seen the faint flicker of a light, but it was gone now. She pushed her way through the vines and cobwebs to where Kael waited with the orb. Their trail had emptied into a clearing.

"We can camp here," Vian said as he stepped out in the opening.

Kael shook his head and took off for the other side of the clearing. "It's not safe."

"This is ridiculous." Desmond dumped his bags on the ground. "We can't keep going like this."

Ayianna glanced around at the puckered tree trucks twisting above them. She fingered the wood flute that hung from her neck. Did these trees have dryads as well? Were they watching them right now?

"This way." Kael stepped back on the trail.

"No," Desmond said, his voice resolute. "We will camp here, tonight."

"I agree." Vian limped up next to Desmond, rubbing his back. "We need the rest."

Kael glared at them. "Saeed said to stick to the Naajiso trail."

"But," Desmond raised his finger, "he didn't say anything about not taking a break, did he?"

Kael hesitated, and then shook his head.

"He wouldn't expect us to traipse through this forest for a few days without resting, would he?" Desmond crossed his arms.

"If you are so adamant—"

"We are," Vian and Desmond said in unison.

"—we will need firewood and plenty of it."

Soon a fire blazed in the open space, its light bobbing up and down on the deformed trees. The darkness seemed to press in closer in its attempt to extinguish the flame.

Ayianna closed her heavy eyes and leaned against Liam, her muscles burning. *Only for a moment . . .*

The forest sang to her. Its ancient song was sad and weary. Sleep. Beneath it, a dull warning throbbed, demanding her to wake and fight. But the voices rose above it, weaving together life's colorful tapestry in song. The dark colors twined with light. Had she heard this song before? The faint strains of the melody pulled at her. The tapestry grew darker. Grief outweighed the joy. Life held no joy, it marched toward darkness to what end? Death. Bitterness stung her soul. What was the point?

She surrendered, and her body succumbed to the forest's silent request—sleep.

In the shadows of her mind, something hunted her. Fear twisted her insides and muddled her thoughts. The forest's song had ceased; its thick silence crushed her. She gasped. Padded steps drew nearer and nearer. She tried to run, to move, but her limbs hung heavy and lifeless at her side. Her lungs constricted; she couldn't breathe. A twig snapped.

Ayianna started. Her pulse pounded in her head, ripping her from the grip of her dream. She glanced around.

The men were lounging around the fire, nibbling on what little food they had left.

Her stomach rumbled. She dug through her knapsack and found a heel of stale bread and a chunk of moldy cheese. She scraped away the mold and broke off a piece. She offered it to Liam, but the wolf refused.

Ayianna's exhaustion was greater than her hunger. Soon her eyelids drooped, and she gave in to the forest's demands.

Again, the unseen beast hunted her, gaining on her with every stride. Its hot, hissing breaths stung the back of her neck. She stumbled and fell, paralyzed. The curse would consume her as well. She would die in the forest like all the others. She glanced up.

Two glowing eyes raced toward her. The creature snarled and hissed.

She screamed.

"Ayianna!" a hoarse voice said as a hand shook her shoulder.

She shot up from the hard ground, gasping for air, drenched in sweat.

"Are you all right?" Desmond stood over her, concern etched into his face.

She glanced around. Everyone was staring at her. "Y-yes, it was only a nightmare."

"Are you certain?" Kael fingered the feathers of an arrow.

"Don't be stupid, adding to the girl's fear like that," Desmond said, but, underneath the words, his voice wavered.

"You don't know what haunts this forest." Kael fitted the arrow against the bowstring. "Or how they hunt."

"What do you mean?" Desmond reached for the hilt of his sword.

"What did you see, Ayianna?" Kael asked.

"I-I don't know." She looked between Kael and Desmond. Her breathing and heart rate slowly returned to normal. "It was only a dream, right?"

"What did you see?"

"Something was chasing me. It had glowing eyes."

"A tu'yan mutat."

"A what?" Vian leapt to his feet. He looked about the clearing as if something was going to jump out and get him right then and there.

"It's a creature of death, bred by Lord Stygian. A few escaped the purge after the fall of Raemoja and made Inganno their home."

"Bard's tales!" Desmond slammed his fist into his palm. "Are you attempting to make us mad with fear?"

Kael didn't respond. His attention diverted to the trees.

Ayianna followed his gaze, afraid what she might see. The firelight flickered, slowly dying. The shadows danced, but the deeper darkness chanted of the forest's deadly secrets.

"They are lazy creatures, preferring to prey on the weak and immobilize them in their sleep." Kael ventured to the edge of the small glow of their campfire and peered into the forest, his bow at the ready. "Stay awake and keep the fire going,"

"Where are you going?" Vian fumbled with his sword.

But Kael didn't reply as he paced the perimeter of the fire's glow. Sometimes he disappeared into the darkness and then reappeared moments later.

"What's he doing talking about nonsense like that?" Desmond threw a branch onto the fire and peered into the trees. The flames sparked and sizzled.

Weak? What did Kael know of her? Ayianna gritted her teeth.

Liam left her side and circled the clearing. Her ears twitched back and forth, her nose to the ground and then in the air. A low growl rumbled from the wolf's throat.

"Liam, come here, girl." Ayianna forced the words out.

The wolf loped to her side, but only for a second, and then she was off again pacing the ground.

The old forest's floor crackled underfoot. Ayianna jumped.

"Easy there—it's just me," Desmond said, drawing his sword. "Better stoke the fire. We don't want it going out anytime soon."

Ayianna dragged a couple of stray branches toward the fire and dumped them on. The flames sputtered.

Liam growled.

Ayianna spun around, her gaze darting from one shadow to another.

Two gleaming eyes emerged from the darkness. The rest of the creature's body remained hidden, but it blew out its breath in a low hiss.

A scream lodged in her throat. She had to warn the others. She tried to speak, but her tongue refused to move.

The creature stalked closer, its hissing breath growing louder.

She should do something. *Run, hide, scream!* Instead, her limbs trembled and her knees buckled.

The creature leapt from the shadows. Its mottled, catlike body stretched out, sailing through the air. The creature's claws reached for her. Its mouth could have swallowed Liam whole.

"Move!" Desmond catapulted himself in front of her, colliding with the beast. His sword pierced the cat's belly.

The cat landed and swatted the sword away. Snarling, it lunged for Desmond, but an arrow pierced the animal's humped neck. It stumbled.

"Get that fire going!" Kael bellowed as he charged into camp, sword raised. The blade swept down and severed the creature's head from its monstrous body.

Ayianna scrambled out of the way as the head flopped toward her.

Course fur lined its face and hid its glowing eyes. The head came to a stop. Its stubby snout fell open and revealed jagged fangs. A rancid smell rushed out.

She spun away and retched. Before she had finished, Desmond dragged her back toward the fire.

Another beast lunged from the shadows.

Kael whirled around and nocked an arrow. The bowstring twanged.

The cat somersaulted through the air and landed on its side at the edge of the clearing. Desmond slashed the beast's throat, ensuring its death.

Ayianna nearly vomited again. She turned away from the dead beasts and closed her eyes. She took long, deep breaths until her body stopped shaking. Weak. The word sank into her heart like a branding iron. Finally, her pulse slowed and her senses returned.

Sparks flew up from the fire and danced around the clearing. Shadows shifted. Had she seen something? She glanced around. She had to do something. She joined Vian in gathering the remaining wood together, but kept her eyes on the darkness beyond the old, knotted trees.

Kael arranged mounds of broken limbs and vines into a ring around them. The dry wood quickly caught on fire surrounding the campsite with flames.

Ayianna stared out into the darkness as several pairs of glowing eyes appeared.

"Nobody sleeps tonight!" Kael yelled as he shot an arrow into the trees.

16

THE EMBERS OF the dying fire fizzled. Acrid smoke hung in the air, burning Ayianna's eyes and lungs. She gathered up her belongings and peered around her. Light dribbled in from above and painted the blemished trees in blotchy gray tones. The forest didn't look as scary as it did last night, but the massive beasts sprawled at the edge of the clearing reminded her of its dangers. She kept her eyes averted, but Liam had pranced over to inspect them.

"This new path is practically a road compared to what we have been following," Desmond said after he had returned from exploring the break in the trees.

"We need to keep to the trail," Kael shoved his sword into its sheath. He picked up his quiver and counted the remaining arrows.

"What if those creatures come back?" Vian rubbed the red-blond bristles already covering his chin.

"They shouldn't harm us if we stay on the trail. Besides, they hunt only at night," Kael said as he slung the quiver over his shoulder. "By then we should be through this forest and into the hills of Ruzat."

"That's what you thought yesterday. But we've been winding through this forest with no destination in sight, our clothes are ripped to shreds, and now we have deadly creatures hunting us. And you want us to continue on that thread of a trail?" Desmond stood with his hands on his hips. His hair bobbed around his head in a tangled mess. The dirty blond stubble covering the lower half of his face enhanced his allure.

Ayianna's father, being an Esusamor elf, could never grow a beard. What did it feel like? An urge to touch his bristly face swept over her. Ayianna averted her eyes as heat flooded her cheeks.

Kael grabbed his pack. "It's the only way to Raemoja."

"How do you know?"

"Nevin Saeed." Kael pulled out the orb and spoke the incantation. A dim glow flickered to life, but it remained weak.

"How do we know we can trust him?" Desmond asked.

Kael raised an eyebrow. "Because he is a guardian."

Desmond hesitated. "Nobody knows where this road leads because nobody has ever taken it. Everyone is too afraid to deviate from tradition. I say we take this road and then map it out so that all of Nälu will know that it leads right to that bloody city. No more thorns slapping against our face, tearing at our clothes. Plus the way is open—we would see the filthy beasts before they had a chance to eat one of us."

"Calm down," Vian said. "Obviously someone made this road, and it leads somewhere. I opt for the wider path."

Kael hung the quiver over his shoulder. "I beg your pardon, Prince Vian, but what good is a guide if you aren't willing to follow him?"

"Guides tend to know the place they are attempting to navigate." Vian pulled a green cap over his disheveled red curls.

Ayianna shook her head. "This isn't getting us anywhere. Saeed is the High Guardian, the leader of the Guardian Circle. Don't you think he knows what he is talking about?"

"But what about the forest?" Vian glanced around at the twisting trees. "Maybe it did something to the trail—changed it or something—and we've been running in circles instead of moving forward. Didn't you say that the forest is alive and deadly? Why wouldn't it take over the trail, especially one laid down so long ago?"

Kael concentrated on securing the blanket to his pack. A deep frown cut into his forehead and scrunched his face, causing the scar across his temple to bulge even more. The same expression since she had known him, only harsher. Did he ever smile?

He hoisted his pack and said, "We must remain on the Naajiso trail."

"We don't have to follow you." Desmond glowered at the half-elf. His hand rested on the hilt of his sword.

"True." Kael shrugged. "But Saeed asked me to escort Ayianna to Raemoja. Feel free to go your own way, but the girl will be coming with me."

Girl? Ayianna crossed her arms. "Wha—"

"I don't think so." Desmond pushed the words out through gritted teeth.

"Then we have no choice." Vian tightened his lumpy bundle on his back. Desmond spun around, but, before he could say anything, the prince continued. "But mark my words, if there is the slightest inclination we are running in circles, your term as guide will end."

Ayianna raised her brows. Even if she didn't like Kael, Saeed's trust in him was enough for her to listen to him. She had heard the guardian say follow the Naajiso trail. But if the forest was cursed . . .

"It's settled then. Let's not waste any more time." Kael turned away and hiked off into the forest.

Ayianna started after him but then noticed a sleeveless riding cape, a robe, and a fur-lined blanket lying on the ground. "Vian?

"Yes?" A scowl distorted his expression, but his green eyes reflected weariness.

"You've forgotten some things." She pointed to the mangled heap of clothes.

"Well, it's, uh, dirty." He adjusted his sword belt. "Not the time or place to worry about laundry, right?"

Ayianna shook her head and stepped onto the constricted trail. If she hadn't been so tired, she might have smiled.

They traveled in silence for a long while. The forest's eerie stillness settled in around them again, consuming the sporadic swishing and chopping of the woody vines from their path. Ayianna eyed the shadows for tu'yan mutats or other creatures that might be hunting them but saw nothing. After a while, the fear of the cursed forest drifted from her exhausted mind as she focused on the decreasing glow of the sphere.

"How did Lord Stygian not know about the fairies living in this forest?" She pushed the woody vines aside to join Kael.

Beads of sweat dribbled down his face, and he wiped them with the back of his sleeve. "He didn't know a lot of things."

"But this forest is so close to Raemoja. Surely, he would have known—seen something or investigated it."

He shrugged and continued moving down the trail.

Desmond came up behind them. "Isn't it about time we take a break?"

"The more we stop, the longer we'll be in this forest."

"Just a little time to breathe." Vian leaned against one of the wrinkly tree trunks. "We are only human—we don't have your kind of endurance."

"Vian!" Desmond turned on him. "How dare you lessen our noble race? Your father would be ashamed."

Vian raised his eyebrows. "I was merely stating a fact. Besides, how would you know what my father is ashamed of?"

Kael sheathed his hunting knife and crossed his arms. "You may have your break, but it will be short. Make good use of it."

"Thank you." Vian flashed a faint smile, but Desmond huffed and shook his head, mumbling something about the prince's kingdom.

Ayianna brushed debris from the path and sat down. The black stones glimmered. Their orange flecks seemed to pulsate. She blinked and they stilled. Perhaps she was seeing things. She focused on something else.

Liam crept up to her and settled her head into Ayianna's lap. She ruffled the wolf's silver fur. Dust leapt into the air, tickling her nose, and Ayianna sneezed. Did the forest muffle the sound, or was her ability to hear dulling?

She needed more noise—birds, squirrels, something in the awful silence—or she'd go mad.

"At least I have you." She cleaned the cobwebs from the wolf's back and then gathered her into her arms. The weight of the wolf squeezed the little wood flute against her chest.

Ayianna pulled the flute out and rolled it between her fingers. Were the trees cursed as well? Being a flute bearer made her a friend to all dryads. Perhaps they would be able to help them find their way out. She hesitated. What if she was wrong? A little sound couldn't hurt, could it? She brought the flute to her lips and blew.

Kael unsheathed the knife. He glanced at Ayianna, his face marred by his constant frown. "Break over, let's go."

Ayianna and the others stood. Disappointment mingled with relief. What had she expected? The curse probably killed the dryads . . . but could trees live without them? She continued after Kael, but he halted.

Ayianna peered around him.

A pair of gleaming eyes blinked in the darkness. Dry leaves crunched as the eyes drew near. A short creature stepped out from the trees and into the soft light of the orb.

She gasped—a dryad.

Diseased bark peeled from his shrunken body. Brown, tousled leaves stuck out from his head, wiggling in the shifting light. He seemed harmless enough. Ayianna stepped closer. Ghastly white maggots squirmed amidst the dead leaves on the dryad's head.

She recoiled. He was nothing like Ashby. What had she done?

"Who passes through unannounced and uninvited?" A guttural voice escaped the wooden lips. His glittering eyes settled on Ayianna.

Kael stepped forward and pulled her behind him. "I am Kael, son of Aiden. We mean you no harm."

"A woman companion . . . " The dryad sneered. He ventured forward, reaching for Ayianna.

Kael raised his sword and knocked the dryad's wooden arms away.

The dryad withdrew his hands and rubbed the peeling bark where the blade had nicked him. "Mighty testy are we, son of Aiden. I was just admiring the flute, quite unique indeed for a . . . " He sniffed the air. "I might suspect a witch."

"But . . . " Ayianna hesitated. Had the Durqa woman been a witch? "I had thought those who bear the flute were considered friends and ambassadors of the dryads."

"Dryads have no friend among the high races. Give me the flute, witch."

"Mind your own business." Kael leveled his sword at the creature's throat.

"Well, this is my business since you are passing through my forest. What is your destination?"

"Raemoja."

"Raemoja!" The dryad cackled.

"The Guardian Circle awaits us. You'd do well not to hinder us."

The creature gasped. His breath whistled like wind blowing through a cracked door. "Well, don't let me hold you back," he said as he receded into the shadows.

Kael strode forward, but the dryad's rasping voice halted his steps. "Are you sure you want to go this way?"

"Yes."

"Does the orb not glow brightly?" The dryad's wooden lips splintered into a sneer.

Ayianna glanced at the orb in Kael's hands. The light did seem weaker. She could barely make out the black stones of the path beneath the dry leaves and lichen. What if they had strayed from the right path?

"This place is cursed." Kael spat and shifted his weight.

"Or perhaps you and your friends have lost your way."

"Narrow is the trail that leads to Ruzat, the mountain of old. From hence the ancient tales of Trygg are told. The . . . "

Kael paused from his recitation, and the light flickered.

"Poems and riddles are tools of bards and fools, not directions to a city." The dryad clicked his wooden tongue. "What a pity."

"No." Kael clenched his jaw. "We must follow this trail."

"Be my guest," the dryad said and disappeared into the trees.

Kael trudged forward, hoisting his blade a little higher.

Ayianna and the others hurried after him. "What was that all about?"

"A dryad." Kael hacked at the vines swaying in front of him.

"I know that much. I have met one before."

"Not many people have met dryads." Kael faced Ayianna, and she halted. His gray eyes flickered on her for a second, measuring, questioning, but then he turned away and pressed on through the narrow trail. "Why was he so interested in that flute?"

She tried to duck as a vine swung toward her face, but she was too slow. Its thorns tore into her forehead. She gritted her teeth. "Because it was a dryad's flute."

"What are you doing with it?"

"What is a dryad?" Desmond asked as he chopped the swinging vine down.

"It is the spirit of a tree. They were nature's storytellers when people used to listen to them, but now they usually remain hidden." Kael glanced back at Ayianna. "A few of the older bards of Zurial claim their tales and songs came from them."

"And how do you know so much about these things?" asked Desmond.

"Books and—"

"You can read!" Desmond choked out.

"Of course I can read! What kind of question is that?" Kael rounded on Desmond, and Ayianna stepped out of his way. "Can't you read?

"Ah—of course I can," Desmond stammered, his face reddening. "It's just that, considering your position in society, it was only natural for me to assume you hadn't had a proper education. I mean, you were only a guard at Dagmar. No one teaches soldiers to read."

Kael glared at him. "Denying people the opportunity to learn based on one's birth is primitive. No wonder you humans are so far behind the rest of the world."

"We humans happen to believe that it is not necessary to learn outside of one's position in life. Just ask any of the peasants. They'll tell you they have no use for mindless lessons on topics that don't pertain to them."

Immediately, Ayianna was grateful for having been born in Zurial. She remembered the villagers' distaste for books. If she had been born among them, would she feel the same?

Prince Vian cleared his throat. "As much as I would like to join in on this little debate, I would rather you lead us out of this dreadful forest."

Desmond and Kael eyed each other for a moment, and then Kael turned away.

Desmond grasped Kael's arm. "What if the dryad was telling the truth?"

"The dryads within this forest cannot be trusted." Kael jerked his arm free.

"Why not?" Desmond asked.

"Because the curse touches everything in the Forest of Inganno." Kael turned and pushed through the vines and cobwebs, following the narrow, disappearing trail.

After a couple of hours of steady hiking, the trail emptied into another large clearing. Kael slumped to the ground and cradled the darkened orb, thankful for the concealing shadows. No one would see the doubt and frustration sure to be etched in his face.

"*Yetakoith taheza,*" Kael whispered.

The orb flickered, but did not relight.

How could he keep going like this? Evening would find the travelers yet again in the dismal forest. They should have made it to Raemoja by now, instead, they would have to spend another sleepless night in the cursed forest.

"We are going in circles!" Desmond flopped wearily on the ground.

Ayianna collapsed next to him. "If we were, we would have found two dead beasts and Vian's discarded robes."

"Unless the forest consumed them. Maybe we should . . . " Vian started, but he fell to the ground next to Desmond. "I think my feet have given up."

"Why would you believe the forest consumes things?" Kael couldn't let his doubts get to him, even if the prince echoed them.

"Look!" Ayianna sat up. "I see a faint light."

Kael followed her gaze. A small sphere glimmered blue, increasing the darkness even more. Its glow chilled him. Hadn't the bard's tale spoke about such lanterns? Some kind of trickery of the forest? The light flickered green, and he shivered. Was he seeing things? He blinked. The blue light had returned. He blinked again and again, but the orb remained blue. Perhaps he had imagined it.

"Where?" Vian asked.

"Over there." She pointed in the direction of where the light had been.

"I don't see anything."

"Are you sure you aren't seeing things again?" Desmond moaned from the ground.

"No, I see it, too!" Vian stood.

"What?" Desmond climbed to his feet. "Come on, let's take a look."

"Wait." Kael grabbed Desmond's shoulder. "It could be a trap."

"A trap?" Desmond sneered and shook Kael's hand off. "This forest lacks the intelligence required to set a trap."

Kael dropped his arms as doubt riddled his resolve. What if Desmond and Vian were right? What if the forest had changed, rendering the narrow trail useless to their journey? He rubbed his head. He had to think, but his thoughts were muddled. The silence tugged at him. The pull grew stronger the longer they remained within the cursed trees. The barriers he had placed around his mind were weakening.

Kael clenched his jaw. The evening would be upon them, and the tu'yan mutats would be back. They would have to make camp soon—and a really big fire.

Desmond must have taken Kael's silence as an assent, because he and the prince charged down the wide path with a vigor Kael hadn't seen in them since they had entered the forest. He had no energy to battle their protests.

He glanced at Ayianna.

Her eyes were closed as she leaned against her pet wolf. She hadn't complained once since they had entered the forest. Remarkable, although her betrothed more than made up for her quiet demeanor. Why had Teron never mentioned Desmond?

"Come on." Kael held out his hand to her. "Desmond and Vian have taken it upon themselves to explore the unusual light."

She frowned, but took his hand and stood. "Do you think this is a good idea?"

"No." He started after them. "But we need to stick together."

Luminous orbs dotted the path and disrupted the shadows with their soft light. The orbs bathed the formidable forest in an ethereal glow. As Kael passed, the lights vanished, and the hovering darkness swept in and reclaimed the forest.

He had to admit the going was much easier, too easy. He tried to discern the path's direction, but his senses were dead to him. He could no longer feel the foreboding presence of the curse. Was that a good thing?

Time droned on. Despair tainted his mind with the ever-increasing thought of becoming lost. He dragged his feet along the path, his whole body protesting. Each time his foot touched the ground, a warning echoed in his tired mind. They shouldn't be going this way. But, he reasoned, they could always go back.

An old man limped toward them, dragging his crippled foot behind him. He halted in front of Kael and glared at him with one watery blue eye. A bloody hole was all that was left of the other one.

Two snakes wove around his arms and hung off his neck. They slithered and reared, their red eyes studying Kael.

Desmond's sword flashed, but Kael only stared at the old man. He shook his head, trying to clear his senses. His eyes told him he should be repulsed, but he felt nothing. Kael glanced at Liam.

The wolf simply sat on her rump and yawned. Strange.

"Turn back!" the old man barked.

Everyone jumped.

Kael hesitated. The man was vaguely familiar, yet when he tried to focus more intently on him, his gray body shimmered and nearly dissolved. "Who are you?"

"You must turn back."

"Why should we listen to you?" Desmond waved his sword underneath the man's nose.

The snakes hissed at him, but the man stroked their bellies. "You fools! Turn back before it is too late. This path leads only to destruction."

"This forest is cursed, and so are you!" Desmond tightened his grip on his sword.

"Am I?" The man leered, his pale eye glaring straight at Desmond, then the man shouted, "*Uchita, wijons*, evil, curses—they have consumed the forest! You have traveled the *kotul dilu*, traitors! You knew the way, but you are here."

Kael shuddered. The man's voice, like a hundred screaming harpies, raked his soul. His failure overwhelmed him. He took a step back and gasped for air. He was succumbing to the curse of the forest. He spun around. The trees crowded them. Where was the path?

"You're possessed by the forest!" Desmond shouted.

"Then release me!" the man screamed.

Kael looked back just as a sword swept the man's head from his neck. The watery blue eye glared at him. Kael's breath caught. Then the head fell and the body vanished. Kael found himself on his knees.

Liam whined and nuzzled his shoulder.

"You shouldn't have. " Kael stood. "It wasn't necessary."

"Do you think he was speaking the truth?" Ayianna asked.

"Of course not." Desmond sheathed his sword and then looked up and smiled. "This forest is cursed, remember? We must be heading in the right direction."

Kael's stomach sank. The old man was right. He had known the way, but instead here he was on the path to ruin. He had failed.

"Rather appalling individual," Vian said. He shifted his lumpy, but smaller, load of blankets on his back and added brightly, "All right then, shall we proceed?"

17

AYIANNA TRUDGED ALONG the wide path, the old man's warnings ringing in her ears. Doubt, like the ancient forest, closed in around her. He couldn't be trusted, could he? He was part of the forest, and nothing could be trusted in the forest. But then, why had Kael been so shaken?

The way turned, and she halted. In the distance, an elaborate gateway glowed in the darkness. Giant marble gates towered above them set between two pillars spiraling into the treetops. Her doubt fled.

"The old fairy kingdom," Kael said. His face had returned to its usual scowl.

"Is that good or bad?" asked Vian.

"I don't think anything good can be found here."

Desmond shrugged. "It doesn't look bad."

Ayianna agreed. The strong walls and bright gate seemed secure and inviting. She welcomed an opportunity to rest without fear of the forest or its curse.

"Need I remind you three," Kael said through clenched teeth, "that we are still in the Forest of Inganno."

Ayianna reached for her talisman. Her heart lurched—it was gone. Fragmented chidings from her father and Kael scolded her, exposing her weaknesses, her laziness. Couldn't Osaryn, the True One, protect her more than a trinket of stone?

"What happened to the fairies?" asked Vian as he strained his neck to see the top of the gates.

Kael stared at Vian. "Did you receive any worthwhile education?"

Vian crossed his arms. "I've received the best education there is to be had on this side of Nälu."

"Clearly you weren't paying attention then. The fairies were slaughtered during the Naajiso Revolt."

"So, the Revolt cursed the forest?" Ayianna peered into the shadows behind them. In the presence of the old fairy gates, the forest was less fearful, less threatening. Maybe they could camp outside of the gates. No need to bother the inhabitants.

"No. Several nymphs had—"

"Nymphs?" Ayianna looked up at Kael.

"Young fairies that haven't sprouted their wings yet. The nymphs had discovered a portal to the underworld and grew entranced with the Tóas Dikon. They convinced many other nymphs to follow them."

Ayianna frowned. "What exactly is the Tóas Dikon?"

"It's the tainted powers of Taethza, queen of the underworld." Kael rested the tip of his longbow on the ground. "The nymphs deposed Queen Leora and overthrew the fairy kingdom, but lost control of the Tóas, cursing the once enchanted forest."

"Isn't Leora one of the guardians?" Vian asked.

A look of surprise flickered across Kael's face. "Yes, she is the last surviving fairy."

"So who lives here now?" Ayianna glanced back at the gates. Had the inhabitants already noticed their presence?

"The bad fairies that won, obviously," Desmond said.

"No, the guardians condemned them to the Abyss. They are what we know today as the imps."

"What?" Ayianna asked. "How could those wretched, furry creatures be anything like fairies?"

"It's a long, complicated story," Kael said. "Some say Taethza had pity on them and gave them fur to cover their nakedness. Some say it was the touch of the Tóas Dikon, others say it grew on them while they adapted to life in the hollows of the Abyss."

"You're not a bard are you, Kael?" Desmond eyed him. "These stories seem a bit colorful."

Kael arched an eyebrow. "I'm surprised at you, Desmond. As a merchant in search of royal offices, surely you could have afforded an education."

"More than you—my education was practical, not storytelling."

"Enough, already." Ayianna glared at them. "What should we do? The path ends here. Do we go back the way we came?" She gestured back. The light had ceased, and darkness had retaken the road.

"No, we shall see who inhabits Sammara now." Desmond started walking toward the polished gate.

Kael shook his head. "Nothing good can live there now. We must go back."

"We're tired, hungry, and evening is upon us. Those beasts will come back." Vian tilted his head and rubbed his lower back with his free hand. "I don't know about you, but I don't think I have the energy to spend another sleepless night fending off those tuyo-muts—whatever you called them." He took off after Desmond.

Ayianna tried to think, but exhaustion garbled her thoughts. She glanced at Kael, torn. His gray eyes pleaded with her. Did he actually think she had a choice? She turned away. She'd take her chances with the inhabitants rather than spend one more night in the forest.

The gates grew larger as they drew closer. Two guards, clad in silver robes, stood at attention on either side of the shimmering gate. A pair of folded wings hung from their shoulders.

"Are they fairies?" Ayianna asked no one in particular.

"No." Kael came up behind her. "Hamadryads."

"What's a hamadryad?"

"They are dryads of magical trees, and they are female."

"Oh, interesting . . . " Ayianna slowed her pace. "What kind of magic do these trees have?"

Kael fell into step beside her. "It varies on the tree and their location, but these trees are cursed."

They neared the gates, and Vian cleared his throat. "Allow me the honor of speaking, since I am a prince. I doubt any of you have been schooled on the etiquettes of the court."

Kael shrugged.

Before the prince could announce their arrival, the guards clanked their halberds together and thundered in unison, "Who seeks to disturb the kingdom of Mandar?" They didn't look to the left or the right, but in a constant stare out into the dark forest.

Vian stepped forward and puffed out his chest. "We are but weary travelers, journeying to the Mountains of Ruzat. We seek only rest and peace within Mandar."

"See," Desmond leaned over Ayianna toward Kael, "it isn't Sammara, but Mandar. You got your castles mixed up, storyteller."

Kael ignored him.

Ayianna focused on the guards as they spoke quietly to one another.

After a while, the hamadryads faced the travelers, stepped aside, and smiled. "Very well, enter, and be at peace."

Ayianna didn't like their smile, but before she could figure out why, the white gates inched open, giving her ample time to process the incredible view.

The foreboding trees gave way to a clear night sky. Brilliant stars twinkled high in the heavens. The full moon hung its blue-white head over the treetops, splashing the city below with a luminous glow. Massive walls held back the gloomy forest, making way for a white marble castle towering above well-kept gardens. Slender trees glistened in the center of the gardens, surrounding a large one adorned with gold apples.

A young hamadryad glided toward them. A wide, black belt gathered her green robes at the waist. Her face was that of a sapling tree, the bark smooth and bright. Long, golden vines wrapped around her head like hair, glittering as if stardust had fallen from the heavens and had settled on her head. Her fluttering, iridescent wings brought her near.

"Welcome, weary travelers," she said. Her melodic voice floated on the breeze. "I am Tivona, maidservant of the Queen of Mandar. I will show you to your quarters where you all may rest. You are here just in time for the festivities. The Queen will be delighted."

"Festivities?" Ayianna yawned.

Tivona motioned for them to follow. The fatigued travelers obeyed and stumbled into the marble halls. Liam's toenails clicked along the marble floor, echoing off the vacant walls as Tivona led them deeper into the castle. The corridor opened into a courtyard filled with sweet smelling flowers and fruit trees. Three archways encircled the aromatic garden.

"The menfolk will stay in these rooms. We have separate quarters for our female guests."

Ayianna twisted the straps of her bag. She didn't want to be separated from the only familiarity she knew, but she was too tired to protest as she was guided away. Tivona led her back through the corridor into the main hallway and then down another hall to the right.

The hall emptied out into a massive courtyard filled with flowering bushes and water fountains. Marble walls surrounded the garden, stretching toward the sky. Archways in the walls led to other parts of the castle. A second floor with four doors and a balcony sat above the archways. Smooth stone steps led up to those rooms.

Tivona glided up the steps to the right.

"You shall stay the night here." She pressed open the heavy wooden door into a dark room. She cupped her hand and blew upon it. Little lights danced upon her hand. Then she flung the dancing lights across the room and immediately the room brightened as if the sun had popped its head in and smiled.

To the left of Ayianna lay a gigantic bed filled with pillows. To her right, a half-wall separated the bathing area, and a plush armchair sat next to the wall. A green robe and a white nightgown were draped over one of its arms. A thick bath towel hung over the other.

"Your bath has been prepared," Tivona said, and instantly steam rose from behind the half-wall. "Rest well, my dear." Then she bowed her way out of the room and closed the thick door behind her.

"Liam, this is beautiful!" Ayianna exclaimed. Desmond's plans for their future fleeted across her mind. "I could definitely live in a castle."

She slipped off her cloak and smiled. The guardians would straighten everything out, and then she and Desmond could be married within a year. She knelt down and untied her boots. Her brother's dagger slid out.

The cold blade anchored her to reality and sobered her short-lived giddiness. What secret took her father's life? Who had taken her mother? Would the guardians help her?

She pulled off the boots and slipped the dagger back inside. "We must not think on these things. Right, Liam?"

The wolf cocked her head, shook her body, and strutted off to investigate the room. Ayianna pulled her brother's clothes off and placed them over the half-wall. Tattered and stained from the trip, they would have to be replaced soon. Should she wash them? Maybe in the morning.

She reached up and removed her betrothal pin. The burning, aching chasm of grief reappeared. The blue stone glimmered in the soft light. Its delicate petals were bent like a broken flower in a windstorm. Why hadn't she packed it away? She blinked back tears, set it down on the half-wall, and undid her braid.

Steam wafted up from the sunken bath, welcoming her tired and sore body. She oozed into the hot water, savoring its warmth and support. Her scratches burned, but she sank deeper. For once, she was safe. No more running. No more beasts to hunt her in her dreams. The men who pursued her, gone. They would never find her now. She lingered in her moment of peace, but exhaustion weighed heavily on her. Sleep would come soon, and she would welcome it. After a while, she dabbed her tender face and hands with a sponge she found lying next to the bath.

Liam growled.

Ayianna jolted upright, her heart racing. What had happened? Had she fallen asleep? Disorientated, she climbed out and peered around the room.

Liam sniffed at the base of the heavy door. Its thick wood muffled a knock, and the door began to creak open.

Ayianna snatched the towel from the chair and dashed behind the half-wall. How could she be so foolish? Why hadn't she locked the door? She waited, but Liam didn't attack. She gripped the towel around her and peered over the tiled wall.

"Forgive me, please." Kael turned away.

What was he doing here?

"I—ah—give me a moment." She grabbed the nightgown and slipped it over her head. Donning the green robe, she joined Kael at the door.

"Would you like to sit?" Ayianna pointed to a large, stuffed chair against the wall.

"I'm not staying long." Kael fidgeted with his sword belt. "Doing all right then?"

"I guess so." She pulled out a brush from her knapsack and began untangling her long hair. "Why are you here?"

"Well, you looked a little frightened earlier. So, I thought I would check in on you."

"Really?" Her brush snagged, and she untangled the knot. "Well, I'm fine now."

Kael nodded and glanced around the room. "Nice quarters. All we have are small, stiff cots for sleeping, and we're all in the same room, no less. As soon we got settled, Desmond fell asleep. Didn't know somebody could snore that loudly. Did you know he snores?"

Ayianna frowned "I suppose you didn't come all the way up here just to compare rooms, or to get me in trouble with Desmond again. If he knew you were here . . . "

He clenched his jaw. "Saeed wouldn't have given the warning to stick to the trail if he knew a place of refuge could supposedly be found in the Forest of Inganno. Something about this whole place isn't right."

"Maybe, maybe not . . . " She yawned.

"Either way, we'll leave at daybreak."

He stepped through the doorway and disappeared into the night. The heavy door swung shut behind him. Exhaustion pushed his warning from her mind. She checked for a lock, but didn't find one. She shrugged and climbed into the gigantic bed, sinking into its soft pillows. For a moment, she lingered, enjoying the comfort, and then she fell into a deep sleep.

18

"AYIANNA! AYIANNA, WAKE up. You must rise, dress, and go at once."

"Yes, Mother, I am awake." Ayianna moaned and sat up in bed. She blinked the sleep from her bleary eyes. Then the realization hit her stomach like an avalanche of boulders. She wasn't home.

Climbing out of the bed, Ayianna caught sight of a beautiful yellow gown set out for her. It had layers and layers of chiffon gathered at the waist. Tiny white flowers dotted the bodice, and its lengthy sleeves drooped to the floor. She changed into the gown and then looked for Liam, but she wasn't there. Odd. Where had she gone?

The door opened and Tivona entered.

"The queen has requested your presence." She smiled and motioned for Ayianna to sit in the armchair.

Ayianna did as she was instructed.

Tivona brushed the gnarled mess out of Ayianna's hair. Then she proceeded to sweep it up into an elaborate bun. "Ready." Tivona stated, rather than asked, and directed Ayianna out the door.

Their steps were quick, and the halls a blur, as they glided through the castle. Ayianna couldn't keep up with the twists and turns. Soon they were standing outside an ornate door, engraved with a large tree and round, gold apples.

The door swung inward. White, polished columns spiraled upward and branched out across the ceiling. Large windows opened the great hall to the east; the horizon brightened with the expectation of the rising sun. For a second, the marble walls seem to waver. Ayianna strained to see what lay beyond the wavering walls, but her attention was diverted by Tivona's tug, leading her toward the throne.

The hamadryad queen sat upon plump, green pillows, which covered the large marble throne. Her iridescent wings shimmered behind her. She wore a pastel pink chiffon robe that draped the steps before her. Long gold tresses of vines spiraled down her back. A wreath of green and gold circled her head. Among the woven vines glittered tiny rubies.

"Ayianna," the queen said, her voice hypnotic. "Such exotic beauty you possess. Where are you from?"

"Um . . . the Prathae Plains." Ayianna's ears burned.

"What brings you to the Forest of Inganno?"

"I . . . " Ayianna hesitated. Should she trust the queen? What had Vian said? "We are traveling to the mountains of Ruzat."

"We? Oh yes, your traveling companions. How is it a girl, such as yourself, is traveling with three men?"

"I am betrothed to one."

"Betrothed!" squealed the queen. "Does that practice still exist? Amazing! And how has your journey been?" She picked up a mirror and gazed at herself. Two other hamadryads dressed in silver robes fanned the queen with broad feathery plumes.

"Uh—fine, thank you."

"You are weary of your journey, I can tell. I see you bear the flute of an ambassador of the dryads. I could use you." The queen smiled. The same haunting smile the hamadryad guards had.

"How do you know?" Ayianna's hand went to her neck, but the flute wasn't there.

"I know all the forest's secrets. Why don't you stay with us?"

"I don't know."

She gazed into the mirror again. "Beauty is wasted on the young, don't you agree, Ayianna?"

"Wait—how do you know my name?"

"I know more than your name. I know that you have suffered great loss and that you seek peace and answers."

Ayianna stared at the interlocking circles embroidered in the rug beneath the hamadryad's throne. The queen's words ripped away the remaining veils of sleep, and the consuming grief returned, plunging into her heart like a knife.

"I could set you free from all that. I could give you peace."

The queen's voice swirled in her head. Peace? How it evaded her! Could she really be set free from the guilt and sorrow? No. How could she think like that when her mother needed her? "I can't. I need to save my mother. I can't stay—"

"Your mother is gone."

Ayianna clutched her fists against her sides. "What do you mean?"

"Do you think she could have survived the very men that killed your father? Or the curse that now controls the plains?"

"How do you know these things?" Something didn't feel right. Maybe it was the way her vision would sway and blur, or the way her mind felt hot and unwilling to think. Like someone was probing around in her head. She shuddered.

The queen gazed at the mirror, stroking her face. She appeared older somehow. Fine cracks slowly crawled across her cheeks, and her golden hair darkened. "I have my ways."

"But—"

"I hate to be the bringer of unfortunate news, but it appears your companions have left without you." The queen looked up.

Ayianna gasped. A cold hand seemed to grab her lungs.

"They must have thought you would choose to remain behind, or maybe they did not want to endure the extra burden." By now, the bark had peeled from the queen's face, revealing diseased wood. "Of course, it would be easier if you would be willing to join us."

In the distance, Liam growled.

Ayianna turned to look for her, but couldn't find her.

The queen leaned over and consulted with Tivona. A ray of light splashed across the marble walls. The sun was rising—daybreak.

Liam's growls grew in their intensity.

Ayianna struggled for clarity as her world pitched and turned. Then Kael's warning echoed in her head—must leave at daybreak. Was she too late? Had they really left her behind? She tried to reason, to think, but her mind swarmed with doubt and fear.

The queen's voice roared in her head. "Tivona, she is perfect. Young and beautiful."

"No." Ayianna gasped, her breath cut short. She fell to her knees as the pressure in her head mounted.

"I am sorry, Ayianna." The queen stood above her. "You had your chance."

"My queen, the feast is almost ready," a voice said.

Ayianna looked up. Blurred images surrounded her and disappeared as her vision faded. What was going on?

"My queen, the cooks await your presence." Another voice sounded above her.

"Yes, of course. And bring Ayianna. I shall be young and beautiful again. Start the fires!"

The marble walls wavered and dissolved into blackened bricks. Ayianna sought escape, but the room spun. Something grabbed her by the stomach and yanked her away.

The lights went out.

Ayianna couldn't breathe. Where was she? Something pressed down on her face. Her arms were pinned. She thrashed and squirmed, and her lungs screamed for air. She brought her knees up and kicked, thrusting her assailant from her.

She shoved a pillow from her face, gasping for air. She was back in her room. Where was her attacker? She leapt from the bed and something crunched beneath her feet. Roaches scattered, and she yelped, kicking at their retreating bodies. Light sifted through rotting timber. Human-looking skulls lined the filthy walls. Her knees buckled, and she stumbled backward. Away. She had to get away. Warn the others. Where was Liam?

At the edge of the bed, Tivona lay crumpled on the floor. Scaly wings replaced the iridescent ones. Strips of discolored bark hung from her wooden arms. Her face was taunt and hollow, framed by the dirty vines that wrapped around her head. Tattered rags replaced her fancy clothes, barely covering her wooden body.

Ayianna looked down at her own borrowed nightgown. Her skin crawled. She ripped it off in disgust and threw it across the room. She pawed at her skin to remove any bugs that might have inhabited the filthy gown.

She forced herself to calm down and pulled on her own clothes and boots. She slipped her brother's dagger back behind the laces, stuffed her belongings into her knapsack, and swung it across her shoulder. As she tied the cape around her neck, she realized her wooden flute was gone.

One glance at Tivona's ragged hands revealed its whereabouts. Her long nails curled around the vine necklace.

Ayianna yanked the flute from the hamadryad's hands and stashed it in the bag.

The door shuddered. A loud growl erupted from the other side.

Ayianna opened it, and a gray blur tore into the room, stopping at Tivona's crumpled body, before returning to Ayianna.

"It's good to see you too." She bent down and hugged Liam.

She straightened and stepped outside. The once-marble castle, pristine in the night, was now rotting timbers by daylight. The great wall surrounding the castle crumbled in places where the forest had broken through. Thorns and brambles choked the once magnificent garden.

A hiss ripped the air behind her, and Ayianna spun.

Tivona's limbs shook as they grasped the air around her.

Ayianna jerked Liam down the rickety wooden steps. She traced her way back through the hall toward the men's chambers. The rotting doors were wide open. She peered into the shadows of the room. The cots were lined up against the wall, their bedding folded and untouched. They had left without her! Her hands trembled and her chest constricted. What would she do now? Where would she go? She fought back tears and darted inside the room.

In the corner, she found Kael's longbow and quiver of arrows. His knapsack lay next to the head of the bed. Certainly, he wouldn't have left those behind. She swung the quiver over her back and snatched up the longbow. On the other side, Desmond's and Vian's gear sat against the wall. Once she had finished gathering everything, except Vian's lumpy ball of clothes and blankets, she crept back through the halls, swaying underneath the clumsy load.

Ayianna scanned the hallway. No sign of Tivona or any other hamadryad. Where would they've taken her companions? She staggered deeper into the castle, moving as quietly as she could under the weight of her burden.

Most of the rooms off the corridor were vacant. Dead leaves and branches littered their floors, and nothing hung on the walls. It smelled like the decaying forest beyond its shabby borders. Liam scouted ahead and ducked into a room. Ayianna gritted her teeth. *Foolish wolf, she should be more careful!*

Reaching the doorway, Ayianna discovered a darkened stairway leading down. She peered into the darkened hole and clenched her teeth. "Liam?" She listened for the wolf's padded feet and clicking nails, but heard only the distant drip of water. She tightened her fists. "You better come here."

Nothing.

Ayianna groped for a railing but found only cold, damp stones. She gritted her teeth. Why couldn't the wolf just listen? But her anger quickly succumbed to the fear pounding in her heart. She took a deep breath and descended into the darkness.

Each step drew her away from the light and into certain death. The air grew clammy and stale. Here, the stench of unwashed bodies and fecal matter wiped away any smell of the decaying forest above.

At the bottom of the stairs, her eyes adjusted. Light from the doorway revealed a long row of cells stretching into more darkness—a dungeon. Surely they would have taken the travelers here. A strange sound rose from the cells. A low, mournful tune. The dungeon's inhabitants were humming.

"Hello?" Ayianna peered through the rusty bars. A small creature, the size of a cat, sat in the shadows. It lifted its head and stepped into the light. A bald man dressed in rags stood before her with wings folded against his back. His silver eyes were sharp yet ancient.

"Who are you?" His voice was scratchy and barely above a whisper.

"My name is Ayianna." She eyed the prisoner. "What are you?"

He stretched his wings and bowed. "I am a Naajiso, a fairy."

"A fairy?" Her eyes widened. "But I thought all fairies had been killed?"

He shrugged. "We might as well be dead. There is no life to be had here but to mourn the passing of days."

"Did they bring an elf and two men down here?" Ayianna scanned the rows of cells.

"No." The fairy tilted his head. "No one comes to the dungeons. Except to mock us or feed us to their horrid trees. Why are you here?"

"We got lost in the forest." Ayianna dumped the heavy load from her shoulders. "The hamadryads have taken my companions."

"What were you doing in the forest of curses?"

"We were traveling to Raemoja."

"Raemoja?" The fairy's brows lifted. He gripped the iron bars in front of him. "Is it time?"

"Time for what?"

"The fulfillment of the prophecy. How is Karasi, the Sacred Pearl? Is she well? Tell me, what is happening in Nälu?"

"Um, well, Karasi has been kidnapped, and Dagmar's been destroyed. We are meeting the Guardian Circle. They should have the answers."

"Oh." The fairy sank to his knees.

"What is your name?"

"I am Eloith." His eyes narrowed. "If the hamadryads have your companions, they are in grave danger. These hamadryads have been poisoned by the forest. They eat people. They think they can prolong the life of their trees by doing so, but it curses them instead."

"Well, let's get out of here. Where are the keys?" She glanced around the dungeon. A few broken benches and debris littered the floor, but nothing that looked like a key.

"Give me your hand." Eloith pressed his forehead against the iron bars and stretched out his arm.

"What?"

"I will not hurt you. We have to hurry if we want to save your companions."

Ayianna knelt. His hand, no bigger than a cat's paw, gripped her palm. Tiny blood vessels pulsed beneath his papery skin. He flinched, and his complexion paled.

"You have suffered great loss." His watery eyes wandered over Ayianna's face. "It is no mistake you are here. The enemy hunts you; you have something they seek."

Ayianna pulled back, but the fairy's grasp held firm. Her thoughts flicked back to the men who murdered her father, ransacked her home, and took her mother captive—so much death, so many secrets! She clenched her other hand. "I know that much. What do I have that they want?"

"I cannot tell you what I do not know. Clear your mind and close your eyes."

"Why?"

"I will show you where the keys can be found."

She hesitated, but he continued to stare at her. She closed her eyes. *Clear my mind? How am I supposed to do that?* Drip . . . drip . . . drip echoed somewhere in the dungeons beneath the faint humming and breathing around her. She had to hurry. Kael and the others were in danger.

"Focus!"

She jumped.

"Focus on the feel of my hand."

Clammy and frail . . .

"I am not frail."

Suddenly, Ayianna's vision exploded in the darkness. A slurry of images swept her through a maze of corridors and rooms and stopped in front of a tall cupboard. The cupboard opened, and she saw a ring of iron keys. Then everything dissolved.

"Keep your eyes closed and follow the vision."

Ayianna's eyes flew open. "What?"

"There is no light in the dungeons."

"But you're a fairy. Can't you create light or fire or something?"

"We are imprisoned in cells we, the Naajiso, crafted." He shrugged. "Naturally, we could not allow our prisoners magic."

"But—"

"Explanations are best saved for when we are no longer in danger. Close your eyes."

Ayianna frowned and closed her eyes. Instead of darkness, the dungeons were lit with torches. "What is this? Magic?"

"We cannot perform magic within the cells. I only shared a memory with you. You do not have much time, for I am sure they will soon discover that you are missing."

She nodded, inhaled deeply, and took a step. The torches flickered. She moved toward the end of the dungeons, but her vision went dark. "Eloith! The memory is gone!"

"Fear not, young one. Turn and, when you see again, go forth. The vision will not fade unless you go the wrong direction."

She turned, and the dungeon came to life again. She passed through a doorway into a corridor. After a couple of blackouts, she finally figured out how to trick her body into trusting what her mind's eye saw.

Reaching the final room, Ayianna strode toward the cupboard and grasped its handle, but her hand came away empty. Her heart pounded in her ears. Had she gone the wrong way? No, she could see. Lit torches hung from the wall, their flames dancing and casting shadows. The cupboard stood tall before her, but her hands found nothing.

Ayianna wiped her hands on her pants and tried to calm her breathing. Something was wrong. *No, think. Don't panic.* She cracked her eyes open. A black void swooped down and swallowed her whole. She strained to see something—anything—but her eyes burned until she closed them again. She groped in the darkness for the cupboard, but tripped over something and fell to her knees. The stone floor bit through her pants, and pain erupted in her legs. The apparition of light wavered. She slid her hands along the floor, though her vision showed nothing was there. Her head spun as she tried to do the opposite of what her eyes told her. Then she bumped into a solid object and felt along its edges. The musty wood crumbled beneath her touch.

Something clinked.

Ayianna froze. She grabbed the wooden object and shook it. Clink, clink. The keys! She plunged her hands inside, and her fingers brushed against a hard, cold ring. She seized it and pulled her hand from the decaying cupboard. The iron keys clanked in her hands. She did it! She had found them. Her chest filled with pride, and she raced back to the cells, keeping her eyes closed until she reached Eloith.

Keys in hand, she darted to each cell and unlocked them all. Soon, the dungeon fluttered with wings and excitement. She smiled. Perhaps it was a good thing they had come to Mandar. She sought Eloith and found him next to Liam, speaking to her in a strange language and stroking her fur. The wolf, who was nearly three times his size, sat on her haunches and wagged her tail.

Ayianna gathered up her awkward bundle. "Any idea where they would have taken my companions?"

"I do not know, but I would guess the courtyard where the hamadryads' trees exist, or perhaps they have now developed some other device to drain the flesh of its blood."

"Eloith!"

"Forgive me." He dipped his head. "The Naajiso will meet you in the courtyard, but first we must gather our weapons. I hope we are not too late."

19

AYIANNA AND LIAM snuck toward the great hall. Hollow laughter interrupted the discordant music drifting through the castle. Since the courtyard had been empty, Eloith had suggested the great feast hall. Where else would they roast people without catching their precious trees on fire?

Eloith and the other fairies fanned out and prepared for an ambush while Ayianna searched for an inconspicuous place to hide. The arched windows didn't help. She doubled over and slid along the wall, keeping low enough to avoid discovery.

Beneath one window, she found refuge behind old, rotting barrels and clay pots the size of horses. She shifted the bags on her back to the floor. Their contents clinked and rustled. Her heart jumped. She took a deep breath and exhaled, forcing the panic out through her nose. *They didn't hear that, they couldn't have.*

She mustered her courage and peered through an opening between two clay pots. Her stomach twisted. Desmond, Kael, and Vian had been bound to spits and hung over a large smoldering fire pit in the center of the hall.

Long tables stretched across the room, surrounding the fire pit. More barrels and jars sat beneath soiled tapestries along the far wall. Scores of hamadryads chatted in small groups, while many others admired the craftsmanship of their victims' swords.

Small brass horns resounded off the walls, and in fluttered the queen just as beautifully dressed as she was in Ayianna's dream.

Liam growled. Ayianna glanced over her shoulder.

The flapping of wings vibrated the air. Someone was coming, and she was in a hurry.

Ayianna sank to the floor behind the wooden barrels. She caught a glimpse of the tattered dress as the hamadryad buzzed through the corridor and into the feast hall. Ayianna touched the fairy sword Eloith had given her and popped her head up in time to see the queen strike Tivona across the face.

Tivona somersaulted through the air and crashed into a stack of barrels. The barrels rocked, and one careened forward into the glowing embers of the fire pit. Its contents spewed everywhere. The fire pit hissed and sparked as plumes of steam swirled into the air.

The queen screeched and clenched her fists. "All of you! Out! Find the girl!"

"But, what about the—"

"And what? Do you think they will unbind themselves and crawl down from their posts? You fools! Find that girl, or I will eat you instead!"

The queen charged out of the room, the others flying close behind.

Ayianna held her breath as they flew past her hiding place. A few stragglers lingered.

"She is lying, you know. We would taste awful, and she knows she would not reclaim her lost beauty while munching on our rotting wood."

"Aye," the other replied as they drifted past Ayianna. "Things were better when the fairies reigned."

"Better not let the queen hear you say that."

Ayianna stood as soon as the two hamadryads disappeared around the corner. Fairies poured in from all sides of the hall. Ayianna dropped the knapsacks and sprinted to a water barrel. She slid behind the barrel and pressed against it, inching it closer to the pit. She pushed as hard as she could, straining against the heavy barrel.

Finally, it tipped and water gushed out. The remaining embers hissed in protest. Steam surged and billowed, filling the hall with a milky fog. Ayianna scanned the hall. Could the hamadryads hear the hissing? Would they fly in any moment and catch them? But no one returned.

Ayianna sloshed through the drenched ashes, trying not to linger in one place for too long. Desmond and Vian were on the other side. Kael was the closest. She darted to his side.

Kael's breath came in short gasps against the thick ropes binding him to the spit. Beads of sweat covered his face. He opened his eyes at her approach and surprise flashed across them.

"What?" Ayianna sawed through the ropes with her brother's dagger as her feet grew warmer. "Didn't expect to see me?"

"No," he said through gritted teeth. His usual frown returned. The ropes gave way, and Kael tumbled into the wet soot. He scrambled out of the ropes and hauled Ayianna out of the pit.

"Where did the hamadryads go?" He set her down and shook the soot from his clothes.

Ayianna handed him his quiver and pack and then glanced at the doorway. "They've gone looking for me."

Eloith darted over and hovered above the steaming ashes. He nodded at Kael. "Captain Eloith at your service." And then he turned to Ayianna. "The queen will return soon, we must leave now."

"The great fairy captain?" Kael's eyes widened. He glanced around at the other fairies aiding Desmond and Vian. "Where did you all come from? I thought the time of the Naajiso had come and gone. We had no idea a remnant had survived."

"Ah, yes." A faint smile brushed Eloith's lips. "A remnant indeed survived, but for how long, we shall see. The world has undoubtedly changed since our absence. Perhaps our presence would be unwelcomed." He shrugged. "And here we thought we would have to wait until the end of Nälu before we tasted freedom again."

"Well, it might as well be if we don't get out of here," Kael said.

Eloith pursed his thin lips together and nodded. Desmond and Vian sloshed through the wet ashes and joined them. Ayianna handed them their belongings.

"Sorry, Vian, I couldn't bring everything."

He wiped the sweat from his forehead and took his things. "Don't worry about it."

Kael finished strapping his sword belt and swung his bow over his shoulder. "Captain Eloith, how do we get out of here?"

"We must go through the front gate." Eloith rose into the air. "Follow me."

Ayianna and the others slipped from the great hall after the fairy captain. The other fairies fluttered above and behind them, keeping a look out for the hamadryads. When Ayianna caught sight of the wiry grass of the courtyard and the looming gates ahead, a smile sprang to her lips. They would make it!

"Fairies!" The queen's booming voice bounced off the stone walls and shattered Ayianna's hope of escape. "Guards! The fairies have escaped!" the queen screeched as she came into view.

"To the gate!" Eloith rounded on the hamadryads and raised his sword.

"You!" The queen dove for Ayianna. Her eyes burned like red coals within their sockets and bark peeled away from her cheeks. She raked the air with her sharp nails.

Ayianna unsheathed the fairy sword and swung, clipping the queen's arm. The hamadryad lurched and howled.

"To the gate!" Eloith yelled again.

Ayianna raced through the courtyard. Desmond and Vian were close behind. Desmond rammed his shoulder into the gate, but the great door only shuddered.

"To the gate, to the gate," he mumbled under his breath. "How are we supposed to get through the gate?"

Ayianna looked for a chain or lock that held the doors closed, but found nothing.

The rumble of a hundred flapping wings echoed in the courtyard. A flood of hamadryads swept over them. Eloith and the fairies struggled to hold back the surging tide as hamadryads rained rocks from above.

"*Edile!*" Eloith yelled, and the gate swung open.

Ayianna rushed through the gate, but halted.

A line of hamadryads bore down on them, brandishing swords and spears.

Kael nocked his arrows as fast as he could. They sailed through the air and sunk into the wooden bodies, but the hamadryads didn't falter. Desmond swiped his sword, clipping off an arm or leg here or there, but they wobbled on while some took flight.

"How do you kill them?" Desmond asked over the clunking of the metal blades on wood.

"By chopping their trees down!" Ayianna dodged a blow from a hamadryad.

"How would you know?"

A hamadryad took advantage of the distraction and swooped in, gouging Desmond's shoulder with her claws.

Vian jumped to his rescue and knocked the hamadryad off.

"Where are their trees?" Kael swung his sword around to decapitate a hamadryad, but the tree spirit ducked and lashed at Kael's stomach with her dagger.

"Back—*njöbul*—in the castle—*njöbul*," Eloith said. A hamadryad's limbs froze up, and she plummeted to the ground.

"There are too many." Vian struck the hamadryad in front of him.

Ayianna yelped as one grabbed her arm, its thorny wood biting into her skin. She jerked free and slammed the hamadryad to the ground. More filled the sky. Buzzing back and forth, they steered clear of the swords. The queen hissed and brandished her own sword.

"This way," Vian hollered over his shoulder as he dashed into the forest. Desmond and Kael followed.

Ayianna raced after them. She would not be left behind.

"No!" Eloith yelled. "Come back!"

Vian disappeared, swallowed up by the cursed forest. Then Kael and Desmond vanished.

Ayianna skidded to a stop as the ground gave way. She clawed at the protruding roots and vines, but their thorns only tore her skin. She tumbled to a stop, but dirt continued to rain down on her, threatening to bury her alive.

20

IN THE ANCIENT ruins of Raemoja, Nevin Saeed waited, his gaze settling on the crumbling altar. An old reminder of a price paid for freedom so long ago. Although many years had passed, he could still see the horror that once gripped the entire world of Nälu. Could still hear the echoes of his brother's final scream as the dagger plunged into his chest. Blood drenched the altar and dripped onto the marble steps below. Saeed closed his eyes against the barrage of memories.

He turned away and glanced at the sky for the hundredth time. What was taking her so long? He twisted the braids of his beard until they pulled at the skin of his face. The Guardian Circle could not convene until she returned with her report.

A flutter of wings drew Saeed's attention back to what was once the outer bailey. Nevin Leora flew over the broken walls. She wore a simple blue tunic and gray breeches, not what he would expect from a fairy who had once been queen.

"*Prözam* Leora, how are you?" Saeed asked as the fairy hugged his neck, her dainty toes barely reaching his midsection.

"My dear Saeed." She pulled away and looked the headmaster over. Her violet eyes hadn't lost their sparkle. "It is so good to see you, although I must say you have aged since our last parting."

"I cannot say the same for you. You've appeared the same since the first day I met you."

"Your vision and your memory must be failing." Leora chuckled. She flitted atop a crumbling wall and folded her iridescent wings against her back.

Saeed shook his head. "I remember more than I would like. Have you finished your latest project?"

Leora nodded. Her curls bounced around her head in wild excitement. "I finished the history of the Naajiso ages ago. Although, I have not settled on a title yet. I have a few I am considering, perhaps you could help me. I would value your suggestions."

"Of course. But then, what has kept you so busy? I have neither seen nor heard from you since the king's wedding."

"Busy, indeed." She nodded again. "I have nearly finished *Irryn Strii Edztumosar* for Nevin Eldwyn, a wonderful book discussing the variations among the elf-kind of Nälu, and I will soon begin illuminating *Strastuvec, a Gukvec ka Roklom*, a heavy tome detailing the Klovan dwarves rise to power and the construction of their great city."

Her voice tinkled like chimes in a gentle breeze. If he had closed his eyes, he was certain she would have lulled him to sleep. He crossed his arms and leaned against the broken half-wall. "It is a pity none of the other races have been able to learn the art."

"Yes." Leora grew solemn for a moment and then snapped out of it with a bob of her head, sending her golden curls bouncing to and fro. "But no bother. I have heard that the Stozic dwarves are creating something in a manner of secrecy. They claim it will change the future of illuminated manuscripts."

"I see." Saeed raised his eyebrows. "Well, I must speak with Hadrian about it. Perhaps he would be able to enlighten us."

"I doubt it. You know how those dwarves are." She pressed her lips together and shook her head.

He knew all too well. He rubbed his temples as an elf glided into the courtyard upon a brightly woven *zrakha*. "I see you've brought Eldwyn with you."

"Yes, yes, I am staying with the elves. But he could hardly keep up with me on his silly little rug. Dwarves are not known for their superior weaving skills."

"I do not think they were overly concerned about the appearance of the rug, but its ability to fly. No other nation has been able to create such a marvel."

Leora snorted. "The Naajiso could have, but obviously we had no need for them." She glanced around. "Have the others arrived?"

"Unai and Lazar are inside." He motioned toward what was left of the great hall. A few broken pillars and the stone outer walls remained; the wood long since decayed. Only squirrels and rabbits held court now. "We will find you there."

She nodded and flew off.

Saeed turned to welcome Eldwyn. The elf's long, black hair and slender face still showed no signs of aging. How many centuries had he served as guardian, and he still looked the same? Except his gray eyes. They had lost their youthful glimmer of hope. Eldwyn unfolded his willowy legs and stepped off the tapestry. He rolled it up and slid it into a bag that hung from his shoulder.

Saeed brought his fingertips together briefly in the elven salutation. Eldwyn did likewise.

"*Striidamor* Eldwyn, are you still using the *zrakha*?"

Eldwyn cocked his head. "I trust it enough, and it's faster and cleaner than a horse."

"You are either brave or foolish." Saeed smiled and grasped the other elf's shoulder.

"Neither, I am resourceful."

"Of course. And how is Zurial?"

"Peaceful and without mischief—I cannot say the same for the rest of Nälu. It seems someone is trying to bring the Abyss upon us." The elf held up a small, rolled parchment. "What is the meaning of this?"

Saeed dropped his arm. "I will explain soon enough."

"It is true then—the rumors I am hearing about Dagmar?"

"Depends on what you have heard. Come, Lazar and Unai are waiting for us." Saeed turned to go.

Eldwyn grabbed Saeed's elbow. "The Nutraadzi . . . is it destroyed?"

"Only in building, not the heart." His gaze settled on the old altar.

Eldwyn's grip tightened. "And the students?"

"A handful escaped. And those who were away in the Observation Phase are still alive."

"We can start over . . . rebuild the school. We must."

Uneven footsteps crunched over the rubble. Nevin Hadrian shuffled into view, favoring his left foot. His bushy, brown eyebrows furrowed in a constant state of petulance. The stout dwarf swung a heavy battle-axe down from his shoulder.

"Nevin Hadrian, good to see you." Saeed bent to embrace the dwarf.

"A simple handshake would do, Saeed." Hadrian shifted his weight to his right foot.

"Come, come," Saeed said. "We have not seen each other in years."

"Yes—and, it would seem, only in time of need."

Saeed snorted. "I have always been available to assist the dwarf-kind in their time of need. It is not my fault you are too stubborn to ask."

Hadrian squinted and tilted his head. "And it is a good thing, too. These humans make enough trouble for us all. Mark my words, they will be the ones issuing in the final days of Nälu."

"I must agree with Hadrian," Eldwyn said. "Perhaps the destruction of Nutraadzi is a sign."

"Let us not speculate." Saeed turned. "Come, the others are waiting."

He ushered them through the arched doorway and into what was left of the great hall. Inside, Nevin Lazar sat atop a large stone table engrossed in a conversation with Unai and Leora. His black, disheveled hair stuck out from his pale skin and crawled down the sides of his face. A simple dark tunic and pants covered his lithe form. At Saeed's approach, Lazar jumped off the table with a grace of a panther.

"Where is Nerissa?" Leora asked as she settled on top of the stone table.

"The merfolk are on the other side of the world." Lazar settled on a makeshift chair and added, "I would not expect her anytime soon."

"Right." Unai scratched his round belly. "Her old dragon is probably winded. I doubt that beast could make it all the way here without a rest or two."

Hadrian chuckled, but Unai glared at him. "That was not meant to be funny."

Hadrian shrugged and shuffled past. "As if you knew anything about dragons." He found some dislodged bricks, dragged them over to the table, and stacked them across from Unai. When he had finished, he sat eyelevel with the others.

"What?" Unai raised his hands. "You do not like our seating arrangements?"

Hadrian raised a bushy eyebrow. "I like to see the people I am speaking with, unlike you, who would rather eat your way through the conversation."

"Guardians, please." Saeed grimaced.

Lazar shook his head and crossed his arms. "Why have you called this urgent meeting?"

"Are the Haruzo so far removed from Nälu, they know nothing of the attack on Dagmar?" Eldwyn slid his bags from his back and sat down next to Hadrian.

Lazar shrugged. "We are. I do not deny it, but I doubt the elves know much more."

A loud shriek rattled the old buildings. Saeed glanced up and held his breath.

A large dragon soared above, blotting out the sun. It dropped from the sky, and the earth trembled as it landed in the outer bailey. The great reptile stretched out its leathery wings one final time and folded them against its emerald body. An older woman sat in its leather saddle. She gathered her gray robe and slid to the ground. Her white hair swung in several braids down her back. Her silvery skin glinted in the sun; opalescent colors danced as she strode toward them.

"*Naweliha*, Nevin Nerissa." Saeed touched his fingertips to his lips and bowed. "That was quite an entrance."

"*Naweliha*, Headmaster." Nerissa returned the bow.

"What news do you bring us?"

"The Perimeter remains untouched. I saw nothing out of the ordinary among the pillars. The gryphons are healthy and well-sustained by their appointed villages." Her words rolled off her tongue like waves at sea. "The Manoa Stones are smooth and vibrant. They display no signs of aging as of yet."

"Thank you, Nerissa." Saeed nodded and motioned for her to join them. "We were just about to get started."

Nerissa sat at the table, her movement graceful and purposeful. She glanced around at the others and nodded her head. "I see Nevin Darin is not here."

"He has been detained for the moment, but he will arrive soon."

Saeed scanned the familiar faces before him. He had led the Guardian Circle for the past five centuries and had grown quite fond of them. Much like a father, he had enjoyed watching them grow and mature before his very eyes. Out of the eight he would have to choose his successor and soon. Death's fingertips tickled his soul. He sighed. Of all the times he could have led Nälu against such an attack, it would have to be now; an aging elf whose best years have been spent. Couldn't his time end in peace?

"Nevins of the Guardian Circle." Saeed scanned their faces. His heightened sense brushed against their well-warded minds. "Three nights ago, an army of a hundred men, a legion of imps, and a giant troll attacked Dagmar. The vault has been emptied of its secrets, and the Sacred Pearl has been taken."

The guardians stared at him. Shock and confusion poured from their minds, and then anger swallowed the rest of the emotions. He girded his thoughts again and waited. The dragon's breathing measured the silence.

"Do you know who did this?" asked Lazar.

"I believe it was one of our own." Saeed nodded at Unai.

"An apprentice of mine." Unai closed his eyes and his shoulders slumped. "His name is Imaran. But I do not think he did all this for his own personal gain."

Saeed nodded. "The men who attacked carried the Muzal banner."

"But how can that be? Stygian has been banished to the Abyss. Who would embrace such monstrosity?" Leora stamped her foot and tightened her small hands into fists. "This generation mocks the sacrifices of our ancestors. They know not the significance of their rash and thoughtless behavior."

"Calm yourself." Saeed lifted his eyebrows. "You are perhaps one of the few remaining who have witnessed the death and destruction perpetrated under his tyranny, but we are not ignorant of it. If people have not seen it, it does not mean they have not heard of it."

"Only in the songs of bards," Leora crossed her arms, "and then the people are too drunk to remember."

Unai cleared his throat. "People still fear him despite his defeat and the strength of the Perimeter."

"Perhaps they do not fear him enough." Hadrian eyed the others.

"Stygian is not the one we should fear." Saeed glanced around the table. "He was merely the vessel."

The dwarf grunted. "What fool would kidnap the pearl and seek to frighten the Guardian Circle with a bit of black cloth?"

"I can think of one." Eldwyn leaned forward. "Semine."

Unai shook his head. "Her past offense places her under suspicion, but we have no evidence as of yet."

"Then why not find some evidence and banish her to Durqa." Leora strutted across the table toward Unai, her hands on her hips. "If she embraces the Muzal, why not banish her to the Abyss so that she may taste the horror of Stygian's tyranny?"

Lazar leaned his elbows on the table and peered over his fists. "Even if she is the one behind the attack, and we banish her to the Abyss, it won't solve the heart of the problem."

Saeed nodded. Lazar was an ambassador who had watched his nation fall away from Nälu. If anyone could see the path the nations were rushing down, it would be him.

"I am afraid that the Guardian Circle is failing," Saeed said. The guardians broke out in protest, but he raised his hand to silence them. "Imaran's mentality is merely a reflection of a greater apathy permeating the plains and slowly infecting the rest of Nälu. Look at Arashel—no longer part of the council, returning to the old ways. And what about Zurial?"

"Zurial!" Eldwyn said, standing. "The humans of the Prathae have ushered this . . . this mentality in, embracing the Nuja, falling away from Karasi's edicts and neglecting the law of Thar'ryn. Durqa is the perfect example. How can we banish criminals to a desolate place and expect cha—"

Unai slammed his palms on the table. "Well, it is a lot better than chopping their hands off for thievery or a hangman's noose for trespassing as is done in Arashel."

"Is it, Unai?" Eldwyn leaned forward. "Branding not only the thieves and murders, but their children as well? We are creating generations of outcasts and criminals."

"Not to mention a population ripe for war," Saeed added.

"What do the elves know of criminals and punishment? You live separate from the rest of us. But tell me, where do your pirates and murderers go?" Unai asked.

"Fellow guardians, please," Saeed interrupted. "We do not always agree with the decisions the rulers of Nälu make, but it is our duty to teach them and protect them."

"True." Eldwyn folded his arms and sat down. "But one cannot teach a person who does not want to learn."

"And here we are." Nerissa held out her hands, the movement graceful despite her age. Of course, she wasn't as old as Saeed.

He rubbed his fingers together, unable to hide the tremors anymore.

Nerissa's fluid voice continued, her features stoic. "Karasi kidnapped, and the Nutraadzi destroyed. Clearly this is an attack against the guardians. What other evidence do we need?"

"Have I missed anything?" a husky voice asked. A tall man strolled into the room. A leather eye patch stretched across his bald head while his good eye surveyed the assembly.

"Not a thing, Darin." Hadrian tilted his head all the way back. "Only the end of the Guardian Circle."

The other Nevins nodded their greeting while Darin settled into the chair next to Hadrian. A golden eagle landed next to him and began preening its feathers.

"*Pyaadunai*, Darin," Saeed said. "What did you find out?"

"King Valdamar has been thrown into the dungeons while Lord Derk reigns in his place."

A stunned silence descended on them.

"How?" Eldwyn asked. "Was there no battle?"

"None. Thanks to Captain Wistan and, as far as we can tell, a curse that has stretched beyond the walls of Badara." Darin glanced over at Saeed. "You were correct. The inhabitants of Talem are effected, but it would seem the curse did not reach Praetan. King Teman will allow us to meet there."

Saeed nodded. "Good."

"What curse?" Eldwyn asked.

"We do not have all the details yet." Saeed faced the elf. "But during the Feast of Daeju, a spell was cast. I did not see it, but it gave me a tremendous headache."

"That proves it, then." Hadrian slammed his fist on the table. "Derk's presence is enough evidence of Semine's involvement. And if she was the one responsible for the spell, she will be tried for high treason. She has gone from a deserter to a full-fledged sorceress."

The sky filled with the hum of flapping wings. The guardians drew their swords.

Harpies? Had the Perimeter failed? Saeed's heart told him neither. He glanced around. Beyond the broken walls of the hall, the dragon only yawned and slumbered on. A beast like him had nothing to fear.

The rays of the afternoon sun refracted on a shimmering cloud as it descended upon them. A small man, about the size of a cat, landed atop the stone table. Thirty or so other similar winged-men settled in the large arched windows.

"Naajiso!" Lazar sheathed his sword. "What—where did you all come from?"

"Queen Leora!" The lead fairy knelt on one knee. The other fairies whispered among themselves and bowed.

"Eloith?" Leora's eyes brimmed with tears. "Captain Eloith! You are alive." She darted across the table and embraced him.

"Where have you been? How are you here—alive?"

"We have been held captive in our own dungeons. Ayianna helped us escape. She told us of the meeting here, but she and her companions are now lost in the tunnels of Grenze. I am afraid they are heading for Nganjo. We must send help."

Saeed closed his eyes and whispered. "May Vituko have mercy on them."

21

AYIANNA RUBBED HER backside. The dirt had finally stopped raining down on them. The forest's smell of decay saturated the air and squeezed her lungs. How far had they fallen? A shiver crawled across her scalp and down her spine. She shook her head and tried to brush the debris from her hair and clothes, but it was useless.

"Is everyone all right?" Kael asked. He rummaged through his pack and pulled out the orb.

"Minus a few minor scrapes and bruises, I'd say we're fine." Vian patted Desmond's shoulder. "Right, my friend?"

Desmond frowned as he brushed the dirt from his torn doublet. "The next time you decide to go charging off into uncharted territory, watch your step."

Ayianna picked up the sword Eloith had given her and sheathed it. "At least we aren't on the dinner menu anymore."

"True enough." Vian adjusted his much smaller knapsack across his back.

"*Yetakoith taheza,*" Kael whispered. The orb's light sputtered and then faded. He shoved it back into his bag.

Desmond and Vian circled beneath the break in the ceiling. Light sifted through but couldn't reach the shadowed corners of the pit. Behind Kael, an opening split the wall, and patches of light spilled into what looked like a tunnel or a burrow. What other creatures lived in the forest? Did the cat-beast live underground like a mole or a gopher?

Ayianna's stomach sank. "Wait, where's Liam?"

"She's a wolf. She can take care of herself," Desmond said.

"But the hamadryads—they might try to eat her." Ayianna swallowed against the rising knot in her throat.

"Captain Eloith will take care of her. Come on, let's get out of here." Desmond stepped through the opening and disappeared.

"Hey." Vian hesitated. "Shouldn't we wait for the fairies? Couldn't they help us out of here?"

Kael ducked back into sight. "I doubt it, given the circumstances."

"But . . . " The prince glanced back up at the gaping hole far above them. "Shouldn't we discuss this?"

"What is there to discuss?" Kael gestured toward the ceiling. "We can't climb out, and we can't wait for the fairies. They are in the middle of a battle with creatures who won't die and won't give up. What if the hamadryads decide to send someone after us? We need to get out of here before we are completely out of food and water."

"Come on, Vian." Desmond gave the prince a little push. "We'd like to get out of this hole today."

"I only want to evaluate our circumstances before we charge into some other disaster."

Desmond grunted. "Perhaps if you had thought of that before, we wouldn't be in this predicament."

"Come on," Kael interrupted. "We're wasting time." He disappeared into the tunnel, and Desmond darted after him.

Vian glanced back at Ayianna. She couldn't read his expression. Had concern flickered in his green eyes? Or was he feeling guilty? He turned away. Ayianna took a deep breath.

She hoped Kael was right, but then, had he ever led them astray? She stepped into the black hole after the others.

After an hour of stubbing fingers on protruding rocks and tripping on mossy roots, Ayianna and the others stumbled out of the half-darkness and into a steep chasm. The dirt gave way to stone as layers of shale and sandstone curved upwards and outwards into the bright, blue sky above them. A stream trickled along the bottom of the ravine and a few straggly bushes dotted the rocky banks.

Ayianna knelt at the edge of the cold water and drank deeply. Its metallic taste lingered in her mouth. After refilling her waterskin, she reclined against a slab of stone. The sight of the sky above and the odor of fungi-rich soil had a calming effect, and a sense of peace settled in her heart.

"How are you doing?" Desmond asked as he sat down next to her.

"Fine." She glanced at his soiled clothes and disheveled curls and wondered if she looked just as bad. "How about you?"

"I have been better." He rubbed the blond stubble on his dirt-smeared face. If the plains people preferred women to cover their heads, then they also preferred men to keep their faces shaven. "I would've dressed differently had I known we'd be crawling around in the dirt."

"Wouldn't we all?" Ayianna smiled as she thought of the prince and his many colorful robes and fur blankets.

"Well, I can't say I'm not impressed," Desmond said. "You have proven to be a strong, determined young woman. A man might be proud to call a woman like you his wife. Just don't get too comfortable in those masculine clothes. I still want a woman when we finish our business with the guardians."

How could he compliment her in one breath and criticize her in the next? She looked down at her brother's old clothes and boots and was suddenly thankful. Hiking through forests and falling down holes weren't exactly dress-wearing activities.

"Rest time is over." Kael slung his longbow over his shoulder and started down the chasm.

Desmond snorted. "As if he knows where he is going."

He stood and helped Ayianna to her feet. He slid his arm around her waist and pulled her close. Her heart leapt into her throat. She was all too aware of the strength in his arms and his sour smelling clothes. She dared a glance at his face, and his blue eyes paralyzed her.

"Just think, in a few months you will be planning a wedding instead of running for your life."

Ayianna nodded, and he released her. She pulled her cloak over her shoulders and stepped away. Relief collided with disappointment in a torrent of conflicted feelings.

Vian clasped Desmond on the shoulder and smiled. "Right, my friend, don't forget the etiquette training, which the Lady Mavia of Sharad has graciously offered."

Ayianna managed a smile, but her stomach twisted. She didn't want to think about wedding plans and etiquette training yet. How could she? Grief severed her heart. It would consume her if she let it. Didn't Desmond understand? She would avenge the death of her father and her brother, and find her mother. She would make things right. Then she could think about marriage. Besides, didn't her father's death change everything? But the disappointment lingered. Had she really wanted Desmond to kiss her?

Desmond winked as he grabbed his pack. "Let's not keep the half-breed waiting, shall we? The quicker we're out of here, the quicker we start planning the rest of our lives." He flashed a smiled and took off after Kael with Vian in tow.

Ayianna hung back. Half-breed. The words stung. What would he think if he knew her secrets? Could she really marry him under such pretenses? But then, he chose her. Surely, a man would investigate a woman before committing his life to her. Her father's words returned. Humans regarded their wives differently. What did he mean?

As the day wore on, Ayianna noticed, with growing trepidation, that the chasm was narrowing until the layered walls almost touched, forcing the bruised travelers to turn sideways at times to continue their slow progression.

"I hope this leads somewhere other than to our deaths," Ayianna mumbled. Shuddering, she pushed her legs to keep moving as she slid sideways along the narrow corridor of stone.

Dread oozed through her bones and clawed at her mind. A childhood memory sprang to her mind's eye. Her brother had locked her in an abandoned cellar, and she had screamed until Mother had found her, hoarse and needing a bath. Those same suffocating feelings gripped Ayianna now, but her mother wasn't here to rescue her this time. A scream pressed against the back of her throat. She closed her eyes and pushed it into her gut.

Desmond touched her shoulder and urged her forward.

She shook her head. "I can't do this."

"Yes, you can." His voice held conviction and kindness, anchoring her. He gripped her shoulder tighter. "Vian and Kael are bigger than you, and they're doing just fine."

Ayianna turned her head to him and rested her cheek on the cold stone. Tears stung her eyes as her breath caught in her lungs. "I can't . . . "

"You have to." Desmond wiped a tear away. "Now, keep moving."

She turned around and braced herself against the rock, her fingers trembling. The walls pressed in on her. She closed her eyes and inched sideways along the ravine. Her knee collided with a sharp edge, and pain exploded down her leg. She gasped, her knees buckling.

"Steady, there." Desmond's hand was on her shoulder again. "Give me your hand."

Nausea surged through Ayianna's stomach as he grabbed her hand and leaned close. His presence shoved the fear back. If only he could wrap his arms around her and swallow her whole, banishing the fear and the trembling tormenting her body.

"Don't think," he whispered. "Just keep moving—one step at a time."

She nodded and moved forward, bumping a stone with her foot. It didn't scrape against another rock but disappeared, echoing off a cavity. She moaned. Was there a break in the chasm's floor? Desmond squeezed her hand. She concentrated on sliding one foot, then the next in a slow shuffle.

The ground crumbled away.

Ayianna screamed. She reached out, her arms scraping against the stone as the darkness closed in around her. More rocks fell with her. She hit bottom.

She gasped for air and tried to blink the darkness from her eyes. She threw herself at the stone embankment and tried to claw her way up, but she only wrenched loose more pebbles and dirt. She was trapped.

"Ayianna!" Desmond grabbed her and pulled her away from the wall.

She collapsed, her lungs burning. Desmond held her, but she struggled and shoved against him. Why weren't his arms enough? She needed more air, the sun, the sky! Freedom from the death trap she had fallen into. Suddenly, cool, calloused hands pressed against her head.

"*Dreyu Osaryn thadziwo roh tóhe.*"

A breeze brushed across her face and peace settled the raging fear within her. Kael stood over her, invoking the elven god. She closed her eyes and inhaled deeply of the dank, underground air.

"Osaryn, vuryn thassada ry ida adzisaryn. Rodzijo unu."

Out of habit, she repeated the refrain, and an image of her father's face flashed in her mind. A flood of grief strangled her heart. She opened her eyes to get away from the pain only to see it reflected in Kael's. He stepped back.

"What did you say, half-breed?" Desmond lifted his head. "I'll have none of your elven incantations spoken over her."

Pebbles shifted and continued to rain down as Kael moved away. She blinked the dust from her eyes and slowly sat up, uncertain whether the balm of peace would soon dissolve or not.

"Vian?" Desmond called out.

"Here." Vian broke into a fit of coughs.

Rocks clattered and Ayianna held her breath. Was it caving in?

"What's going on?" Desmond turned and scanned the shadows. "Was that you, Vian?"

"It was me." Kael's voice echoed in the darkness. "There is an opening over here."

"Why should we follow you?" Desmond asked. "You seem to be leading us into worse situations as we go."

"Do you see any other way out?"

"What kind of question is that?" Desmond lifted Ayianna to her feet. "As if anyone could see anything in this darkness."

Silence answered him, but Kael's patience had to be wearing thin. Ayianna leaned on Desmond to steady her trembling limbs. Had Desmond heard her? Why had she repeated the refrain? Did she really believe Osaryn could help or was it only out of habit?

"All right there, Ayianna?" Desmond kept one hand on her waist as she tested her footing.

"I think so."

"Hey, I found an opening over here!" The prince's voice rang out and bounced wildly off the walls of the cavern.

Desmond tensed. "Not so loud." He tightened his grip on her arm and hauled her toward the direction of Vian's voice.

Ayianna slid her feet along the ground, feeling for holes or protruding rocks. Fear prickled at the edges of her mind. He was going too fast, but then he stopped.

"So nice of you to join me," Kael replied. "This crevice actually widens into a tunnel—a man-made tunnel."

22

AYIANNA TIGHTENED HER grip on Desmond's tunic as she slid her hand along the slimy, cold walls of the tunnel. Somewhere in the distance, water dripped and a rat screeched. They turned a corner, and an orange glow beckoned at the end of the tunnel. They quickened their steps.

Reaching the end of the tunnel, Kael held up his hand. He leaned forward, looking left, then right, and then led them into an adjoining hall. Iron braziers lined the carved walls, casting their fiery light on the moist rock and smoothed floor. More tunnels branched off in different directions.

"Which way?" Ayianna peered around Desmond at the openings. None of them looked inviting.

Kael inspected the openings. A few minutes later, he motioned to the others. "This way."

Desmond eyed him. "How can you be sure?"

"It's bigger, and the air is fresher in this one."

A gentle breeze cooled the perspiration on her forehead. She had to agree with Kael, the air was fresher. Travel should go faster.

"Well, the tunnel looks just as good as the other ones." Vian followed after Kael.

Her courage bolstered by the light, Ayianna moved away from Desmond and entered the tunnel. The solid slab of rock arched high above them and sweated. Light from the braziers pooled along the floor, pushing the darkness into the farthest corners. "Did the fairies make these tunnels?"

"No." Kael unsheathed his sword and eyed the tunnels. "They don't like dark, cramped places. It doesn't bode well with their wings."

The tall ceiling did not feel cramped to Ayianna, but then she couldn't fly. The dark holes and crevices between the tunnels glared at her as if otherworldly eyes spied on them.

"So, who made them?" Desmond asked. "By the look of these torches, I'd assume these tunnels are still in use."

"I agree." Kael scanned the walls. "That's why we must proceed with caution."

Ayianna jumped as a creature scurried across her path. She gripped the hilt of her sword and exhaled.

Desmond chuckled. "It's only a rat."

She wheeled around. "How would you like it if it had leapt out at you?"

"Hey, you might want to take a look at this." Vian's voice drifted through a corridor to the right.

Ayianna walked into the adjoining tunnel and froze. People—hundreds, maybe thousands—lined the walls. No, they were encased in the stone. A strange fire burned around them, but did not consume them. Some were unmoving, frozen in place like statues. They slumped against the wall, hands hanging at their sides or laying in their laps. Dejection reflected in their vacant eyes and long faces. Others struggled against their chains, mouthing silent pleas—their eyes imploring an unseen adversary or advocate.

"Miss? Can you tell me what's going on?" Ayianna stared at a young woman weeping silently. "Can you hear me?"

The woman continued to weep.

She inched closer to touch the woman, but her hand passed through her and into something incredibly hot. Ayianna jerked back. "Ouch!"

Kael lunged and grabbed her hand. "What happened?"

"I don't know. It felt like I stuck my hand into a bowl of hot porridge."

"Your hand seems fine." Kael's scowl deepened. "Next time, don't be so impulsive."

Ayianna yanked her hand away. "How was I to know?"

He shook his head and strode back to the main hall.

Ayianna gritted her teeth. A chained man turned toward her, his pleading eyes bore into her soul. She glanced away. Did he see her?

"What is this place?" Vian's gaze slid over the inhabitants as he wandered farther into the tunnel. "Wait a minute, I know this man. Desmond, this is your old friend, Cuthbert."

Desmond joined Vian. "This isn't right. They are here, but yet they aren't."

"This is the work of the Tóas Dikon," Kael said from the opening. "We are on enemy territory."

"How?" Ayianna's eyes returned to the people. Would she see anyone she knew? Did she want to? She tried to look away, but their plight held her. How could she help them?

"Those who corrupt the gifts of Vituko find ways." Kael sheathed his sword and stepped toward her. Did he think she would be dumb enough to touch the wall again?

"Wait." Vian's head jerked up, and his tangled mass of red curls spilled out from under his cap. "The Shadow God is responsible for the dark magic?"

Kael furrowed his brows. "It's not magic. Vituko gave gifts—the Yenzo Tanil—some to the guardians, some to the nations. But the queen of the underworld twisted them for her own desire."

Ayianna turned to the wall, and her mother's face stared back at her. She gasped.

Fear saturated the woman's bleary eyes as tears streaked her dirty cheeks. She struggled against the chains binding her wrists and ankles. Her mouth moved, pleading, but no sound escaped her lips.

"Mother!" Ayianna rushed to embrace her, but Kael grabbed her arm and wrenched her back. "Let me go! That's my mother."

Her mother turned and reached for her. The others moved with her, their arms outstretched. Faint whispers filled the hall like wind, all of them crying, pleading. Could they hear them, see them? What was going on?

Kael's grip tightened as he wrapped his other arm around her shoulders. "We have to get out of here."

"No, we have to save her!" Ayianna reached for her mother's outstretched hand, but her fingers passed through the wall and into scalding heat. She jerked back, shaking her hand. There had to be an entrance at the other end of the tunnel, if she could just find it. She lunged forward, but Kael held her in place. She twisted and shoved against him. "Mother, where are you? We can save you."

"She isn't here." Kael dragged her back toward the main tunnel.

"How do you know?" Hatred and anger surged through her. She slammed her elbow into Kael's stomach, but he didn't falter. "Let go of me!"

"Desmond, would you give me a hand?"

"Hey, there's the blacksmith from Badara." Desmond pointed at a large man crumpled on the floor, crying. Similar chains bound his wrist and ankles.

"Let go!" Ayianna yelled.

Kael yanked her around and pressed her against the wall. "Listen to me. There is nothing you can do here."

She pushed her breath out through her nose and avoided his eyes.

"Ayianna . . . " His grip lessened. "I'm sorry."

She pulled away and wrapped her arms around herself. A fresh wave of tears spilled over her cheeks. She quickly brushed them aside and sought Desmond. He bent over next to the prince, studying the blacksmith.

"We shouldn't be here." Vian grasped Desmond's shoulder. "Let's go before someone discovers us."

"I'll be back, Mother," Ayianna whispered as Kael pulled her away. "I'll find a way to save you." She fastened her eyes to the ground and tried to stem the flow of tears.

Back in the main tunnel, everyone trudged in silence, but Ayianna's thoughts roared through her head. Her mother's haunting face chastised her; her tears and cries for help raked her heart.

What were they up against? Would the guardians know what to do? She took a deep breath. Things were spiraling out of control. First it was the betrothal, the lies, the secrets. Then her father's death, her brother's death, and her mother's disappearance. Now this. How much more of this could she take? She curled her fingers into her palms. *Where are you, Osaryn? My father trusted you.*

"There's an opening." Kael's voice broke through her tumultuous thoughts.

Ahead, a gray light seeped into the passageway. Ayianna's breath caught. Freedom.

They piled outside. Ayianna squinted, blinking away the underground's darkness. Images blurred into view as her eyes grew accustomed to the light. She halted. Dread swept over her like a black tarantula attacking its prey.

Dark clouds overshadowed a somber castle in the distance. The land was barren and vacant. The stale stench of decay hung on the crippled trees dotting the rocky terrain. She shivered and covered her nose with the edge of her cloak.

"To the very edge of evil we stumble." Kael rested his hand on the hilt of his sword. "Nganjo—the warden of the Abyss. Let us hope we go unnoticed."

Kael stepped away from the group and looked up at the towering cliffs behind them. Ayianna followed his gaze and her stomach sank. Hundreds of caves pocked its harsh face. Stone outcroppings like thousands of jagged teeth threatened to eat anyone foolish enough to scale them.

"Well, is there a way out?" Vian's pale face seemed even more insipid as he stared at the looming barrier of stone.

"Sure. Death," Desmond exclaimed.

"And I thought you were the optimist here," Vian said.

Kael motioned toward the cliffs. "The Ruzat Mountain Range is to the west. If we head that way, we might find a spot to climb out."

"Might." Desmond shook his head. "And which way is west?"

"That's easy." Kael scanned the terrain some more. "You can't get much farther north than Nganjo. But we must make camp before dark."

"We can't camp here." Ayianna glanced at the darkened castle with its spiky ramparts and piercing towers. "We've gone beyond the Perimeter. Don't you realize what that means?"

"We are in the company of the greatest evil that ever was." Vian tugged his cap off and shook out his red curls. "It is the breeding grounds for the Tóas, imps, and all manner of wickedness."

Ayianna looked at Vian in surprise.

"I didn't sleep through all my courses of study." Vian returned the cap to his head and adjusted his soiled tunic.

"But don't you see?" Ayianna drew the edges of her cloak together. "All those things you mentioned—they're held back by the Perimeter. We are trapped. Nothing can cross over from here."

"Nonsense." Desmond faced Vian. "Quit filling our minds with fanciful stories. Vian, I'm disappointed in you. Didn't your tutor teach you anything beyond infamous legends? What good has it done for you but instill fear in your heart?"

"Well . . . I . . . suspect the tutor had his reasons." Vian looked away. "It is imperative that Badara knows its neighbors."

"Suppose you're right, Desmond." Kael swung his bow from his shoulder. "If all these bard's tales are untrue, how do you explain the Perimeter and its lovely Manoa Stones?"

"Maybe the Manoa Stones are there to keep us out of Nganjo." Desmond raised his hands and gestured toward the darkened castle. "And perhaps to prevent us from achieving immortality."

Kael raised his eyebrows. "Now who is telling fanciful stories? Let's move out before we are discovered."

"I still don't want to camp here." Ayianna tightened her cloak against the chill snaking down her neck. "I feel exposed. As if something foreign and cold has wrenched away my heart."

"Don't worry, Ayianna." Desmond placed his arm around her shoulders. "You'll be fine. Just stay close to me."

23

KAEL TIGHTENED HIS JAW and scanned the dim horizon.

A sliver of the sun seeped between the clouds, clawing its red fingers across the sky as if fighting its descent. And then it was gone. Night painted the terrain in varied shades of charcoal gray, except for the faint, eerie glow emitting from the earth beyond the castle. Its unnatural olive light lengthened the shadows and plagued him.

The prince chuckled at Desmond's ridiculous tale. A venture Desmond swore his father and him had endured in the Zriab Desert hundreds of miles to the west—a venture, no doubt, at the expense of the inhabitants of Zajur.

"Oh, that's enough." Vian twirled his cap on his fingers.

Kael tightened his jaw

"One more?" Desmond took a swig from his waterskin and wiped his mouth.

"Okay, one more." Vian yawned, stretching atop his blanket.

"Well, this story was passed down to me by my uncle, Lord Ramiro." Desmond rocked backward. His blue eyes sparkled in mischievous delight. "You see, my great, great grandfather had several lovely daughters."

"Are you drinking mead?" Kael eyed Desmond's waterskin. Did he detect a whiff of fermented honey?

"No, and don't interrupt." Desmond grunted. He capped his waterskin and stuffed it into his pack. Turning to face Vian, he continued. "These young virgins were so enthralled with the legend of the unicorn they had decided they would be the first to capture one. They knew that only a virgin could actually beckon one. Thus, they absolutely refused the thought of marriage. They would sneak out and go in search of them for nights on end.

"Well, one night, they met a most handsome man named Nach. They forgot about the unicorns and became mesmerized by him instead. He invited the ladies to dine in his castle. He entertained them with wine and dance. He was, in every way, genteel and regal, but an ominous curse weighed heavily on his soul. Little did these love-struck maidens know, he was cursed to survive on the blood of virgins. The young women were never seen again, but some say they heard their screams as he drained the blood from their bodies."

Vian stared at Desmond. "That's not true, is it?"

"True or not, this story has always quickened the heart of any reluctant virgin and sped them toward marriage." Desmond glanced across the camp. "Perhaps I need to share this tale with her."

Kael followed his gaze to where Ayianna lay, curled up in a ball, looking wretched and alone without Liam. At least she had Desmond, even if he was an arrogant boar, but that thought left him nauseated. Why did her elven father betroth her to someone as despicable as Desmond? But her father was dead now, why would she continue with such a match? What did she see in him? Surely, she could do better.

"Well, it's a good thing we aren't virgins, then." Vian plopped his cap over his face. "We wouldn't want to worry about someone emptying us of our blood."

Desmond doubled over with laughter. Vian joined him, but humor had evaporated from his voice.

Kael shifted away from the others, pulling the wool blanket over his shoulders. His gaze rested on the withered tree at the edge of their campsite. No breeze whistled through its twisted limbs. Dead. Nothing lived in Nganjo, except the dead. How long had the land been cursed?

His thoughts drifted back to his wife and son, their warm smiles fading. His carefully buried grief exploded in his chest. Was the Shadow God bent on tormenting him? Was it not enough he had lost his wife already, but to lose his son and sister too?

Kael shut his eyes against the rising anger. The images flooded his mind for the thousandth time. The imp carcasses, his sister's throat slashed, his son's mangled body. He had failed them. Teron had put up a good fight, but one person against so many . . . The vow of friendship twisted his heart as he saw his best friend's headless body again.

Kael opened his eyes as bitterness rose like bile in his throat. He took a deep breath and forced his feelings into a dark corner. He didn't have time for sorrow or self-pity. He glanced at the darkened sky and vowed to Osaryn—if he was even listening—he'd never love again.

The night progressed without incident. A breeze picked up and moaned through the stark trees. He scanned the area for movement, but found none. He refused to reach beyond his sight. With the pocked cliffs at their backs, the only thing that stood between them and the Abyss was the old castle and a few outlying buildings. Who had built the castle? Had Stygian survived? Where were all the exiled creatures? Perhaps the queen of the underworld made her abode here rather than in the depths of the Abyss.

Too many questions and not enough answers. Kael shifted between the gnarled tree roots, but their knots still managed to poke his back. He glanced at the others. None remained awake. His own eyelids drooped. He should keep watch, but exhaustion muddled his thoughts. He closed his heavy eyes. Rest . . . that's what he needed.

Kael jolted awake.

Vian's pale face hovered over him. "It's Ayianna. She's gone."

"What do you mean gone?" Kael sprang to his feet and glanced around the campsite as he gathered his bearings. He caught sight of her wool blanket discarded a few yards away.

"Ayianna!" Desmond shouted in the distance.

"Tell the fool to hush. He'll bring the Abyss upon us," Kael snapped, trying to keep his own voice down.

Desmond stormed into the campsite. "I'm going to kill her!"

"Keep your voice down. She wouldn't have gone off by herself." Kael peered into the green-yellow glow immersing Nganjo.

"Traipsing alone all over the countryside? Remember Dagmar?"

"That was different." Kael dumped his blanket on his pack. "She wouldn't have gone off on her own in a place like this."

"Maybe she had to, you know . . . " The prince shrugged, his face flushing as red as his hair. "Relieve herself."

"Well, let's spread out. We can find her quicker that way," Desmond said.

Vian nodded. "I'll go with Desmond, and Kael, you can go that way."

"Spread out . . . right." Kael shook his head. He had never met anyone so spineless. And *this* was supposed to be the next king of Badara? He looked back over his shoulder at Desmond. "And no shouting—she couldn't have gone far."

Ayianna mounted the steps of the castle. She did not know what had awakened her, perhaps a soft melody or a gentle touch. Maybe she was dreaming. A dark splendor called to her, drew her near. She desired it. It beckoned, and she pursued. She was the huntress. Where was her quarry?

She glided through the halls. Torches sprang to life as she passed by, giving light for her passage and then quickly extinguishing. She caught flashes of crude stonework and faded tapestries, but her intent was farther ahead. The air chilled the deeper she went, cooling the perspiration on her skin. She welcomed the cold against the heat rushing through her body. She was getting closer.

At the end of the hall, two double doors graced the wall, disappearing into the darkness above. She pressed against them, and they swung open silently.

A fire burned in a large stone hearth, flooding her vision with light, but the air remained cold. The brick walls and the polished floor gleamed. The room was barren, except for a small couch in front of the fire.

"How pleased I am to finally meet you," a voice said. "You have no idea how dreadfully lonely it can be here."

Ayianna turned. A handsome gentleman dressed in burgundy and black stood before her. A grin broke his sallow face as he gazed at her. His bright, hungry eyes swallowed her whole, and she dared not look away. Fever burned in her veins. Why was she so hot? Was she sick?

She stepped closer. "Who are you?"

"Do you not know? I am the object of your desire, pretty one."

Yes. She desired him, yet somewhere deep in her soul a faint warning repulsed her. She shouldn't be here.

"Come, recline by the fire. It is rather chilly."

Ayianna glided toward the hearth, the attraction growing stronger, the air growing colder. She shivered, but welcomed the icy breath on her feverish skin. Inside the room, a layer of ice covered the bricks, sweating and creating ribbons of icicles down the wall, pooling and refreezing along the floor. Was she dreaming? Soft music slithered through the air and tugged at her. She glanced up at him.

"Or perhaps, my lady, you would like to dance?" He stepped to her side and held out his hand.

She could scarcely breathe. She slid her hand into his, his skin cool against hers, soothing the fever raging in her body. He never broke her gaze as they waltzed around the room. He drew her closer, so close she could feel his pulse race.

At the edge of the cliffs, Desmond, Kael, and Vian regrouped. No sign of Ayianna. Kael clenched his teeth. How could she be so foolish?

Vian yelped. "There's a light in the castle!"

Desmond gasped. "She wouldn't."

"We are not alone," Kael said.

Shadowy objects bobbed across the barren land, going in and out of the stone dwellings surrounding the castle.

"What is she doing in there?" Desmond asked. "*Women*!"

The men rushed to the castle. They darted between boulders and scraggly, nude trees. Kael slowed as he reached a wide river. Its sluggish waters wended their way through the rocky terrain and separated them from the castle. Farther down, a stone bridge rose from the riverbanks.

A chill ran down Kael's spine as a thought pricked his mind. "Desmond, is Ayianna a virgin?" Kael asked as they reached the bridge.

Desmond raised his eyebrows. "Pardon me?"

"Well, you two are betrothed, and you don't strike me as the kind of man who likes to wait."

"That is none of your business!"

"Believe me, I'd rather not know. But what if your uncle's tale was true? Look." Kael pointed to a large boulder in front of the bridge with a faded inscription. Characters of an ancient language had been etched into the rock.

"What is that?" Vian bent over, his hands on his knees, and took deep breaths.

"It's Táchil." Kael studied the characters.

Vian peered closer. "It looks like a drunken chicken with a hammer wrote that."

"I thought that all royalty was schooled in the ancient arts and languages."

"I might have missed that class," Vian said, his face coloring.

"What does it say?" Desmond asked.

"*Kotáwisil twamns, isür wileíth ulin, ruza isür wileíth lechin taechil. Taltan* Nach." Kael read aloud.

Desmond placed his hands on his hips. "In the common tongue. You don't have to flaunt your knowledge."

Kael rubbed his nose. A sour smell like a clogged privy rolled up from the river and burned his eyes. "For the most part, it states that Lord Nach welcomes you and warns you can never leave."

"That's impossible." Desmond's eyes widened. "It was only a fable."

Vian covered his nose with the edge of his cloak. "What is that smell?"

Kael unsheathed his sword and started across the bridge. His elven senses stretched out before him, searching for the familiar essence of Ayianna. Nothing. What if they were too late?

Kael shoved his doubts aside and tried to remember everything he had read about Nganjo.

"But the sign!" Vian ran up behind him. "What about the sign? If we cross this bridge we won't be able to leave."

"We will worry about that later."

Kael glanced into the strange river as he rushed past. His eyes stung and watered from its stench. Thick waters churned through the channel as corpses of men and women of all races rolled beneath the poisoned waves. He caught only glimpses of their bloated and discolored faces—faces stricken and frozen in horror. He averted his eyes.

"Dead people—in the river!" Vian blurted out.

"Quiet, you fool." Kael ducked behind one of the giant pillars jutting up from the ground and waited for the others to join him.

"Oh." Vian slumped against a pillar. "We're going to die."

Kael ignored him and scanned the castle grounds. Large, stone steps led up to a great doorway. No guarded gate, no heavy door, no barricade built to keep trespassers out. He could sense nothing but a great void. What would possess Ayianna to enter the castle?

What if she hadn't come this way? Kael inhaled and tightened his grip on the sword's hilt. She'd better be in there, or they'd risk waking the residing evil for nothing. He turned to Vian.

"I'll go first," Kael whispered and scanned the area again. "Where's Desmond?"

"He was right behind me." Vian glanced over his shoulder.

"Never mind." Kael inched around the pillar. "Once I reach the stairs, you follow."

Vian raised his eyebrows, but nodded.

Kael sprinted from his hiding place and slammed into a giant troll holding a crude mace.

"Where did he come from?" Kael dodged a swipe of the troll's weapon.

"Who cares—just get rid of him." Desmond appearing suddenly from behind a pillar next to the castle's steps.

"Me?" Kael jumped out of the way from another swing as the mace swooshed past his ear.

"He doesn't look too bright to me, or fast." Vian peered from the other side of the pillar. "Maybe you could outrun him."

"You slay the troll, and I'll go rescue the girl." Desmond bounded up the steps.

"Vian!" Kael yelled.

"Oh no, I don't slay trolls."

"Just distract it." Kael swung, but his sword bounced off the troll's thick, bumpy skin.

The troll laughed. Its booming voice echoed off the surrounding cliffs.

"How?"

"Figure it out. Throw rocks at it or something." Kael rolled to the side as the troll's stubby foot nearly squashed him.

Vian scooped up a large rock and threw it at the troll. The stone thumped against its face and bounced off. The troll shook its head and turned its beady eyes toward him.

"Ah, Kael, your plan?"

The troll lumbered toward Vian. Its footsteps thundered in the eerie stillness, kicking up plumes of dust. The prince darted behind a pillar across the courtyard. Kael grabbed his longbow and nocked an arrow, waiting for an opening.

"Any day now!" Vian yelled, weaving between pillars.

The troll bounded after him.

Kael leveled the arrow, but couldn't get a clean shot.

Vian dodged the troll's mace, but tripped. He hit the ground hard, and the troll's gnarled fingers enclosed him. The monster's pocked face broke into a toothless grin as it swung Vian by the foot.

"Now would be a good time!" Vian shouted. He flailed his fists against the troll's rough hide.

Kael sent the first arrow flying into the creature's neck. The troll gagged and gasped. It dropped Vian as it scratched at the embedded arrow.

Kael aimed his next arrow at the monster's eye. The arrow plunged into its soft target, sinking deep into the troll's small brain. The troll roared and collapsed.

Vian stood and dusted his clothes. He glared at Kael, his face as red as his hair. "Never, ever use me as a distraction again."

"Come on." Kael dashed up the steps.

24

CAPTIVATED BY HER delightful partner, Ayianna continued to whirl about the room in an enchanted waltz. The gentleman's presence kept her questions at bay, her fever in check, and she decided she must be in a dream—a strange, but wonderful, dream. His hands pressed against her back, and she leaned into his compelling embrace.

"My lady," he whispered softly in her ear. "You are ssso graceful . . . ssso beautiful and pure. So innosssent."

He kissed Ayianna's temple. Her pulse raced. For a moment, she felt his passion become hers. He wanted her, and she was willing.

She would promise him anything. Ayianna glanced up, but her insides went rigid as revulsion ruptured her dream-like trance.

His sallow face contorted. His lips parted into a hideous smile, revealing two slender eyeteeth. A forked tongue flickered between his teeth as his eyes devoured her.

Ayianna tried to pull away, but his embrace imprisoned her. He wrenched her against him and nuzzled her neck. She screamed as the sharp fangs pierced her skin. A burst of icy venom poured into her body, and her vision darkened.

Kael's blood ran cold as Ayianna's scream echoed throughout the castle. The eerie music had ceased and sounds of scraping drew near. Certain the scream had come from ahead, Kael rushed toward the large double doors and slammed through them.

A man lifted his head—no, not a man, a beast. Blood dripped from his gaping mouth. In his arms, Ayianna hung lifelessly.

"Nach!" Kael yelled. He charged, sword in hand. "Let her go."

Nach flung Ayianna aside and leapt into the air. Large, leathery wings burst from his back, ripping his clothes. He belched a ball of flame, and Kael dove out of the way. The winged-lord circled the room and shrieked.

Kael ran to Ayianna, but Nach lunged and slashed at him. Sharp nails raked across Kael's shoulder. He spun and drove his sword deep into the monster's belly.

Nach collapsed, but a laugh gurgled in his throat. "You cannot kill me." His forked tongue licked blood from his lips, and he glared at Kael. "It isss ussselesss. She isss dying."

He slumped over, crushing his leathery wings beneath him. His eyes closed, but his lips cracked in a sardonic smile.

Desmond burst into the hall, followed by the scratching of a hundred scurrying feet echoing through the halls. In the distance, came the sound of flapping wings and high-pitched screams. A chill ran down his back.

"Where have you been all this time?" Kael gritted his teeth and rushed to Ayianna's side.

"I got—" Desmond faltered.

Kael lifted Ayianna. Her body sagged in his arms, and her head flopped against his chest. The weight of his failure escalated.

"What happened? Is she all right?" Desmond strode over to where Nach lay and prodded the lord with his foot.

"What in all of Nälu is this?"

Kael hoisted Ayianna over his shoulder. "Where's Vian?"

"Run!" Vian burst into the hall. "Harpies!"

Kael and the others rushed outside and into an angry mob of trolls. He darted left and passed by large, cage-like buildings made of stone. Shimmering eyes glared at him from behind the iron bars, but he didn't stop to investigate. The ground shuddered as the trolls gave pursuit.

Desmond and Vian flanked Kael as they outran the trolls, who were now peering in and out of stone buildings, looking for them. Dogs snarled and howled behind them.

Kael ducked between boulders, but a large hound leapt in front of him. Tremors shook its hairless, wrinkly skin, and slobber dribbled from its long incisors. White eyes bore into Kael as if they alone could destroy him.

Kael stumbled but caught himself before he fell. He repositioned Ayianna and fumbled with his sword. Footsteps pounded behind him as the hound advanced. He couldn't get a proper grip on the hilt. The hound lunged, but Desmond's blade plunged forward and slashed its throat. Kael shifted Ayianna and dashed to the right. Ahead, the eerie light rose from the Abyss.

"They're here!" Vian gasped, his eyes wide with horror. "Oh, we are all going to die!"

A large, bat-like creature dropped from the sky. It bore the slender face of a woman, too narrow to be human. Dirty, scraggly hair topped her head like a rooster's comb. Her shriveled skin stretched across sharp bones, and her eyes burned with an insatiable hunger. She dove for Kael, no doubt to retrieve her master's dinner.

Kael leapt out of the way as the harpy sped past. She soared into the air and corkscrewed back to earth. Her lizard-like tail swung dangerously close to his head. He ducked, but one of the poisonous barbs scratched the back of his neck, blasting fire through his skin.

Vian jumped to Kael's side, his blade hissing through air, and struck one of the harpy's wings. Shrieking, she tumbled to the ground. She flipped the knotted hair from her face and scrambled after Kael. He lifted his sword arm to fend her off, but it wavered. Or was it him? Was the harpy's poison so quick?

He staggered back as his vision shifted and nausea burned his throat. The harpy's thin lips twisted into a sneer. Her knobby arm shot forward, and Kael jerked Ayianna out of the way. Her claws bit into Kael's thigh instead.

He stumbled away as Vian decapitated the harpy. Dazed, Kael shook his head, but the world kept spinning. Ayianna's weight doubled. He'd drop her, if he wasn't careful.

Desmond grasped his shoulder, whispering, but the words didn't make any sense. The merchant's frown twisted into anger. He grabbed Ayianna's arm and pulled.

Of course. Kael shifted her limp body to Desmond's shoulder, but the lack of her weight unbalanced him, and he fell to his knees. His vertigo slowly lessened and a headache blossomed in the back of his skull. He rubbed his neck. The harpy's barb had only brushed the surface of the skin, and hopefully its poisonous effect would be short-lived. For that, he was thankful, if not a little nauseous.

"Look out!" Vian exclaimed.

Shrieks filled the night sky as more harpies descended upon them. Would this be the end? Kael clenched his jaw against the dizziness and headache. He would not go down without a fight. He stood, grabbed his bow, and hurled arrows into the mass of wings and claws. His unsteady aim still managed to hit some of the harpies.

More hounds burst from the shadows. He nocked his last arrow, but it sailed above their heads. Vian charged and swung into the pack, cutting one down. Déjà vu slammed into Kael, and it was Teron rushing, sword raised, defending his family from the imps. Kael shook his head, and his vision cleared. He wrenched his sword free of its scabbard and slashed at the others.

Vian yelped. A brown splotchy hound had the prince by the leg and was dragging him away. Kael lunged to Vian's side and ran the hound through. He helped the prince to his feet and scanned the area for Desmond and Ayianna.

Desmond stood several yards to the left in the middle of a harpy's assault. Ayianna lay crumpled on the ground. Anger surged through him. How could the fool have discarded her like that? He rushed to her side.

The harpy dove and swiped. Kael ducked, but her claws caught Desmond across the ear. He swore and jabbed the sword into her side. She flopped to the ground and wobbled away.

Kael bent to pick up Ayianna.

"Kael!" Vian hollered.

The last hound barreled toward Kael, snarling. He grabbed his sword and swung, catching the hound's front leg.

The hound yelped and tumbled forward. It scrambled for traction, but its momentum carried it over the edge of the cliff.

Kael knelt to catch his breath. Below, howling winds tore at the creviced canyon stretching forever into the depths of the earth.

He inched away from the mighty vacuum of the canyon and glanced over at Ayianna, but Desmond held her. At least she was safe for the moment.

Vian stood next to them, favoring his right leg. He brandished his blade in front of him. Kael tightened his grip on his sword and turned to face the creatures he was certain he'd find.

A dozen harpies surrounded them, perched on boulders and other stone formations jutting from the rocky soil. Their red eyes glared as if daring them to flee. Why didn't they attack?

A sallow face loomed above them as his thin lips curved into a sneer—Nach. He stood next to a particularly large harpy and ran his slender fingers through her wild hair. "Did you think you could essscape?"

"How are you alive?" Desmond shifted Ayianna in his arms. Where was his sword?

"I am immortal." Nach laughed as he stretched his leathery wings. "But you are not!"

The winged-lord rushed toward Desmond.

Brilliant flames exploded from the ground in front of Desmond. The force knocked Nach backward and dispersed the harpies. The winged-lord shrieked and clawed at his eyes as prisms of light soared into the darkness. The fiery streams swelled and converged into two giant men, but just as quickly they dissolved into the flames and formed a dome of flickering white. Ruwachs? Kael whirled around, searching the shadows. Who had summoned them?

"To the caves!" a rough voice commanded. A tall, bald man materialized out of the shadows and strode into the dome. Around his neck hung a stone, pulsating with light. He quickly drew his cloak about him and concealed the pendant. A leather patch covered his left eye, but the remaining one reprimanded them. Nevin Darin.

Kael sheathed his sword. "How did you—"

"No time. Go!"

Kael raced toward the great cliffs towering in the night. The blinding light arched high into the sky and dissolved as they charged into the caves. Spasms of light stung his vision until his eyes adjusted to the darkness around him. Vian and Desmond stood next to him, Desmond still cradling Ayianna in his arms.

A rush of wind and heavy steps echoed off the walls as the tall form of Darin strode into the cave and stopped. Kael held his breath.

"What happened? Why did you stray from the trail?"

Kael lowered his head. "I am without an excuse."

"Darin, I presume?" Desmond shifted Ayianna to his other shoulder and exposed his right ear. Three slashes cut across it and dribbled blood on to his neck and tunic.

"We have no time for pleasantries," Darin snapped, and then his gaze fell on Ayianna. "What is wrong with the girl?"

"Nach," Kael said.

Darin turned Ayianna's head and examined her neck. Blood trickled from two small wounds, her skin ashen and her lips blue.

"The venom is fast. I will take her, and you three will have to keep up," Darin lifted Ayianna from Desmond's arms and rushed ahead through the dark cave.

Kael ran to keep up as guilt and anger surged through him. He had known better, but instead he had listened to lies. He had been weak, and he despised weakness.

25

IT SEEMED LIKE hours to Kael as Nevin Darin navigated the Grenze caves. Every second drew Ayianna closer to death. By the time they had reached Raemoja, green streaks of poison stretched like spider webs across her neck, face, and arms.

Kael rushed after Darin through the ruins and into the old courtyard as the eastern horizon began to lighten. The crumbling walls shadowed a handful of tents. Dawn's silence enveloped the world in a false sense of peace. A layer of frost lined the stones and crunched underfoot. The mountain air already tasted of winter's first breath and stung Kael's lungs.

Darin strode toward one of the tents and ducked inside.

Kael and the others piled in after him. In the shadowy recess of the tent, he could make out a single cot and a lump of someone snoring softly.

"Saeed!"

The elderly elf scrambled to his feet and grabbed the blanket falling from his shoulders. "What is the meaning of this? *Yetakoith taheza!*"

A light sprang up in the center of the tent, and Kael blinked in the sudden brightness. A small globe, much like the one he had, chased away the shadows of the tent. He glanced at the others. Filth and blood covered their faces and clothes.

Darin's presence filled the tent as he hunched over, cradling Ayianna against his chest. Her face was deathly pale, her lips blue. The green web-like streaks spreading across her skin darkened to black and stretched down her arms to her fingers.

He shuffled forward, the back of his shoulders brushing the canvas ceiling. "The girl has been bitten by the harpy lord." He laid her on Saeed's now vacant cot. "She is nearing death."

"Harpy lord?" Saeed pushed Darin out of the way. He bent over Ayianna and pressed his fingers against her temples. He cupped her chin in his hand, turned her head, and inspected her wounds. "Darin, get Nerissa. She might have enough kulin to save her."

Darin stepped out of the tent, and the flaps slapped back into place, but not before a draft of cold air slithered over them. Kael shivered and pulled his cloak tighter around his shoulders. He stared at the young woman before him, her breathing shallow, her skin hauntingly green. He prayed, hoping he hadn't failed again.

Before Kael could get lost in his thoughts, Darin returned with a merwoman. Her white braids were swept up into a tousled bun above her ridged forehead. She gathered her gray robe, knelt down, and examined Ayianna's wound. She inspected her arms and legs. "Why did you bring her here? The venom has almost completed its task." She glanced up at Darin, her eyes as cold as the icy rivers of the north. "Stand ready in case we are too late."

Kael clenched his jaw as an anger burned in his gut. How dare she reprimand them for trying to save Ayianna's life! Were the merfolk so heartless?

"How did she find him?" Nerissa shook out her satchel and grasped a dark bag. From it, she slid a vial. "Is he not confined by the Perimeter?"

Kael exhaled his mounting tension and told her what had happened.

Nerissa's fingers brushed against the small puncture wounds on Ayianna's neck. She uncorked the vial and dribbled the contents into them. Kael held his breath as the liquid fizzed and sizzled. Holding her hand over Ayianna's forehead, Nerissa closed her eyes and spoke in her native tongue.

"*Nawaeli Akonamalihi, ako powakolua'i kakoha li hi. Naloa'hi, lipeya'hi. Kua kakoha li hi. Naloa'kua li hi lakipe. Maloa lewapohi akiwo maeko mawa. Lakipe'in hi.*"

"Another blanket please," Nerissa said, her voice fluid and soft.

Vian yanked one from his leather bag and handed it to her.

"Is she going to be all right?" Kael crossed his arms and leaned closer.

"We will not know until evening. By then the kulin may have consumed the poison and restored her body, if we were not too late." Silence hung on her words. "She must stay warm and observed. If her condition worsens, give her three more drops of this." Nerissa rose and handed Kael the vial.

"Will her neck remain scarred?" Desmond rubbed the back of his neck.

Nerissa paused at the entrance of the tent and faced Desmond. "Cursed wounds never heal. If she survives, she will have more than a scar to worry about."

Kael twisted the vial in his hands, the weight of his failures suffocating him. He needed some fresh air. He handed the vial to Desmond.

"Wait a minute, what about my ear?" Desmond lifted his hands.

Kael clenched his jaw. "What about it? It's not going to kill you."

"Those claws weren't exactly clean." Desmond glanced up at the prince.

Vian stepped back. "Don't look at me. I'm not cleaning it. If you'll excuse me, I have some questions that need answers. I'll put in a word about your ear." He grimaced. "What's left of it."

Desmond's eyes narrowed. He turned his back to the others and sat down next to the cot.

Kael took one last glance at Ayianna and followed Vian out of the tent. They made their way across the courtyard. Smells of blended herbs wafted from a black pot bubbling a few feet away, reminding him he hadn't eaten in days. Or was it? He rubbed his tired face.

Leora and Eloith fluttered past, carrying a loaf of rye bread between them.

"Rabbit soup. It is a couple of days old, but it will fill you," Leora said. She and Eloith placed the loaf on the table. "Darin, can you bring the bowls? Be careful, they are hot."

The half-giant grunted. "One mother was enough for me."

"Tisk!" Leora fluttered into the air. "Would you rather I serve it cold?"

"Nobody likes cold soup."

Darin strolled over to the small fire. Moments later, he returned with three steaming bowls. He handed them out and sat next to Kael. Kael nodded his thanks and sloshed the chucks of potatoes, onions, and rabbit around in his bowl. His stomach growled. He closed his eyes and reveled in the pungent smell. Food—even if it was soup.

Nevin Saeed reclined at the table and toyed with his braided beard. Even though he just woke up, he had already donned his traveling cloak, a knapsack, and his sword. Did he expect trouble so early? Next to him sat Nevin Unai, Saeed's deputy headmaster and the only teacher who survived the massacre. Aside from Darin, he was the only other guardian eating.

Eldwyn sat across from them. Rigid and dressed in fine embroidered silks, the Esusamor Elf could have passed for royalty or a pompous noble, but Kael knew better. He had been a good friend to his father when he was still alive. Lazar, the only Haruzo this side of the desert, conversed with him. His lithe form draped over his chair with feline grace and casualness the other guardians lacked. He was also the youngest of them.

Nerissa sat adjacent to Lazar with the content of her satchel spread out before her, minus the vial of kulin. She replaced them in their appropriate pockets. A few conch shells, a worn journal, and an inkwell remained.

Toward the back of the courtyard, the stout dwarf kept to himself, scowling as he sharpened his battle-axe. His bushy, brown eyebrows furrowed even more as he concentrated on the rhythm of his whetting stone. Out of all the guardians, Hadrian was the busiest, being responsible for three dwarven clans. He was also the most stubborn, at least according to Saeed. Kael had yet to work with him.

Kael tore a chunk from the loaf of rye and sopped up the remaining broth. Behind him, Leora and Eloith spoke in hushed tones, their voices like delicate chimes singing on a breeze. If he listened long enough, he'd certainly fall asleep.

Saeed cleared his throat. "How did you end up in Nganjo?"

Kael finished chewing the bitter bread. What was he going to tell him? That he strayed, allowed his companions and the forest to sway his thoughts? He knew he should have stayed on the Naajiso trail, but he didn't. Why? He could blame Desmond. He could create reasons and explanations, but none of it mattered. He glanced up at Saeed, expecting to see fury in his amber eyes, but instead they held compassion.

Kael sighed. "I failed to stick to the trail."

"Quite an adventure, I hear." Saeed motioned toward the fairies. "In failing, you succeeded. Interesting how it all worked out, no?"

Kael frowned. "How did Darin know where to find us?"

"Eloith told us you had fallen into the tunnels, most of which lead to Nganjo." Saeed twisted a braid between his fingers. "I had suspected the enemy of using those old caves."

"When we were down there, we saw people in chains. They were present, but yet they weren't." Kael folded his arms and leaned forward. "When Ayianna tried to touch a young woman, she said it felt like she stuck her hand into hot porridge."

Saeed's brows knitted together. "That is peculiar indeed." He stroked his beard and leaned back in his seat.

"We recognized some of the people. They were from Badara." Kael glanced at Vian and returned his attention to the headmaster. "Ayianna saw her mother."

Saeed tugged on a braid. "If I am not mistaken, the people you saw are connected to the spell the dancers had cast." He glanced at Unai. "What do you make of this curse? Have you come across anything like this in your studies?"

Unai finished his last bite and smoothed the few strands of hair he had left across his head. "Well, did anybody see how the curse was actually performed? Was blood involved?"

"I didn't see any blood," Kael said. "But during the festival, these dancers chanted and danced in the inner courtyard. One of them had a pronged staff. The longer they chanted, an orb of energy began to form and grow brighter on the tip of the prongs, but that's all I know. I grabbed Ayianna and jumped into one of the pools of water."

Unai raised an eyebrow. "Interesting, I doubt I would have thought of that, but nevertheless effective. Then what happened?"

Kael shrugged. "Later, we saw the dancers give a man called Derk a goblet, and he made a toast. I didn't sense any other spells, except when he called down fire to consume the book of Thar'ryn. Then they hailed him as king."

Unai scratched his ear and leaned forward. "If what you saw underground were the souls of the people influenced by the dancers' spell, then I would assume the plains people have been placed under the Twammurt Curse. It binds people's souls, locking them into eternal bondage and servitude to the curse's source, or seed as we call it. It appears," Unai turned his attention to Saeed, "that Semine has chosen Derk to be the seed."

"Then it is as I feared." Saeed ran his fingers over his braided beard. "Semine has tainted her soul with the breath of the Tóas Dikon."

The guardians grew silent. Kael glanced around. They sat there, staring at the table.

But before he could speak, Vian coughed. "What exactly is the Tóas Dikon?"

Saeed eyed the prince. "It is a pity when the future rulers of Nälu do not even know their own history. We will all pay the cost of ignorance."

Eldwyn snorted. "Speak for the humans. We in Zurial see to the education of our people."

"Badara seeks to educate its citizens of what they need to know and not in fanciful philosophies." Vian lifted his chin. "I, on the other hand, have been instructed in such knowledge, but I've only seen the Tóas to be nothing more than words to scare people, to give meaning to the meaningless, an assumption to hang all of our fears, unmet desires, and dreams."

"Well spoken." Saeed nodded. "For many people that is true. But tell me, does your experience in Nganjo suggest otherwise?"

"Perhaps." Vian held the headmaster's gaze. "As High Guardian, what do you say the Tóas Dikon is?"

"Apart from what I have witnessed, I speak only from what Karasi, the Sacred Pearl, has revealed. The Tóas Dikon is the tainting of the gifts the Shadow God had bestowed upon his servant Taethza, before she rebelled against Zohar."

"The queen of the underworld?" Vian fell back in his chair and shook his head. "This gets more convoluted as we go. Do you actually believe that?"

Saeed smiled. "Where do you think Semine got the power to bind the souls of people?"

"So what you're saying, then, is that the Tóas Dikon is power to do one's bidding."

"Not exactly." Saeed tugged at a braid. "It is power to a certain extent, but overall it carries out only one agenda, Taethza's, who would like nothing more than to defeat the Shadow God."

The prince eyed Saeed. "I have to agree that something is at work here, but, to be honest, I'm not sure what it is."

"Fair enough."

"So, how do we break this curse?" Vian raised his hands. "There must be a way."

Unai scratched his round belly. "Some people can fight it, like Saeed did, but most do not have the strength on their own to withstand such a spell. If I remember correctly, there is a tonic called Dwalu. When a cursed person drinks it, he or she receives clarity and the ability to overpower the bindings of the mind."

Vian's eyes narrowed. "How do we find this tonic?"

"Well, that is the problem." Unai raised his hands in a half-shrug. "All the scrolls and tomes of the guardians have recently been destroyed or stolen."

"Someone else must have it." Vian glanced around the table. His gaze settled on Kael. "What about the elves?"

Before Kael could say anything, Eldwyn spoke. "No nation has been granted privilege to the guardians' sacred knowledge."

"You can't be serious?" Vian's face flushed. His eyes sought the headmaster. "This is ridiculous. How has the Guardian Circle ever helped Nälu? You hide away in the north as the nations go about their business. You do not care whether they succeed or fail, and now, when Nälu needs you, you don't have the answers?"

"Calm yourself," Saeed said quietly. "You do not fully understand the situation."

Vian stood. "I am Prince Vian of Badara. My father is missing, his kingdom overthrown, and his subjects cursed. I want to see action on the part of the people who call themselves guardians."

Kael tore his gaze from Vian's red face and glanced at Saeed. The headmaster studied the prince. His amber eyes blazed clear and focused. His presence carried so much wisdom and strength. Didn't Vian see that?

"The plight of your father and the plains people has been duly noted." Saeed raised his bushy eyebrows. "But action based on insufficient information brings about inferior solutions and, at times, greater problems."

Vian clenched and unclenched his jaw in the prolonged silence. His glare softened. "I'm not that big of a fool to go rushing into something unprepared." Vian sat back down. "So what do you suggest?"

"Saeed?" Leora fluttered down to the table. "I know where we might find some information about the tonic.

Remember when Njira appointed the first guardians? Perhaps you were still too young, but the chieftain of the Haruzo hosted the Guardian Circle for centuries until they built Dagmar."

Saeed nodded. "You are right. Then we shall send someone to Bonpazur."

"What about my father?" Vian asked.

Darin stretched his legs out beneath the table. "He is in the dungeons."

"Then we should free him."

"We cannot go marching into Badara right now." The half-giant adjusted the leather eye patch and leveled his remaining eye at Vian. "We must have a plan."

"Then, let's make one." Vian glared at the guardians.

"Be patient, young one." Leora glided over to him. "You of all people know the formalities of ruling a kingdom. The Guardian Circle oversees much more."

Kael shifted in his seat. The lack of sleep and a full stomach pulled at his eyelids. Couldn't they finish the conversation later?

Saeed let go of his beard and stood. "So where does this leave us?"

Leora held up her hand and counted on her fingers. "First, we have the attack on Dagmar, the thievery of the vault's contents, and the kidnapping of the Sacred Pearl. Second, we have a missing king and a curse. Third, I think it is safe to say that Semine and Derk are behind it all. Have I left anything out?"

Saeed shook his head. He clasped his hands behind his back and paced the hall.

"Wait, what about the people after Ayianna?" Kael's gaze followed him. "Maybe they're connected to all this."

"It is difficult to tell." Saeed's forehead furrowed. Had Kael detected a slight shake of the head? Saeed shrugged.

"Perhaps when she wakes she will have more information for us."

"Do you believe the attack on Dagmar and the happenings at Badara are related?" Vian asked.

"Perhaps." Saeed tugged at his beard and continued pacing.

"If you ask me," Unai glanced at the prince, "Semine obviously discovered the curse in the records Imaran stole from the vault." He turned his attention back to Saeed. "If you would have listened to me and had those scrolls destroyed, we would not be dealing with this."

"I support your theory that Semine is the culprit behind the attack and the curse, but . . . " Saeed shook his head, his voice thin and tired. "Knowledge in and of itself remains neutral. It is what we do with it that makes it dangerous. Ignorance will bring us to greater ruin."

"Yes," Kael said. "And with knowledge comes responsibility."

"Spoken like a true elven lord." Eldwyn clasped the table's edge and dipped his head. "Your father would be proud."

Kael bowed his head momentarily. "May he rest in peace."

"As guardians." Saeed faced the table. "We have the ultimate responsibility to the Shadow God for the care of the nations. If Semine and Derk are employing the Tóas, we can assume that their plans are influenced by Taethza." He glanced around at the others. "I do not think they will stop at the plains."

"What are you suggesting?" Eldwyn leaned forward and braced himself on the table.

"That each of you return to your respected cities. Inform them of the threat that gathers in the plains. Ask them to take up the Alliance colors once more for the sake of Nälu."

"That is it? That is your plan?" Hadrian's moustache jumped with each word.

"Will not happen." Lazar shook his head. "The highlanders have severed ties with Nälu."

"The dwarves care nothing for the plains people." Hadrian stood. "Their kind has brought it on themselves, I tell you. First, the empty religion of the Nuja, and now this."

"True enough." Eldwyn nodded his head in agreement with the dwarf. "Man has chosen the path of Arashel. We should leave them to their demise."

Saeed's gaze wandered over the guardians' faces, flickering for a moment on Kael's. "We cannot. We have the prophecy to consider."

Kael cocked an eyebrow. What prophecy? The others remained quiet, their gazes locked on Saeed. The headmaster retrieved a tattered, old book from his knapsack and flipped it open.

"The Morning Star shined in the dark, blinding the sighted." Tremors shook his gnarled hands as he held it open. "Death and her loyal subjects defeated, but in shadows, they remain. Twice more Zohar's Star will shine, but let not Death find him, nor the dagger. So listen well, Guardians of Nälu, guard the dagger that in slewing released the Star, lest they be found and the enemy unbound." Saeed closed the book and returned it to his knapsack.

Kael glanced at the others.

Pensive scowls etched their faces except Nerissa. She reclined, her angular face smooth and calm, her eyes closed. Prince Vian merely raised his eyebrows and shrugged.

"You have read only a part of the prophecy." Unai's fingers brushed a pendent hanging from his thick neck. "Is there not something about the shield of Chai and the nine stones becoming one?"

"Yes, Unai, you are correct, but the Perimeter stands strong. We are not in the final days as of yet." Saeed clasped his hands together and sat. "But I believe Semine and Derk are taking it upon themselves to usher in the end of Nälu."

"Bah!" Hadrian shuffled over to the table. "What evidence do you have?"

Saeed cocked his head. "Have you not been listening? What of Dagmar's destruction, the kidnapped pearl, and the overthrow of Badara?"

"Perhaps, but how do you connect them to the prophecy?" Hadrian folded his arms over the butt of his battle-ax.

"Mostly rumors and speculation, but, at this point, we need to at least consider it."

Kael rubbed his face. How long was this meeting going to go on for? He had more questions than answers, and the need for sleep buzzed in the back of his mind.

"I have heard some of the Nuja worshippers mention the dagger." Unai leaned over the table. "I believe Semine is searching for it again."

"Perhaps that is why she attacked Dagmar." Leora paced the table top.

Saeed shook his head. "She knows we do not have it." He leaned forward. "Taethza seeks the end of Nälu, and anyone who embraces her power will find themselves achieving her goal."

"Why does she want to destroy Nälu?" Vian asked.

"Revenge." Unai adjusted the robes over his belly. "Vituko banished her from Zohar. Of course it is more complicated, but we do not have time to get into all the details."

"And most of it is speculation." Saeed raised his bushy eyebrows and sat back. "Semine is only the pawn. A means to an end, and in order for Taethza to be released from the underworld—"

"She would need the dagger." Unai straightened. "That is where the prophecy comes into play."

How did Ayianna and her family tie into all this? Kael stifled a yawn and shifted in his seat. What did the prophecy say again? He rolled its words around in his mind. Something about a star and a sacrifice and dagger. Guard the dagger, but the guardians didn't have it.

Kael straightened. That had to be it. The men after Ayianna were searching for the dagger. He opened his mouth to speak, but Saeed raised an eyebrow, his eyes alight with dawn's approach, and then glanced away.

"If we do nothing," Saeed continued. "Derk and Semine will release Taethza from the underworld and ravage all of Nälu. Their destruction will be far worse than we can imagine. The prophecy warned us of this danger, and today we must face it whether or not Man has provoked their own destruction."

Kael glanced around the table. The guardians fell silent, their faces wrinkled in thought. The tension in the air was heavy like a great storm on the horizon, its foreboding thunderclouds building in the sky, impatient to empty its rage on the lands below.

Saeed lifted his head. "If Taethza is released from the underworld, we, the guardians, will have failed the people of Nälu. Do not think your nations will remain unscathed from her wrath." His gaze swept over the guardians. "If we refuse our responsibility, the blood of the forsaken will be on our hands. Then when our silver cords of Zohar are cut, we will find our golden bowls smashed against the rocks. We will be cast into the Abyss."

Kael stared at his dirt encrusted nails. Was his bowl already smashed? He certainly failed enough for Vituko to remove it. He hadn't refused any of his responsibilities. He had fulfilled his duty to his father, taken care of his son and sister . . . until the attack on Dagmar. What was left except to become a guardian? Would Saeed even want him now? Then his thoughts returned to Ayianna and his oath to her brother. His stomach sank. *Osaryn, please, do not let her die. I'll try harder next time. I won't fail you again.*

Eldwyn stood. "I shall carry your message to the elves." He bowed his dark face before Saeed. His thick, black hair fell over his shoulder.

A chorus of agreement echoed from the others, and one by one the guardians stood and strode away. Then a thought occurred to him.

"Saeed?" Kael waited for the headmaster's gaze. "Why would Semine curse the people if she was only after the dagger?"

"What do you do with people who are bound to your will?"

Kael shrugged. He heard a sharp intake of air and glanced at the prince.

Vian stood. "She's building an army, isn't she?"

Saeed nodded. He turned back to Kael. "I must ask that you and your companions journey to Bonpazur and find the Dwalu Tonic."

Kael's stomach sank even further.

"Great!" Vian crossed his arms. "We're on a child's mission while the rest of the world is preparing for battle."

"Young master Vian." Saeed ambled over to the prince and gripped his shoulder. "We each have a part to play in this life, and if we cannot prove trustworthy in the little parts, how can we handle the greater parts?"

Vian studied the headmaster. "What about my father?"

"We will do what we can to save him."

Vian's shoulders slumped and Saeed lowered his hand. "I don't like it, but I will trust you." He stretched his arms and yawned. "I'm beyond exhausted. Where might I rest?"

"Leora?" Saeed turned to the fairy, who was still pacing atop the table. "Please show the prince where he may rest."

She nodded and fluttered away, Vian in tow.

Saeed gripped Kael's shoulder. "Walk with me."

He nodded and followed Saeed out of the courtyard and up a small hill overlooking the ruins. The pale blue sky and the fading stars stared down on them.

"Headmaster, I'd prefer to go alone."

Saeed studied him, his gaze gentle, but firm. "Two fair better than one and defeat comes slowly to a cord of three, does it not?"

"So the Thrar'ryn says." Kael tightened his jaw. "But what if the person is considered an enemy?"

"Do you believe that one of your companions is the enemy?" Saeed raised his eyebrows. His wrinkles bunched up and distorted the dark ruins on his forehead. "Or is it merely a clash of differences?"

Kael frowned, resigned to the truth. No matter how hard he disagreed, Desmond wasn't the enemy. He sighed. "A clash of differences."

Saeed smiled faintly. "Kael, you are like a son to me. Eldwyn is right, your father would have been proud of you." He placed a withered hand on Kael's shoulder. "The evening after next, you and your companions will set out. Darin will see you as far as N'dari and secure supplies for your trek across the desert. Once you have what you need, meet me in Praetan, unless you are informed otherwise."

Kael nodded. "What about Ayianna? Do you think her father was hiding the dagger?"

"Yes." Saeed tugged at the braids in his beard. "Eloith told me he senses an ancient evil surrounding her. The enemy knows this and is hunting her."

They lapsed into silence as Kael gazed at the ruins below. So many questions tumbled in his mind. "Does Semine know where we are?"

Saeed shrugged. "She is a sorceress now. She operates in a realm of power forbidden to us. She will go to any means to achieve her goal, and she is not concerned with the cost."

"So." Kael crossed his arms. "You're saying we should keep a low profile."

Saeed smiled. "Perhaps it is divine intervention that Ayianna is here with you."

Kael thought it was more like a horrible fluke of cruel circumstance.

Saeed turned to go. "And Kael, time is of the essence. I do not think the people can survive at length in such a binding of their wills. The curse will ultimately destroy them. If you fail, Nälu will fail. No matter if the alliance is formed."

"I will not fail."

Saeed stared up at the approaching dawn, and Kael followed his gaze. Layers of red swelled on the eastern horizon as the sun lifted its head from slumber and disappeared into the clouds. Suddenly, he was overwhelmed with gratitude for the headmaster's presence and wisdom in the difficulties soon to come.

Saeed put his hand on Kael's shoulder. "Your journey is perilous, take care in whom you trust, but do not forget to trust."

He nodded, despite his misgivings.

Saeed smiled and squeezed his shoulder. "I trust you will do fine. You will make an excellent guardian. Rest well, son of Aiden, the evening comes quickly, and who knows what manner of nights you will see in the days ahead."

26

AYIANNA BLINKED AT the hazy images surrounding her. Dingy canvas stretched up and created a low ceiling. Where was she? She turned her head, but pain speared her neck and sizzled down her spine. Its heat chased away the numbing cold from her limbs. Waves of spasms seized her muscles. She held her breath and waited for them to subside.

Why did her body ache so terribly? She took a deep breath and tried to sit up, but the room spun and her muscles screamed. She fell back. What was wrong with her? She couldn't remember ever feeling so sore.

"Good morning, Ayianna."

A woman's angular face blurred into view. Where her eyebrows should have been, a ridge of flesh dipped between large, oval eyes the color of murky sea water. An inscription darkened the woman's high cheekbones and three faint slits slashed her neck. She had seen the inscription before, but where? The strange woman moved closer. White braids spilled over the edge of her head and tickled Ayianna's cheek. She touched Ayianna's forehead, her fingertips were cool but comforting.

"Who are you?" Ayianna tried to prop herself up again, but a tremor rippled through her body, and she lay back down.

"Be still, young one." The strange woman massaged her arm. "My name is Nerissa, and I am a Kaleki, from Ganya."

"Oh, you're a mermaid," Ayianna said. The ridged face made sense now. She peered over the side of the cot. "Do you really have a green tail?"

"I am a bit old to be referred to as a mermaid." She scooped up a blanket from a wooden stool and folded it. Her face remained somber and unreadable. Aside from the white hair, the merwoman's appearance bore no sign of old age. "And, yes, I do have a tail, but it is black and only forms when I am submerged in water." She sighed. It was a beautiful sound like that of a gentle, welcoming rain. "Kaleki cannot go long without their beloved waters."

Ayianna shifted in the cot. Had she offended her? She turned away and tried scanning the room from her position. A handful of scrolls littered a corner of the canvas tent opposite of a large bag and a broadsword in its sheath. A fear sliced through her daze. She gripped the edges of her blanket. "Am I . . . dead?

"No, but you have been very sick."

"Where is everyone? Are they all right?" She tried to sit up again, but her vision swirled, and she pitched forward. Nerissa caught her by the arm. "What happened? Why am I here?"

"Your questions will be answered soon enough." Nerissa stuffed the folded blanket and pillow behind Ayianna. "Your friends are fine, but right now, you must eat and regain your strength. A bit of breakfast will settle your hunger, but not upset your stomach."

She picked up a bowl from the floor and handed it Ayianna. She peered at the contents. Cold, lumpy porridge never looked so good.

Nerissa sat across from her and pulled out a blue velvet bag. "We must discuss your wound."

"Wound?" Ayianna asked through a mouthful of porridge.

"You are fortunate Darin found you when he did. You had an encounter with a harpy lord, which has left you with an incurable injury."

Ayianna reached up and felt her neck. Her fingers rubbed across two puncture wounds. A ripple of pain shot through her spine, and she jerked her hand back.

"The pain will eventually subside, but the scarred flesh will remain sensitive. However, you must keep the wound clean and administer the contents of this vial once every three months or so." She slipped a crystal bottle from the velvet pouch and held it up.

Ayianna's eyes shifted from the small bottle to the pearly scales covering the merwoman's arm. She tore her gaze away and drank more of the porridge.

"The *kulin maekoha* is the sacred water from my home," Nerissa explained. "Merfolk need it to live, and a drop of it will heal most anything. Your wound, however, will never heal completely."

The last gulp of porridge caught in Ayianna's throat, and she began coughing. Nerissa handed her a cup of water, and Ayianna washed the rest of the porridge down. She took another drink to ensure the fit of coughs had finally dissipated.

Finding her voice again, she asked, "What do you mean?"

"The venom that entered your blood stream is cursed. I was able to stop it from destroying your body, nevertheless damage remains. The wound will seep, infections are inevitable, and there is a chance the kulin only slowed the poison rather than eradicating it from your body, making you vulnerable to . . . " Nerissa trailed off as her pale green eyes averted for a second. "You could still be vulnerable."

"Are you saying that this—this venom could still be in my body? And that it could still kill me?"

"Or worse." Concern flickered across Nerissa's large eyes.

Ayianna raised her eyebrows. "What could be worse than death?"

"Harpies are dreadful creatures, an abomination." She clasped her hands and rested them in her lap. "You could become one."

The words slammed into Ayianna. She tried to make sense out of them, but the words washed over her and away, unable to penetrate her muddled mind.

"But if you do as I said, one dose every three months, you will be fine."

"For the rest of my life?"

Nerissa nodded.

Ayianna stared at the empty bowl. What had happened? How did she end up here, cursed for the rest of her life?

The merwoman said something about preparations, took the bowl, and left.

Ayianna laid on her side and pulled her knees to her chest, feeling cold and exposed. She tried to remember the last couple of days. Slowly images of fairies battling hamadryads shifted through her thoughts. She had escaped, only to find herself trapped in the horrible underground tunnels. A shadowy memory of an eerie, empty Nganjo slipped past her mind like a slippery fish. What had happened?

She closed her eyes. *Cursed. For the rest of my life . . .* Her stomach churned and threatened to eject its newly eaten contents. What would her mother say? Desmond? Would he still want her? She could add it to all the other secrets she was supposed to keep from him and live a double life just like her father had done and expected her to do. Tears burned behind her eyelids.

"Ayianna?"

A male's voice disrupted the flood of anguish drowning her. She swallowed the knot in her throat and looked up. An old elf pushed through the tent's opening, his bronze face full of wrinkles and concern. He looked like a kind grandfather with his white beard and receding hairline. And like Nerissa, his cheekbones bore an inscription that seemed to have blurred with time. Then she remembered. He was Saeed, the High Guardian. But how did she know him?

"Nevin Nerissa told me you had awakened." He sat down on the stool.

His golden eyes bore into hers and never once strayed from her face. Still she couldn't help but feel he was staring at her neck. He must know the horror that she had become.

"We've made it to Raemoja, then?" she managed to ask.

"Yes."

Ayianna sighed. She should have been relieved, but the emerging despair overwhelmed her. They had reached the guardians, but—why did they have to come here again? Slowly, the shattered memories of recent events came together: The death of her father and brother, the escape from Badara, getting lost in the old Forest of Inganno. The image of her mother's stricken face and silent pleas resurfaced.

Ayianna bolted upright, but immediately wished she hadn't. A searing pain shot through her head and the room spun.

Saeed clutched her elbow and repositioned the blanket and pillow. "Calm yourself. You will have to move slowly until your body fully recovers."

Ayianna nodded and leaned back. "Did Kael tell you we found my mother? We saw her and many other people locked in chains. We must return and rescue them."

Saeed shook his head. "He told me, but she is not physically there. A sorceress has bound the souls of the plains people, your mother included. We have determined to send a delegation to Bonpazur to find a tonic that will free them."

"But then, where is she?"

"We will do what we can to find her, but we need the tonic. You must help Kael find it."

"Kael doesn't need my help. Besides, I'm not going to run all over Nälu while my father's dead body rots in the woods without a proper burial."

"His body is no longer there."

"What?"

"We looked, but did not find him."

She blinked back tears. "No peace in life or in death."

He leaned forward, placing his elbows on his knees. His eyes filled with tenderness. "We know what your father was hiding. If you can remember anything he told you about the secret he was keeping, you must tell me. It might help us find your mother."

Ayianna stared at the old elf sitting in front of her, wishing she'd wake up any minute and find herself someplace else. She nodded. She closed her eyes and forced herself to remember the last time she saw her father alive.

The trees had been clothed in their autumn splendor. She and her father walked along the trail discussing their future, her future. Then the men ambushed them. Her father fought valiantly against so many. Then his crushing weight fell upon her as he took the sword that had been meant for her.

Ayianna glanced up at Saeed through her tears.

He reached for her hand and held it firmly. His calloused hands were warm and comforting.

She brushed away the tears and took a deep breath. "He said to tell my brother, the sun has set and that the morning star is forever locked in stone."

"Daughter of Arlyn, you have strength and courage in your blood. Thank you."

"But what does it mean?"

"I must think upon it. Perhaps, in time, the meaning will become clear." He patted her hand and stood. "I am certain the others are anxious to see you, now that you are awake." He turned to leave.

"Wait . . . what secret was my father guarding? What were those men looking for?"

Saeed tugged at his braided beard and studied her.

She twisted the wool blanket in her hands. Its rough fibers bit into her skin. The silence lengthened, and he still didn't respond. What if he wouldn't tell her? She gritted her teeth. "There have been too many secrets. I have the right to know."

He studied her and then slowly nodded. "You are right. For whether you knew it or not, your life has been and still is in danger. The men seek a dagger. I am assuming your father hid it, otherwise they would have found it already."

She frowned. "A dagger? Anyone can buy one for a handful of dlaquis."

"This dagger was a tool created by Taethza to connect mortals to immortality but at a very high cost." He tugged on his beard and nodded to himself. He raised his bushy eyebrows. "It would be best if you did not mention this to anyone."

She nodded as a chill ran down her spine. "Do you think they are still looking for me?"

"Perhaps." He hesitated. "I am certain they have your mother, and if she is not cooperative, they might think to use you to persuade her to reveal its whereabouts."

She stared at him. How did her world fall into such chaos? Saeed disappeared through the tent's opening. Its flaps settled back in their place, closing her off from the rest of the world. Ayianna exhaled. A fresh wave of tears spilled down her cheeks, and she quickly wiped them away. She clenched her trembling hands together. She had to stop crying. Desmond would be there soon. What would she tell him? Maybe he already knew.

"Ayianna!" exclaimed a booming voice.

Her heart jumped into her throat as Desmond blew through the opening, carrying with him the chill of late autumn. His long strides covered the distance quickly. Dirty blond curls hung past his bristly chin, nearly reaching his shoulders. He grasped her hands, but his eyes strayed to her neck. Shame engulfed her. How much did he know? Would he still accept her?

"Come on, Desmond." Vian suddenly appeared behind him and pushed him out of the way. He clasped her in a hug. "We were worried about you." He pulled away. "You wouldn't believe what we had to go through to rescue you. There were these trolls and harpies and this—"

Desmond elbowed Vian in the ribs. "We're just thankful you're better."

"How are you feeling?" Kael stood at the entrance. His bow and quiver already strapped across his back. His left hand fidgeted with the hilt of his sword.

"As well as I can be." Ayianna forced a smile. She didn't want to sound ungrateful. "Thank you—all of you—for saving me." She glanced back at Desmond. He squeezed her hand. She'd tell him about the wound later. No one else needed to know. "Saeed tells me we need to find a tonic."

Desmond's face crumpled into a scowl. "The old bird seems to think we need to help the half-breed. The prince included."

"Desmond." Kael's eyes narrowed. "You should show the proper respect for the High Guardian."

Desmond straightened. "He *is* old, isn't he? There's no disrespect in speaking the truth is there?"

Kael clenched his jaw. "We leave for N'dari the evening after next." With that, he turned and disappeared through the tent's opening.

"I guess the gods have blessed us with more time to harass the half-breed." Desmond chuckled.

"Go easy on him." Vian rapped his knuckles against Desmond's shoulder. "He might be a bit stodgy but he's on our side."

Desmond's eyebrow shot up. "Don't tell me you're taking a liking to him? What would your father say if he heard you talking like that about half-breeds?"

"Now, gentlemen," Nerissa said as she reentered the tent. "Ayianna needs to rest, especially if Kael insists you will leave so soon."

"Right." Desmond turned to Ayianna and gave her hand one last squeeze. "We'll see you later."

Once the men had left, Nerissa placed a conch shell and the blue velvet bag containing the vial of *kulin maekoha* in Ayianna's hands.

"If you travel as far as the Maekoha Sea, my horn shall bring you aid. There you may refill the vial when the kulin begins to diminish. And there is one more surprise I think you shall like." Nerissa reopened the tent's flaps, and a large blur of gray fur leapt into the air.

"Liam!" Ayianna grabbed the wolf's neck. "How?"

"Eloith took care of her."

Tears slid down Ayianna's cheeks as she buried her face into Liam's fur.

27

ON THE EVE of the second day, Ayianna tightened the straps of her leather knapsack and prepared to embark on a journey she didn't want to take. She took a deep breath and grasped Liam around the neck.

"Come on, let's go find the others before Nerissa changes her mind."

She strode out of the tent, thankful for the opportunity to rest for the past couple of days, but glad to be finally free. Nerissa had kept her isolated, to rest, she had said, but a different reason burned in her eyes. Had she really expected Ayianna to turn into a harpy? And what if she had? Ayianna shook her head. At least in sleep, her thoughts had not tormented her.

Above her, the ruins of Raemoja protruded from the mountainside like a blight. Its empty hulls of stone expanded across the valley and up toward the peak, except where mudslides had knocked them down. She found it difficult to imagine the decrepit city was once great and formidable. Now, lichen and other vegetation covered its crumbling walls as nature reclaimed its scarred land.

The sun slid behind the trees, taking with it any thread of warmth. She tightened the cloak around her neck and entered the outer baily. She was met with a flurry of activity and energy in the air. Six more guardians packed away their tents and assisted Kael with supplies. Fairies buzzed from one place to another while Desmond and Vian strapped on their swords. She caught bits and pieces of conversation.

"We will purchase more waterskins in N'dari." One guardian towered above the others and wore only a vest and pants. What was his name again? A gusty autumn breeze hissed through the courtyard and sent the tree limbs clicking and scratching against the ruins. She shivered. How could he be warm?

The large man continued. "I have a good friend there, Aberim. He will be able to assist you and hopefully guide you."

"You aren't coming with us?" Kael asked.

"If Saeed wishes to resurrect the old Alliance, I must speak with the Pauden myself. The giants have closed off any communication with the rest of Nälu. Personally, I think it will be a waste of time."

Giant? Ayianna stepped closer. A patch covered his left eye, and inked runes not only marked his face, but his hands as well. Hadn't Nerissa told her about him? Darin, the half-giant who had carried her to Raemoja.

"Well, if it is such a waste of time, you could just come with us."

Darin chuckled. "Nice try."

Kael turned, his eyes catching hers. Had his frown deepened at the sight of her? The others must have seen her too as a chorus of welcomes and hellos echoed. Her face burned. She thanked them, and everyone turned back to their tasks.

"From N'dari, I suggest you take the southern route through the Zriab Desert. There, you will be able to rest in Zajur," the tall man continued.

"Zajur! You cannot be serious, Darin."

A voice growled behind Ayianna. A dwarf hobbled up. His leathery face displayed the same inscriptions that the other guardians bore, but barely legible above his bushy, brown beard. He handed a braided rope to Kael. "Never be found without a good rope." He grunted at Kael before rounding on Darin. "Why not Mútni?"

"Because Mútni takes them too close to Durqa." Darin folded his canvas tent and tucked it in a bag.

"I suppose." The dwarf eyed Darin, his face tilted to the sky. "They would be better off not mixing with those folks, if Derk considered wasting manpower on a small, insignificant settlement. The northern desert is less sand and more rock. The traveling would be quicker and easier."

"Durqa isn't as small and insignificant as you might think." Darin tied a bedroll to his pack. "I will not have them taking any chances."

"Have you crossed the desert before, Kael?" Desmond asked as he walked up behind him.

"No."

"Well, I've crossed it plenty of times—not an easy trek."

"Right." Kael frowned as he attached the rope to his belt.

"Nevin Darin," a small voice said.

Ayianna smiled.

The fairy captain, Eloith, fluttered atop a broken pillar. "With permission from my Queen Leora, I ask that I may accompany Kael and the others to Bonzapur. I owe them my life."

"Ah . . . " Desmond shouldered his knapsack. "Crossing the desert might prove too much for a little guy like you."

"You underestimate me." Eloith nodded curtly, but turned his attention upon Darin.

Darin slipped a heavy cloak around his shoulders. "Your request is granted. I have a special task for you then, Eloith.

After we reach N'dari, you must fly on ahead and deliver this letter to King Runako."

Eloith accepted the sealed parchment, folded it, and slipped it into a pouch at his hip. "I will make you proud, Nevin Darin. The heat does not affect my ability to fly, nor the dry air, for I will be in Bonzapur by the fourth night."

Eloith bowed low as another fairy joined them. This one a female and wearing a long, blue tunic with gray breeches. Her gold hair curled up into a bun like a crown. Was this the Queen?

"My fellow fairies and I have stayed up into the wee hours of the morning making special cloaks for the *kuathza*, the quest, or we could call it the *nata'kovidi*—"

"And you are?" Desmond interrupted. "You'll have to forgive me, but there are so many of you fairies, it's hard to remember who is who."

"I am Leora, queen of the Naajiso, and a guardian." Leora clasped her hands together and addressed Kael. "We are excited to be able to be of service to you and all of Nälu once again. Please accept our gift."

Kael nodded as he accepted a bundle from one of the fairies.

"I already have a cloak." Desmond slid his fingers over his. "What's so special about these?"

"They are designed to protect you from the desert heat," Eloith replied.

Leora smiled. Her eyes glittered like amethysts. She snapped her fingers and several more fairies appeared, carrying tan cloaks. She nodded, and they handed them out.

Ayianna slid her fingers along the cloak's smooth edges. Its lightweight fabric flowed through her hands like silk. Threads of gold wove through the cloak in gentle swirls and shimmered in the setting sun.

Desmond fingered the material. Surely, a draper would have considered it a wonder. Instead he stuffed it into his bag. "All right then, are we ready?"

"Ready?" Darin chuckled. "Hardly. Nevertheless, we must proceed. We shall reach N'dari by tomorrow's eve."

28

THE DESCENDING SUN painted the nude landscape in hues of burnt orange and red. The Zriab Desert stretched to the west and disappeared into the fiery sunset. Ayianna lifted her hand and tried to shield her eyes from the burning light. Below, a small city squatted amidst the foothills of the Ruzat Mountains. Home to the desert elves of N'dari.

Hundreds of rounded buildings huddled behind high walls, except for a few towers scattered throughout the city and those standing guard at the gatehouses. Unlike Zurial, where the elves strove for the heights, N'dari hugged the ground as if it were afraid of being blown away.

Leaving behind the last trees for miles around, she trudged behind the others as they began their descent. Liam pranced at her heels. The wolf darted this way first and then that way, inspecting and exploring. Ayianna smiled. At least one thing remained constant in the chaos around her. What would she do without her?

Darin's step quickened, and she hurried to keep up. Prince Vian and Desmond hiked behind the half-giant. Their strides grew shorter and heavier until the prince tripped. Desmond grabbed his arm and cursed under his breath. Vian's foot never failed to find a rock or a hole in the sloping landscape.

Kael strode past and not once looked in their direction. Ayianna frowned. Why did Saeed have to insist they worked together? Maybe Desmond's dislike for Kael had merit. He was a little too proud for a half-elf. And rude too. His demeanor had certainly irked her on several occasions and left her more than a little confused. She clenched her jaw. Maybe they could part ways once they reached Bonpazur. Then she'd be able to rescue her mother, wherever she was.

Ayianna glanced at the sky. The few, scattered clouds had turned purple and red, but already the vibrant colors faded. Somewhere above, Eloith flew or perhaps he had already made it to N'dari and was waiting on them. Either way they weren't going to make the main gate before nightfall. She hurried after the others, hoping otherwise.

Once the ground leveled out, Darin turned suddenly from the path and lead them toward a few scraggly bushes near the city's eastern wall. A large, golden eagle swooped out of the air and landed on his outstretched arm. It ruffled its feathers and nuzzled Darin's fingers.

He whispered something, and the eagle shook his head. Stretching its wings, it leapt into the air and flew over the wall of the city. Ayianna scanned the horizon. Just maybe she'd catch a glimpse of Fero. Would she ever see her brother's falcon again?

Desmond brushed past Ayianna and approached Darin. No doubt to complain, but before he could open his mouth the side of the wall shuddered and revealed a secret entrance.

"Darin! *Prözam,* my friend!" A stout man greeted from the shadows.

"*Prözam,* Aberim. That was quick." Darin ducked inside. "I expected to be waiting till midnight."

270

"Will you ever stop tormenting me? Last time I had been in the middle of an important meeting of sorts." Aberim held the door open as Ayianna and the others slipped into a long, narrow alleyway.

Long splays of light and shadow stretched along the adobe homes. Ayianna slid from the entrance and slammed into a fetid odor. She yanked her scarf over her nose. What was wrong? Elf-kind weren't supposed to stink. How far had the Saryhemor's society deteriorated? She pushed away from the others, but the stench saturated the air.

"I'd not wander too far in that direction." Aberim motioned toward her. "The cleaners don't come through here until tomorrow. You wouldn't want to step in a fresh dumping of refuse, now would you?"

Ayianna shook her head. She peered down the alley and could just barely make out the smelly heaps along it. She clenched her teeth against the rolling in her gut. She glanced back at the others. Why were they taking so long?

"You should be tormented." Darin squinted down at his friend. "It was in the middle of winter."

She glowered at him. *I bet he's so tall the smell doesn't even reach him.* She grabbed Liam's thick fur and pulled the wolf closer.

Aberim grunted.

"You had not seen me in five years," Darin continued. "And you forgot that I was standing outside freezing my—"

"Hey, if your bird would've found me sooner."

Darin drew his shoulders back, and the shadows swallowed his head. "Kimir is an eagle. One of the great Golden Eagles of Moruya."

"A bird is a bird." Aberim smiled, but quickly added. "I'm sure you'd be glad to know that Eloith arrived this afternoon. We've spent the rest of the day preparing for your arrival and recovering from the shock of seeing a living Naajiso. You're full of surprises, you know."

"I am a guardian—it is expected."

Vian stepped around Aberim and scanned the long, narrow ally they had entered. His lip curled. "This is why Badara doesn't have secret doors."

"That you know of." Darin leaned closer to Aberim. "We shall save introductions for later."

Aberim nodded and slid the door shut behind them. "It really isn't a secret, more like a forgotten door. One that the shepherds used before the king made N'dari his capital." He strolled past them and smiled. "Cook is preparing a meal as we speak. We can get cleaned up, and then we can talk."

"Lead the way." Darin sniffed. "I do hope the smell does not linger."

Aberim scurried off. He led the travelers down a zigzagging path, dodging the main streets, and finally stopping at a large adobe house. He pressed open the double doors.

"Niyah!"

"Have you no caution, old man? The neighbors will hear you." Darin looked down the dusty street and stooped to follow his friend into the house.

"Bah! Let them. It'll give them something to talk about." Aberim turned around and pointed at the hooks lining the wall. "You may hang your packs and cloaks there."

Ayianna slid her leather bag from her back and found an empty hook. Bunches of woven satchels and pouches already occupied most of them. Lumpy canvas sacks slumped against the wall, filled with who knows what. Did he have other visitors? She followed the others through the entryway into a greater room.

Ayianna glanced around, unsure what she had expected from a desert elf. But what she saw wasn't it. Paintings of mountains and jungles hung between mounted deer heads, while bear and tiger skins littered the floor. A large stone fireplace protruded against the far wall. Above it hung an odd assortment of crude iron weapons. An overstuffed red couch and matching chairs sprawled in front of the hearth spoke of a feminine touch.

A petite woman waddled into the room, her hands resting on her burgeoning stomach. Her dark hair was pulled into a sloppy bun except for a few strays that hung across her forehead and pointed ears. Her face broke into a wide grin.

"Niyah, darling." Aberim put his arm around his wife. "Look who finally decided to show up."

"It's about time." She reached up to embrace Darin.

"Niyah, you are glowing!" Darin kissed her on the cheek. "Your husband did not tell me you were expecting."

Aberim snorted. "Well, the fault's your own—you're never around."

"Rubbish!" Darin clasped Aberim's shoulder, his tattooed hand nearly covering it. "There are ways of communicating, you primitive being!"

"Primitive!"

"Now, now." Niyah tugged Aberim's other hand. "We have guests! Let's make them welcome."

"Of course."Aberim's face broke into a wide grin. "Darin, would you do the honors?"

Darin nodded and introduced everyone. Niyah brushed her fingertips together and curtsied. When Darin was finished, Aberim looked around and asked, "Where are the children? They've been a riot since Eloith arrived. They would've been banging down the doors to see you, you know."

"I've sent them outside to bed down the goats before supper. I figured our guests would like a little time to rest before they're bombarded with a bunch of noisy questions." Niyah gestured toward the stairs. "The rooms are ready, if you'd like to wash up."

Aberim turned to Ayianna. "But the wolf must go outside."

"Oh." She fumbled for a reply. "I didn't mean to offend you."

"You didn't." Niyah smiled and patted Liam's head. "Our youngest starts sneezing around the animals. We had to give away my mother's long-haired cat when he was born." She smiled. "For the love of children, eh?"

Aberim strode to the other side of the living room and opened a door. Liam didn't even wait for a command as she sprinted out into a small courtyard. Ayianna smiled. The wolf would be happier outside.

"If you'll follow me." Niyah waddled over to the stairs.

"Darling, you should rest. We don't need to be having that baby anytime soon." Aberim rubbed her belly and kissed her on the forehead.

Ayianna smiled as she followed Aberim up the stairs. Excitement tickled her spine. A baby. One day she'd have her own, maybe a son first or maybe a girl. She glanced at Desmond, and the thought withered like a water-starved plant. How could she love out of duty? At a distance, he had looked appealing, she couldn't deny that. All the girls of the villages had been fascinated by him, many of them had swooned over him. Where had all the girly feelings gone? The rushing of love? The fluttering of the heart? What was wrong with her?

Once inside the guest room, Ayianna undressed and took a cold sponge bath, scrubbing away the dirt from the trip. All the while she tried to make her heart and head agree. Perhaps the feelings would change over time, but time didn't change secrets or the lies. She stood naked in the small room like the truth before her eyes. She shivered and pulled a robe over her shoulders. Who else would love her? She was cursed.

A knock at the door startled her. She wrapped the robe around her body and cracked the door open.

Cleaned and shaven, Desmond leaned on the door frame. A pungent smell saturated the air around him. Had she detected a slight fluttering of her heart?

"How are you?"

"Um . . . I'm . . . " Ayianna adjusted the robe. "I'm fine, thank you."

"Well, are you going to invite me in?"

"No." Her eyes widened. "It wouldn't be proper. I'll dress, and we can go down to the courtyard."

"The robe will do," Desmond said, his eyes sweeping her small frame.

Heat flooded her face. She closed the door and ducked behind the dressing curtain in the corner. She donned a plain dress Niyah had laid out for her. A moment later, she came back out only to find that he had already entered and was sitting upon her bed.

Fire rushed up the back of her neck and across her face. She tugged on the linen sleeves. "You shouldn't be in here." She glanced at the closed door. Had she heard footsteps?

"And why not? We're betrothed, aren't we?"

"There are other places we could go."

"But we wouldn't be alone." Desmond stood and crossed the distance between them. He grasped her hands and pulled her close. "I thought I had lost you."

Ayianna stopped breathing. Her mind had been wiped clean of her thoughts. Every nerve tingled in a heightened awareness of her body next to his. His breath tickled her ear. His hand slid to her waist and drew her against him.

Her heart pounded; surely he could feel it. She should pull away, but her knees weakened as she hung limp in his embrace. His fingers stroke the sides of her face. She looked past him, scarcely breathing. He lifted her chin.

"Do you dislike me so?"

"No. It's just that . . . "Ayianna glanced into his eyes. "So much has happened, changed. I don't know what to think or feel anymore."

"Well, why don't you let me help you?" He pressed his lips against hers.

She trembled. His kiss unleashed a torrent of mixed feelings. He was desirable. Why couldn't she let go and embrace him? What was holding her back? The kiss deepened; his fingers slid from her chin to her neck.

Pain shot through her body, and Ayianna gasped and jerked away. "Don't. The wound is still fresh."

"Oh." His gaze settled on her injury.

"Nerissa said it will never heal."

Desmond frowned. "The fish-woman told me that much."

"But," Ayianna quickly added, "she gave me this special water from her homeland. All I have to do is apply it every three months, and I'll be fine. I'm sure the pain will subside eventually." Her throat closed up, and she swallowed. Should she tell him about the harpy's curse?

He ran his hands through his hair and glanced away. "I guess you will keep it covered. No one has to know about it."

The truth died on her tongue. She slowly shook her head. "It doesn't change anything, really . . . you and me?"

"No." He straightened, and his expression brightened. "No, it doesn't." He flashed a smile. "Dinner will be ready soon, and Vian will need my assistance. The prince is lost without me."

She nodded and watched him disappear down the hall. She slumped on the bed. Why was she so difficult? She had to make this work. The wife of a merchant. She could grow to love him, couldn't she? Unless . . . did he regret his choice now? Could he marry a tainted bride? She clenched her fist. *Not to mention a deceitful one. All these lies, Father, did you ever think of that?* She bit her lip against the threat of tears.

Should I have told him? But what is one more secret? Oh, Osaryn, where are you? What should I do?

Ayianna glanced down the hall and then found her way to the courtyard to check on Liam and get some fresh air.

A high brick wall enclosed Aberim's home. The sun had long since departed and left the world full of shadows. Two lanterns sat atop pillars and flung their light on the cobbled path below. Ayianna made her way to the barn and willed her thoughts to wander. Animal odor mingled with hay and grain. One of the goats lifted its head and bleated. Where were the children? Tuffs of straw still clumped together lay in the goat pen, evidence enough of their haste to see their guests. Most likely they were preparing for dinner or hanging on Darin's long arms. He seemed the fatherly type. Did guardians marry?

An occasional cluck or hoot escaped the handful of chickens roosting along wooden perches in the back. Something grunted behind her, and she whirled around. A large animal stood in the corner and snorted at her. She peered closer. The animal looked like a big fuzzy horse, but had a large hump on its back.

"It is a camel, a creature of the desert." Eloith fluttered down from the rafters and landed on the railing. "Aberim calls him *Treviko*, Big Chief."

"I thought the Saryhemor elves bred horses?"

"Some do, but Aberim is a *luddzim ot thawodzi*, a camel-puller."

"A what?"

"He takes care of the camels on a caravan and leads them through the desert. This afternoon, he told me he is one camel away from owning a full file, and then he will hire his own camel-puller."

"Oh." She peered over the railing at the camel. He just stood there, eyes closed, and chewing on something, or was he looking down his nose at her.

"But he will have to wait until next year. The caravan has already left without him."

"Because of the baby?"

Eloith grinned. "Aberim loves children. He would not miss the birth for the world."

Ayianna sighed.

"What bothers you?" the fairy asked, his silver eyes searching hers.

She glanced away. What could she say? Maybe he already knew. She eyed him. "Can't you read my mind?"

"I could if I wanted to, but that would be improper."

"But back in the dungeons of Mandar you did."

"That was different. I needed to convey images to your mind in order for you to find the keys. When I touched your hand, I could hear your thoughts, but elves can learn to guard their thoughts, even those who are not a full-blooded. Kael could teach you."

"No." Ayianna stepped back. "How did you know?"

He studied her. "You hide from your ancestry."

It was more of a statement than question. She looked away and clenched her jaw. "I must."

"You need not explain your actions."

She glanced back at him. Despite his baldness, his smooth face gave him the appearance of a youth in his prime, but his eyes held the secrets of the long forgotten. How old he must be! She shifted her feet and leaned against the boards.

"You said that the enemy is hunting me. What did you mean?"

"A long time ago, the Naajiso, the Fairy-folk, had deep connections to Karasi, the Sacred Pearl. We have not the gift for prophecy like she does, but through her, we have the gift of discernment. We can sense disturbances."

"Like the elves?" She laced her fingers together.

"Yes and no." He crossed his arms and paced the railing. "Obviously, we can read your thoughts, feel your emotions, but unlike the elves, we can sense a disturbance beyond your emotions."

"Then, you sensed a disturbance in me?"

"It is difficult to explain. People and objects have an essence, and they can leave a trail."

"How can an object have an essence?"

"It can come from the creator of the object or the user, and whether or not it was designed or used for good or evil."

"Oh." Her pulsed race. It had to be the dagger. What had Saeed said? A tool to connect mortality to immortality. That's what the enemy wanted. But she didn't have it. She straightened. No, she did have a dagger, her brother's. "Do you still sense it?"

"Yes."

Her brother's plain, old knife couldn't be what they were after. Wouldn't a tool like this be more grand looking? Wouldn't her father have hidden it better? She tilted her head and ran her hands along the boards. Could Eloith pinpoint the object? "What do you sense?"

"An ancient, consuming evil."

29

AFTER DINNER, ABERIM kissed his wife goodnight and settled into the overstuffed chair next to the fireplace. Ayianna sank into the couch as exhaustion rolled over her, and all she wanted was to sleep.

Darin threw another log into the dwindling fire. He grabbed the metal poker and started stabbing the embers. The flame spat and hissed, but slowly its tendrils wrapped around the wood.

At Aberim's request, they hadn't discussed the nature of their meeting during dinner. He didn't want his wife to be disturbed with such talk. He believed a happy pregnancy equaled a happy baby. He had three children already, and they had entertained their guests like cheerful birds, chattering away throughout dinner. The floorboards overhead rumbled with footsteps as Niyah chased them to bed.

"Don't stay up too late." Her voice drifted down the stairs.

Aberim chuckled as he pulled out his ceramic pipe and pouch of tobacco. He stuffed the pipe and lit it.

Desmond dropped next to Ayianna. She jumped. Had she fallen asleep? He leaned back and stretched out his legs.

"Well, let's get this over with. I could sleep forever." He cracked his knuckles and placed his hands behind his head.

"Me too." Prince Vian sat down beside him. His back remained rigid, his shoulders squared, such a contrast to Desmond who nearly took up the whole couch.

Ayianna inched closer to the polished armrest but only found that his body followed her. Why was she trying to avoid touching him? He was her betrothed, her future husband. Did propriety matter anymore? Her world spun in chaos, and all she could worry about was proper decorum.

Kael sat cross-legged on the floor in the corner, partially hidden by the evening shadows. His head rested against the brick wall, his eyes closed. Eloith flew through the rafters overhead and fluttered down next to Kael. His silvery wings folded against his back, and his watery eyes reflected the fire flickering in the hearth.

Ayianna shifted in her seat and gazed at her hands clenched in her lap. How much did Eloith know about her? When he held her hand, did he have access to all her thoughts and secrets? Protocol might forbid him to read her mind without her permission, but he still knew things about her much like Kael did. Oh, how she needed to learn to guard her mind. But Eloith could sense a person's or an object's essence. Could he sense the harpy's poison running through her veins, even now?

"So," Aberim cleared his throat, "what brings you to N'dari?"

"Dagmar has been destroyed, and many of the teachers and pupils are dead." Darin settled into the red armchair across from Aberim. "The Pearl is missing. Badara has been taken without bloodshed, and the people of the plains are suffering under a curse. Nälu is under an attack."

Aberim drew long and hard on the pipe. The smoldering leaves hissed as air was pulled through the ceramic barrel. He gazed at the fireplace, his face wrinkled in thought. The silence lengthened. Ayianna wondered if he had fallen asleep, but then he suddenly exhaled and sent the bitter smoke into a cloud above him.

He pulled the pipe from his mouth. "All of Nälu?"

"Semine has bound herself to the Tóas Dikon. She and Derk will not stop at Badara."

"Derk, wasn't he a teacher or an apprentice in the Nutraadzi?" Aberim rubbed the pipe across his teeth, its ceramic barrel clinking above the murmur of the fire. *Click, click, click.*

"He was once studying to be a Nevin, but he and his friends found the realm of the underworld more appealing. They fled three or four decades ago into obscurity, but they have returned. They have placed the plains people under the Twammurt curse. We cannot hope to overcome it without the aid of the Dwalu Tonic—"

"And I don't suppose you have the ingredients for it?"

"No."

"So you want me to accompany this band of youths to find the ingredients?" His pipe rattled on his teeth again—*clink, clink, clink.*

"All I ask of you is to take them across the Zriab Desert to Bonpazur." Darin stretched one leg at a time and then crossed them.

Aberim eyed him. *Clink, clink, clink.* "When?

"Tomorrow."

Aberim coughed out smoke. "Tomorrow?"

"The guardians will shake the sleep from the rest of Nälu, but if we are without the tonic, we will have no army."

Aberim frowned. "I just got back from the last caravan. My camels need their rest, and Niyah is due in a month. Surely, you can find someone else."

"Can you recommend someone else?"

Aberim turned his gaze to the fire. *Clink, clink, clink.* He ran his pipe harder across his teeth.

Ayianna watched the flames dance along the log. The heat drew her in and baked her face. Her muddled thoughts slipped, and her head nodded. A sharp pain ricocheted through her neck and body, jerking her awake. She glanced around, but no one was looking at her. She took a deep breath and shifted in her seat. How long was this going to take?

Clink, clink, clink. Aberim grunted. "It's ten days to Zajur, another three to Bonpazur and then the return trip. I can't do it. I need to be here for Niyah."

"I've crossed the desert before. We go straight west. How hard can it be?" Desmond leaned forward and placed his elbows on his knees. "Why do we need a guide at all?"

"The desert is never constant. The sands shift, the sun distorts, the heat kills," Aberim replied without looking up from the fireplace. "It's not a trek to be taken lightly."

"Can you get them to Zajur?" Darin asked.

Clink, clink, clink. "I hadn't planned on going anywhere for the next couple of months. Treviko needs rest, and I don't have the funds for more camels." The pipe clinked across his teeth again. "Unless of course you're prepared to cover the cost?"

Darin shook his head. "I have enough for the supplies. That is all."

Aberim squinted his eyes at Darin. "You owe me."

"I figured we would come up even, considering the letanili tusk I brought you back from Moruya."

Letanili? Ayianna raked her mind. She had heard of it before, but where?

Aberim grumbled, but his eyes sparkled. "Let's see—" *Click, click, click.* "We will need—" *Clink, clink, clink.*

"Would you stop?" Darin glared at him. "It is rather annoying."

"Sorry about that—bad habit." He pulled the pipe from his mouth. A guilty grin broke across his face.

"So, will you take them?"

"I will need at least a day or two to get all the supplies together." Aberim eyed the others. "Are all of you going?"

Darin shook his head. "Eloith will fly on ahead, announcing our arrival to the Chief of Bonpazur. I will leave for the old King's Highway to Zjohedaryn in the morning."

"That old pirate den!" Aberim eyebrows arched. "What for?"

"I must sail for Moruya and meet with the Pauden."

"Good luck with that." Aberim rubbed his jaw. "Do you think you could bring me back the hide of a letanili? I hear their skin is near impenetrable as a dragon's but softer when tanned."

Darin shook his head. "They are protected beasts. It would be foolish to be found in possession of such."

"Oh, well, I thought I'd ask." Aberim crossed his arms and touched the pipe to his lips. "I suppose Treviko could make the trip to Zajur, but we'd probably need another camel to help carry the supplies."

"Travel light, my friend." Darin stood and stretched. His fingertips brushed the rafters. "I will leave you to figure out the details. I must rest." He turned to the others. "And I suggest you all do likewise. I doubt you will get much sleep in the desert."

30

SEMINE CLENCHED HER gloved fists and whirled around. "What do you mean he wasn't there?"

Her servants fell back and withdrew to the flickering shadows. Hundreds of tall, fat candles burned along the walls and atop shelves, but the air remained cold. Etched ovals darkened the wax and watched those who entered the circular room like sentries at their post.

A single servant remained in their glare.

"No one has seen him, Holy Mistress. Not even his father."

"Must I do everything?" Semine bit back her anger and took a deep breath. "Leave me."

When the last of the servants left, she paced the room. *It's only a minor setback. I'll find him myself, and then I . . . but what if I'm wrong?*

She halted. Goddess Raezana would never forgive her. She bit her knuckles and closed her eyes. She returned to her desk and the heavy book Imaran had snatched for her. She caressed its pages. Names and dates filled column after column. Meaningless to most people, but here, she found her salvation.

Thirty years ago, Raezana had given her a vision. The birth of a baby boy. Born under the death star, he was marked. Semine crosschecked the dates of her vision and the birth of Prince Vian of Badara. The closest match she could find. His blood would release Raezana from the underworld . . . if she could find the dagger. Semine clenched her jaw. Raezana was growing impatient.

A muffled knock interrupted her thoughts. She huffed and lifted her head.

"Don't disturb me, I'm busy." She strode over to the faded map hanging on the wall. Its edges curled and split. The words, For Her Glory, marched across the Prathae Plains. *Where are you, Prince?* She could consult the uisol stones, but searching the entire world would be too strenuous, time-consuming, and require too much blood. But if she had to, she would do it.

"Holy Mistress, you have a visitor."

Semine spun around, but her rebuke caught in her throat.

A hooded figure filled the doorway. "Well, well, well." A husky male voice carried across the room. "Are you going to invite me in?"

"What are you doing here?"

"I will take that as a yes." He slipped into the shadows and closed the door behind him.

"So," the husky voice continued, "have you found the dagger?"

"What do you think?" She tightened her velvet robe and settled in her chair. She paged through the heavy tome again. "I'm busy, Nevin, so if you have something to say, get it over with."

"Semine, Semine . . . " Even in his sighing, she heard derision. "You are hardly one to rush to business so soon."

"With you, it's only business."

"You were my brightest pupil." He took a step closer. She caught the glint of his eyes from the wavering candlelight. "Perhaps you will change your mind."

"Not tonight."

"Mistress." He bowed back into the shadows. "Then business it is, for now. But the Goddess demands a tithe, does she not? A renewal of covenants?"

"Don't tell me what she demands." Semine stood and braced her arms on the desk. "If you withhold information from her, you'll quickly outgrow your usefulness."

He chuckled.

Semine crossed her arms. "You're wasting my time."

"Well, where shall I start? It has been so long." He placed his hands on his hips. "Perhaps I should commend you for the fall of Badara—without bloodshed no less. And how clever, you think to manipulate prophecy with a curse."

"Your point?"

"Cannot a master praise his pupil?"

"Raezana is my only master."

He grunted. "Does Raezana know about the quest?"

"What quest?"

"Did you think the Guardian Circle would not recognize the curse? Saeed has sent Kael, son of Lord Aiden, and a small party to obtain the tonic."

This time she laughed. "The library is destroyed. They won't find it."

"You have forgotten Bonpazur."

She scowled. "Enlighten me, then."

"The first Guardian Circle resided in Bonpazur until Dagmar was built. The royal library there might still contain copies of the ancient texts."

She tapped her fingers on the book and turned toward the map. "They must be stopped."

"Of course, Mistress, leave it to me. I know just the way to do it."

"Oh?" She faced him.

He stood on the other side of the candles. Their flames danced in his glittering eyes, but the shadows consumed the rest of him. "They are crossing the Zriab desert as we speak. They will soon reach the oasis of Zajur. We can send the Tögo, and the guardians will not know of their demise until it is too late." He touched his fingertips together. "And we can focus on more important things like the dagger and getting reacquainted."

"We?" She leaned against her desk. "So you need my help?"

"Do we not serve the same end?"

"Perhaps." She eyed the shadows where he stood. "What are the guardians preparing to do?"

"They seek to unite the nations."

She smirked. "Good luck with that. Where has he sent you?"

"Oh, here and there." He crossed his arms. "We convene in a month at Praetan. I will report to you then."

The shimmering flames drew Semine into her thoughts. Could she have the dagger and Prince Vian in a month? Perhaps Derk's little demonstration could buy her time and maybe even lure the prince out of hiding. She must send him word to proceed. If she could keep the guardians guessing she might be able to hinder their schemes. Or if their leader was somehow disposed of . . .

"Sorceress, are we done here?"

"Not quite, my pet." She smiled. "I have a task for which Raezana will reward you richly."

His eyes lit. "Speak it, and I will see it done."

She leaned forward. "Kill Saeed."

Silence hung between them, and for a moment, Semine questioned his loyalty.

"It will be done." He bowed and turned to leave.

"And Nevin?" Semine smiled. "I'll need your blood."

He eyed her. "What for?"

"The Tögo."

"But of course. What is one more sacrifice when I will soon savor the sweet reward of our Goddess?"

Semine stood in the inner sanctuary of the temple and exhaled a cleansing breath. Incense burned beyond the thick curtains separating her from the chanting priestesses. She guarded the small flame she carried and stepped over the oil-filled channel. She lit the candelabra towering above the large stone basin. Its dark, placid waters consumed the dim light.

She pulled the vial of blood from her robe, still warm in her hands. She poured it out across the basin and dropped the uisol stone. It plunged into the water. A glow sprang up from the center of the basin and grew with the ripples.

She closed her eyes and sang.

"Kozan, Koletu, Aenlu, Ninol
Thöm uisol thil
Sram za sil
Shoza isür thil."

"Seek eye, in the Zriab desert, Kael, son of Lord Aiden of Zurial." She slipped the dagger from its sheath and slid it across her arm. It stung, nothing more. The blood swelled black against her pale skin. She turned her arm over and with each drop the waters trembled and grew brighter.

Semine blinked. An image appeared and cast the room in orange-yellow tones. A small caravan of two camels and five people trudged wearily through the sand.

"Death to you and your quest."

She began to chant. The fire grew within her and smoke curled from her mouth. She blew on the basin. Tendrils of flames shot forth and stirred the waters. Steam hissed and filled the room. She glared at the image before and willed the Tögo to Zajur. Sand dunes dissolved and the city emerged among palm trees and ferns.

The image swirled and slowly faded.

"Seek eye, and show me Kael again."

The lean elf hiked next to an older elf who led the camels. He wore the typical headcloth and dress of the Saryehmor elves. Behind them, a young woman and two men trudged.

She chuckled. What was Desmond doing on the quest? His companion had swaddled his head in a linen cloth as well, but there was no mistaken the red tuft of hair framing his face.

She froze. She had to hurry if she was going to beat the Tögo to Zajur.

31

AFTER NINE DAYS of hiking in the desert, Ayianna's determination was near spent. The stifling heat drained her energy and her focus. Each step sank into the loose sand and brought pain. Dust and grit invaded the many layers of her long tunic and leggings and rubbed her skin raw. Just when she didn't think she could go any further, Aberim signaled a rest.

Ayianna dribbled the warm liquid into her parched mouth. She swallowed, but the water was gone. A film covered her tongue like paste, and her body ached for relief. Liam leaned against her leg. She craned her neck and nipped at the tuffs of torn fabric wrapping her paws. If Ayianna hadn't been so weary, she might have laughed. Instead, regret gnawed at her for dragging the wolf along. She bent down to share her water.

"We should reach Zajur by tomorrow evening." Aberim tugged the headcloth off his face and drank from his waterskin. The long folds of his tunic and linen robes billowed around his legs as he circled the camel.

"Oh! Real food for a change." Desmond exhaled heavily. He dabbed his red and blistered face with a dingy handkerchief.

Prince Vian uncapped his waterskin and took a swig. "Your face is burning."

"Don't you think I noticed?"

Aberim turned to Desmond. "If you'd wear the cloth, it would protect you."

Desmond shook his head and muttered, "Women's clothes."

"Fool." Aberim dug a small clay jar from one of the camel's pouch. "Then put this on."

"What is it?"

"A balm crushed from the aloe plant." He shoved it into Desmond's chest. "You don't want to scar that handsome face of yours."

Desmond frowned, grabbed the jar, and started smearing it all over his face.

"I thought you had crossed the desert before." Kael stood in the shade of the camel and adjusted his headcloth.

"Not like this."

Ayianna touched her face, but she didn't feel the burn of the sun. Just sweat and grime. She wrapped the large headcloth around her face again and pulled the fairy cloak over her shoulders. Was the cloak working? She still felt the heat of the desert. The others wore theirs, except Aberim, of course, and Desmond.

"I'm ready for a change of scenery." Vian lifted a cloth-wrapped hand and shielded his eyes. He scanned the horizon. "I don't see how anyone would want to live here."

"Well, after the miles of sand and heat, the oasis is very refreshing and beautiful," Aberim said.

Desmond grunted. "Not to mention the perfect location for business. These people are rich."

"Why?" Ayianna asked, prying her thick tongue from the roof of her mouth.

"It is the crossroads of merchants." Desmond stuffed the pouch of salve into his knapsack. "Well, Bonpazur is really, but

Zajur is the only good place for water and food through this awful desert."

"All this trouble for a handful of yettus—I wouldn't live in a desert for a bucket of gold," Ayianna said.

"Suppose the inhabitants of Zajur wouldn't mind us dropping in on them?" Vian asked.

Desmond shrugged. "They won't exactly roll out their best rugs, but they'll welcome us for the sake of news from the greener parts of Nälu."

Ayianna remained quiet, her muddled thoughts drifting in and out. Her shirt stuck to her back, damp with perspiration. She closed her gritty, burning eyes. Soon, she'd bathe in the cool waters of the oasis and wash the desert from her body and mind. Liam nuzzled her leg and whined. Ayianna bent down to pet her.

She looked back over the way they had come and saw nothing but sand dunes stretching for miles. The desert had swallowed up their tracks. A bloated dune rippled and rolled toward her. Ayianna blinked, and the dune deflated. Perhaps the heat was getting to her. She was almost used to the sweltering sun's deception and the sands constant moving and changing. A breeze picked up, its hot breath scalding her face. She pulled the headcloth over her nose and turned back to the others.

"The desert plays tricks on the mind." Kael glanced over Ayianna's shoulder. Perhaps he saw something too, but he stalked away. "We should keep going."

Aberim nodded. He tugged on Treviko and started their small caravan west. Kael fell in step with him, and Vian turned to follow, but stopped next to Desmond.

"You're not looking so well, my friend."

"We'd get their faster if we could have ridden or at least traveled at night." Desmond hoisted his waterskin over his shoulder and glanced at Ayianna. The whites of his eyes were bloodshot, and Ayianna wondered if she looked just as bad or worse.

"You well enough?" he asked.

She nodded. Fire burned in her neck and shoulders, and thirst clawed at her throat, but her burden was no different than the others. Her waterskin slouched against her hip. The liquid sloshed inside, and her mind begged her to drink. She tightened her jaw. The rationed water would last one more day. One more day, and she would be in Zajur. An oasis. She shook her head and focused on putting one foot in front of the other.

The ground exploded next to Desmond, and sand shot into the air.

Ayianna jerked back, shielding her eyes.

Orange scales flashed in the sun as a giant lizard-like creature sprang toward Desmond and clamped down on his foot. He bellowed and battered its large snout with his fists. The lizard rolled away, dragging him with it.

"Skink!" Aberim cried and rushed after it.

The camels jerked away and nearly stepped on Ayianna. Vian caught Treviko's rope and held.

Aberim lunged for the skink and managed to grab its tail. She stared in horror as the tail snapped off and continued to writhe in Aberim's hands. He growled and threw it aside.

The skink hissed and whirled around, its stubby bottom flinging sand everywhere.

Kael darted into the swirl of dust and decapitated the skink. Its body shook and flopped, spraying everything with crimson blood. Finally, it slumped against the ground.

Ayianna stepped back and scanned the sand for more movement. The dunes wavered, the sand shifted, but it could have been the wind or the heat. Were there more scaly creatures lurking just under the surface? If there was one, then there were more, waiting to burst from the sand and devour them. Her skin crawled, and she shuddered. She took a couple of steps, trying to shake off the intense need to flee.

"What was that?" she asked, ignoring the real question demanding an answer.

"A türuza, the largest variety of the desert skink." Aberim pulled Desmond's boot off and inspected his leg. "Be thankful for that leather, boy. It prevented you from losing your leg, all right. You'll have a nice bruise for sure—some scratches and nothing more. You'll be fine."

Desmond only grunted and massaged his leg. He pulled his boot back on, grumbling under his breath.

"I owe you, Prince." Aberim stood and grabbed the rope from Vian. "We need to move out, now. They hunt in packs."

That was not what Ayianna wanted to hear. The need to flee surged through her again. She quickly gathered up Desmond's belongings and shook the sand from them. She handed them to him, but he snatched them away.

Ayianna gaped. "What—"

"Move it." Kael strode past, his sword dripping blood. "I don't want to have to save your hide again."

She clenched her teeth and hurried after Aberim. She glanced back at Desmond. He threw his waterskin over his shoulder and limped along behind them. *Ungrateful bugger!* She was almost glad he had been bitten. He deserved it.

She turned around and came face to face with another türuza. The skink snapped at her, and she fell back into the hot sand. She scrambled out of the way as it dove beneath the dune. Someone grabbed her arm and yanked her to her feet. The sand bulged and rolled toward them.

Ayianna's eyes darted back and forth. Where was it going to strike next? Kael brandished his bloody blade, and Vian unsheathed his sword, but the skink had disappeared. Should they run? She reached for her own sword, but the türuza vaulted out of the sand near Kael.

He jerked right and kicked the skink in the head. It recoiled, and a second türuza sprang from the sand. The two skinks charged, followed by a third. Kael lunged forward and decapitated one. The other skink advanced on Vian, but Desmond stabbed its back. The creature hissed and went rigid, its limbs twitching.

Ayianna's heart raced as the third skink swaggered toward her, its tail lashing left and right. She stumbled back and fumbled for her sword, but she couldn't pull it free. Remembering her brother's dagger, she reached for it just as the skink leapt toward her. She plunged the dagger into its gaping mouth. Its teeth raked against her skin. Its limbs flailed, pawing at her, and its claws shredded her clothes. She wrenched the dagger out of its throat as the creature fell to the ground. Her hands shook, barely able to hold the weapon.

"Make sure you clean the blood from the blade." Kael stood over her and inspected her arm. "Filthy creatures—we need to clean those cuts."

"No, don't waste the water," Ayianna said, but Kael opened his waterskin and splashed some of the warm liquid across the wounds.

"I've got more than enough. Besides we should reach Zajur tomorrow."

Ayianna flinched as her arm burned. She dug out the small vial that Nerissa had given her. "Put a drop of this in them."

Kael opened the vial and dribbled its contents into the slashes. The liquid fizzled and disappeared.

"Full of surprises, aren't we?"

"Nerissa gave it to me." She slipped the vial back into the pouch around her waist.

"Let's get out of here before any more tuza-whatever you call it show up!" Vian said, breathless.

"But it's almost dark." Ayianna lifted her face to the fading light.

"We can't stay here."

"We'll just have to travel in the dark." Desmond shot Aberim a gloating glance. "You will find it obviously easier to travel by night."

Aberim shrugged. "The night has its own dangers."

32

AYIANNA SHIVERED AND pulled the wool blanket tighter. Her teeth chattered from the cold as she pushed herself to keep up with the others. She scanned the vast darkness that descended on the desert—no moon, but thousands of stars stared down upon them. Darker still were the shadows between the sand dunes.

The scorching desert that seemed so dead during the day had now come to life. Creatures scurried and twittered in the night beyond the light of Kael's orb. Shining eyes gleamed and danced away. Were the animals investigating them? Or were they hunting them?

A sharp noise yelped in the distance, and Ayianna jumped

"It's only a fox." Aberim pulled on Treviko's halter. The camel grunted, but continued its slow, alternating stride. The other camel followed in the same manner.

Ayianna hesitated as the others fell back into line. Liam turned her head and loped after the camels. At least she was enjoying the cool reprieve. Ayianna clenched her jaw and willed herself to trust Aberim. He was the guide, after all.

Dawn burned fiery red on the horizon. The landscape slowly changed, even if the difference was only subtle. A few rock formations rose up out of the sand dunes. At one of the arched stones, Aberim halted.

"What's going on?" Desmond asked.

"We need rest." Aberim eyed the sky.

Desmond straightened. "We should almost be there. We can rest then."

"Without a proper break, we will travel slower."

"But we could be there in several hours. Certainly that would give us enough motivation to keep going."

Aberim turned and stroked the camel's neck.

Desmond kicked at the sand. He scratched his bearded chin and then drained the rest of his water in one gulp.

"Easy there." Vian uncapped his waterskin. "You don't want to get sick."

Desmond sneered. "As if you know anything about the desert."

Vian frowned and walked away, leaving Ayianna alone with Desmond. Vian had finally convinced him to wear the headcloth, but blisters had already formed on his forehead. His bloodshot eyes roamed the desert landscape and then settled on her.

"What are you looking at?"

"I . . . um." Ayianna glanced away. "It's just that you look like you're in pain. You shouldn't be so hard on Vian. He is only looking out for you."

"Not you too." He snarled and shoved her away. "Why don't you and your dog go cozy up with the prince."

Ayianna stumbled, but quickly caught her balance. She clenched her teeth and bit back a retort.

"Don't take what he says too seriously." Kael leaned against the stone outcropping and crossed his arms. "The fool is losing his mind."

"Don't call me a fool." Desmond growled and lunged for Kael.

Kael darted to the side, but Desmond caught him by the arm, flipped him over, and pounced atop of Kael. They wrestled to dominate the other, but all they managed to do was stir up the dust and fling sand everywhere.

Ayianna jumped out of the way. "Shouldn't we do something?"

Aberim shook his head. "Heat, lack of sleep, and scant water destroys the mind."

"Fools." Vian dropped his bag in the sand. His gaze never left the grappling men as he paced around them.

Kael spun free. He scrabbled toward the outcropping, but Desmond grabbed him. Kael elbowed Desmond in the ribs. Desmond roared and shoved Kael against the rocks.

Finally, Vian caught Desmond by the tunic and jerked him back. Desmond grunted. He flailed his arms, but Vian threw him into the sand.

"Get a hold of yourself." Vian's eyes flashed with a fire Ayianna hadn't seen before. "Or you really will be a fool."

"Aberim!" Kael yelled. "I've been bitten or something."

Ayianna whirled around.

Kael sat in the sand, holding his arm.

Aberim rushed to his side and inspected his hand. "Where?"

Ayianna searched the ground. What had bit him? Was it still here? A black shadow caught her eye as it scurried across the rock. She fell back. "Aberim, there. What is it?" She pointed, but it dove into the sand.

He grunted as he dug out a pouch from his belt. "A scorpion."

"Is it deadly?" she asked.

"Ha!" Desmond bellowed. He bent over and laughed. "I can't believe my good fortune."

"Hush, you fool." Vian growled, and his green eyes darkened.

"Of all the stupidity in Nälu." Aberim grit his teeth. He tied a strap of cloth around Kael's wrist. "Vian, Desmond, back a ways was a vine-like plant. Bring me back its fruit. Ayianna, I need your help."

She drew closer and knelt down.

"It burns." Kael massaged his right hand. His skin swelled around his forefinger and formed a blister.

"Stop rubbing your skin, you'll push the venom into your blood more quickly. Ayianna, apply pressure here." Aberim indicated near the makeshift tourney.

She placed her hands around Kael's hand and squeezed as tight as she could. He gritted his teeth. Aberim dug a clay jar out of his pouch. He poured out an amber-colored serum from the jar into a small cup.

"This is crazy! What kind of creature does this?" Kael gasped. "It's like fire moving under my skin."

"Don't worry, it shouldn't kill you." Aberim mixed something into the serum. "But the pain will make you wish you were dead."

"Well, that's a relief." Kael clenched his jaw. "Does it get worse?

"Drink this." Aberim held up the cup.

Kael lifted his head and drained it. He sputtered and gagged. "Yuck. Can I have some water?"

Aberim offered him his waterskin.

Kael swallowed and took a breath. "How long?"

"I don't know. Maybe a couple of hours to a day, if you make it past day three you should be fine."

Kael groaned.

"I have something that can lessen the pain." Aberim stood and went to his camel.

Kael dropped his head and leaned into Ayianna's shoulder. Ayianna's breath caught in her throat. His closeness caused her head to spin, but she focused her attention on squeezing his hand.

"I'll kill him," Kael said through gritted teeth. "Or maybe I'll drop a scorpion on his head."

33

DESMOND'S LITTLE INCIDENT cost them another day in the heat. Ayianna stared at the outcropping's surface and jumped at every flickering shadow. The small campfire burned against the cold, but she could not sleep. Finally, sometime before dawn she slumped over, unable to keep her eyes open.

Aberim roused them as the last stars started to fade. They set out with great expectation, but the day wore on without a glimpse of the oasis. It wasn't until the afternoon sun baked the desert, that Ayianna remembered Nerissa's vial.

"Kael," she whispered. It took too much energy to talk, but she added. "I'm sorry." She held up the vial and pulled back the dingy cloth wrapping his hand. She dribbled a bit of the kulin into the blistering wound. The tissue was discolored. That was a good sign, Aberim had assured them. *It's the stings you can't see you need to worry about.* At least it would heal up and go away. Unlike her wound.

"Is it painful still?"

"A little." He studied her. "I'll be fine."

She nodded, suddenly feeling awkward. Why did it bother her? Did she feel responsible for Desmond's actions? She fell back and was glad when Aberim signaled them to move on.

The air shimmered with heat. Silhouettes of buildings danced on the horizon—another mirage. Ayianna had quickly learned her lesson the first time when, after alerting the others, they arrived only to find desolate sand stretching as far as the eye could see.

The caravan shuffled on ahead. She yanked her boots against the weight of the sand in a monotonous rhythm, but with each step, she fell further behind. Her muscles burned and her limbs trembled. Absurd thoughts flew through her subconscious, but she couldn't muster them into coherency. She stumbled. She tried to crawl to her feet, but her boot caught the edge of her tunic, and she toppled into the sand. The heat of the sand seeped through her clothes and warmed her legs. How nice it would be to fall asleep and never wake up?

Liam whined and pawed at her back. A shadow broke from the caravan and glided toward her. Everything stopped moving except the hot wind on her face. Kael dropped next to her and offered her his waterskin. She shook her head.

"I can't do this anymore," she whispered through parched, blistered lips. Her heavy tongue scratched the roof of her mouth.

"Yes, you can."

"Let the desert take me."

"We are almost there."

"No, we aren't. Aberim said tomorrow, and tomorrow has come and gone twice over."

"We're closer than before. Drink, it will help." Kael uncorked the waterskin and held it up for her.

Ayianna drained the last drop in a swallow. "Now, there's no more." She coughed.

"Come on." He grabbed her elbow and pulled her to her feet.

Ayianna staggered after him and squinted in the glare of the setting sun. Faint outlines of buildings appeared on the horizon. Could it be? No. She couldn't bear the shattering of her hopes again. Oh, how she tired of the desert's games!

Liam whined. Ayianna closed her eyes, afraid to look at her faithful companion. Would the desert take her too? The wolf nudged her leg and whined again. Ayianna scratched Liam's furry head. Sand blanketed the wolf's fur and burned her fingers.

Ayianna frowned, but her lips cracked. She touched them with her swollen tongue and tasted blood. A sudden gust of heat scorched her cheeks, and she glanced up. In the distance, a wall of billowing sand darkened the eastern horizon.

She gasped. "Look!"

The men turned around and froze. The turbulent sand cloud boiled and seethed. It stretched forever north and south, and as it approached, it swelled to the heavens.

"We must run," Kael said.

"No, we should hunker down." Aberim coiled the camel's rope around his wrist and jerked his scarf over his mouth and nose. "Everyone, cover your faces."

"We will never last in that!" Kael thrust his hand to the west. "Zajur is near, we can see buildings and trees from here. We must try to reach it."

"And what if it's the trickery of the desert?"

"If we're wrong, then we can hunker down."

Aberim glared at Kael. "So be it."

Ayianna scrambled after the men as they raced toward the western horizon. The closer they drew, the more defined the structures became. The raging storm was almost on top of them. The wind tore at her clothes and whipped the edges of her headcloth. Sand pelted her exposed face. She glanced up, but the men had disappeared.

Reaching the city, Ayianna rushed through the open gate and into a maze of low buildings connected by clay awnings and narrow pathways. She yanked on the doors, but none gave way. Her stomach knotted. Liam pushed ahead, nosing the walls and scratching in the sand.

Someone grabbed Ayianna's arm and pulled her aside. She screamed for Liam, but the roar of the wind drowned her voice. Nevertheless, the wolf spun and dashed toward them. Once inside, Kael pressed the wooden door shut just as the wall of sand swept over the city.

The dark room muffled the howling winds. Leather covered the small windows to keep the storm out, but cracks were evident as small streams of sand poured through the edges. Kael slipped the orb from his knapsack.

"*Yetakoith taheza*," he whispered. The orb responded, and a faint glow filled the room.

"I hope the others made it." She sank to the floor next to Liam. Her eyes stung and watered as she tried to blink the grit away.

"Yes." Kael leaned against the opposite wall and closed his eyes.

They sat in silence. The winds wailed, and the leather shutters quivered at their gusts. Except for the piles of sand and two entryways, the area was bare. What kind of room was this? The door they came through rattled in its hinges. Suddenly, the strap binding the windows broke, and a blast of sand exploded into the room.

Kael scrabbled to his feet, grabbed Ayianna, and shoved her through the interior door.

"Hey!" She glared at him. "What is your problem?"

He reeled. "You are. I don't know why Saeed thinks that I need to play nursemaid for him."

His words tore into her. Her shock turned to hurt and then anger. "Why do you hate me? I've never done anything to warrant such . . . such behavior from you."

"I . . ." He clenched his jaw and looked away. "I don't hate you. It's just that dragging you along makes things harder."

"Me? How have I made things harder?" She paused as the realization hit her. "You mean Desmond? And if you hate him, you hate me."

He threw his hands up in the air. "This whole mess is no place for a woman."

"And where is my place?" She gritted her teeth against the tears stinging her eyes. She wouldn't cry. Not in front of him. She curled her fingers into a tight ball. The coward wouldn't even look at her.

"That's not what I meant."

"Then what did you mean?"

"Forget it." He pulled away and strode down the hall, holding his arm tight against his body.

She chased after him. "I can't."

Kael rounded on her. "Can't you just accept that I don't want you here?"

She stared at him. Something deep inside broke, and the truth seared her soul. She was completely, utterly alone. What had she thought? That he was her friend?

"Do you think I want to be here?" Her voice trembled. No. She fought it, but the harder she fought it, the more the tears came and spilled down her cheeks. She turned away and wiped them away.

"Ayianna . . ." Kael's voice cracked.

"You are nothing but a jerk." She pushed past him and rushed through the empty corridor. He wouldn't see her cry, not if she could help it.

Deeper inside the building, the howling of the winds diminished. Exhausted, Ayianna leaned against a wall, but Kael continued down the hall. The sand crackled underneath his feet and then ceased. She glanced up as he entered a room. She sighed, pushed herself from the wall, and followed him.

Large plump chairs sat in a circle. Elaborate tapestries adorned the brick walls. Zajur certainly looked rich—rich, but dirty. The sand covered everything in a fine, gritty film. She could never live in the desert.

Where was everyone? Was it normal to leave the gates unattended? Perhaps they didn't guard their gates. Who would expect an attack in the middle of the desert, especially, if they could see the enemy coming miles away? Hadn't they seen them coming?

"We'll rest here." He shook the sand from his blanket and flung it on the floor. Without another word, he stretched out on top of it and closed his eyes.

Ayianna clenched her teeth. She leaned against the wall and slid down. Liam curled beside her. She closed her gritty, burning eyes. How she longed for a bath and a tall pitcher of fresh water. She fell asleep, too tired to realize how unnatural the silence and absence of people were in Zajur.

34

KAEL SAT UP. His arm burned and nausea twisted his gut. He bent over and willed the queasiness to stop. He took a deep breath. How long would the scorpion haunt him? He forced his mind beyond the immediate discomfort of his body. An odd presence lingered in the room, but he heard nothing. The empty silence unnerved him the most. Where was everyone?

Ayianna lay in a heap against the wall and her head, kinked to the side, rested on Liam. She resembled her brother, except in a more delicate manner. Her dark eyelashes were thicker and longer, her face slender, and her rounded ears denied the elvish blood running in her veins.

Liam lifted her head and swiveled her ears first one way, then another. She looked at Kael. Did the wolf sense the odd presence as well? She stretched and rested her head on her paws, but her eyes remained on him. Ayianna shifted, and her braid fell away to reveal the puncture wounds on her neck.

Guilt slammed into him. He closed his eyes. *I knew. I knew what we were supposed to do, but I didn't do it. Why? Oh, Teron, it seems I cannot keep my oath.*

Kael stood. He shouldn't have to, she was betrothed. Didn't Teron know that? The situation irked him. In fact, everything irked him. He clenched his jaw. *She's right, I am a jerk. Osaryn, what have I become?*

He snatched his blanket and rolled it up. "Ayianna?"

"Mmmm?"

Her eyelashes fluttered against the gobs of dirt and sweat stuck to them. Desert grime smeared her face where she had wiped her tears away. Tears he caused. He ground his teeth and shook her shoulder.

"What?" She stretched her arms over her head and looked around. At least, her gaze had lost its glare.

He stuffed his blanket into his bag. "We need to go."

"Right." She staggered to her feet and leaned against the wall.

"We'll find the others and some water."

She nodded. Liam strolled around the room and sniffed the chairs and walls.

"All right there, Liam?" Ayianna asked. At the mention of her name, the wolf loped toward her. Ayianna ran her fingers through her fur and shook out the dust. "Liam, you need a bath worse than me."

"I'd have to disagree." Kael stepped out of the room.

She frowned. "You aren't too fresh either."

They wandered down the corridors, their footsteps echoing off the walls. Kael ran his hand along the yellow bricks. It reminded him of Dagmar. So much had happened since the attack. He was a world away from his old life, but none of that mattered anymore. He had nothing to return to. Sorrow choked him, and he quickly drove those thoughts away.

Down the hall, metal scraped against stone. Kael unsheathed his sword and listened. He crept forward and allowed his thoughts to reach out into the darkness. His mind touched a malevolent force, ancient and filled with bloodlust. It pulled at his conscious. Another presence mingled with the first, it was stronger, but guarded. He withdrew and tightened his grip on his sword.

Footsteps echoed ahead of them. Kael glanced back at Ayianna and inched forward. Who could guard their presence besides an elf? Perhaps the Haruzo? If they were in feline form, they could mind-speak but at least he would sense them. Where were they? He slid along the wall, reached the end of the hall, and peered around the corner. He jumped back as Desmond barreled into him.

"Ah, it's just Desmond and Vian." Kael shoved his sword into its sheath.

Desmond frowned. "How is it I always find you two together?" He shoved past Kael and strode down the hall to Ayianna.

"Perhaps if you'd be more responsible, I wouldn't have to keep doing your job."

Desmond kept his back to him as he spoke with Ayianna.

Kael shook his head and leaned against the wall. Why couldn't he sense Desmond? He reached out again, but this time his mind slammed into a barrier much stronger than a mere human could put forth. He recoiled and doubled his own mental defense. Desmond couldn't be that strong, could he?

"Have you seen Aberim?" Vian asked.

Kael shook his head.

Vian planted his hands on his hips. "I'm telling you, something is not right here. Storm or no storm, nobody leaves their gates abandoned."

"They're riding out the storm deeper inside," Desmond said as he walked up.

Ayianna stood next to him, tucked under his arm like a package. She avoided Kael's gaze and stared at the wall in front of her. What rubbish did Desmond tell her this time?

Kael turned away.

"Desert people have different customs." Desmond flashed a smile. "I mean, you can't expect them to sit outside guarding the gates in a sandstorm. Follow me, I have been here before."

He directed them back the way he and Vian just came and led them to an entrance. He pointed at the low ceiling. "All buildings in Zajur are connected, that way the people never have to face the desert's harsh elements unnecessarily."

The glow of the orb slid across barren walls as they passed through long, narrow corridors. A foul odor hung in the air and worsened as they drew nearer to the keep.

"What is that smell?" Vian sniffed. "Are the Haruzo a dirty race? Can't they smell this?"

"The Haruzo are impeccable when it comes to cleanliness," Desmond said over his shoulder. "I don't remember it smelling like this the last time I was here."

"I wouldn't think that's possible with all this sand and dirt everywhere," Ayianna said.

Kael slipped his headcloth over his nose and mouth. They pushed on without a soul in sight. A hall, a room, another hall, and soon they came upon the most interior room of Zajur. Desmond halted.

Kael pushed past him to see why he had stopped and wished he hadn't. The stagnant air rotted with death and sour body odor. Hundreds of gaunt bodies lay strewn about the room. Stark bones stuck out from shriveled skin as if they had outgrown its coverings. Hollow sockets stared back at him where eyes had once been.

"What is it?" Ayianna asked.

"Don't let her in here." Kael blocked the doorway.

Desmond flinched and buried his nose in the crook of his arm. He stared wide-eye at the scene before them. Vian peered over Desmond's shoulder and gagged.

"Get away from me!" Desmond scooted out of the way. He inspected his clothes and then turned his glare on the prince.

"What happened?" Vian wrapped the headcloth around his face.

Kael eyed the shadows. "Do you really want to know?"

"What if it's still here?" Desmond's face blanched, and he blinked furiously as he scanned the room.

"Let's not find out," Kael said.

Ayianna glared at him. "What is going on?"

"Trust me." Kael grabbed her shoulder and spun her around. "You don't want to know." She went without a fight, and for that he was thankful. He glanced back and shivered. Was there no one left?

"We'll retrace our steps." Desmond's voice trembled. "We can go to the kitchen, scavenge for food, and refill our waterskins. Then we leave."

"We can't leave until the storm is over." Kael glanced over his shoulder.

"What if *it* finds us?" Vian asked.

Kael shook his head. "We'll worry about that later. Let's get out of here."

Vian nodded. Desmond didn't wait any longer; he turned and fled down the corridor. Kael and the others rushed to keep up.

Hours later they trudged into the kitchen. Ayianna searched for signs of life, be it benign or otherwise, but it was empty. Bowls, rotting food, and cooking utensils lay scattered atop a long table in the center of the room. A massive black pot hung in the hearth. The fireplace filled one whole wall of the kitchen while barrels lined the other.

"I thought you said you knew this place?" Kael grabbed a wooden bucket from a shelf and stepped over to a barrel of water.

"Well, I've only been here a couple of times." Desmond plunged his head into the barrel and resurfaced, dripping wet.

"And it takes you hours to find the kitchen?" Kael's jaw tightened.

"I hadn't exactly come to cook." Desmond shook his head and ran his hands through his hair.

Kael's eyes narrowed. "It wouldn't hurt you to be a little more considerate of others. Nobody wants to drink that water after you've had your filthy head in it."

Kael dipped the bucket into a different barrel. He held it out, and Vian reached for it.

"Have you no manners, Prince?"

Vian lifted his chin. "Of course, I do. I'm royalty."

Kael handed the bucket to Ayianna, but she hesitated.

"Oh, right. I had thought . . . well . . . " Vian grimaced. "No, go ahead, Ayianna. Ladies first."

Although she didn't feel like a lady with her dirty clothes and parched throat, their actions softened her frustration. She took it and drank. The cool liquid spilled down her neck and soaked her clothes. All her cares and weariness drowned in the water. She handed the bucket back to Kael.

Kael gave it to Vian. "At least you have more manners than Desmond."

After filling their waterskins and scavenging for food, Desmond and Vian discovered the cellar and passed out on its floor. Kael circled the kitchen, scanning the walls and ceilings. Ayianna sat down at the long table and laid her head on it. Liam curled at her feet. Exhausted, she wanted to sleep but couldn't. Her skin burned and itched. Her body ached.

Pots, pans, and odd bits of cookery lined one of the kitchen's tall walls and hung above her head. At the back of the kitchen was an adjoining room with a large basin loaded with dirty dishes. Between the scullery room and the stairs leading down to the cellar was a door. Perhaps it led outside.

Her mind drifted back to the other room. What had the men seen? Fear blazed in their eyes and strained their voices. All she had experienced was the horrid stench, but the men's reactions lingered in her mind.

"Why don't you rest?" Kael sat next to her.

"What happened in that room?"

He ran his hand along the worn table top. "Evil."

"Why didn't you let me see it?"

"No one should have seen that."

"Dagmar was bad."

He shook his head. "Not this bad."

A shiver crept down her spine. "What do you feel?"

"Feel?"

She lifted her head. "You are an elf. You can sense things while others, like humans, can't. We are a dimwitted bunch."

"Some humans, yes, and I could name a few, but all the races have their share of dimwitted fellows. And according to Desmond, I am only half-elf, remember?"

"If that's the case, then you're more elf than human."

"Is that a good thing?" He leaned on his arm. Strands of hair had escaped the confines of his braid and framed his angular face. The shadows hid the scar across his eyebrow, but she could see the slender arc of his ears and the glint of the gold hoop piercing his right earlobe.

"I guess it depends on who is doing the judging, huh?" She tried to smile, but her swollen lips cracked in protest.

His face relaxed. "But you are part elf. What do you sense?"

Her breath caught in her throat. "How do you know that?"

"Is it not common knowledge?"

She shook her head. "Not among the humans."

"Do you despise your elven heritage?"

"Of course not. I'd give anything to return to Zurial."

"So why do you hide . . . " He straightened and eyed her. "You *want* to marry Desmond."

She flinched. The tone of his voice sharpened and pierced her. Did he detest her even more? She shook her head and covered her face with her hands. Her heart ached. If she could just be free of all the secrets.

"My father . . . " She pushed past the knot in her throat. "At my mother's insistence, he thought it best to betroth me to him."

"So you choose to live a lie?"

"Why do you care?" Ayianna glared at him. "I am nothing to you. After this is all over, I have nothing but the betrothal."

"It isn't right."

"Don't you think I know?" She stood and turned away. But where could she go? She was trapped. *Osaryn, I don't want this, but I don't have a choice, do I?*

"Ayianna?"

She clenched her jaw. She had just given him more reason to hate her, and he didn't even know about her curse. Why did she care? She glanced along the shelves against the back wall. A couple of clay jars sat undisturbed. Perhaps she'd find some food.

"Ayianna," he whispered. "I won't tell him."

35

AYIANNA HAD DRIFTED in and out of sleep while Kael and Vian searched for Aberim. She huddled under her blanket and watched the flickering candles burn down. The cellar was a nice change from the constant scorn of the sun, even if it did get a little chilly. The underground room ran the expanse of the kitchen as far as she could tell. Shelves lined the walls, and the room contained an assortment of jars, barrels, sacks, and wooden crates.

At the other end, Desmond opened a barrel. Guilt jabbed her. It wasn't right to live a lie. She was deceiving the man she would marry, but what would he say if he knew the truth? He could reject her, and then she would be free of the betrothal. But would he punish her? Could he? She tired of wrestling with her thoughts.

She stood and wandered to the end of the cellar. How would she tell him? Her stomach twisted, and her heart pounded in her head.

"What did you find?" Her voice sounded small in her ears.

Desmond grinned. "A barrel of honey mead. Come, join me." He got a second cup, filled it, and handed it to her.

"Thanks." She accepted the cup and took a drink. The liquid was sweet yet sharp.

"This mead is milder than most, but it's still good." He brushed stray hair from her face. "How are you?"

"All right, I guess." She sipped the cup and glanced up at him.

Candlelight shimmered in his blue eyes, making them look green. His blond hair hung in greasy, tangled locks, and a dingy beard covered half of his face unlike Kael, who could never grow one. Still, he remained handsome. The facial hair added character, but what did it feel like?

She reached out and touched his cheek, the coarse whiskers prickled against her skin. "How about you?"

He smiled, leaned forward, and kissed her. "It's getting better already."

Warmth flooded her face. He slipped his hand around hers and pulled her closer. The smell of the honey mead filled her nose and almost covered his rancid body odor. He nuzzled the side of her head, his beard scratching and tugging her hair. "I wish we could've had a normal courtship."

"I need to tell you something." She forced the words out.

He pulled away, but kept her hand in his.

She took a deep breath. "I-I need you to know something about me—my family." She couldn't look at him, but plunged on before she lost her nerve. "My father was an elf."

She glanced up.

His countenance hadn't changed. He simply smiled. "You thought I couldn't figure that out?"

She stared at him speechless. He already knew and still wanted to marry her? "You don't . . . mind?"

He threw back his head and laughed.

"But I thought, as much as you hate Kael, you couldn't have known what I was."

He sobered up. "Kael is arrogant and a fool. He doesn't respect my culture, thus he doesn't respect me." He paused, his eyes twinkling. "But you, on the other hand, are different. You are better than he is."

He drained his cup and tossed it aside. He slid his arms around her and kissed her again.

Ayianna trembled. Why did she fight it? If she was going to spend the rest of her life with him, she had to be willing. She swallowed the knot in her throat and kissed him back. Excitement ravaged her insides. Yes, she could be willing . . .

She lingered in his embrace, his breath hot against her hair. The chaos around them forgotten, husband and wife forging a new life. She could accept that.

He pulled back, his eyes alit with a new fire. "Do you have any other secrets I need to know?"

She hesitated. "Actually, there's more."

"Well, why don't we sit, and you can tell me all about it." He drew her over to a bench against the opposite wall. "Marriage is built on trust. Man and wife should have no secrets."

She nodded and sat next to him. He faced her, leaning his left shoulder into the wall, and continued holding her hand. She couldn't remember him being so affectionate, but then, they hadn't been alone for any length of time. Or could it be the mead?

She took another drink. Was she being hasty? He didn't need to know about her father, did he? But what if those men came looking for her again, how would she explain it to him? She drained the last drop of the mead. If her father chose him, then she should trust him.

"My father was a secret keeper. He left Zurial and tried to keep his identity hidden, but these men found us and tried to kill me." Her voice wavered. Tears slid down her face and pooled on her chin. She wiped them away with the edge of her sleeve.

He squeezed her hand.

"Instead they killed my father and now, I think they're after me. At least they were. They followed me to Dagmar and then Badara." She glanced up. "And they've kidnapped my mother."

"Why didn't you tell me this before?" He brushed the tears from her cheeks.

"I don't know."

"What did these men want?"

She hesitated. Everything within her told her stop, but it felt so good to trust, to feel his hands on hers. "They were looking for a dagger."

"They killed your father for a dagger?"

"It's a special dagger, created to do horrible things."

A look of concern flashed across Desmond's face. "Did they get it?"

She shook her head.

"Do you know where it is?'

"No. My mother might, maybe my brother, but I don't know. They kept so much from me."

"I'm sorry your father didn't trust you with something so important, but he probably had his reasons, seeing as those men tried to kill you."

"I should've died that day. The sword that killed my father should've killed me."

"Don't say that." He put his arm around her.

She pressed into his chest and cried. She released the guilt, the anger, the condemnation. It was over. She had nothing to hide from him. Grief poured out of her wretched soul, and she allowed it.

He stroke her hair in silence, and when she calmed down, he asked, "Did your father give you a blessing when he died?"

She shook her head. "He only had enough life in him to give me a message for my brother."

"Oh? I'm sorry." He squeezed her shoulder. "But maybe it was blessing in disguise."

"He said, tell Teron the sun has set and something about the morning star being locked inside a stone. Then he was gone."

"It sounds more like a riddle, than a blessing." He stroked her hair. "I'm sorry, Ayianna. Soon, this will all be over, and we can put it behind us."

"I can't wait." She snuggled deeper into his arms.

"Hey!"

Ayianna jumped, her heart thudding against her ribs.

Kael stood at the base of the stairs; his arms braced against the narrow stairwell.

Desmond stood and stretched. "What do you want?"

"The storm's over."

Kael's voice was harsh. Fury burned in his eyes, but he would not meet hers. Why was he so upset?

"Did you find Aberim?" She wrapped her arms around herself.

"No."

"Maybe he already left." Desmond picked up the barrel's lid and replaced it. "He wanted to get back to his wife quickly, and we were behind schedule."

Kael narrowed his eyes, but his face remained unreadable. "Maybe. Vian found some extra knapsacks we can use. Pack what you can carry."

"Are there no camels we could take?" Desmond lifted his hands. "Riding would be better, and we could pack more food and water."

"It's only a two-day journey." Kael's frown deepened, but he dropped his arms. "I'll check the stables. Maybe I'll find Aberim there."

Ayianna's stomach plummeted with each of Kael's footsteps as he climbed the stairs two at a time. Had she done something wrong? No. She had revealed everything to Desmond like any good bride should. Almost everything. She had no more secrets, except the harpy's curse. But he didn't need to know the specifics, did he? Kael couldn't have known she had told Desmond the truth. Was that why he was angry? Why should she care? Once this was all over with, it wouldn't matter what he thought.

36

"KAEL SHOULD'VE BEEN back already." Desmond paced the cellar.

"Would you sit down?" Vian leaned against the wall and stretched out his legs. "With our luck, we'll be walking to Bonpazur. Besides, you're making me dizzy."

Ayianna sat crossed-legged atop her blanket, but the chill from the stone floor seeped into her legs. She picked at the crusty stains on her pants. The long passing hours gnawed on her nerves.

She glanced up. "Maybe we should go check on him."

"No, he said to wait here for him," Vian said.

"But what if . . . " She didn't want to think about that. She stood and shook out her clothes, but they were stiff with dirt and dried sweat. Perhaps she'd start pacing too.

"Well." Desmond crossed his arms. "If he's not here soon, we'll leave without him."

A muffled thump sounded above them.

"See, that's probably him right now." Vian gathered his bags and waterskin.

"It's about time." Desmond charged up the stairs.

A clanging noise ruptured above them as if someone knocked one of the kettles from the wall. Ayianna jumped. Why would Kael be messing with the pots and pans?

Desmond froze. "What's he trying to do, scare us?"

"Kael wouldn't make that much noise." She inched closer to Desmond. "He's an elf."

"He could be making noise to let us know he's back, so he doesn't scare us half to death when he opens the door," Desmond said, but he didn't move up the stairs.

"Listen!" Vian's voice came out in a hiss.

Ayianna forced herself to breathe slower and strained to hear over her thudding heart.

"Kael!" a voice cried out. "Vian . . . Dethmond?"

"It's Aberim!" Vian laughed, but his voice held no humor.

"Feeling a little foolish now?" Desmond bounded up the stairs, thrust the door open, and rushed into the kitchen.

Ayianna and Vian followed close behind. She scanned the kitchen. "Aberim?"

Desmond and Vian looked in the washroom.

"Help!" Aberim cried. His voice was thick and garbled.

Ayianna ran to the other side of the table. He lay on his side, his back to her. His outer robe was gone, and his tunic and pants hung in strips. Yellow sand lay strewn about the floor around him.

"Aberim!" she shouted.

Desmond and Vian darted across the room, dodging the table, and skidded to a stop on the sandy floor next to her.

"Away!" he shrieked. Guttural sobs shook the man's broad shoulders. He dropped his sword and tried to push up from the ground, but his arms collapsed beneath him.

Ayianna knelt by his side. His exposed skin appeared shiny and tight. Red splotches covered his arms and neck. He turned over to face her.

She screamed. His friendly eyes were gone, and, in their place, shriveled hollows glared at her. He grappled toward her, his limbs flailing in the sand. She fell backward as she retreated.

"Kill me, pleath." His mouth moved oddly, and his face twisted in pain.

"What happened?" Desmond stepped back.

A desert breeze blew through the kitchen, and Ayianna shivered despite its warmth.

"They're coming!" he screamed. "Kill me. Don't let them get me. Pleath!"

Aberim slumped to the floor, and the kitchen grew silent. Had he died?

Desmond peered closer.

Then Ayianna noticed a small child cowering beneath the table.

She didn't know whether to scream, laugh, or cry. She had never seen anything like it before. Void of clothes and gender, the small child wrapped its long spindly fingers around the table's leg and inched forward. It lifted its head from the shadows and looked up. Large blue eyes glimmered like sapphires and drew Ayianna closer.

She bent down, but Desmond's hand was on her shoulder.

The child-like creature trembled. Its gaze never left Ayianna's face.

"Hey little one, are you all by yourself?" Ayianna asked.

"Um, Ayianna." Vian stepped back. "Creature—remember? Dead people?"

"You think he did it?"

"Don't touch it." Desmond's grip tightened, and he tugged Ayianna closer. "I don't like the way he is looking at you."

The creature glanced at Aberim and then back to Ayianna. It limped forward, its big eyes fixed on her. It tilted its head. The blue of his eyes swirled black as it opened its mouth wider than should have been possible. Rows of tiny, jagged teeth lined the fleshy insides of his lips.

It lunged and latched onto her arm, its touch like fire.

Ayianna screamed as hundreds of sharp teeth pricked her skin. She shook her arm and banged it against the table, but the creature only squeezed harder.

Desmond ripped it off and threw it across the room.

The creature shrieked. It slammed into the wall, but quickly scrambled to its feet and leapt back in a single bound.

Desmond unsheathed his sword and caught the creature midair. Yellow sand showered the kitchen.

"What was that?" Vian brushed the sand from his face and clothes.

"It's gone now." Desmond turned. "Are you all right?"

Ayianna nodded, but stared at her arm where the creature had bit her. Blood oozed from the many tiny teeth marks, and she wiped it off on her pants.

"Did it suddenly get hot in here?" Desmond asked.

But Vian didn't respond. His pale face mirrored horror as he stared up at the ceiling.

Ayianna followed his gaze and froze.

They were everywhere, climbing along the walls and ceiling. They crawled toward them like bobbling waves along the shore. They opened and closed their fleshy lips in a chant. Their harsh voices filled the kitchen.

"*Quatat! Quatat!*"

Then they dropped to the floor.

Ayianna pulled her fairy-crafted sword from its sheath. Vian drew his blade and waved it in front of him. Desmond charged, swiping and chopping away at the onslaught of the yellow monsters. Bursts of sand exploded around him.

Still, they advanced.

Ayianna threw a large kettle and knocked several over. She swung her sword clumsily around her, trying to keep them at bay.

A hot, gritty hand grasped her neck. She whirled around, clawing at the creature's rough yellow skin. It fell off, and she kicked it across the room. Two more leapt upon her. They tugged and ripped her clothes. She spun, swiping at them with her sword.

Desmond and Vian plowed through the hordes, but it was no use. They just kept coming. There were hundreds of them with the same yellow skin and big blue eyes. When one was killed, three more were in its place.

"*Quatat! Quatat!*" Their guttural chants continued undeterred.

Ayianna's sword fell from her hands. Several suctioned themselves onto her arms and now exposed legs. Their touch burned. Many more pulled at her hair and remaining clothes. She stumbled to the ground, feeling around for her sword. She gasped for help, but Vian and Desmond fought their own losing battles. The creatures clung to their bodies, some already latched on, sucking away their lives.

Ayianna gripped the side of the table and pulled herself up. She swayed under their weight. Her ears roared with the pounding of her heart. Her body was on fire. She tried to cry for help, but her throat was dry, her tongue thick. She was so thirsty. The room swirled around her; her vision blurred. Her strength dwindled fast. Only one thought lingered in her hazy mind—water. She saw the large drum in the scullery room. She stumbled toward it and fell to the ground.

Liam's snarling grew louder as the wolf bounded toward Ayianna, scattering creatures everywhere. Liam sunk her teeth into one on Ayianna's face and tore it off. Ayianna gasped. The creature hissed and attacked Liam with its spindly fingers. *No, not Liam!* Ayianna pummeled it, but it kept clawing the wolf. Its hands stained with blood.

Ayianna remembered her brother's dagger. She grabbed it and stuck the creature in the back. A burst of sand rained down on her and Liam. The wolf was a blur now, but at least she still moved. Voices hollered around her, but Ayianna couldn't understand them.

She crawled to the drum and pulled herself over the edge. The water hissed and steamed as it washed over her. The creatures sputtered and shrieked, releasing her. They fled.

Ayianna tried to stand, but sank beneath the surface of the water. She scratched at the sides of the large barrel; her lungs cried for air. Someone grabbed her hands as she slipped into darkness.

37

AYIANNA STRETCHED, HER arms sore and heavy. On the edge of awareness, she burrowed deeper into the softness surrounding her and sought the oblivion of sleep again. An odd mix of happiness and grief followed her from her dreams and clung to her mind like veils of mist. What had she been dreaming?

She blinked away the sleep and sat up. The room spun. She doubled over and closed her eyes. In the darkness, the world righted itself, and she took a deep breath. She caught a familiar yet strange scent. The smell drew her back into her dreams.

She had been at a wedding, her wedding. She wore a midnight blue dress swathed in layers upon layers of palest pinks and purples. People stood in lines swirling and spiraling out to the edge of the large, sacred ring. Inside, she would find the sanctum, and there her beloved waited. Her heart rushed, but she would not.

She danced slowly through the circular lines of people. White flowers rained around her. She stood on her tiptoes and tried to catch a glimpse of her betrothed, but it was no use. The people's arms waved and more flowers fell.

Her mother appeared and slipped a delicate, star-studded crown on her head. Beyond the rings of dancing people, her father and brother conversed. She called to them, but the clamor drowned out her voice. She continued to dance. She needed to find her beloved. Closer and closer she drew until at last she passed the last person and stepped into the inner sanctum.

Her beloved was not there.

The happiness and love had felt so real and the loss even sharper. Ayianna rubbed her face. *It's only a dream.* A dream which she already knew its outcome. Desmond. What had changed between them? Had she begun to trust him?

She straightened and glanced around. Light streamed through an open window. A large oval hung from a wall and reflected light, brightening the room even more. A cushioned chair and a wooden wardrobe sat against the other walls. Where was she? What happened? Glimpses of smelly camels and tall, dark men slipped through her mind. Had they made it to Bonpazur?

Ayianna crawled out of bed, and her long hair fell loose down her back, brushing against her naked skin. She gasped. Where were her clothes? She grabbed the frail linen blanket from the bed, wrapped it around her, and darted to the wardrobe.

Inside, she found her knapsack, her hairpin, and a few sleeveless tunics. She donned one of the shirts. The embroidered bottom hung at her knees, and the squared neck drooped around her shoulders, but at least she wasn't naked anymore. She twisted her hair into a loose bun and stuck the hairpin into it. *Now to find the others.*

She glanced out the window. A golden city sprawled in a lush oasis. Beyond its curtain walls, square adobe homes stacked atop each other and lined narrow streets. In the distance, the sand dunes of the Zriab desert stretched forever into the horizon.

Home . . . she'd never been so far from it and now a vast sea of sand lay between them. She'd have to endure the heat, the sand, and its dangers all over again just to return. She wrapped her arms around herself and tried to quell the rising nausea.

Below, people flowed in and out like the ocean surf. The dust from the desert swirled in the streets and most likely made its way into their homes. A brief memory of the grit covering the floors and walls of Zajur flitted through her mind. She couldn't imagine having to deal with the sand day in and day out. Her skin crawled just thinking about it.

A knock broke her reverie.

"Good morning, child." An elderly, dark-skinned woman greeted her with a nod. She carried a tray of flatbread and fruit in her hands, while a white towel and a blue garment draped over her arm. Tight gray curls hugged her dark face. A brown smock swung loosely above her bare feet as she walked. She set the tray on the small table next to the bed.

"Good morning," Ayianna replied.

"I am Golma. Have you slept well?"

"Yes, thank you."

"Please eat, you must be starving."

Ayianna nodded. She selected a round flatbread and bit into it. It contained a nutty sweetness, and her stomach growled its thanks. She glanced up at Golma. "Do you know where my . . . travel companions are? My wolf?"

"They are well. You have had a devoted visitor, but you were asleep. He is making sure the wolf is well cared for."

Desmond. Ayianna couldn't help the grin. "Where are they now?"

"They are with the king. I am here to prepare you to meet the queen. Come." She disappeared through the doorway.

The Queen?

Ayianna stuffed the rest of the flatbread into her mouth, grabbed another, and followed after Golma. The elderly servant led her through the castle's halls and upstairs into another hall, passing several guards on their way, each one dark-skinned and wearing only a deep green loincloth. Gold bands circled their biceps. They stood alert with a halberd in hand.

"Have you been to a *zaporza*?" Golma asked. She stopped at a large door and pushed it open.

Ayianna shook her head.

The elderly woman went on to explain. "It is a bathhouse customary in Bonpazur. The waters have been freshly heated."

The elderly lady pushed open a second door, and Ayianna halted. Naked women of all ages filled the spacious room. Some bathed in a large pool while others sat in a cloud of steam. Scores of female servants, dressed in white smocks and gold bracelets, attended to their needs, bringing towels, combing hair, and rubbing bodies with fragrant oils. Several servants fanned the fires and placed heated stones in the pool. The rocks hissed, sending steam rolling out of the water.

"My child, wash and dress." Golma set the towel and blue garment on a stone bench and turned to go.

"But where are my clothes?" Ayianna tried to focus on Golma's face, but caught sight of a bare-breasted woman behind her. She glanced away and saw the backside of another woman. Finally, Ayianna just stared at the floor.

"They are not fit to wear, so the queen has supplied you with new clothes. The maidservants will assist you when you are finished bathing. I leave you now."

Ayianna glanced up.

Golma bowed her head and ducked out of the room.

Ayianna turned toward the wall, and her hair fell down over her face. She quickly braided it, piled it atop her head, and jabbed the pin it again, but this time she pricked her scalp. She gritted her teeth. *Of all the things, I have to go and poke my head!*

Her trembling fingers tugged at her nightgown. Her temples tightened as heat flooded her face. She glanced at the pool. The other women chatted, quite comfortable with each other's nudity. At least they all looked alike. Not her. Her olive skin glared out of place like a weed in a lovely flower garden.

Ayianna swallowed, took a deep breath, and then pulled off her nightgown. She darted to the edge of the pool and stepped in. She sank beneath the surface until only her head remained above. The waters were hot and perfumed. She closed her eyes.

The embarrassment slowly subsided, and her thoughts slipped to her betrothed. Desmond had checked on her. Devoted, Golma had said. It thrilled her and scared her. Was she ready? Marriage . . . Oh, her heart was a fickle thing! She had to see him again. She needed confirmation. *Osaryn, what am I to do? If he is my chosen husband, what else is there to do but accept? I've not been good at this praying thing, but please—*

"*Zabbi!*" A voice wrenched Ayianna from her thoughts as a young girl emerged from the water next to her. "*Zja azur li?* You are not from here. Are you the new *yzaharo*? The king's mate?"

Ayianna's hand slipped; her head went under. She came back up, spitting out water. The perfumes left a bitter taste in her mouth.

"Are you fine?" the girl asked. Her accent weighed on her words as if she was talking through her teeth. Colorful beads adorned her black braids swirling tightly around her head and spilling down her neck. Long eyelashes lined her eyes, and her dark, round face was youthful, full of expression, and without a care.

Ayianna coughed, but nodded. Aware of how close the young girl was, Ayianna inched away, but the pool's cold ledge halted her retreat.

"Well, are you?" The young girl stared unflinching into Ayianna's eyes.

"Am I what?"

"The new mate? How you call it, the new wife? Everyone has been speaking of her. The king announced it last week. Tonight we celebrate the *hazzerquer,* the—ah—union."

Ayianna crossed her arms. She couldn't remember how clear the water was, but she wasn't going to take any chances. "How many wives does the king have?"

"Five."

Ayianna raised her eyebrows. How could a king have more than one wife? Badara might allow its men to take as many as three wives, but not the king. The birthright would be a mess. Who would succeed him?

The girl toyed with one of her braids. "So what are you doing here?"

"Here?" Ayianna frowned. "I'm trying to bathe."

"Without a sponge?" The girl laughed. She swam over to the other ledge where a basket of sponges sat. "Silly foreigners." She flung the braids over her shoulder and returned.

"Here, you use this sponge to clean your pale skin. It has come from Ganya. The Kaleki harvest them. Can you imagine how fine it would be to meet a merman?"

Ayianna accepted the sponge.

The girl stared off into the distance, her eyes grew wistful. She couldn't have been more than ten years old. Not enough time for the world to crush her dreams.

The girl's attention returned to Ayianna, and she tilted her head. "Sand and water do not mix, do they?" She shrugged and began scrubbing her own body. "Everyone is preparing for the king's wedding feast and speculating about the new mate." She leaned closer and whispered, "It will be the biggest celebration of them all. The other mates have been preparing her room, but no one has seen her yet."

"So, the others are not jealous?" Ayianna asked.

"How could they be? They are married to the king of Bonzapur!" The girl splashed the water.

Ayianna tilted her head. "Does that mean there are five queens?"

The girl laughed. "No, he has one *franth-haro*. The other wives are called the *yzaharo,* and their firstborns are entitled to rule one day. They may rule the cities of the desert, but only firstborn of the *franth-haro* may rule Bonpazur. I am Liara, firstborn, but my mother is a *yzaharo.* One day I shall rule one of the desert cities like the wind!" The little girl flung her long, thin braids over her shoulder.

"I wouldn't be too excited about living in the desert." Ayianna scrubbed her arms with the sponge. She cringed under its rough texture, her skin still tender.

"You are beautiful. You could be the new mate." Liara smiled.

"Thank you, but I'm betrothed to another man."

"Oh, I see." Liara tossed her sponge at the basket, but it missed and tumbled beyond it.

Their conversation lilted, but then Ayianna caught sight of a man walking across the smooth stone floor.

Ayianna gasped. "What's he doing in here?"

"That is Siloo. He is a *habor pujath*—um—he is not a *haru*. How do you call it? He is a eunuch."

"A what?"

"He has no . . . " The girl bit her lower lip and glanced away. "You know, he has been cut. He is safe. The king trusts him to guard his harem."

"Harem?"

"Where do you come from? You know nothing of our culture. You must be *puzpa*, a commoner."

"I'm from the Prathae Plains, on the other side of the Ruzat Mountains. I am quite sure you know nothing of my culture or the culture of the elves or dwarves either," Ayianna replied.

"Perhaps, but I have read about their cultures."

"You can't learn everything in books."

"What would a *puzpa* know about books? In your culture, you do not teach the people to read except the nobility."

Ayianna stared at her. Why was she even bothering to argue?

Liara lifted her head. "I must go. You finish bathing before your skin wrinkles or the oil will . . . fall off." She neared the shallows and stood.

"Oil?" Ayianna averted her gaze away only to see another woman in all her naked glory step into the pool.

"The servants will oil your skin to make it smell good and protect it from the dryness of the desert." Liara shook her head as two maidservants engulfed the little girl in the towel. "Obviously, you should try not to be so ignorant of other cultures."

Ayianna took a deep breath. Why did the girl rile her so?

She swam to the edge, climbed out, and stormed to her towel. She rigorously dried her body, but then noticed the two maidservants drawing near. One held an ornate jar filled with oil. The other took her towel. Ayianna's anger fled and embarrassment rushed in as the maidservant poured the contents of the jar over her shoulders while the other rubbed the fragrant oil into her skin. Ayianna closed her eyes and counted.

Once she had dressed, she breathed easier. The servants led her past a polished metal rectangle that hung like a painting on the wall. She paused. A young woman with her mother's face and her father's hair stared back at her. She titled her head.

The soft blue blouse buttoned down the front and then split into several flowing long rectangular strips of fabric that covered a deeper blue pants that swirled when she walked. She loved it.

"Beautiful!" Golma had returned. "The Queen is waiting."

King Runako hadn't moved since Kael had relayed what happened in Zajur. The king stood at the large window and looked upon his golden city. He wore no clothes except a white skirt-like wrap which contrasted with his dark, polished skin. A wide, gold belt circled his waist. The ambassadors of the northern and southern province conversed quietly across the room, glancing every so often at the king.

Lord Nyason, ambassador to Parzanth in the south, was tall and skinny like a graceful hound. On the other hand Lord Mahdi, ambassador of Zaffa, was short and stubby like an old bulldog. Each wore a white linen tunic and a woven band of colorful threads around his forehead.

Runako turned from the window. "I am thankful my warriors made it in time to save you, but sad we had not heeded Eloith's advice sooner. You will be safe here. My library is at your service, and I hope you find what you are looking for. I am uncertain what Eloith has accomplished, but my nephew, Tariq, will aid you in your search."

"Thank you, your Majesty." Kael bowed.

One of the lords cleared his throat, and Mahdi stepped forward. "If I may be permitted to speak, *Fraaro Zhiipa*?"

King Runako nodded.

Mahdi smiled. His yellowed teeth blinked against his dark lips. The folds of his weathered skin hid his eyes, except when he arched his brows and exposed their creamy whites.

"Does this mean you have made your decision to join the Alliance?"

"Lord Mahdi, you are here on behalf of my brother to discuss this, why would I decide before then?"

He bowed. "But of course, I mean no disrespect, but are you not now giving assistance to the Nevins by allowing these . . . persons access to the royal library? Might I remind you that the Nevins refused our request for aid during your father's reign?" He paused but quickly added, "my *Zhiipa*."

"Mahdi," Lord Nyason spoke up, "we were not the only nation with difficulties during that time. Do not waste the *Zhiipa*'s time on grudges."

"Well-spoken." Runako turned to Mahdi. "What I decide to do with my library is my business. What the nation of Bonpazur will or will not do will be decided the day after tomorrow. Let us not get ahead of ourselves. Tonight, I and all of Bonpazur will celebrate my union."

"Of course, my *Zhiipa*." Mahdi bowed deeply.

"Kael, please rest today and join us in our celebration this evening. I will see that you and your companions are well accommodated."

Kael nodded. "Thank you, your Majesty."

He turned and strode from the room. He clenched his jaw. Merriment was the last thing he needed. Where was Vian? Desmond? They couldn't still be sleeping, could they? He'd wake them this time, and then he'd find Eloith and see what he had uncovered in the library.

38

AYIANNA FOLLOWED GOMA through the great halls of the palace. Great tapestries hung from the ceiling against the beige stone. Woven in its threads were the stories of the seven races of Nälu: Man, Elf, Dwarf, Pauden, Kaleki, Haruzo, and Naajiso. Then the hall emptied into a large round room with a dome ceiling.

Elaborate murals depicting epic battle scenes and grand celebrations adorned the round room, each scene fading into another. The rays of the sun spilled through the narrow arched windows and caused the paintings to glimmer. Copper paneling ran along the base of the walls. Hazrul runes embossed the shiny metal and told the story of the murals above. But what they said, Ayianna couldn't tell.

"You like the paintings?"

The Haruzo queen stood in the arched doorway. Tall and dark-skinned, she wore a white linen sheath-dress, adorned with delicate embroidery and tiny emeralds that glittered when she walked. Her black hair was braided into a bun that exploded with tiny curls. She didn't wear a crown like the queens Ayianna had read about, but instead, bright emeralds dotted her braids and temples.

"*Zhiipa-Naaru*," Golma said, bowing.

"Ah . . . " Ayianna stammered, not sure what to do. She glanced at the maidservant and bowed as well. "Uh—yes, I do, *Zhiipa-Naaru*."

"Rise, Golma, please bring Turina to the merchant hall."

"*Isoth*, my *Naaru*." The maidservant bowed and disappeared down the hallway.

"The mural tells the birth of Nälu." With a smile at Ayianna, the queen pointed to a wall, and her wooden bangles clicked together, echoing in the room.

A black shadow stretched to the ceiling and threatened to destroy the peoples beneath it. Its outstretched arm reached for a young elf riding a white horse. Many young men and women lay scattered over the ground, a bloody cavity in their chest where their heart should have been.

Ayianna shivered.

"A thousand years ago, Nälu was overshadowed in darkness; a divided land, it had no name. Lord Stygian had forged a forbidden union with Taethza, the queen of the underworld. She gave him immortality and the Tóas Dikon. In return, he worshiped her with the blood of the innocent. The seven races formed an Alliance to defeat them."

The dark Haruzo woman lowered her arm. Everything about her radiated grace and elegance. Not even the elves could compare to her fluid movements and lovely poise. She glided to the next scene. The shadow contrasted with white, glittering rays of light. The young elf lay dead at the feet of Taethza, his heart in her hands. The queen of death's face contorted in pain.

"Trygg, the only person to return from Zohar alive, did so, but not without a cost. His death released Karasi, the Sacred Pearl, from her confinement, breaking the wretched covenant between Taethza and Lord Stygian. Thus ended the dark age, and the land became Nälu."

340

Ayianna touched the mural's cool surface. Had not her father told the same stories when she was a child? But at the time, they seemed mere folklore, rather than the history of nations. Moving onto the next scene, she recognized the castle of Dagmar. People from all races streamed through its gates. Painted banners representing different nations overlapped the image.

"Njira, the only guardian to have survived Stygian's evil Dwäza, built Dagmar and the Kayulm'sa Nutraadzi, the guardian's School of Nevins, choosing the next generation of Nevins to complete the Guardian Circle under the leadership of Karasi."

"You speak about the Sacred Pearl as if it were a person." Ayianna stepped back from the wall.

The queen nodded. "There is mystery surrounding her. Some say she is one of the Chai, the twelve immortal rulers of Zohar, kidnapped from her paradise and confined to this world in a pearl of great size. Some say she is the mother of the Naajiso. For when she was taken from Zohar, she wept, and the fairies sprang from her tears." She rubbed the gold bangles around her wrist. "Karasi used to appear before the guardians, but she has been silent for centuries now. Some say she has died, others say she is biding her time until the end of Nälu when she will return home."

Ayianna stared at the large, white globe painted on the wall. The pearl was more than another idol fashioned by hands and tools to be worshipped like her mother's Nuja, but how did it fit in with Osaryn or the Nevin's Shadow God? And there was that strange word again. Chai. The woman from Durqa had used it and now the Queen. "What do you mean, 'the end of Nälu'?"

"The Thzaj Prophecy speaks of it. Where Njira will return with all the armies of Zohar in a final battle against the queen of the underworld."

Ayianna gazed at the final painting. A shadow rose up against Nälu. Great fire danced at the shadow's feet. Death and darkness shrouded Nälu once again. A man stood to fend off the imposing black cloud, holding only a silver shield. A thread of gold circled nine colorful stones and three pearls on its center. All the nations fled into the rising sun, but they were met with five great men astride white horses, adorned for war. Light clashed against Darkness again for the last time.

"What is the prophecy?"

"It is a two-fold warning, but of vigilance and hope. When all seems dark and the days grow evil, Zohar will not forget the people of Nälu, but in order to regain that which was lost, Nälu must end."

Ayianna brushed her fingertips on the silver shield. "Who is he?"

"The Chosen One—only he will know how to use the great shield of Zohar."

"Do you think we are in the days of the prophecy?"

"Prophecies are difficult to understand, and the Thzaj Prophecy speaks of the dagger and the shield. Each serves its purpose but at different times and reasons." The Haruzo raised her arm to the archway. "We should proceed."

Dagger? Ayianna tore her eyes away from the paintings and followed after the Haruzo woman down another corridor. Was her father guarding the prophecy's dagger? If only the queen would elaborate. Who else knew? Kael? Eloith. She'd ask the fairy.

The queen led Ayianna into a large room. "I am certain after such an ordeal in the desert you must be exhausted. How are you feeling this morning?"

Ayianna hardly heard the queen as she took in the explosion of color. Amid the twisting marble pillars, tables of fabric, trinkets, and pottery filled the room. Bright tapestries adorned the walls. Then, when things couldn't have gotten more overwhelming, several large cats with glossy, black velvet fur glided through the arched doorways and sat on their haunches.

Realizing she had been asked a question, Ayianna quickly replied. "I'm sorry, my-my *Naaru*. I'm a bit sore, but I feel quite rested."

"Yes, well, you have slept for three days."

"Three?"

A man approached, flanked by two older women. He bowed low. "*Zhiipa-Naaru*, it is a pleasure to serve you and your young guest. How can I be of service?"

"Her name is Ayianna, and she is in need of new clothes, especially an outfit for this evening's celebration."

"*Isoth*, my *Naaru*."

The man snapped his fingers. One of the women darted to Ayianna and began to measure her.

"I understand you are betrothed. You must be pleased to have such an attentive man."

Ayianna's heart quickened. "Yes, my *Naaru*."

"He was quite vigilant, always checking on you and making sure the wolf, Liam, was well cared for. He must care for you very much."

Did Desmond really love her like that? A warmth blossomed inside Ayianna, flowed throughout her body, and burned her cheeks. But it didn't quell the unease in her stomach. Why couldn't her feelings cooperate? Here was a man who wanted her. Despite the curse, despite all that had happened thus far, and he was determined to marry her. Shouldn't that be a good thing?

Fragments of her dream lingered in her mind, and with it, the fading images of her dress and the star studded crown. If she did marry Desmond, there would be no traditional elven wedding.

The queen stepped to the side and picked up a gold vase. "Do you not love your betrothed?"

"Well," Ayianna swallowed, "I don't know. What is love when one is betrothed?"

"You may grow to love him. Arranged marriages sometimes work well, but if your heart is not willing, then it will not work."

"I am trying. He is nice to look at, but I have seen sides of him I do not like." Ayianna tried not to move as the woman tucked the measuring string beneath her arm. "Perhaps even scare me."

"My dear! What is it about Kael that scares you?"

"Kael?" She stared at her. "I am not betrothed to Kael. No, I am betrothed to Desmond."

"Oh, forgive me. I have not met Desmond. That is most interesting . . . " She trailed off as she put the golden vase back on the table. "Only seek the truth, be honest in your dealings, and with the grace of Parzanah, your path will be made straight."

"If you don't mind me asking, my *Naaru*?" Ayianna lifted her arms, and the woman placed the string around her waist. "Who is Parza . . . Parzna?

The queen smiled. "Parzanah is what we call the Shadow God of Zohar. I believe the guardians call him, Vituko. The One-With-Many-Names. We tend to think of him less of a shadow and more of a compassionate father."

"My *Naaru*." The man came forward with an armful of delicate, colorful rolls of fabric. "Which fabric will you be purchasing for the young lady's garment?"

"The green one."

He nodded and left.

Ayianna couldn't stop her sinking heart. Why had Kael seen to her and Liam instead of Desmond? Perhaps he had been detained or was still recovering. She hated the unanswered questions and the doubt tainting her thoughts. She needed to see Desmond again, hopefully before the celebration.

The woman finished measuring Ayianna, gathered her things, and faced the queen.

"My *Naaru*, I will have the garment ready for fitting this afternoon." She bowed and followed the man into adjoining room.

"Ayianna," the queen turned to her, "it has come to my attention that you need some formal teaching in combat skills."

"What?" she asked and then quickly added, "my *Naaru*."

"If you are required to battle, then you must be prepared."

"But I don't know how to fight."

She tilted her head, sending her curls bouncing and the emeralds sparkling in the light. "Life begins without knowing how to do many things, but it is through learning and practice that life begins to take form. You did not walk or talk when you left the comforts of your mother's womb, did you?"

"No." She had learned those things, and how to read and cook. She could learn to fight. Like diamonds in the rough, tiny nuggets of confidence glittered amid her anxiety.

Golma entered with a woman dressed in leather armor. They bowed in greeting.

The queen smiled. "Ayianna, I would like for you to meet Turina, one of my best *paqzronas*. She will teach you while you are here."

Excitement tingled down Ayianna's spine and into her toes. She would learn to fight, and then she could take care of herself and her mother. She might not need a man's covering after all. A weight lifted from her shoulders.

39

DESMOND STOOD OUTSIDE a door in one of the outlying taverns. He crumpled the note in his fist and lifted his hand to knock, but hesitated. The clamor grew downstairs. As the afternoon turned into evening, the tavern got busier and noisier. Merchants and drifters mixed below with the locals swapping rumors and stories. They wouldn't pay any heed to a foreigner, would they?

He gripped the door knob and twisted. He took a deep breath, trying to quiet his thudding heart, and swung open the door. The light from the narrow corridor spilled into the darkened room and chased the shadows into the corners.

"Come in, you fool!" A female voiced hissed.

He darted inside and closed the door. Darkness swallowed him whole. He held his breath, his pulse drumming in his ears.

"*Yetakoith taheza*," the voice whispered, and the room was bathed in a dim yellow glow.

A woman cloaked in shadows sat at the edge of a bed, her hood hiding her face. Shadows hid most of the sparse furnishings, but didn't reveal any bags. The woman traveled light and without an escort.

"You're late." She pulled her hood back and coppery red curls cascaded down her shoulders and back.

"Semine." Desmond swallowed. "How did you—what are you doing here?"

The sorceress smiled. "How did you like my little welcoming party at Zajur?"

"That was your doing? You almost got me killed!"

"I figured you could handle a few Tögo."

"A few! Try a couple hundred or so." Desmond scowled. "What brings you all the way out to Bonpazur?"

"Change of plans, my pet. You see, I've discovered something very important, and I need you to secure it for me."

"Oh?" Desmond crossed his arms and studied her painted face.

She stood and untied her cloak. "I want you to bring Prince Vian to Gwydion, unharmed."

Desmond thumbed the crushed parchment in his fist. "What do you want with him?"

"That is my business, pet." Semine draped the cloak over the side of the bed. Her black dress barely held her generous chest. The silky fabric flowed over her hips and brushed the tips of her boots as she glided toward him.

"Unless, of course, you have changed your mind?" Her green eyes rooted him to the floor.

He shook his head, but kept his gaze on the advancing woman.

"Do you have the dagger?"

"Not yet."

"Why not?" Semine drew closer.

Desmond lowered his arms and took a step back. "I've been a little preoccupied."

"Preoccupied with a woman of impure bloodlines? I do not believe you would prefer her over me." Semine cocked her head and ran her gloved hand along his tunic.

Desmond's breath caught. The scent of muskroot hung in his nose, reminding him of the temple's incense and when he had first met her. His faithful pilgrimages to Gwydion had rewarded him generously, but he was no fool.

"Yes, unbelievable as it may seem." She circled him. "She is a descendent of the elven lord, Dloryian. His duty was to guard the dagger and his sons after him, but the dagger has been lost. For thirty years, I have searched everywhere for the dagger. Its presence evades me." She faced him again. "I had hoped you would have had something for me by now. She must know something."

"She claims to know nothing, but I'm gaining her trust."

"Trust?" Semine's dark eyebrows arched. "This is not the time for wooing games. The goddess demands retribution, and if you cannot fulfill this request, I will find another."

"No, may the Goddess live free." Desmond raised his right hand. "I have other information. For one, she bears a harpy's curse."

Semine cocked her head, and her gaze grew distant. "That is interesting." She refocused her attention on him. "What else?"

"A message her dying father gave her to give her brother." He took a breath. "He said, 'the sun has set. The morning star is forever locked in stone'."

A smile brightened Semine's face, and her eyes shone. "I love riddles. Thank you, pet, you've been most helpful. Her mother wasn't as useful, but she did have this." She slipped something from a pouch and held out her gloved hand. A polished black marble the size of a small egg sat in her palm. "Take it. It will glow if it nears an object the Tóas Dikon has touched."

He took it and slid it into the leather pouch at his waist. "What about this silly quest?"

"Put an end to it any way you like, but make it look natural. We don't need the Nevins getting wind of our plans. We'll let them think it is going fine, and then when the time is right they will discover their failure." She rubbed her arms. "And bring the girl, if you like. I might have a use for her."

Desmond's frowned. Why would the sorceress want her now? Ayianna was his . . . unless Semine made him a high priest, not that he wanted to be a priest. But what was a title when he had the sorceress? But how did Vian fit into all this? He slowly nodded. "I will see to it."

"I know you will, my pet. That is why I chose you." She peeled off her gloves and revealed heavily scarred arms.

He flinched.

"Do my arms bother you?"

"No."

Semine smiled and pulled the silver dragon pendent from her neck. "Blow on this pendant when you are ready to return to me. I have two dragons and a handful of imps prepared to assist you, but I must warn you, if you tarry, the imps will get a little . . . impatient."

She slipped the satin cord around his neck and lingered, her face close to his. He stared into her green eyes unable to breathe. She withdrew and ran her finger along his temple. A rush of desire slammed into him.

"The goddess desires vows to be consummated as tradition dictates."

Finally! He tried to calm his racing heart, afraid she'd see him trembling. But it didn't matter now, did it? He smiled. "Let's not disappoint the goddess."

She pulled him closer, and he lifted her chin. He caught sight of the black spider inked into her skin and a vein pulsated beneath its red dotted abdomen. There was no going back, no turning around. Tonight the sorceress belonged to him.

"Together," she whispered and kissed him. "We shall free the goddess from the tyranny of the underworld."

Desmond wrapped his arms around her. Fire burned in his veins, a desire too strong to deny. This was how it was supposed to be, him and the sorceress—forever.

"*Uzath taheza!*" And the room succumbed to darkness once again.

40

AYIANNA STOOD AT the doors to the great hall. Her stomach squirmed like a heap of wiggling worms. What if she didn't know how to eat properly? What if she spilled her drink, or worse, tripped and fell?

She smoothed her green dress and slowed her breathing. She rocked her head back and forth. It had the sensation of a pin cushion. Golma had assured her the pins holding her hair in place had been necessary. She reached up and touched the flower petals of her parents' betrothal gift and sighed. At least she had convinced the maidservant her need of it. Desmond would be pleased to see it.

Ayianna slid along the wall, scanning the room for her companions. A sea of dark faces and black hair converged in the hall. The women dressed in colorful linen sheaths with matching sheer scarves flowing from their shoulders. Their hair swirled in elaborate braids atop their heads, pinned down with glittering gems. The men wore only white linen wraps around their waist and a beaded belt. Their bare, oiled skin gleamed in the lanterns.

Vian's flaming red hair and pale skin stood out like a dragon in the plains. Oh, the wonder of familiarity in the midst of the unknown! She could've hugged his neck. She made her way to him.

"Ayianna!" He closed the distance and embraced her. "You look wonderful. How are you?"

"Good, thank you." She fingered the edge of the sheer scarf draped over her shoulder. "How are you? Did you sleep for three days too?"

"Not quite." He frowned. "I feigned sleep until Kael came and yanked me out of bed."

She smiled. "And where is he?"

"Eloith is trying to drag him out of the library. He's pig-headed if you ask me."

"Ha, that is the truth." She laughed, but then quickly sobered. "Have you seen Desmond?"

He shook his head. He looked beyond her and grinned. "Well, look who decided to show up."

Ayianna turned, and her breath caught.

Kael strode toward them, dressed in a white linen shirt and brown pants. He had smoothed his dark hair into a braid, accentuating his elven features even more—the high cheekbones, the curved ears, and the smooth face, except of course where a scar cut across his eyebrow. The gold earring piercing his right ear caught the light.

He stopped when he saw her. His gray eyes softened and a smile brushed his lips. Her unease melted like frost on a warm spring day.

He touched his fingertips together. "It's good to see you well."

She nodded. She should say something, anything. She cleared her throat. "Didn't Eloith come?"

"No, he doesn't—"

Trumpets blared, and the king entered with a woman swathed in a gossamer veil. The translucent layers of her dress hung on her dark curves. Ayianna glanced away. She didn't see what she thought she did, did she? One look at Vian's red face confirmed her fears. *What is it with the Haruzo and nudity?*

The great hall exploded in activity as everyone found their seat. Servants hurried into the great hall, carrying plates of steaming food and pitchers of honey mead. Ayianna sat with Vian and Kael as the room grew quiet. At the front, the king, his new wife, and his harem sat on an ornate platform. Colored veils hung from the ceiling and swirled around the white pillars interspaced through the hall.

From the side of the hall another batch of servants poured through the arched doorways, hauling silver trays of giant lizards. They placed them on the tables amidst platters of sugared figs, nuts, grilled cacti, and baskets heaped with flatbread.

Somewhere in the room, drums and lutes sang a lilting song, and the room rumbled once more as the people continued their cheerful chatter between mouthfuls.

Ayianna turned back to her table. A huge, dead lizard sat on a silver platter in front of her, its orange skin blackened. A large red fruit gagged its pointy snout, and its vacant eye sockets stared back at her.

"I say," Vian leaned over, "we should eat him just for spite." He stabbed the lizard with a knife and tore out a chunk.

She shuddered and grabbed a handful of nuts instead.

When everyone had finished eating, the king called for a dance. Drums pounded out a lively rhythm and other instruments joined in. Ayianna's stomach lurched. Surely, he didn't mean for her to dance, just his loyal subjects—many of whom had sprung to their feet at the invitation. Vian was close behind. Where was Desmond?

She stared at the sugared figs in front of her, her cheeks growing hot. If she appeared busy or uninterested, maybe no one would notice her or maybe she could excuse herself. She grabbed a fig.

"Do you like to dance?"

Ayianna looked across the table at Kael. "Why do you ask?"

"Teron loved to dance. I just thought you might as well."

"How well did you know him?" she asked.

"He was my friend." A shadow passed over his eyes, and he looked away. "He was going to marry my sister."

Ayianna dropped the fig. "He never said anything about getting married."

"He was going to tell you and your family when he returned home."

She frowned. "Why didn't you tell me earlier?"

"It didn't matter."

"Of course, it mattered." She swallowed her rising grief. "It . . . it changes things."

The look in his eyes was a world away and pierced with sorrows of his own. Suddenly, the music broke into a frenzied drumming. He leaned closer. "We can talk later when it's quieter."

She nodded.

"So, would you like to join in the festivities?" His eyes sparkled with life she hadn't seen before, and a trace of a smile warmed his face. Maybe it was the mead. He pulled back. "If you don't want to, that's all right."

"No," Ayianna said before she could stop herself. "We should celebrate with the Haruzo. They might take offense if we don't."

He grinned. "That is exactly what I was thinking."

She rose to her feet. Kael took her hand in his and led her to the dance floor. The touch of his calloused hand sent a tingling sensation throughout the rest of her body.

He said something, but the drums drowned his words. His eyes twinkled as he spun her around. She followed his lead and was soon swept up into the dance. Circles of people swirled around the room, weaving in and out, switching partners as they went. Twice Vian was her partner in the vibrant song, but her eyes kept drifting, searching for Kael.

Then the music faded, and the dancing stopped. She scanned the crowd for Kael as the people chatted and made their way to their seats. To her delight, he appeared next to her as he placed his hand under her elbow and guided her back to her chair.

Ayianna sat down in a daze. The thrill of the dance coursed through her, the drums lingering in her heart. The brush of his fingertips across her skin sent a shiver down her back. What had just happened?

Kael sent her a reassuring smile, and an unexplainable joy rushed through her. For a moment his mask came off, and she caught a glimpse of the elf beneath the icy exterior. Kael had been a friend to her brother and would've been family if the attack on Dagmar hadn't happened. He was an elf of heavy sorrow, and it broke her heart.

The king stood up to address the crowd, but Ayianna didn't hear a word he said.

Ayianna floated down the hall to her room, humming. Her stomach satisfied with figs, nuts, and flat bread. The roasted lizard now a distant memory, and the warmth of the Haruzo's famous sweet amber mead lingered. The events of the night replayed in her mind, and each time she reached the moments with Kael, her heart skipped a beat. She hadn't had this much fun in a long time. She sighed and pushed open the door to her room.

"Oh!" A male voice exclaimed.

Her thoughts scattered like dry leaves before a wintry storm. Desmond bumped into the bed, causing it to screech across the floor. The lamp beside the bed flickered as a breeze swept into the room through the open window.

Her pulse drummed in her ears. "What are you doing here?"

"I was . . . " His gaze averted for a second, then returned to her. "I was looking for you." He flashed a bright smile. "You look beautiful. The wedding feast over already?"

She crossed her arms. "Where were you? Why weren't you there?"

He shrugged and sat on the bed. "I had things to do."

"In Bonzapur?" She frowned. "What kind of—"

"I'm a man of business." He stood and strode toward her. "You think I would cross the desert without a thought of taking advantage of the situation?"

"Well, I guess not."

"I mean, look at this fabric." He slid his fingers along the silk neckline of her dress.

Ayianna stepped back as a shiver raced down her spine.

"Imagine. In a year's time, we'll be celebrating our own wedding." His blue eyes pierced her through and through. "I was thinking we could stay behind and get to know each other a little better."

"But the quest?"

"Kael and Eloith are more than capable of carrying on without us, don't you think?"

Ayianna shifted her weight to her other foot. Why did it feel like he was setting her up? "But Saeed—"

He placed his fingers over her lips. "He is busy with the affairs of the nations. He doesn't care about your mother. He wouldn't even let you bury your father. He's a good man—I mean elf—but he has a lot on his mind as of late. I think we should split from this quest and return to the plains." He took her hand in his. "Can you imagine what the hunters are doing to your mother? *If* she is still alive. She harbors your father's secrets, and they'll do anything to extract them."

Ayianna shuddered as he rubbed his cold thumb over her fingers. For a moment, she was back in the caves, her mother's stricken face desperate for help. Desmond's proposal made sense.

"I'll talk to Vian tomorrow, and we can make arrangements to return to Badara as soon as the next caravan heads east."

Her heart quickened. Could it be that simple? Could she head home so soon and rescue her mother? That is what she should do, right? She pulled her hand from his. "Where will we look for her?"

"Gwydion." His eyes narrowed. "If the sorceress is behind this, your mother will be there. If we aren't too late."

"They wouldn't kill her like they did my father. She is the only one who knows the secret."

A smiled tugged at the corners of his mouth. "Oh, I think you know more than you realize, but you're right. Let us hope they've not worn her down."

She took a step back. "I've told you everything I know."

"Let's not think on that anymore. We have more pressing circumstances that need dealing with first." Desmond grasped her hands and smiled. "How was the wedding feast?"

She shifted her feet again. "It was lovely. Lots of food and music."

"Did it make you think of our wedding? Were you thinking about you and me and our future together?"

"I, well . . . " She averted her gaze.

"Or were you thinking of Kael?"

Her eyes shot up and met his. "What?"

"You heard me." He dropped her hand and paced around the room, her stomach sinking deeper with each footstep. "You have no idea what I risk for you."

Her face burned. He could see right through her, there was no denying it. Her heart had betrayed her. Hours ago, she had been willing to accept the fate her father chose, but now she clung to a few moments of delight that had probably been influenced by mead. She remained quiet, waiting for his rebuke, but instead he smiled. She wasn't sure if she liked his smile.

"Do you delight in shaming me?" Desmond reached out and wrenched a lock of hair free.

She shoved his hand away. "What are you talking about?"

"You are betrothed, yet I find you in the arms of another man."

Ayianna stared at him. "I wasn't—"

"I saw you dancing with Kael."

"I-I danced with others too. It meant nothing."

"You couldn't keep your eyes off him."

Ayianna stared at the floor as his words ripped away the excuses. The truth glared at her, naked and cold. Shameful behavior—she knew it. Everyone knew it. What must Kael think of her? She gritted her teeth. Her reputation soiled. To the world she was Desmond's, and he could expose her.

"Do you think he would want you if he knew the risk of the harpy's curse?" He smirked. "Sure, after a little mead and some fine clothes, he's all nice to you, but have you told him of the poison running through your veins?"

Harpy's curse? How did he know? She slowly shook her head.

"No elf would want a cursed bride." Desmond rested his hand on her shoulder. "I know all your secrets, and I am still willing to have you as my wife."

358

"I . . . I'm sorry. It's just, we—I didn't want to offend the king. I thought it was the proper thing to do, but I was wrong." She straightened. "I won't let it happen again."

Desmond lifted her chin, and she met his blue eyes. He could demand anything of her, and she would give it.

The tension in his face disappeared. "I don't entirely place the blame on you. Kael should respect the bonds of betrothal. If he can't respect that, what would stop him from violating the union of man and wife?"

Ayianna scarcely breathed. Kael couldn't—he wouldn't. But Desmond was right. She was betrothed, yet Kael had danced with her. Shame and guilt sliced deeper. He wasn't responsible for her heart, she was. She allowed it to betray her father and her future husband.

"But I must admit my own failure." Desmond's face grew somber. "Since I haven't announced our betrothal publically, who's to blame, but I?"

She wrapped her arms around herself. Why did he even bother with her? If she can't be trusted now, how could she be trusted in marriage? Horror gripped her. She didn't deserve his love or anybody's love for that matter.

"What token of my love have you received from me? None," he said. He pulled a delicate box from the pouch at his waist. "Until now."

Ayianna took the box and opened it. Inside a gold bangle gleamed in the candlelight.

"Tomorrow, I will announce my intentions to the world. One yettu should be enough to let others know that you belong to another man."

"One yettu! Desmond, I can't accept this," Ayianna said. "That's almost a year's wage."

"You can and must." He smiled. "It's a sacrifice for the one I love."

He ran his finger along her cheek, down her arm, and grasped her hand in his. He slipped the bangle over her hand. "My feelings for you and our future together haven't changed one bit. I hope this gift will remind you of that."

Desmond pulled her into his arms and kissed her. A trace of incense clung to his clothes. She had to be willing. She returned the kiss, but inwardly, she wept.

He released her. "I am the luckiest man in the world."

A hand strayed from her shoulder to her waist, and he nuzzled her ear, his breath hot against her skin. "It's a pity to waste a beautiful evening like tonight."

She held her breath. Fear speared her and sent her pulse racing. He tightened his embrace and kissed her again, awakening desires she didn't want. They screamed and raged within her.

He pulled away, but she clung to him. *Don't leave, not now . . .*

"Desmond," she whispered and glanced up at him.

He smirked. "Goodnight, Ayianna, sleep well."

She watched him disappear into the darkness. Her burning desire gave way to emptiness. Panic wrapped its cold fingers around her heart. *What am I doing?*

The brick walls of her room closed in on her. She had to get out. Where would she go? The library? Why was she always thinking about Kael? No, she'd go to the gardens, maybe the stables. She needed Liam. She took a deep breath and fled.

41

KAEL RUBBED HIS face. He tried to read the clay tablets in front of him, but his mind wouldn't cooperate. Dwarven chicken scratch couldn't compete with the lovely Ayianna. Oh, how she plagued his mind!

"You should go to bed." Eloith fluttered down from the tall bookshelves lining the library and settled on the table next to him.

Kael shook his head. He pushed the tablets aside and leaned back in his chair. "I have to solve these riddles."

"A tired mind, and a distracted one at that, will not accomplish much."

Kael glanced up at the arched ceiling and the pattern of colors swirling into each other. The design was too chaotic, too much like his life to be enjoyable, but the bright colors weren't right. He needed, wanted to get lost in a dull brown. His returned his gaze to Eloith. "Tired or not, an accomplishment is still an accomplishment no matter how small it is."

The fairy captain grinned.

"What?"

"You sound like Saeed."

Kael sighed and sat up. "I hope he's having better luck than we are. I still have to finish his letter."

"Am I to deliver it?"

"No, I'll send it with King Runako's response." Kael ran his finger over the tablet's carved runes. "Do you think Bonpazur will join the Alliance?"

"Yes."

"At least Saeed will have some good news then." Kael picked up a parchment and angled it in the light of the lamp. Eloith's distinct scrawling words translated the tonic's recipe and directions.

"She is a good woman."

"Who is?"

"The young lady who is seeping into your thickly calloused heart."

Kael glared at him. "Isn't there a law against mind-breaching?"

"No," Eloith grinned and crossed his arms. "The Naajiso were thought to be destroyed. Why clutter the kingdoms with unnecessary rules? Still, I did not breach your mind. It is written all over your face and in your eyes."

"I don't suppose I could lie to a Naajiso."

"Some have tried, but why fear the truth?"

"You don't understand. I can't." Kael clenched his jaw. "My concern for her is nothing but a vow to her brother."

"Is it?"

"And she is betrothed."

Eloith rested his hand on his sword belt and studied him. Finally, he said, "I do not like him. He should not be allowed to continue on this quest, in my opinion."

"Having a little clash of differences, are we?"

"His essence reeks."

"All right, so maybe it's a little more than that, but Saeed didn't think he was the enemy." Kael shook his head. "Don't misunderstand me. I would love to leave him behind."

"But where he goes, she goes."

Kael clenched his teeth. He shouldn't care. He didn't want to care, but he did and that complicated things.

Concern flashed in the fairy's eyes. "Her essence dims. If you do not do something, I am afraid—"

"Hey, how's it going?" Vian stood outside the doorway.

Kael straightened. "What are you doing up?"

"I couldn't sleep." He slumped in the chair next to Kael. "Besides, we have a tonic to find."

"Eloith has already found the recipe. We just need to figure out what it means."

"Uh! Guardians and their riddles." Vian slapped his head. "So, what does it say?"

Kael smiled. "Well, the tonic consists of three ingredients: a silver pinecone from the belly of the earth, healing water from an underwater garden, and roots from the Famor tree where giants roam."

"Oh, that's easy." Vian shrugged. "We just sail to Moruya Island and chop off some roots and anything to do with underwater would be the kingdom of the Kaleki."

Kael frowned. "We've figured that much, but what of the silver pinecone?"

"Well, that's a good one, isn't it?" Vian leaned forward and propped his elbows on the table. "What does the riddle say?"

"Silver pure, mind secure. Into the belly of the earth, grows a tree of hailed worth. Through a maze of dark and stone, hangs the silver pinecone."

"Oh?" Vian glanced around the room. "Any leads on that one?"

Eloith stepped over to the parchment, which was as big as he was. "From what we can gather, it's hidden away, buried deep in the ground. In order to find it, one must 'climb the highest to reach the lowest. From within become the lowest to enter the highest to reach the lowest'."

Vian groaned. "Must it be riddles?"

"There you are, Vian!" Desmond's voice boomed through the library. His face glowed as he strutted into the library like a rooster. "I've been looking all over for you."

"Where've you been?" Vian asked.

Desmond's step faltered. "I've had a few things to take care of. You three aren't working on that tonic thing already, are you? We just endured the desert and escaped from some blood-sucking creatures. We should take a break, enjoy the sights a bit." He stopped and shrugged. "Or not."

"What do you want?" Kael asked.

"Nothing to do with you, that's for sure." Desmond turned his attention to Vian. "Let's go down to the kitchens to see if they have any food left."

"I'm not hungry." Vian fingered Eloith's parchment. "Besides, I'm working on a riddle."

"Oh?"

A frown marred Desmond's perfect features. Kael would've liked to permanently mar the man's face. Instead, he picked up the clay tablets and focused on translating the cramped runes of Tarôc.

"Well, then." Desmond worked his jaw. "Have a pleasant night, Prince."

"And you as well."

Footsteps disappeared from the library. Kael ground his teeth and shifted the clay tablets to the table. Where had the man been all day? If only he could think of a way to detain him without leaving Ayianna behind. Not that she needed to be hiking through dangerous mountains and jungles. A quest was no place for a young woman, even if she held up better than many of the men he knew. His chest constricted. He couldn't leave her behind.

Kael turned the map. "Since the Kha Vaaro Mountain Range is considered the highest point in Nälu, perhaps our pinecone is hidden somewhere within."

Eloith and Vian nodded.

"Have you met Tariq yet?" Eloith asked.

"Briefly at breakfast. Why?"

"He has expressed interest in joining our expedition. He says he can serve as our guide and translator. He is fluent in Tarôc, Nihi and Pyamor. He mentioned a fourth, but I cannot remember it."

"The king's nephew?" Vian raised his head. "We're practically the same age. Shouldn't a guide be a little older, more experienced?"

Kael shrugged. "If he knows what he says he does, he could prove to be invaluable to our cause. But don't you think we have too many people already?"

Vian glanced between Eloith and Kael and raised his hands. "Hey, I've got a special interest in this tonic. I won't stand aside and do nothing. My kingdom needs her prince to do something."

"Of course, Vian." Eloith clasped his hands together and paced across the table. "We weren't suggesting we'd leave you behind."

"We can figure it out later." Kael stood and stretched. "If Tariq is fluent in Tarôc, then I'm going to bed. He can tell us what these clay tablets mean tomorrow."

Back in his room, Kael stared out the window at the starlit sky. Ayianna's warm smile lingered in his mind's eye, no matter how hard he tried to shove it aside. *Her essence dims.* What did Eloith mean? If only Vian hadn't showed up. Still, he shouldn't take his frustration out on the prince. He had proven himself a better man than Kael had figured him for. He had potential. There might be some hope yet for Badara.

Kael leaned against the stone windowsill. Celebratory lamps twinkled throughout the foreign city. The Haruzo would celebrate the king's union until morning. A sickening knot twisted in his stomach. That chapter in his life was closed. He pulled away from the window and turned his thoughts to the coming quest. The knot in his stomach sank.

Their journey would cross mountains, jungles, and plunge to the depths of the sea. They'd face dangers, harsh weather, and who knew what else. It wasn't a risk he wanted to take with a young woman and her demented betrothed. Perhaps he could convince Desmond to stay behind, but as Eloith pointed out, where he went, Ayianna went.

Yet, Kael couldn't see himself saying goodbye to her, at least not if that meant she'd be staying behind with Desmond. Why hadn't Teron mentioned the betrothal? Of all the times her brother had tried to convince Kael of a double wedding, he had never once mentioned Desmond.

So what did he feel for her? Was it only a promise to Teron? A transfer of friendship or was there something deeper? Kael clenched his jaw. No. He'd chosen to join the guardians; she was betrothed to a jerk. Their paths were already sealed. What could he do about it?

Kael sighed. If he couldn't sleep, he could at least finish Saeed's letter. He returned to the small desk, pulled out the parchment and ink jar, and settled into the chair. He fingered the quill. Should he share Eloith's concerns? It seemed trivial compared to the events at Zajur and the upcoming quest. How would he tell Saeed about Aberim? Maybe a second letter addressed to Darin or Aberim's family.

He dipped the quill in ink, but the words wouldn't come. He shoved the parchments aside. What was his problem? He stood and stretched. He needed some fresh air. Maybe Osaryn would break his silence.

42

AYIANNA SCRATCHED LIAM'S ears. The silent stars sparkled in the dark expanse above, while a cool desert breeze whispered through the courtyard much like the quiet pleas of the masses chained in their underground prison. She shuddered. Was her mother still among them? Had Saeed found her?

She leaned back against the bench, and Liam dropped her muzzle into Ayianna's lap. They had made it to Bonzapur. Surely, Saeed didn't expect her to continue on the quest. They had found the tonic; what help could she be? Wouldn't it be better to return with Desmond and rescue her mother?

"Ayianna?"

She started, her heart pounding against her ribs. At the entrance of the garden, Kael stepped out of the shadows and into the warm glow of the lanterns. She glanced at Liam and pursed her lips. "Why didn't you warn me?"

Liam only cocked her head and nestled deeper into Ayianna's lap.

"What are you doing out here?" Kael asked.

"I just needed some fresh air."

He looked up at the sky and then back at her. "Do you mind if I join you?"

She opened her mouth to speak, but the gleam of the golden bracelet caught her eye, and the words choked in her throat. She stood. "I'm sorry, I can't. I have to go."

"Wait." His hand on her arm stayed her. "Are you all right?"

She searched his eyes. The desire to pour her heart out to him overwhelmed her. "I—I'm fine, really. I have to go."

He dropped his hand. "You're not fine."

"I don't suppose I can lie to you, can I?" She straightened. "You probably already know what I'm thinking."

"I can't read your thoughts like the Naajiso can, but I can sense your emotions, the disturbance in you."

"Oh." She eyed him. "Why can't I sense yours, then?"

"I shield myself."

"Can you teach me?"

He raised his eyebrows. "Of course, but I thought you had to go."

"I do, but . . . " She rubbed the bracelet against her wrist. "I'm betrothed, and I shouldn't be talking to you."

"Desmond?"

The icy tone in his voice sent a shiver scurrying down her spine. She glanced away. "Look, I've already told you. I don't have a choice."

"We always have a choice."

She glared at him. "Not for women."

"Even women have choices." He cocked his head. "But are you prepared for the consequences?"

"What's that supposed to mean?" She ground her teeth. Why did he infuriate her so?

"No matter what you choose, there will be consequences. Whether you chose to live a lie or seek the truth, whether you allow—"

"I told him the truth, okay?" She wrapped her arms around herself. "It doesn't matter to him if I'm a stupid half-breed."

Kael clenched his jaw. He knotted his hands atop his head and turned around.

Tears sprang to her eyes. She whisked them away and started toward the exit.

"Ayianna." His voice was quiet.

She halted. She ached to flee, but a deeper desperation rooted her to the ground.

"Don't ever refer to yourself as a stupid half-breed."

She spun around. "Why do you always make me so mad? If you were such good friends with my brother, why do you . . . " The flood of tears burned her eyes. She steeled herself. She wasn't going to cry in front of him. She took a deep breath. "Well, we've made it here, so now you won't be encumbered by me anymore. Is that what you want? I'll be going back with Desmond." She clasped her hands together. "He's making the betrothal public tomorrow."

"No." He stepped closer. "You can't."

"I thought you said I had a choice."

"You do." He lifted his hand as if to touch her, but then lowered it. "Just don't decide too quickly. We're in the middle of a mess, there's no telling how it will all end. Don't let Desmond force you into making a decision or," he glanced away, "or make you do something you might regret. If he truly loves you, he won't force you to marry him." His gaze returned to her, his eyes pleading. "Promise me you'll wait until this is all over with."

Ayianna searched his eyes and swallowed the emotions clogging her throat. "Why should I? What does this decision have to do with you?"

Kael stepped aside and looked up at the starlit sky. "I made a vow to your brother."

"Oh." Ayianna's heart sank. What had she expected? That he'd actually cared for her of his own accord? She was too tired to be angry.

"Teron asked me to give this to you." Kael untied the small leather pouch at his belt. He pulled out a silver ring and handed it to her.

Teron's ring. Tears blurred her eyes as she rubbed the silver braided vines. Life had seemed so much simpler, easier, when she had made it for him. She slid the ring on her forefinger and twisted it.

"He was with me when the battle horn was blown."

Ayianna shook her head. She didn't want to relive the horror she'd found at Dagmar. Kael reached for her hands. His touch soothed her.

"He gave me this ring," he continued, his voice low. "He said if anything should happen to him that I should find you."

Ayianna stared at the ground. Her mind swam with images of Dagmar and her brother's headless body. Her emotions catapulted her into a haze as thoughts, and memories tumbled one after the other. Kael's touch anchored her to reality, and she drew comfort from his presence. She lingered. Why couldn't things have been different?

"You should know, he died valiantly, doing his best to protect my sister and . . . "

She raised her eyes, but a wave of anguish washed over her, burdened by guilt and condemnation. Suddenly, she realized, she was sensing Kael's emotions. Something he had always blocked.

Kael pulled away. She could no longer feel his pain, but the memory of it was enough. Her heart ached. She wanted to say something, to comfort him, but the words escaped her.

He glanced at her neck. "How's your wound?"

"Well . . . " Ayianna stammered and trailed her fingers through Liam's fur. He didn't need to know the truth. "It's healing."

"That's good to hear."

"Are you having any luck with the tonic?" she asked, glad to have changed subjects.

"I suppose. We have three ingredients to find." Kael leaned against the stone wall surrounding the garden. "Eloith has translated it, but we still have to figure out the rest of the riddles. Even Vian came to help."

She frowned. "Does that mean we'll be leaving soon?"

"Maybe in a week or two, depending on how helpful the king's nephew is. The sooner we leave, the better. If we don't return with the tonic before Derk and the sorceress march to war, the alliance won't have an army, and the whole of Nälu will be plunged into darkness."

"How comforting."

"I know." He shook his head. "We'll need to map out our journey, gather supplies, and leave as soon as we can." He looked at her. "I hear the queen has arranged for you to do some training with her elite warriors."

Ayianna nodded.

A smiled brushed his lips. "Good. Although, you shouldn't have to use the training, except maybe on Desmond, if he doesn't behave."

"Very funny." But she didn't laugh. She mulled over the possibility of besting Desmond in a duel. No, she'd never be as good as he with a sword.

The silence lengthened, and the mirth faded from Kael's eyes. "I should go. I don't want you to get into any more trouble on my account." But he lingered, his eyes on hers. "When we finish getting the tonic to Saeed, I will help you rescue your mother. I promise."

Kael would too. He turned and disappeared into the shadows.

She scratched Liam's head and glanced up at the silent stars, now more confused than ever. Did she want to go on the quest?

"Well, Liam, perhaps we should get some sleep while we still have a bed to sleep in."

After putting Liam up for the night, Ayianna made her way to her room. Her nerves had settled a bit, her heart lighter, but exhaustion muddled her mind. She slipped the gold bangle off and tossed it in the wardrobe. She didn't need to make a decision tonight. She twisted her brother's ring on her finger. Maybe Desmond would change his mind.

43

TURINA, THE QUEEN'S *paqzrona*, had awakened Ayianna before dawn to start their lessons. By midmorning, Ayianna stood in the practice field and gripped a polished stick in her hands. Her makeshift sword until she proved competent. The hot breeze burned her bare legs and arms. The linen tunic and shorts covered the necessities, yet she felt even more exposed than in the public bath.

Turina's clothes mirrored Ayianna's, except now they were damp. Her feet hardly touched the ground as she slid forward and executed the moves with more grace than an elf. How was that even possible? How was she ever going to move like Turina? Turina came to the end of her routine, turned and faced Ayianna. Her dark skin glistened in the glare of the desert sun. Her amber eyes scanned the area, then settled on Ayianna. She nodded.

Ayianna was supposed to copy that? She shifted the stick to her right hand. She lunged and thrust her sword arm up to the left, then right, down to the left, then right. Repeat.

"With fire!" Turina punched the air with her fist.

Sweat poured down Ayianna's face and neck as she went through the repetitions again and again, but still the female warrior shook her head. She tried to summon the fire as Turina called it, but the heat sucked her energy.

Finally, Turina signaled a break.

The lazy sun hung above the practice arena, nearing the midday break, but food was the last thing on Ayianna's mind. She stumbled back to the canvas canopy where several swords, wooden poles, and a jug of water sat. She wiped the sweat from her forehead and took a drink.

"Not bad." Turina set her sword down. "But you must focus. Think of something that makes you angry, a person who has wronged you, then focus that energy into your movements."

Ayianna nodded.

"Yes, good." Turina smiled, the white of her teeth shone bright against her dark, polished skin. "Again."

Ayianna groaned, but took her stance at the end of the practice field.

"Think now." Turina stood to her left. "Anger. I know you are grieving, but turn your grief to fuel."

Ayianna took a deep breath and recalled the recent events. Her father and brother dead. Why? Secrets. She lunged forward. Her mother kidnapped, because of secrets. She thrust her arm up to the left, right. Society's rules, duty to her family. All of it, locking her in a cage, the door snapping shut. She brought the stick down to the left, then over to the right. She wouldn't let it overwhelm her. She would fight it. Arm up, left, right. Her cursed wound. Down left, right. Desmond. She gritted her teeth and charged through her paces. Again and again.

"Enough," Turina said.

Ayianna collapsed in the hot sand. The afternoon sun glared overhead, but the flames within scorched hotter.

"You did well. Tomorrow we shall attempt sparing." Turina bowed. "Golma will see you bathed and rested."

Ayianna groaned. Not the bathhouse!

44

KAEL POURED OVER Tariq's notes, comparing them to the clay tablets and his own, but his mind drifted back to Ayianna. Would she give in to Desmond? Couldn't she see he didn't love her? Why did Desmond even choose her? The man could have had any girl he wanted, but instead, he pursued a young woman of mixed race, a thing he disdains. No, something wasn't right, and Ayianna didn't see it. He would have to stop Desmond from making any announcement or taking matters into his own hands.

"I knew I'd find you in here." Vian appeared in the doorway. He had traded his princely attire for Bonzapur's common tunic and pants dyed a deep shade of green, not unlike the colors of Badara. His mop of red, curly hair bounced around his head and nearly touched his shoulders.

"Don't you need a haircut or something?" Kael asked.

Vian ran his hands through his curls. "No, I'm rebelling." He ducked out into the hall. "He's in here."

"Of course." Eloith's voice floated into the library. "I told you he is hard-headed. He would have left three days ago, if he could have had his way."

"I can understand his earnest." Another, deeper voice echoed in the hall. Tariq.

Vian reappeared with Tariq and Eloith in toll. Vian strolled across the study and flopped down on the couch against the wall. Eloith fluttered to the window and stood on the sill. He took a moment to observe the outside before turning his attention back to Kael.

Tariq stopped in the doorway. His black, curly hair flopped looser around his face than the other Haruzo's. His skin was lighter too. He could almost pass as a Saryhemor elf.

Kael stood and bowed. "Welcome."

"Thank you." Tariq returned the bow and strolled over to Kael like a man content with life. "Vian's been telling me about your adventures out east and how you two took down a troll in Nganjo. Very impressive."

"Ah . . . thank you." Kael shifted. "Sometimes we surprise ourselves with our abilities when we are placed in challenging circumstances."

Tariq crossed his arms, rested against the table, and grinned. "That sounds like something Nevin Saeed would say."

"I did spend the last six years under his tutelage."

"Oh, the wonder to sit and learn at a master's feet." Tariq leaned over and sifted through the pile of parchments. "Have you found my notes helpful?"

Kael nodded and picked up one of the parchments. "You've done well, and from your notes, it seems you've already mapped out the journey. I must ask, why did you choose that route? We were considering taking the old highway down to the sea and sailing to Ganya."

"Stark's Peak is closer. We can retrieve the silver pinecone, then descend into the jungles from there and make our way to the sea. If all goes well, I'm hoping the Kaleki will fly us back to the plains. If we were to go the route you suggest, the mountain passages will be perilous in the spring.

We'd have to contend with ornery bears, mudslides, and swollen rivers from all the melting snow."

"What?" Vian sat up. "It'll take us that long?"

Tariq shrugged. "I'm being generous with the calendar. I've calculated extra time for possible setbacks. Once we've crossed the mountains, we can take a boat down the river quicker than it would be to sail through the treacherous waters of Taetuga Sea. Besides, the old highway deposits you right in the middle of Zjohedaryn Cove, a pirate haven."

"Oh." Kael glanced at the map on the table. Sailing had sounded the easiest and the quickest route. He should've remembered the dangers of Zjohedaryn, aside from the fact that the old highway would take them into the land of the Wofsemor elves. He sat back down. "It makes sense, but are you certain you want to join us?"

Tariq lifted the map. "I've spent five years among the Stozic dwarves and was able to observe their interaction with Arashel, and then I spent three years in the jungle." He looked at Kael, his amber eyes so much like Saeed's, but otherworldly. "I think I can be of service to you and your quest."

"And what about the Kaleki?" Vian asked.

"I accompanied my uncle on business meetings a few times when I was a youth."

"You are making Badara sound more and more isolated." Vian frowned. "Not that my father didn't travel. He used to—Zurial, Praetan, Kvazkhun, Stratuvec, even Bonzapur, but when I came along, he stopped." He shrugged. "At least that is what the servants have said."

"Not everyone is so well-traveled or has the means to." Tariq returned the map to the table.

The prince's face clouded. "We have plenty of—"

"I didn't mean to offend." Tariq raised his hands. "I'm merely a nephew, not quite as impressive as a prince."

"Still, I'm impressed." Kael crossed his arms. "You sound like you've traveled as much as the guardians."

Tariq shrugged. "I have no mother or father, and I have no intentions of being a leech to my aunt and uncle, so I decided I would become an ambassador."

"That is noble enough." Kael cocked his head. "Have you considered becoming a guardian?"

Tariq smiled. "Perhaps."

Kael stretched, and then clasped his hands behind his neck. "You're welcome to join us, but I don't think we'll need a guide. The journey seems pretty straightforward."

"You don't need a guide to find a place on a map." Tariq ran his finger along the Kha Vaaro Mountain range. "You'll need someone who knows what's not on the map. The creatures you'll encounter, the customs of the people you'll likely run into. Hopefully, none if you're lucky."

"What do you mean creatures?" Vian eyed the map.

"The dithza-mielis haunt the trails of Kha Vaaro looking for souls to feed on. Then there's the pesky glotuls and their little annoying darts. Although, I don't think we will need to worry about them too much—they're only a bother in the summer and early fall. Then there's the klhordan that roam the jungle at night, some say it's a gorilla, others say it's some kind of beast that escaped the underworld."

"You expect us to believe this?" Vian asked.

"Yes." Tariq folded the map. "And we'll need to update your weapons. Where you are going, your swords and shields will fail to protect you."

Kael leaned forward. "If what you say is true—"

"He speaks truth." Eloith hopped off the window and fluttered over to the table. He rested his hands on his hips. "An ally against the natural and the unnatural world would be greatly appreciated."

"So are we in agreement then?" Kael glanced at Vian.

"Of course." Vian stood. "I don't want to face a dithzy-something-or-another by ourselves when we have someone with experience to join us. More the merrier, right?" He stuck out his hand. "Welcome!"

Tariq looked down at prince's offered palm. "What do you want me to do with your hand?"

"You shake it."

Tariq grasped Vian's hand. "I must journey beyond the desert soon. My travels have only taken me west." He faced Kael. "When do you plan to leave?"

"As soon as we can." Kael stood and smiled. Tariq's presence emanated a sense of peace and wisdom much like Saeed's. It would be like having the headmaster on their quest. Almost. But almost was better than facing the quandary with Ayianna and Desmond alone.

Tariq nodded. "I will see what supplies we can secure for our journey. Shall we check out the weapons?"

"Yes!" Eloith's wings snapped open, and he sprang into the air. "About time."

The wide, stone stairs descended deeper and deeper beneath the palace of Bonzapur. Tariq's torch hissed in the eerie silence. Fine silt covered the steps and walls, and grated beneath their feet. Kael shivered. The memory of Zajur's quiet but deadly halls flitted at the edges of his mind, despite his senses telling him everything was fine.

Entering the armory, Tariq lit the torches hanging against the walls. The darkness gave way to long shadows, revealing rows of tables filled with all sort of weapons and shields. Swords, halberds, spears, and axes lined the walls. The massive chamber smelled of old oil and dust.

Eloith gave a shout of joy and flew off to inspect the weaponry.

Once a captain, always a captain. Kael smiled. He had only been a guard, but the excitement was contagious. He scanned the multitude of weapons. Where were the longbows? Crossbows? He slowly turned. Didn't the Haruzo have armor?

Tariq selected a sword from the wall and tossed it to him. Kael caught it in midair with ease and swung it around.

The runes of Tarôc marched up the blade in straight, tiny columns, rigid but practical, not like the elves' flowing script and detailed scrolling. Why did the dwarves have to sacrifice art? Still, the blade balanced well. Kael handed it back to Tariq. "It's well-crafted."

"All dwarven blades are." Tariq tilted it to the light. "The inscription reads, Skagok honors truth, its blade brings freedom."

"From the Igazin clan?"

Tariq nodded. "Their blades have been treated to give them strength against creatures that do not have flesh. No other sword is as strong as these."

Vian picked up a shield with intricate carving in its metal casing. Rays of gold swirled outward from a circle like an ornate sun.

"The Nahkha shield, it bears the crest of Nälu," Tariq said.

"Badara's crest is not so different." Vian set the shield down.

"All right." Tariq scanned the room. "We will need the belts and pouches over here, but don't open them yet. And those wooden moons over there."

"Wooden moons?" Kael selected a black one with red dots forming diamonds along the smooth wood. The width of the arcs curved outward and stretched the length of his forearm. "This is a weapon?"

"It is the *klhodda zudchiddi* to be exact. The pygmy tribes of the Rimanga Jungle use them for hunting, among other things."

"Like a club?"

"No, you throw it like this." Tariq flicked his wrist, and the wooden moon sailed through the air. "Better duck."

But before Kael could respond, the wooden moon whistled past his head and almost clipped Vian as he dove under the table.

Tariq caught it and stuck it into his belt.

"A little more warning, please." Vian crawled out from the table.

Tariq smiled. "These have been reinforced by the dwarves, making them one of the best weapons against the dithza-mielis."

"That is . . . interesting," Kael said.

"These haven't been used in a very long time." Vian ran his fingers through the thick layer of dust covering everything.

"We haven't had need for them." Tariq picked up some belts and handed them to Kael.

"Didn't you use them on your travels?" Vian asked.

"The Haruzos have other advantages." Tariq smiled. His amber eyes reflected the torches' dancing flames and glowed silver. "Except against the pygmy tribes."

Vian eyed the wooden moons. "I hope we don't meet any of your pygmy friends."

"We will take the four Nahkha shields." Tariq selected the shields and placed them near the door. "Divide the *klhoddas* and belts, Kael, putting each one within a shield."

Kael nodded and did so.

Vian's eyes narrowed. "Are we to replace all of our swords and shields?"

"For the most part." Tariq hauled a ladder to a wall of shelves. "Unless you want to carry a double load."

"He knows all about carrying a double load, don't you, Vian?" Kael slapped the prince on the back.

Vian scowled. "I don't see the difference between your sword and mine."

"You're right. You can't. But the enemies we will fight will know the difference. Have you ever fought against a dithza-mieli, or the klhordan?" Tariq asked as he climbed a ladder.

"No."

"The mielis have no flesh and bones for us to touch, yet they can harm us." Tariq grabbed a sack from the shelf and descended. "These miserable hags are bent on stirring up your past and all your failings. Then they suffocate you with despair and ultimately bring you to your death—self-induced at times."

"So what stops them?" asked Vian.

"The *klhodda zudchiddi*, the wooden moons."

"I see." Vian arched his brows. "What about the klhordan-gorilla thingy?"

"Let's just hope we don't run into one." Tariq held up one of the silk purses he had pulled from the sack. "These contain a powdery substance that will protect us from the klhordan while we sleep."

Tariq divided the silk pouches between Kael and the others.

"I'll need two," Kael said. "One for Ayianna."

Tariq tossed him another and continued to browse through the various weapons.

"How is she doing?" Vian asked.

Kael shrugged. "She is doing all right, I guess. The Queen is helping her prepare for the journey."

"Have you seen Desmond?"

"Not after last night." Kael fingered the silk pouches. "How would you feel if he didn't join us?"

Vian cocked his head. "Are you going to ask him to stay behind?"

"Maybe"

"Well, don't you think having another swordsman would benefit us?" Vian crossed his arms. "I know he can be a little difficult, and he has some issues, but he is my friend. He's just under pressure right now."

"As if we aren't?"

"Point taken, but he's not used to a girl resisting him."

"Don't blame Ayianna for his behavior," Kael said.

"Oh, no. I don't mean that." Vian ran his hands through his hair. "It's probably good for him; maybe it'll teach him a few things. Just give him time. Once this is all over, he'll be back to his old, charming self."

"That's what I'm afraid of."

"Look what I found!" Eloith cried as he flew toward them, carrying a miniature bow. "A Naajiso crossbow! Tariq, where did you get this? And the *noqui*!"

"After the great Naajiso Rebellion, your queen gave us these and more."

"What is a *noqui*?" asked Vian.

"They are small stones used in a sling. Anything you hit will turn to salt," Eloith replied.

"Will they work against those beastly hags?" Vian reached for the bag.

Eloith jerked upward, holding the stones out of reach.

"I haven't tried it." Tariq pried open a barrel. "I'd never wanted to risk it, especially knowing that the *klhoddas* worked."

"And we only have six," Kael said.

"I think." Eloith gave the bag of stones to Kael. "Ayianna should have the stones and my *klhodda*."

"What about you?" Vian asked.

"The dithza-mielis can't harm me."

Vian frowned. "Well, aren't you the lucky one."

"Well, I think we have a good start on the weapons." Tariq gathered his share of supplies. "I'm famished. Let's go eat."

Kael nodded and stuffed the *noqui* into a sack for Ayianna. "Eloith, did you find a sling?"

"I found an elven sling, and it will work. A fairy one would probably be too short for her." Eloith handed Kael a leather sling, and Kael placed it inside the sack along with the silk pouch and a braided belt.

A wisp of excitement fluttered in his stomach. He couldn't wait to see her face when he gave it to her.

45

SITTING IN HER room, Ayianna brushed her hair, the fragrant oil from her bath still drying on her skin. She inhaled its delicate, flowery scent. The public bath hadn't been as humiliating the second time, and the hot water had been relaxing after Turina's grueling practice. She glanced at the mirror and decided to leave her hair down.

The day had passed without a word from Desmond. He'd made an empty promise. She stood and pulled the linen dress over her shoulders. The muscles in her arms and legs burned softly—a relished feeling, a feeling of freedom. She smiled. Time for dinner.

Vian's laughter carried through the halls. What was she missing? Ayianna hurried into the private dining chambers. A marble, circular table filled the room. Vian and Kael sat along the right side, talking with a third man—a Haruzo.

Kael glanced up. His features softened and a smile played at his lips. He stood as did the others. "Good evening, Ayianna."

"Hi." Her face burned. "Have I missed dinner?"

"No." Vian smiled. He strode over to her side and took her by the elbow. "Let me introduce, Tariq. He will be our guide."

Tariq smiled. His amber eyes were kind like Saeed's but fiercer. Thick, black sideburns framed his face and flowed into his wild, curly hair. He bowed graciously, then took her hand and kissed it. "A pleasure to finally meet you."

"Thank you," she said as she sought how to respond. "Nice of you to join us." Could she have been anymore dull?

"Well, it took some convincing, but Kael and Vian think likewise." He and the others returned to their seats. "Have you enjoyed your stay?"

"It's been great, thank you." Ayianna sat in the polished wood chairs. "How has the research been going?"

"Wonderful." Vian shook out his napkin. "So wonderful that we are leaving tomorrow."

"So soon?"

"Well, you know how Kael is." Vian laughed.

"We'll be leaving in a week." Kael took a drink from his goblet. "We still have to get a few supplies. I've got to find some sinew. It seems Bonzapur doesn't see the importance of the longbow."

Tariq snorted. "We aren't much for any bows. Now, you give us a good blade, and we will show you how battles are won."

"Tariq." Kael shook his head, but his eyes twinkled with the challenge. "A longbow can outreach a sword every time. You might as well eliminate half of your enemies with the bow first and then take out the rest with the sword."

"True, unless one has a terrible aim." Tariq laughed.

"I can't argue that." Kael glanced at Ayianna. "Speaking of aim, Ayianna needs to get some practice time with the *noqui*."

"What is that?" she asked.

"It's a stone that will turn your target into salt." Vian raised his eyebrows. "Ever use a sling before?"

"When I was a child, my brother and I would . . . " Emptiness overwhelmed her, but she pushed past it. "We would hunt with them, but that was a long time ago."

"Excellent." Tariq smiled. "I'll take you to the practice field tomorrow. You'll remember how to use them quickly enough." He faced Kael. "I've got to get a few more supplies too, but it shouldn't take me too long."

"Not if you've been turned into salt by then." Vian erupted into laughter, his voice bouncing around the room.

"I won't be foolish enough to be standing where she can hit me." Tariq draped an arm over the back of his chair.

"Is there a remedy for the *noqui*?" Kael asked.

Tariq shrugged. "Not to my knowledge."

Ayianna glanced at Tariq, hoping she still had the knack for the sling. Her face must have mirrored her fear, because Tariq smiled and said, "Don't worry, Ayianna, we won't practice with the real *noqui*."

"Oh, of course not." She smiled.

"Good evening everyone."

Ayianna's stomach sank like a brick at sea. She took a deep breath and glanced up.

Desmond stood, smiling in the doorway. Freshly shaved, trimmed, and bathed. A slight fragrance wafted into the room.

"Desmond, is it?" Tariq stood and bowed. "Nice to finally meet you."

Desmond bowed. "Likewise. So will you be joining the quest?"

"I will."

Desmond strode toward Ayianna and pulled out the chair next to her. "I've been doing some thinking. We don't all need to be traipsing over the countryside looking for these ingredients." He sat down and glanced at Vian. "If we split up, we could free your father, Vian." He reached over and took

Ayianna's hand. "And we could rescue Ayianna's mother while the rest of you find the tonic."

Kael's face hardened. "Saeed wanted us to stick together."

"But he is not here now." Desmond cocked his head. "We've made it as far as Bonzapur. You've got the tonic, and you know where you're going. Why do you need us?"

Kael frowned.

Desmond smiled. "See, you don't need us, or should I say you don't need me?"

Ayianna stared at the black swirls in the white marble table top and focused on breathing slowly.

Desmond stood and pulled her up with him. "Today, I am publically accepting Arlen of Praetan's contract of betrothal to Ayianna. With you three as my witnesses, I make it official."

"Desmond." Kael stood. "This is hardly the time or place for such things, don't you think?"

"A need to protect my interests has come to my attention."

"But we're on the brink of a war."

"So we should stop engaging in life?" Desmond laughed. "I don't follow your logic, half-breed."

Tariq straightened. "There is no need for such slurs. We've heard your announcement. Go and fulfill it in the manner of your customs."

The pounding in her head nearly drowned the voices around her. Her face burned, but she kept her gaze down and steadied her breathing.

"Doesn't Ayianna get a say in all this?" Kael asked.

Desmond smirked. "Not where I'm from." He turned his gaze to her. "Besides, she knows the secrets she carries. She knows her place is with me."

Secrets that killed her father and snatched away her mother. But those were her family's secrets, now she carried her own. No one would have her if they knew about the harpy curse. She shuddered.

"Besides." Desmond cocked his head. "What makes it any of your business?"

Kael's eyes darkened. "Her brother asked me to look after her."

"Is that all?" Desmond chuckled. "Didn't I already tell you she is none of your concern? Her family betrothed her to me."

"Do you have evidence?"

Desmond smiled. "Of course." He reached into his doublet and revealed a folded parchment. He shook it out.

Kael glanced at the certificate. The room grew silent except for the spitting of the torches along the walls. His scowl deepened. "It is true, but it lacks her signature."

"Easily remedied." Desmond snapped his fingers. "Bring me ink and a quill."

Ayianna stared at the certificate as a servant brought the items. Her father's sloppy script scrolled across the bottom beneath an empty space. She glanced at Kael.

His icy gaze bore into Desmond. His concern was nothing more than a vow to her brother. If he knew her secrets, he would despise her. If she signed, he wouldn't have to be burdened with her care anymore, instead she would be on her way back to the plains to rescue her mother.

The servant appeared and set the ink jar and quill on the table. He bowed and returned to stand along the wall.

Ayianna swallowed the knot in her throat. Desmond knew her secrets and still wanted her as his wife. What else did the future hold for her? *Osaryn, what should I do?* She had to trust her father's decision. Before she could change her mind, she picked up the quill, dipped it, and signed her name.

The torches sputtered, startling her, and she dropped the quill. A splotch of black ink bled into the parchment, smearing her name. Her fate sealed. She clasped her trembling hands together and sat. What had she done?

"Dinner is served." A deep-throated voice rumbled in the small room as servants streamed in carrying platters and jugs of mead.

Ayianna's stomach twisted. She had no desire for food. Only to run outside and be swallowed up by the evening sky. She needed air, where she could see the stars and breathe again.

"Desmond." Vian lifted his knife and cut into the chunk of meat on his plate. "I won't be going with you. Saeed will take care of my father. It's more important that we retrieve the tonic."

"Oh." Desmond's eyes narrowed. "It won't do any good to return without you. I suppose we'll join you then."

"But what about my mother?" Ayianna forced the words out.

"I won't leave without the prince." He frowned, but his gaze shifted beyond her.

Ayianna stared at the plate set before. She had sealed her fate for nothing. What had she expected? The promise of home had made her decision easier to bear, but now? The betrothal was official. It was over. She had signed her life away, committed it to a merchant. Could she have refused? The doubts and conflicting emotions burned in her mind and churned her stomach. No one would want her if they knew the secrets she harbored. If Kael didn't love her, than who would?

Desmond slid his fingers over hers and lowered his voice. "We can consummate the betrothal anytime you're ready. Tonight, if you want."

She pulled her hand away as tears sprang to her eyes. She'd grow to love him, just like the queen said, just like her mother said. Did her mother say that? No, she said fools married for love. Her plate sat empty while the others ate. Snippets of conversation drifted her way, but the roar in her ears snatched the words away.

In less than a week, she'd be embarking on a quest, taking her farther and farther away from home, from her mother. Did she even have a home? Was her mother even alive? No she couldn't think like that. They would save her, then she'd marry Desmond, and they would make a new home, but he would have to wait until they rescued her mother. The bars on her heart slammed shut, echoing in the silence of her soul.

Taking a deep breath, she lifted her head and squared her shoulders. She had made her choice. There was no going back. Others had married for less. She would do this and make her father proud.

ABOUT THE AUTHOR

Writing as J. L. Mbewe, Jennette is an author, artist, mother, wife, but not always in that order. Born and raised in Minnesota, she now braves the heat of Texas, but pines for the Northern Lights and the lakes of home every autumn. She loves trying to capture the abstract and make it concrete. She is currently living her second childhood with a wonderful husband and two precious children who don't seem to mind her eclectic collections of rocks, shells, and swords, among other things. Here, between reality and dreams, you will find her busily creating worlds inhabited by all sorts of fantasy creatures and characters, all questing about and discovering true love amid lots of peril. She has two short stories published in *The Clockwork Dragon* anthology, and four short stories set in the world of Nälu. Her debut novel, *Secrets Kept*, was nominated for the 2014 Clive Staples Award.

Stay up-to-date with all things Nälu and her journey as a writer mama at JLMbewe.com.

EXPLORE

THE WORLD OF NÄLU

Learn more about the characters, places, and history at
WorldofNalu.com.